IF O

Born in 1966 and brought up in Gloucestershire, Alice Jolly now lives in Brussels with her husband and son. She is the author of *What the Eye Doesn't See*.

IF ONLY YOU KNEW

ALICE JOLLY

POCKET
BOOKS

LONDON • NEW YORK • SYDNEY • TORONTO

First published in Great Britain by Pocket Books, 2006
An imprint of Simon & Schuster UK Ltd
A CBS COMPANY

1 3 5 7 9 10 8 6 4 2

Simon & Schuster UK Ltd
Africa House
64–78 Kingsway
London WC2B 6AH

www.simonsays.co.uk

Simon & Schuster Australia
Sydney

A CIP catalogue record for this book is available from the British Library

ISBN: 0-7434-5072-8
EAN: 9780743450720

Typeset in Garamond by Palimpsest Book Production Limited,
Grangemouth, Stirlingshire
Printed and bound in Great Britain by
Cox & Wyman Ltd, Reading, Berkshire

In loving memory of our daughter
Laura Catherine Kinsella
who died before birth
19 May 2005

ACKNOWLEDGEMENTS

With thanks to: Stephen Kinsella, Amanda Holmes, Simon Pettifar, Clare Andrews, Susannah Rickards, Gregory Feifer, Igor Panich, Masha Macrae, Nikolay Khalip, Anna Jaquiery, Sam Mitchell, Lucy Hodgson, John Boyle, John Hellon, Vincent Eaton, Loretta Stanley, Jeremy Duns, Andrea Rees, Jeannette Cook, John Lash, Dr Andy Harrison, Miles Warde, everyone at Vindi's nursery, Victoria Hobbs of A M Heath, Kate Lyall Grant and Tara Wigley of Simon & Schuster.

12/20 rue de Lausanne, Geneva

September 1991

His fountain pen, a pad of paper, a green toothbrush with splayed bristles, a folded linen handkerchief, three Metro tokens and his watch, which still ticks. He said to me once that our fear is not that death will be momentous, but that it will be trivial. I pick up each object in turn, unfold the handkerchief, flick through the blank pages of the pad.

I should have known that a man with a talent for being present would have a talent for being absent as well. A suitcase and twelve cardboard boxes – that's all he left. The boxes are sealed with plastic tape and have been used many times before. Instructions have been written on them in Cyrillic script and then scribbled out.

Of course, I should look through these boxes. Those endless blue notebooks must be somewhere, and there'll be other letters and documents. He wouldn't mind me looking. In fact, he'd encourage it. I can almost hear his voice, that gentle American drawl – *Yeah, sure, go through it all as much as you want.*

He wouldn't say – *See it all exactly as it is,* but that's what he'd mean, because that was always his creed. And for a while I tried to make it mine as well, but now he's gone I

can't believe in that any more. He had his secrets but he
can keep them now. I have my picture of him and I don't
want it blurred. I've learnt my lesson: no more meddling
with the past.

I pick up those few scattered items and start to push them
back into his case, but his smell draws me in. Straw, perhaps?
And smoke, and the grime of Moscow, and rough-scented
soap. I move aside two towels and a bedsheet. Underneath
I see a square of golden-coloured wool – his coat. And
beside it, his shoes. I watch my hands lift them, as one might
lift a newborn baby, and place them on the tiled floor. They
stand there, floodlit by cool evening light. The tongues of
those shoes still speak of the high arch of his foot, and the
sole is still attached to the leather all around, its hold unweak-
ened. On one toe is a splodge of white paint, which he
never quite scratched off, and the laces are brown, because
he could find no black in Moscow. My fingers touch the
deep-squeezed creases which would once have marked the
ball of his foot. Those creases laugh like the lines at the side
of his eyes.

I mourn for him, and I mourn for the person I became
when I was with him.

I pick at the plastic tape on one of the boxes. Then I
fetch a carving knife and wriggle the tip of it in under the
tape. Pulling up one cardboard flap, I find a grey plastic filing
tray which used to lie on his desk, and a sea-shell paper-
weight. Then I stop: next to it is a tiny glass bottle with a
rubber skin across its neck. Beside the bottle is an empty
syringe, the needle removed. I remember it lying on the
edge of the sink, between the taps, next to his razor and his
wristwatch.

I'm melting like wax. Soon there'll be nothing left, just
a pile of clothes, with an acrid twist of smoke rising from

them, and a singed mass of hair. My name is Eva Curren. I am thirty years old and I live in Geneva. I'm going to leave here soon. *Just shake up the world and pick out a city. Hope that when you arrive you won't find yourself there.*

I lay the knife down, go to the fridge and take out a bottle of vodka. I pour a glass and drink it, feeling it burn down my throat. Then I pour another and drink that as well. The telephone rings. I wait until it cuts into silence, then unplug it. Sitting at the table near the window, I rest my head on its cool surface. Below, in the communal gardens, the branches of trees spread wide, their leaves flickering orange at the edges. Beyond the garden is a main road, and then the lake, silver-grey, fading into the mist. It's beginning to rain – fine, light rain – which dances sideways in the wind. The day is closing down.

I go back to his suitcase and take out his pen. In a plastic bag I find a bottle of ink. The pen is slim and green. I know exactly how it fitted into his hand, gripped between those fingers which were not as elegant as I wanted them to be. *Write it all down,* that's what he advised. The gold nib of his pen hangs over the expanse of the paper. In my head I try to form words, but I'm unnerved by the sound of my own voice. Its cadences are unfamiliar; it may stutter and evade, or swerve out of control, suddenly rant and rave.

My hand stretches out to open the bottle of ink and unscrew the barrel of the pen. I pull the plunger up and the pen fills. I write my name and then, with a flourish, *Memories.* But even that is wrong. Memories are gentle, sepia-tinted, long ago. This story happened less than a year ago, and remains more vivid than today. The gold nib of his pen goes down on to the paper and remains there, gathering ink. What was it he said? Once a feeling becomes a word, then we are released from its grip.

10/38 Kutuzovskii Prospyekt, Moscow

November 1990

It begins with a party – Maya's party. Except that I don't
even know that it is her party. It's just a place I've come
to late on a November Moscow night, and I'm tired, and
a little drunk, and I didn't even want to come. And as soon
as I arrive, I hear that voice – deep and slurring, a mix of
accents, some words oddly elongated and others cut too
short. For a moment it stops the blood in my veins but then
I decide not to hear it.

Instead I do my Party Girl act. I chat to a man from
the Japanese Embassy, and manage a joke or two with a
bulging salesman from Leicester, who provides me with
a great many details about street furniture, whatever that
is. I'm introduced to a woman called Valia, or Svetlana, or
something like that. She's six foot tall and thin as string.
She wears a backless top, a mini-skirt and ankle boots with
high heels. We talk about nothing. A blonde American
called Estelle pours some clove-tasting liqueur into my
glass and blows cigarette smoke into my face. She tells me
about a German banker who was gunned down in the
lobby of his building. Hallways and stairwells, they're the
most dangerous places. Blah-blah. I've lived abroad enough
to understand what's going on here. The only thing these

people have in common is that they *don't* have anything in common, and so they work hard to make it seem as though that isn't the case.

And none of them notice that my Party Girl act lacks conviction. I'm new in this city, I belong with Rob, and he's popular, or at least respected. He's part of this city in the way that most of the people here aren't. He speaks Russian fluently, doubtless even using the subjunctive correctly. Together we're a charming young couple. The tiny world of Moscow expatriates needs more people like us. But I'm left feeling angry that people are so easily conned.

I move over to a table where food is piled on plates. There's the traditional *zakuski* – gherkins, cold meat, hard-boiled eggs, salted fish. But also food I haven't seen since I arrived in Moscow – smoked salmon, chicken legs and French pastries. I start eating and can't stop. The person who bought this food isn't shopping in the places where Rob and I go. I move towards the window and stare out. I'd rather be out there, beyond the double-thickness windows, part of the silent city. The distant lights of cars move along the Kutuzovskii Prospyekt. A blurred line of black indicates where the Moskva river flows and nearby the outline of one of the Seven Sisters Skyscrapers rises from the frozen mist. No neon, no advertisements, hardly any cars. Most people find the silence of this city chilling but I enjoy it.

I turn back to the room and my eyes travel over parquet floors and double doors. This apartment is three or four times the size of any other Moscow flat I've been in. Pictures, which have the look of Chagall or Kandinskii, cover the walls. Could they even be originals? In the hall, a bust of Lenin wears a rakish trilby hat, while behind him, pale blue wallpaper with gold stars peels at the seams.

When I first stepped into these rooms it felt like stepping back into the grandeur of pre-Revolutionary Russia, but now I notice that the chandeliers are plastic, and their wires loop across the ceiling. They don't appear to work and so the rooms are inadequately lit by lamps wedged in corners. Pipework stands out from the walls and is discoloured by rust. A marble fireplace contains an electric heater.

Then I hear that voice again. Yes, I suppose Maya would live in this kind of flat. There was always something purposefully antique about her. The clove liqueur has gone to my head, and my eyelids scrape over my eyes. I want to go home but, when I look around for Rob, he's deep in conversation with Bill and Sarah. We had supper with them earlier, and they brought us to this party. As usual, the conversation is all politics. Will Gorbachev implement the Five Hundred Day Plan? The Soviet Union and the command economy can't last much longer. The Republics are running their own economies now. Will there be rationing, a famine, a coup? Bill is Rob's American boss and Sarah is his wife. They've been in Moscow five years but their trainers still glisten white, as do their teeth. They appear the perfect couple but Rob tells me that Sarah has threatened divorce if they're not out of here by the summer.

I'm about to go over to them when I hear those familiar cadences again, mixed with the rumble of other voices. What on earth is Maya doing here? But then I remember. She was born in Russia, she told me that when I was six years old. Maya Pototska. Even the name had the power to enchant. It filled my childish ears with sleighs, fur coats, forests of silver birch and roaming wolves.

I stand in the hallway, uncertain, but I can't go to her, so I push through the nearest set of double doors, and find myself in a dark corridor. All along it, hardback books are piled up on the floor, rising to waist-height. I bend to peer at the titles and see that they're all art books. They would be, of course.

I open a door onto a room where a lamp throws slanting light across a desk covered with papers. A bed by the window hasn't been made, and here one whole wall is filled by bookcases. Canvases are propped against the wall and the desk. I step forward into the room then stop, because I'm not alone. A man is standing near the bookcase with his back to me. He turns and, without knowing why, I shut the door behind me.

The man is tall and thin, and he stands straight, his head held high. He has a hawk-like nose and hair which is thick and grey, but might once have been blond. A nervous flutter runs through his hands as they idle through the pages of a book. He turns to replace it on a shelf. Everything about him is neat and proper, except that he has brown laces in his black shoes. His clothes — a grey polo-neck jumper worn under a sharply cut dark suit — are stylish, but it's clear he's had them for years. For some reason, he makes me think of the way in which people who are very old, or desperately sick, are sometimes meticulously well-dressed.

I stand staring at him, and he at me. I'm sure I've seen him before. The back of a grey-golden head retreating down an evening street, the reflection of his face in the shifting windows of the Metro. And he's seen me before, I'm sure, but we've both taken care not to notice. Now I've no choice but to look at him. And really there's nothing exceptional to see. He's just an old man, but for some reason I keep on staring and he doesn't look away. The moment has no drama, no tension. I just think, Oh yes, it's you, of course. Even now I know – and he does too. Already we're haunted by the future.

A shriek sounds in the next room. Of course, I remember, this is meant to be a party, isn't it? So I should introduce myself and start up a conversation. I step forward, trying to turn myself into the Party Girl. But before I've even started I see from his eyes that he's not going to believe in any of that. I turn, stumbling, back to the door and pull at the handle. It doesn't open. I tug at it, once, twice. With a jerk the door swings back and I step out into the corridor, then close the door behind me.

I must find Rob, and my coat. Perhaps I should tell him about Maya. But he wouldn't even remember, he never remembers anything. That voice ricochets out from the sitting room. In the hall, piles of coats have fallen from their over-loaded hooks. Boots and shoes stand in puddles of water. The bulging Leicester salesman drops his glasses and scrabbles for them on the floor. What was in that clove liqueur? People are jostling, they push against me and I nearly fall. A foot in a high-heel shoe hovers over my toe and I step into the sitting room.

A woman lounges on a blue-green sofa, the size of a small boat. It's crammed with cushions and a Chinese shawl is draped over the back of it. As she turns towards me, her over-large eyes blink wide and she stops talking halfway through a sentence. Her hand, draped in a heavy gold bracelet, moves in a slow circle through the air. I don't need to say anything because she already knows. I move towards her across the acres of parquet. 'Oh my Go-o-d.' She pushes herself upright, swings her legs down onto the floor, and stares up at me. I remember how, when I was a child, those eyes always reminded me of a doll I had. You tipped the doll back and its eyes shut, then you held it upright and they clicked open again.

'You used to know——' I speak in a rush, suddenly feeling too hot.

'Eva. Yes, of course, of course. You're Theo's daughter.' Maya's plucked and pencilled eyebrows move upwards and she swallows. Those eyes click open and shut. She looks as though she's received bad news. 'You look so ve-e-ry like him.' That slurring voice seems trapped in her throat. She stretches out a hand, speckled and knotted with veins. She wears a gold ring in the shape of a snake, which winds around her finger and has a tiny red stone for an eye. Her touch feels like the dead. 'My long lost goddaughter. Do sit down. Ple-e-ase, sit down.'

The sofa is over-stuffed and tips me towards her.

'Whatever are you doing here?' Maya wrinkles up her nose, drawing in deep breaths. 'You can't have been here long. You don't have the sme-e-ll of it yet.'

I laugh for a moment then stop. I point out Rob and tell her, in a gabble, that he works for the Democracy Foundation. Maya gestures towards a man with silver hair standing in the hall – her husband, Harvey. He works for an oil company which is hoping to set up a joint venture in Kazakhstan. Maya asks how I am, and I say that I'm fine, really fine. And both of us know that this is all distraction.

A door slams, and someone turns up the music. Maya has a walking stick propped against her knee. Her black hair is still long and thick but her face is deeply lined and her eyes are overly bright and ringed by badly applied eye-liner. Her jewel-coloured velvet clothes, cameo brooch and string of jade are as consciously antique as the décor of the flat. I feel as though a long cigarette-holder should be drooping from her hand.

'So, have you se-e-en your father?'

This feels like a question asked in a foreign language.

'No.'

'No? What never? Oh well, I suppose not. It's just, I always thought that if he'd got in touch with anybody . . .' She shakes her head and shrugs, raises a hand in despair. 'How sad. How ve-e-ry sad. Will you have a drink?' Before I can say anything she's poured vodka in with the clove liqueur.

'You know, I've always missed him.' She looks at me again as though unable to believe in my existence. And as she raises her hand to smooth her hair, I see her as she used to be – the fairy godmother. She lent me her gold high-heeled shoes and I tottered on them through the corridors of Marsh End House. And she painted my nails in pink polish and later I had to pick it off so my mother wouldn't see. In the evenings she used to sit out on the lawn with Rob's mother, Amelia, the two of them surrounded by a blue haze of cigarette smoke. And Amelia wearing that Paisley shawl – red and gold and orange in a pattern like question marks.

'Perhaps you don't remember much about him?' Maya says.

I think of my bedroom at Marsh End House, that china night-light on the chest of drawers. He used to sit beside that light reading to me. It was the shape of a toadstool, and the spots were holes through which the light shone. He'd always read the story of Bluebeard from Grimm's *Fairytales* and I'd look at the pictures in the book. A castle with fountains, and peacocks, and chandeliers. A perfect world – but still the bride always wanted to look in that one locked room. My father's hands turned the pages, moving through the dappled light.

Maya is talking about him – how gifted he was, his paintings, his parties. He often used to come and stay at her flat in London. The man she's describing isn't my father. Such a brilliant talent, she says, at the peak of his career. I want to tell her that that isn't right. My father never sent us any money. Only his early paintings were any good. That's all my mother has ever said about him. Inside my head a kaleidoscope turns so that all the patterns and colours merge. 'But then why did he leave? Why did that happen?' I hear myself say those words and wonder where they've come from.

Maya is trying to pour vodka into her glass. A gust of laughter blows through from the next room. As she looks across at me, her eyes open wide. She starts to ask a question but no words come. The glass slips from her hand and cracks onto the floor. Pieces of it skid across the parquet. I bend down, thinking that I should pick up the larger pieces, but as I do so my head jerks forward as though I'm suffering from vertigo. For a moment I have the impression that I'm on the edge of a cliff with a 300-foot drop below.

I feel Maya's hand grip my arm. 'Leave it, dear. Just le-e-ave it. It re-e-ally doesn't matter.' She's wiping vodka from her blouse with a handkerchief. I feel the muscles in my chest start to tighten. Maya's voice is suddenly loud. 'You know, I went away. The winter before he left.' I look down again at the pieces of broken glass, and as I do so, feet appear. Black shoes with brown laces. They come closer then step away, moving with delicate precision, as though the act of walking is a well-rehearsed dance.

'Ah, Estelle, there you are. You must meet Eva.'

The American woman with the lethal liqueur is suddenly upon us. Ignoring me, she bends over the arm of the sofa and, laying a hand on Maya's shoulder, she kisses her. She's pink and flouncy, wears too much gold jewellery, has nails painted the colour of blood.

'I must go,' I say.

But Maya keeps her hand on my arm. 'No, no. Stay a while.' She turns back to Estelle. 'I used to know Eva's father – many years ago. I remember what he used to say – *Maya, you're so ve-e-ry beautiful, but you will kill yourself with comfort.*'

I stare at my hands, feeling pain swelling in my chest. A smell of pine needles gathers around me. The man with black-brown shoes is standing close to Valia, or Svetlana, or whatever her name is. His hand rests on her shoulder, and he's kneading the skin near to her prominent collar-bone. As I watch I feel his touch, that thumb pressing into my own skin.

'Is he a doctor?' Maya and Estelle are talking about the shoe man.

'Yes, part of some team advising on hospitals,' Maya says. 'I knew his family in my childhood.'

'So he's Russian?'

'Well, American really.'

I'm shivering despite the heat of the flat. 'I must go.'

'No, no. Don't go.'

My throat is closing up and I'm gasping for breath. The scent of pine needles is heavy around me. I know what will happen if I don't go. I can't see Rob anywhere. People are gathering around Maya, coming to say goodbye. I feel the room growing dark and stand up unsteadily. My lungs are shrinking, growing shallow. I begin to see the image of a white-faced child. Maya still holds my fingers in her chilly hand. 'You must come back some other time.'

The floor is slippery under my feet. In the hall I sort through coats lying on chairs but mine doesn't seem to be there. Not another coat lost. I lose them all the time, sometimes two or three in one winter. I go back towards the sitting room, looking for Rob. The flat is lurching forward

– the floors tip, the doors swing. I cling to a chair to keep my balance. The child is pressing into my mind. I see her thin face, and curly hair, just like mine. The lights plunge, the party guests laugh. People reach out but I fight my way through their hands.

I need to get to a window, I need air. My fingers grasp at a metal catch. I pull open the inner window and pieces of cotton wadding crammed into the frame drop down on to the sill. The outer window opens and cold air bursts into the room, carrying with it frozen shards of ice. The curtains blow back, bulging and billowing, their silken surface dragging against my cheek. Rob's hand closes around my arm. 'It's asthma,' he says. 'She'll be all right.'

My fingers claw at my throat. The curtain, flapping in the wind, catches in my mouth, and coats my tongue with dust. My windpipe has shrunk to the diameter of a drinking straw. Papers from the desk rise like a flock of birds and glide around the room. Above me, a light-shade swings, making shadows dash up the walls. I see Rob's hand struggling with the window catch. Then suddenly, a thick line of blood is moving down his wrist. A voice shouts, 'Is there a doctor here?' The man with the black-brown shoes is suddenly close. Maya's voice dances in my head. *I always thought that if he'd got in touch with anybody it would be you.*

The child stands on a path glittering with frost. Above her, moon-light breaks through the gaps in the trees, covering the ground with stripes of pale light. Ahead of her, a half-broken door opens in a brick and flint wall, thick with ivy. The child's eyes are fixed on that door. She's wearing a cloak of black satin which comes down to her knees and is tied at the neck with a ribbon. Her red tights crinkle at the ankles and her red patent-leather shoes have criss-

cross stitching over the toes. The shoes are too big so there's a gap between the leather and the side of her foot, and the bar strap is pulled tight.

The child hears distant sounds – a shout, laughter, the hiss of fireworks. Her mother's voice still echoes in her head – You must go to bed. You must go to bed. The path ahead of her is enclosed in a tunnel of pine trees. It's edged by a zig-zag line of bricks, and to either side the earth is sandy. She turns and looks back. In the distance a bright light flickers, as though a torch is burning. The silhouette of a woman hesitates at the entrance to the path.

The child walks forward to the broken door. A moment ago a figure stood here, a man dressed in a blue frockcoat and a black three-cornered hat. A tall-tall man, he glittered like the frost on the path. But he has gone now, hurrying through the door, his shadow sliding-winding-riding down the frame, smooth as liquid. She moves forward and lays her hand on the wood of the door, feeling the place where the shadow was. She must go with him now. If she doesn't, then she never will.

A voice calls to her, the sound spiralling upwards through the night. She wants to step through that doorway, but her red shoes will not move. She must never go through that doorway. Never-ever-tether. The voice wraps around her and pulls her forward. She stands with her hand resting on the rotten wood, uncertain, amid the cold leaves.

She'll be all right. Asthma. Yes, asthma. It's Maya and Rob. Their voices are distant. Let me help you with that. Bandages? In the kitchen. I'm propped up in bed, lying under a duvet. My breath wheezes in my lungs and my eyelids droop. The kaleidoscope colours are changing again and again. Those voices – No, no, he'll look after her, you need that strapped up.

A shadow above me fills the ceiling. Something rustles and the shadow moves, yawning open like the jaws of an animal. I open my mouth to call for Rob, then turn my head and find the shoe man standing near me. He pulls up a chair and sits down. I try to speak, but don't have enough air.

'Perhaps I can help,' he says. He stands up, takes off his jacket and puts it on the back of the chair, then he rolls up his sleeves. His movements are slow and deliberate. 'No, no, really,' I gasp. 'I'm quite all right.' He takes the pillows off the bed and tells me to turn over. Then I'm lying on my front and he's moved my arms up beside my head, and my jumper and T-shirt slide upwards. His hands are warm as they press down on either side of my spine. The skin of his fingers is rough, his touch certain. 'You need to breathe as deeply as you can,' he tells me.

His fingers pluck at the muscles to the sides of my spine as though he's playing a harp. Then he's still, and I can hear his breathing above me. For a long time he's motionless but his hands still press into me. Then he moves his fingers with a twist. There. He pulls twice at one particular muscle and pain fires into my neck and arms. His fingers massage that muscle, pressing into it. Again a surge of pain, and a sudden image of that child standing on the path. Then my body unknots and my lungs expand, filling with acres of air. His hand comes close to my face as he pulls up the duvet.

He asks me, then, when I was born. It's such an odd question that for a moment I can't think of the answer. Then he says, 'The sixth of March, perhaps?' The eighth, I tell him. He nods his head, as though thinking something through. Then he tells me that his birthday is the tenth of March. He asks what year. 1961. He was born thirty-five years before me – 1926. I can't think what all this is about but it bothers me that his guess was accurate.

He asks me what I'm doing in Moscow and I'm about to start on some long story about the political situation, and Rob, and his work. But instead I say, 'Well, it was an accident to do with bacon and eggs.' He tells me that he doesn't believe in accidents. Everything, he says, happens for a reason. If I didn't feel so tired I'd argue about that.

We talk about how neither of us will be in Moscow for long. Rob's contract may get renewed in March, or it may not. The shoe man says that each day he thinks he'll leave but he never does. Then he says perhaps he just stays in Moscow because it's an easy place to seduce women. And at this point I should think, This guy is a creep and I should get out of here. But instead I'm charmed by his candour.

Then he says, 'So tell me about yourself,' and I can't think of anything to say, nothing at all. 'Well, I teach English, that's what I do,' I say eventually. But really I'm just one of those cardboard dolls which little girls have, and they make them into all sorts of different people – a nurse, or a secretary or a Party Girl – just by putting a paper costume in front of them and folding over the tabs.

And now we're talking and talking and I can't remember all he says. But I'm stealing words from the tip of his tongue, and he from mine. And I can tell him anything because he knows it all already. And I want us to go on talking like this for ever. But the rubber thump of a walking stick sounds in the corridor, and a tall figure wavers at the door. Inside my head, I plead, *Make her go away.* But she stays, without speaking, and I feel her invisible eyes seeing too much. *Make her go, make her go.* Her shape fades, and we've got just a little more time.

So I tell him then about Maya, and how she was a friend of my father's, and how he went away when I was six and never came back. And I tell him about the child on the moonlit path – although I've never talked to anyone about that. And all the time he sits beside me, while I lie in bed. And it feels just right like that. And he says to me, 'So that image – is it something you remember?' No, it's not a memory, I'm sure of that. He says that it must have been, but I know it wasn't.

Then he tells me that I need to find out about my father because otherwise I'll never know who the person behind the cardboard cut-outs is. And I've heard all that before, and I don't believe it, but I behave as though I'm taking it seriously. Then Rob appears at the door, asking if I'm all right. His hand is thick with bandage. I know that I've got to go home, but I don't want to. I say to Rob not to worry, and could he find my coat?

I watch the shadow of the shoe man's hands as he buttons up the sleeves of his shirt. He says that on Thursday next week he's going to Tsaritsyno. I don't know where that is, so he tells me it's a ruined palace out in the suburbs. It's a good place to walk, he says, and by then the snow will surely have come. I could meet him at a café which doesn't have a name but it's in Malaia Bronnaia Ulitsa, the north side of the Patriarch's Ponds. I didn't think there were any cafés in Moscow, but I say, 'Thank you.' And then, 'Thanks for your advice.' And he says, 'Oh, you really shouldn't listen to me, my dear, I'm probably just talking about myself.'

Then he moves towards the door and I realize that I don't know his name. 'Sorry, sorry – I didn't catch your name?' He turns back to me. 'Jack Flame,' he says. 'That must be made up,' I say. And he says, 'Yes, it is. It's a name I've tried to lose many times but it follows me.' He walks to the door and light from the corridor touches the side of his face. Then he turns back into the room and says, 'You know, I wouldn't be too sure it never happened. The past can be unpredictable.'

30/16 Ulitsa Pravdy, Moscow

November 1990

At the time, I was sure that Rob and I were happy in Moscow. Now I don't know. Perhaps we didn't even understand what happiness was? We lived near the Byelorusskaia Station in a block apparently reserved for railway workers, although I never met anyone there who had any connection with trains. Our flat had been broken into so many times that Rob had made the landlord fit a steel door. I never thought that the flat was bugged but Rob was convinced it was.

For Rob and me, the living-together experience was new, and we didn't know how to do it. We felt like children playing house, and being in Moscow only added to our uncertainty. Usually when you live in a foreign place you try, by degrees, to understand it. In Moscow there wasn't any point in trying. One day the city happened, the next day it happened again; you couldn't draw any conclusion from anything.

In the evenings Rob would arrive back – always after eight o'clock – and I'd say, So how are you? I'm fine, he'd reply, and you? I'm fine, and how are you? Fine, fine, he'd reply, and you? And so we'd go on until he got bored, and kissed me, and told me to shut up. Then we'd stand together in our lime-green kitchen wondering how to make supper, and we'd invent handy household hints. How to open a tin with a blunt, left-handed tin-opener. Twenty imaginative things to do with half a pot of sour cream, two pork chops and three carrots.

And that's how it was until Maya's party and that card from my mother, which arrived a week later. Rob gave it to me when he came home from work. It had come that morning, he said, but he'd only just remembered. My mother buys her cards from church bazaars or charity shops and they're usually photographs of ducklings, or fluffy cats with red bows. This one had three puppies in a basket, with sad eyes and drooping ears. I read it and then laid it aside, purposefully taking no interest, then sat down to do some marking. Rob reached out to put the kettle on, picked up the card, and read it. 'I take it that the stuff about your self-respect can be translated as You're living in sin, you nasty slut, and you should get married.'

'Yeah, that's pretty much the size of it.'

'Well, I've heard of worse ideas.'

I allowed one of my books to slide off the table and then spent too long picking it up. When I emerged, Rob was looking at me with raised eyebrows.

'And God ordained Holy Matrimony in order that no one should have to sleep on a lumpy sofa?' I said. This was a reference to the night I'd arrived in Moscow, when the situation between Rob and me was unclear, and he'd offered to sleep on the sofa. I'd told him the sofa looked as lumpy as the Lake District and so we'd finished up in the same bed. That was the only conversation we'd ever had about our relationship.

'Well, the sofa is one question but, seriously, we should

think.' Rob was making mugs of tea with the last of the tea bags I'd brought over from England. 'I mean, these visa issues aren't going to get any easier. When we move somewhere else it'll be just the same problem.'

A coin was lying on the table and I picked it up, turning it from heads to tails, then back again. Was marriage about visas? Was it decided over pork chops and the unwashed breakfast pots? I couldn't imagine being married to anyone other than Rob, but still the thought filled me with panic. *Is this it then? Is this what it's going to be?* I'd loved other men more than I loved Rob, but it had always been the same pattern – two weeks of passion, followed by two years of despair. I held my mother's postcard over the bin. The puppies whinged and whimpered. With their sad eyes and drooping ears, they pleaded with me not to abandon them. So I propped them on the windowsill with the other two cards she'd sent.

I thought of her, sitting in her sewing room at Marsh End House, the night before I left, her expression uncertain. What attitude should she take to my departure? Of course, she was thrilled that I was going to be with Rob – but Moscow? Eva, I'm just not sure it's a good idea, she had said. You know how you are. Remember what Doctor Evans said. Blah-blah. And have you got a good pair of gloves? You can't go to Moscow without proper gloves.

Rob started to chop up the carrots and asked if I'd rung her.

'No. I don't like to deprive her of an opportunity to worry.'

The knife went down through the carrots and Rob sighed and shook his head. For me, one of the advantages of Moscow was that it was difficult for my mother to ring me, and almost impossible for me to make an international call, unless I went to Rob's office. I picked up the coin again. Heads, tails. Rob's hand was still tied up in that bandage. He'd never said anything much about that evening at Maya's, and I was grateful for that, but now the thought came to me – would I have answered yes if he'd asked me before Maya's party? I watched a fat cockroach emerge from a crack beside the door and scurry across the brown tiled floor. 'You know,' I said, 'I was trying to remember how my parents ever knew Maya.'

Rob was busy with the pork chops. 'Um . . . I don't really remember. I think perhaps her father used to rent one of the flats in that big house next door.'

'Which big house?'

'You know, Wyvelston Hall. They pulled it down to make the caravan park. The lake and the boathouse were part of it.'

I knew about the lake but I couldn't picture it. 'Quite interesting to meet her, wasn't it?'

'No, not really,' he said. 'She just struck me as in some other world.'

'Maybe. I suppose she's trying to recreate the world of her childhood.'

'Well, hardly, because she wasn't here before the Revolution, was she?' Rob was right, of course, it did seem odd for someone to live like that. 'Where've the saucepans gone?' He was staring at the shelf above the sink.

'Oh, sorry, I forgot to say. I gave them to the Lady with a Hundred Relatives.'

'What?'

'I thought she might need the money for the children.' The Lady with a Hundred Relatives lived in the flat opposite. People banged in and out of there twenty-four hours a day, shouting and swearing. All of them had the same dark faces and long, narrow eyes. Rob said that they must be people from the south, Chechens or Azerbaijanis, and that they probably had no papers. Often a little girl played out on our landing, making a den out of old suitcases and dust-sheets which were tucked into the corner under the stairs.

'So now we haven't got any pans?' Rob said.

'That's a pretty fair assessment of the situation.'

The cockroach was approaching my socked foot. I remembered that I'd been warned about them before I came to Moscow. I felt annoyed with the cockroach for being a cliché. Taking a glass and a piece of paper, I captured it, and, opening the front door, I dropped it down the stairwell. When I came back, Rob was staring at the carrots on the chopping board.

'Tomorrow I'll go and find some more saucepans,' I said.

'And then you'll give the new ones to her as well?'

'I might do.' I thought of that child with her staring black eyes, cold sores, and thin arms sticking out of the too-short sleeves of her jumper. I'd given that woman the pans in the hope of making the child smile. It hadn't worked but I didn't regret what I'd done.

Rob came to stand beside me and rubbed his hands up and down the back of my neck, under my hair. 'You silly fool.' I liked the way he touched me – not in a sexual way, but gently, easily. It was like that when we were children, and now it went on just the same.

'I'm sure you can cook carrots in a frying pan,' I said.

'Do you think?' Rob chopped up the carrots and filled the frying pan from the tap. I watched him and realized how much I liked the way he looked. I never usually think of that because I've known him all my life. To me, he just looks like Rob. He's not particularly tall or solid, and yet he has a physical certainty to him, a brisk way of dealing with practical problems. And no matter where he's living, he always has the tanned and rumpled look of someone who's just arrived back from some exotic trip.

I sat down and went on marking, moving my books so that I could see them better. The bulb in the central light in the kitchen had broken soon after I arrived, and we couldn't get it out, so now we relied on a lamp standing on the top of the fridge. The walls of our building were as thin as tissue and every sigh, every snore, every argument, travelled up and down the pipes. Now, from somewhere below, I heard a dog bark and a murmur of music – a crackly recording of a U2 track? I was teaching my students question words. How? When? What? Why? At least in the classroom the questions usually had answers. A second cockroach advanced across the floor. I scooped it up, put it outside the door, then screwed up a scrap of newspaper to stick into the crack near the door.

'I shouldn't bother,' Rob said. 'They'll just come out of somewhere else.' A shout came from above, and a scraping noise like a chair being dragged across the floor. Rob and I stared up at the low ceiling. 'Oh no,' he said. 'Not again.' He lifted plates down from the cupboard. We'd heard these noises often enough before, but they'd never been as loud as this. Another creak, a thump and a shout. *'Nyet, nyet, nyet.'* From a crack in the ceiling, a thin line of dust dropped down on to the table. I'd heard the names of the people upstairs – Mariia and Nikolai Balashov – but I'd never seen them. Sometimes I did see a man going up to the floor above but, with his tired face and round glasses, he looked more like an academic than a wife-beater.

'Rob, don't you think we should call the police? There's a woman up there being hit.'

'No one here calls the police.'

'We need to do something.'

I wondered why Mrs Balashova didn't just get out of there. Her husband must have locked the door from the inside. *'Nyet. Bol'she ne mogu.'* I tried to work out what was being said – I can't take it any more? I thought of bleeding lips, a fist smashed into an eye-socket. The frying pan bubbled over and Rob turned it down. Another cockroach emerged from under the sink. Rob followed my eyes, we looked at each other and shrugged. He put the pork chops on plates, and the carrots. I'd bought the chops earlier in the day from a hard currency shop. Imported from Denmark, they cost twelve dollars. And yet only that morning I'd read in the *Moscow News* that Russian farmers were starving because they couldn't sell their produce. That was typical of how it was. Nothing made sense, and the Russians didn't expect it to. They lived in a continual comedy of the absurd.

We sat down at the tiny table, our knees banging together, and Rob poured me some vodka which he'd got through someone at his office. I'd never much liked vodka before I came to Moscow but it had already become a habit. Another Moscow cliché.

'So what do you think?' Rob said.

'Looks good.'

'No, not that.'

'Oh yes. Sorry. Well, I don't know.' A sound like the breaking of china came from above. *'Nyet, nyet, nyet. Vsyo, khvatit. Perestan'.* I tried to translate in my head – No, no. Stop. I can't take it any more – what if he kills her? Or rapes her? Another crash, and a sound of creak-thump, creak-thump. 'I'm sorry. It's just these aren't ideal conditions for responding to a marriage proposal.'

'That's true,' Rob said, and I felt his knees move against mine.

'Also, I just feel . . . I mean, aren't we happy as we are? Surely we don't have to get married because everyone else does.'

'Yes, but often the reason why everybody does a certain thing is because it's a good idea.'

'Is that right? I think often people just unquestioningly do what is expected and it isn't necessarily good for them.'

'Surely it's a question of knowing what you're doing it for,' Rob said, poking at the carrots on his plate. 'I mean, purely as an example, consider cooking carrots in a saucepan. Now you could say we usually do that just because everyone does, but that's not right. Actually we do it because otherwise the carrots are hard as bullets.'

'They don't seem too bad to me. In fact, I rather like them.' I speared three pieces of carrot with my fork. 'I don't know why we ever bothered with a saucepan.' Carrots crunched in my mouth. Above us, a door slammed and footsteps cascaded down the stairs. Suddenly there was silence. I reached out for the vodka bottle but Rob's hand was there before mine. Our fingers met around the thick of the bottle and he moved his thumb up over mine. Rob smiled and, awkwardly, we poured the vodka together, so that our thumbs could stay joined.

I thought back to the summer before. I'd moved to Paris after three years in South America and Rob had come to visit me there. During the six years since I left university we'd covered the globe visiting each other. I'd flown from Sucre in Bolivia to Kenya, and he'd made the journey the other way. He'd also visited me in Lima, and I'd been back to The Hague to see him there. Wherever we were, we always finished up in bed together because it seemed almost necessary, having travelled so far. Rob always found a way of making it seem the only reasonable option. *Shouldn't we discuss this over breakfast? It really isn't safe for you to travel home tonight. Oh no, just look at the time, and there's only one bed*.

When he flew from Moscow to visit me in Paris, I hadn't seen him for two years, but I thought it would be just the same. In Paris he was staying in his father's flat near the Champs Elysées. His father has flats all over the place and they're all the same – cream carpets, gold-plated bath taps, and a mass of technology, none of which works. And, sure enough, the first night Rob just couldn't lay his hands on the buttons required to get us out of the building. And so that's how it was, but I didn't think anything of it. Just Rob, my second cousin, the brother and sister I never had. The buttons turned up next morning under the sofa.

We spent the week together, idling from one café to another. They were all the same, as they are in Paris – on a corner, with a red awning, a curtain halfway up the window, small round tables standing on one ornate leg. Rob was full of Moscow. *Glasnost, perestroika*, the possible collapse of the empire, the change from a command to a market economy, the development of civil society. I suppose I was jealous. Why was it that he had a proper job while I was teaching English? After all, we'd both done the same Master's Degree, and I was the one who'd got a distinction. I'd come back to Europe full of the idea that I needed to make use of my qualifications. But the truth was that I'd moved city four times in the last six years and each time I'd done it with the idea of getting a proper job.

But still I'd had high hopes for Paris. It was there that

I'd walk round a corner, into a certain street, and I'd think, Oh yes, this is it, the place where I was always meant to be. But I never found that particular street. So once again I finished up with the usual underpaid teaching job, and the usual two weeks of passion followed by too much despair. I'd wander for hours through the ungrasped days, through Montmartre or Le Marais, thinking, Should I turn left or right? Drink tea or coffee? Get married or not? And none of it seemed to matter. In the evenings I'd stare out of the window of yet another rented room and think, This is it, my life, here, today. Hurry, catch it. But day after day got away from me, dissolving like a sentence half-overheard, or a face glimpsed through a café window.

The night before Rob was due to leave Paris, we were on our way to see a film, and got caught in a rainstorm. As we ran for the cinema, we jumped across a gutter swollen with rain, his hand gripping mine. 'Look out for the piranhas,' he said. And it was just a silly comment, a reference to a game we used to play as children, but it suddenly struck me that we were the only two people in the world who could laugh about that. And I knew that I'd miss Rob, when he'd gone.

At the cinema, the film we'd wanted to see was full, so we had to make a split-second decision on another one. It turned out to be one of those films you've seen hundreds of times before. Woman meets man, falls in love, complications ensue, true love triumphs in the end. Blah-blah. The rain had stopped and we walked through the dripping streets looking for somewhere cheap to eat. Then Rob bumped into this guy he knew from school, called Tom, or Peter, or something like that. Rob suggested he might like to come along with us. I thought that Tom or Peter would have the decency to refuse but he took Rob up on the offer. As we walked, I told Rob that Paris wasn't really the right place for me, that perhaps I'd go back to Lima again.

Then Tom, or Peter, or whatever his name was, stopped in the street. 'Listen, I've got a better idea. Why don't you two come back with me and I'll cook you some bacon and eggs?'

But at that same moment Rob said, 'Well, why don't you come to Moscow?'

My stomach pleaded for bacon and eggs. 'Oh yes! I'd love that.'

Then I was caught in the line of Rob's eyes, and saw delight dancing there. 'I'd love it if you would,' he said.

'Oh, well, I mean . . .'

'I think I might have some sausages as well.'

'Really, I don't know,' I said.

'Well, it's just as you want. Mushrooms, I've definitely got mushrooms.'

'It could be just for six months,' Rob said.

'Of course,' the Tom–Peter man said. 'It's only five minutes' walk.'

'Yes, perhaps I will.'

'Will what?' Tom–Peter said.

'Have some bacon and eggs.'

But I ended up buying a plane ticket for Moscow instead.

Rob and I finished supper and cleared up the dishes, then I filled the sink with water and added grey Soviet washing powder. Other expatriates in Moscow lived in refurbished flats, with pale Scandinavian furniture, and washing machines, or even spin dryers. Rob preferred to live as the locals did, and I agreed that that was the right approach. We were having an experience of the real Russia, but still I couldn't help sighing as I washed, rinsed and squeezed yet another pile of shirts.

As I filled the sink for the third time, Sasha arrived. He often came round in the evenings and sat for hours, drinking and talking to Rob. Most Russians wouldn't have dared to come to our flat but he had always seemed impervious to the risks. As soon as he arrived, Rob turned the radio up so that it would be difficult for anyone listening to understand what was said. Seeing him do that made me think of low-budget spy films.

Usually Sasha spoke in Russian so I couldn't understand, but now he was speaking in English. 'You know in schools zey stop teaching history. Zey have no more any to teach. All ze old is thrown away but no new history instead. But me, I think zat if you have no history, zen you have no country.'

Sasha was thin, with his hair tied back in a ponytail, and a strawberry birthmark covering half of his face. He wore Levi jeans and a Cornell University baseball cap – clothes he must have bought from some tourist. His long legs were draped awkwardly over the arm of a chair. Sometimes he came with his guitar and, when he'd had a lot to drink, he played and sang. I knew Rob found that embarrassing, but it was also strangely touching. According to Rob, Sasha had grown up in an orphanage, and his sister, when pregnant, had been arrested and then died in prison.

'You know what?' Sasha said. 'In Voronezh zey are wanting to introduce rationing but zey cannot do it because zey have not any paper to print the ration tickets on.' He enjoyed this joke, the birthmark on his face turning red as he laughed. Sasha was involved in the running of an underground newspaper, and Rob had met him because the Democracy Foundation had provided the newspaper with some funding. As a result, Rob had become firm friends with Sasha, and his newspaper colleagues Igor and Vladimir. In the evening he often went to help them, although I sometimes wondered, disloyally, how exactly a foreigner could assist them.

Before I came to Moscow I thought that all Russians would be like Sasha and those other newspaper enthusiasts, but I soon realized that they were the exception to the rule. The Western press made it seem as though every Russian was engaged in a great struggle for freedom and democracy, but the reality was that for most people survival was a full-time job. People weren't much interested in politics because they didn't believe that anything could change. There was much talk of the free market but all anyone saw of it was men in the street selling fur hats, war memorabilia and ancient tins of caviar. *Glasnost* and *perestroika* were words for businessmen and politicians who jetted in from the West. The only other Russians I'd really met were women who worked at my college. All they talked about was how they wanted to get out of the country. An odd mix of vulnerability and aggression, they were fascinated by all things Western, but spoke with frank contempt of *biznesmyen* and *spekulianty* — words which included anyone engaged in a commercial operation, however innocent.

Sasha then started to speak in Russian, and I understood enough to know that he was complaining, as he often did, that nobody bought the newspaper. I watched Rob sitting in the black swivel armchair, listening, and I knew that he cared about every word Sasha was saying. I wanted to care as well but I couldn't. If anything, what I felt was a certain jealousy. Sasha had had a life of terrible hardship so he had an excuse. I didn't. Nobody had ever hit me or locked me in a cupboard. There was only really the casual damage which characterizes any English childhood. If I had a problem it was that I'd never really had any problems.

I stood at the window staring down into the courtyard. I liked the view of the buildings opposite. The black and grey geometry of roofs and windows, the crooked grid of a television aerial, the rusted balcony on every third window. Now, with the lights on, it was possible to see into kitchens, sitting rooms and bedrooms just like ours. Sometimes I wondered whether, if I came home one day and accidentally walked into another flat, I could begin some other life without even noticing the change. I looked at my watch and found that it was past midnight. Turning back to the table, I packed up my books.

My eyes travelled over photocopied sheets and words filled in by my students. *How? When? What? Why?* The place where I was teaching wasn't even a proper college. My boss was an Italian called, improbably and appropriately, Signor Baloni. He claimed to have set up the first ever English language college in Moscow. In reality, his business was an illegal operation taking place in three adjoining flats. His students were all diplomats or the bored wives of businessmen. I wasn't contributing anything to anyone by working there. Rob and I didn't even need the money. In Moscow there was nothing to spend it on, as just about everything was provided free by the state.

As I wandered through the sitting room and said goodnight, Rob and Sasha hardly acknowledged me. In the bedroom, I shut the door and sat down on the bed. In the back of my address book was an envelope which contained a photograph of my father. I hadn't looked at it in years. When I was eighteen I stole it from a cardboard box which my mother kept under her bed. Now my fingers were clumsy as I opened it. There he was –

my reprobate father. The man who never sent us any money, who never painted anything really good, except for perhaps a few early pictures.

I remembered what Maya had said, that I was so very like him. The same corkscrew curls, blonde and red, which stick up everywhere. The face long and mournful and pale as a sheet of paper. Eyes which are green, the colour of willow, and can't help staring. The mouth wide, and containing too many teeth. When I think of him, I imagine my father living in a shack on a turquoise and gold beach, with the sun glistening on the green tops of waves.

But why Mexico, of all places? Had he spent time there before he met my mother? I didn't know. But he was following a family tradition, I suppose. My paternal great-grandfather was an explorer in Mexico; he disappeared there and was never found. My grandfather was a cartologist who worked in Central America. Rob's father was a diplomat. Escape disguised as adventure, recklessness disguised as decision-making, activity disguised as purpose. A couple of weeks ago I was thinking about that and I said to Rob, 'It's a fine line, isn't it, between escape and adventure?' He looked at me narrowly and said, 'Fine, yes, but distinct.'

I looked at the photograph and sorted through the bottom drawer of my mind. Half-formed images drifted in my head, of a time when everything was upside down, a summer of endless cartwheels. My father fizzing down the lawn like a Catherine Wheel, his shoes spreading in an arc towards the sky. A round of applause as I tucked my dress into my knickers and stood on my head with my feet wavering above me, my head pressed into the grass. Marsh End House suspended from the edge of the lawn, my mother's head dangling down into the cloudless sky, the frown on her face changed into a smile.

I was sure that he'd put all the clocks and the pictures in the house upside down, but could that be right? And his shirts fastened up the back and he ate dinner with the plate the wrong way up. From far back in the past I heard rhyming words. Cabbage-rummage-damage-sandwich. Words-at-good-was-he. Those sounds fade but a memory of warmth and ease remains. What was that feeling – happiness?

At Maya's party I'd suddenly said, 'But why did my father leave?' Such an obvious question, but I'd never asked it before. I'd somehow always known that I must never ask my mother, or anyone else, about my father. I thought of Jack Flame and how he'd said, 'Yes, it sometimes happens that if the people around you don't want you to see something, then they pretend it isn't there, and so you learn not to see it. And if something isn't seen for long enough, then after a while it simply doesn't exist.'

I lay down on the bed, which was fake Louis XIV in style, with a tapestry headboard, and one leg resting on a crate. The wall next to me was covered by brown carpet, stuck there with glue. Above me, a five-armed lamp swung from the ceiling, filling the room with ochre light. Trapped inside its frosted glass bowls was a haze of dust and a few dead flies. I kept my eyes fixed on that lamp. And as I lay there, a thought came to me which I had been avoiding all week. Now I couldn't escape from it any longer.

Jack Flame was right, what he'd said was true. If I could understand what had happened to my father, then I'd stop hesitating at street corners, stop asking, *Should I turn left or right? Drink tea or coffee? Get married or not?* And I'd stop moving from one rented room to another, from one dead-end job to the next. I was sure that that was true, but how could I find out anything about my father? I had tried once before, when I was eighteen, but it had seemed as though there was nothing to know. I needed to talk to Jack Flame. He would know what I should do, he'd be able to make it happen. I was sure of that. For once, I'd made a decision.

Tsaritsyno, Moscow

November 1990

The snow has come, just as Jack said it would. I walk
with him along a wide path through trees which are
a hundred different shades of white. Every branch, every
leaf, is covered by its own intricately piled layer of snow.
Flecks of ice cloud the air, settling like dust on our coats.
The only sound is the rustle of trees as the snow collects
in their branches. Under the snow, the path is covered with
packed ice, and so we walk carefully, placing our feet down
flat. Occasionally Jack reaches out as though to steady me,
but I keep my hands by my sides.

The path turns and opens out. The skeleton palace lies
ahead, its vast façade three storeys high. Its arched windows
contain no glass, and it has no roof, no doors. We walk
towards it across what must once have been a lawn. Now
trenches have been dug and pipes are exposed. We pass a
derelict bandstand and rubbish bins. A *babushka* sits next to
a gate, swaddled in layers of black, topped by a pink beret.
She sells gherkins in a bucket, two or three plastic bags, and
two boxes of Chanel perfume. A few other figures move
along the front of the palace, staring up at it. Sagging barbed
wire surrounds the building and it's hung with signs. *Vkhoda
nyet*. No Entry.

Jack finds a place where the wire is low and he puts his foot on it. Then he stretches out his hand to help me over. The ground is uneven and for a moment I wobble. As he catches at my shoulder, I look up at him and see him smile. There's something fresh about that smile. With other people I always see emotions pass through several filters before they're expressed to the world. With him there are no filters.

We set off along the front of the building. The ground-floor doorways are boarded up but he finds a place where the boards are rotten and pulls them away. I'm frightened that someone is going to come and tell us that we shouldn't be doing this, but Jack doesn't hesitate. We step through the boards into a vast deserted room. The remains of a fireplace stand out from a wall and there are marks where stone pillars must once have been. Broken timbers litter the ground. In one corner a pair of boots with no soles lies in the remains of a campfire.

Jack walks away from me. His head is stretched back, looking up through the missing storeys at the sky above. Standing there, he has the stillness of a figure painted on a museum vase. Ever since I met him earlier in that nameless café, I've been trying to work out what quality it is that he has. Now the word comes to me. Savour. Yes, that's it. He sees and feels much more than I do. He's like a wine merchant, holding the day on his tongue and letting its tastes spread on his palate. Or like a tailor rubbing the air around us between his fingers, feeling its warp and weft.

I follow him towards the remains of a stone staircase. He turns back, stretching out a hand. I don't take that hand but I follow him and we start to climb. On a narrow ledge, we stand looking out through a gap where a window must once have been. From there we can see the chimneys and pylons of Moscow made pale by the snow. An occasional onion dome shines gold through air which is white with a mixture of mist and chimney smoke. I feel Russia stretching away from us on either side. More than four thousand miles, all the way from the Baltic Sea to Vladivostok. Forests, lakes, railway stations, villages. A country in which geography makes individuals irrelevant.

The silence folds in on us, broken only by the sound of a lump of snow sliding from a ledge above. Jack moves me in front of him so that I can see more clearly. His breath is warm against my hair. I turn to him and our faces are close. For a moment I feel dizzy and put out a gloved hand to steady myself. My voice echoes against the walls. 'What is it? This . . .'

I don't expect him to know what I'm talking about but he answers immediately. 'It's recognition, that's all.'

'Recognition?'

'Yes. Sometimes you meet someone and they're like a mirror. When you look at them you see yourself more clearly.'

I keep my eyes fixed on the distant shapes of Moscow.

'You know Plato's idea?' he says. 'He thought that before the soul enters the body it exists in a place of great beauty, a place which is infinite, perfect – but when it enters the body, it can no longer remember that place. Until the moment when we fall in love, and then what we experience is a memory of that other place and a yearning to return.'

He's standing too close to me. I move my foot and a stone beneath it wobbles. 'But there can also be other ways to see back into that world, can't there?' I say. 'Like the memory of certain moments. You measure everything against them, and find all of it wanting. And you long to be allowed to go back but you never can.'

'Which moments?'

'Just . . . I don't know.' Despite the cold my neck prickles with sweat. 'I always think of a beach, and the sun is setting in a certain way . . .' I feel tears suddenly gather behind my eyes. 'I always want to go back there. You understand?' Above us, a brick moves and we both look up. Further along the wall we see the brick slide, then fall, bringing with it a shower of snow.

'Come down,' Jack says. 'It's not safe.'

He moves towards the steps, and we climb down from the ledge. As we step out through the broken boards the sun is failing and snow starts to fall again. We take a path which leads downhill, and see below us a wide lake. In my mind I'm flicking through the future. Rob's contract expires in March. Jack says he may leave Moscow soon. So how many more times will we walk together like this? I wonder if he's thinking of that as well.

Jack walks away from me, along the bank of the lake. The evening light brings with it a strange stillness. His head is held high and he's staring out across the frozen water towards a smudge of black trees on the distant shore. And to me it's as though someone has taken a black pen and drawn a thick line around him. Nothing can be added to him, nothing can be taken away. He creates his own limelight. For me he's there – really there – in a way that nothing else ever has been.

As he walks back towards me I see distant figures far out on the ice. What are they doing? Jack says that they are fishermen who have bored holes through the ice and let down lines. I ask, 'Don't they fall through?' Jack says that perhaps they sometimes do and I shudder, suddenly aware of my numb feet and raw lips.

We talk then, as we trudge back up the hill, about that night at Maya's. It's hard for me to speak about those images

– so much sharper than memory – of that child. I usually
don't even admit to myself what I see. Of course, I could
ask Maya about my father, I say, but I don't think she knows
what really happened. She'd already gone away to Rome by
the time he left for Mexico, but all the same, I could ask.
I expect Jack to think that a good idea, but he only says,
'Well, you could do but I doubt you need to. Your mind is
its own detective story. All the information you need is
almost certainly there, it's just a question of whether you
can find it.'

The snow is falling heavily now, blurring the air. When
we come upon the ruins of a Palladian pavilion beside the
path, Jack suggests that we should shelter for a while. Half
of the roof is missing, and graffiti is scrawled on the walls,
but a narrow bench remains under the ruined roof, so we
sit down there.

I take off my gloves and unbutton the collar of my coat.
Then I remove my scarf to shake the snow from it. I see
him watching my throat and the open collar of my shirt.
He puts out his hand and picks up the crucifix I wear around
my neck. His fingers brush against my chin. I move back
but still he holds the crucifix in his hand. 'Does this mean
anything?' he asks.

'Yes, something.'

I have a vision of him bending down and pressing his
lips, cold with snow, against my neck. I imagine placing my
hand on the side of his head, feeling his hair, touching the
skin just below his ear. I jerk my head back and he lets go
of the crucifix. I twist my scarf through my hands as I search
for words. 'You know, if you're like me, and you know you
can easily become the victim of your own mind, then you
need someone larger to hand that over to. Someone to help
keep the lid on.'

'Why keep the lid on?'

I look away from him, unable to answer. My hands are blue because of the cold and I can't feel my fingers. Taking off his own skiing gloves, Jack pushes my stiff fingers into them.

'Tell me,' he says. 'About that beach?'

I struggle to find the right words. 'It's not just the beach – it's also this figure. He's tall, and he's wearing these eighteenth-century clothes – a frockcoat and a three-cornered hat – and he's standing out at the water's edge. And the beach is like the one near our house in England – mud and stones. And I don't know . . . I just feel that's a place I want to go.'

'I think those places exist for all of us. But in your life now, don't you ever feel you're in that place?'

'No, not really. I suppose I once did, for a few months, when I was eighteen, just before I left school. But then I got asthma and – I don't know . . .'

Jack is looking down at me, his eyes intense. 'But you know, Eva, you don't have asthma.'

I'm about to start arguing with him but there's no point because I know he's right. A doctor I saw when I was eighteen told me that, but since everyone else always insists that I have asthma, I say that as well. Now it seems like that moment at Maya's – a sudden hole opening up in front of me, the kaleidoscope twisting, the patterns changing.

'You know, you can always go back to those perfect places,' Jack says.

'How? How can you do that?'

'They're here, now – those exact places. It's just that you can't see them.' For a moment I almost believe him. It's as though his words have summoned up that world. I hear the wash of the sea, and smell salt, and dank seaweed. And it seems as though I feel the sun above, spreading its rays. He puts out his hand and lays it over my gloved fingers.

'And it was that place you saw when we last met?'

'No. No. Well, not really.'

I look down at his hand resting on mine. He should have long white pianist's fingers, but instead his knuckles look sore and chapped. A scar runs across the end of his index finger, and the nail is yellow and misshapen. Suddenly I start to think, This man is thirty-five years older than me, and I've got a boyfriend, and I'm going to marry him. I don't want to become Valia, or Svetlana, or whatever her name is. And this isn't even what he wants, I know it isn't.

I start to slide my fingers out of his gloves. Immediately his hand jumps back from mine. For a moment it drifts through the air, as though to suggest that it was only ever an accident that he touched me. Although he doesn't move, I feel him drawing away from me. 'Please don't mind too much,' I say. 'You know, you're deceived by me. People always are. Somehow I cast spells, quite accidentally, and people think they see something in me, but really there isn't anything there.'

'No. You're wrong. That's not how it is. There is something there. It's just that other people see it and you don't.' He stands up and I try to give him his gloves back but he won't take them. Instead he digs his hands into the pockets of his coat and strides away. I follow, but he's moving too fast. We head back along the icy path, and I'm slipping and sliding, and I want him to come back and offer me his hand but he's brisk and distant now. We reach the Metro and take the train back into the city. I can't believe how stupid I've been. What did I think this was all about?

As we reach the centre I ask him where he lives. He

doesn't answer but says he'll travel back to my stop with me. He says it kindly but still he's all closed up inside. When we reach Byelorusskaia he gets off the Metro with me. A woman in a khaki uniform wields an object like a table-tennis bat as she marshals passengers on and off the train. We're caught up in a mass of people, crossing the vast plat-forms, walking under high marble arches and past statues of Soviet peasants enthusiastically tilling the fields. We travel miles up long wooden escalators, the brown gloom illumin-ated by circular white lights.

As we arrive at ground level and walk through the underpass, men in black leather caps gather around kiosks. They drink from bottles, standing in puddles of melted ice. On the wall, posters displaying Communist slogans have been defaced. People stare at Jack and me as we pass because they know we're from the West. My red hair gives me away but also my clothes. Wearing baggy leggings and Army Surplus boots is a luxury that Russian women can't afford.

In the square the snow has been swept off the streets and lies in piles in the gutters. Cars hoot and crowds of people push towards the station. Women upholstered in layers of black pack up the remains of makeshift market-stalls. We pass through wooden walkways which have been built to protect the pavement from falling masonry. At the entrance to my street, we stop and shelter in the doorway of an office building, standing close. I give his gloves back to him. 'Perhaps we'll meet up again?' I try to say it casually.

'I don't know,' he says. 'My time is very limited.'

'Yes, I'm sure. But at least write down your number for me.'

'There isn't any need. If you want me, you'll find me at that café.'

After that I expect him to say a brief goodbye and leave, but he doesn't go.

'Jack, it's just . . . you understand things. You know, I thought about what you said – about the past – and I know you're right. But I need your help.'

For a moment he closes his eyes and shakes his head. 'Eva, you know I'm not really interested in playing at substitute fathers.'

I feel my lungs suddenly close, and I turn away. My legs are dissolving but I hurry towards home, my head down. He comes after me and catches hold of me. I yank my arm away. We stand together under a streetlight. 'I'm sorry. For some reason I had the impression that you were interested . . . that you could . . .' I can't find the words and flap my hands in frustration.

For a moment both of us stare, wide-eyed, then suddenly we're laughing. I know myself to be ridiculous. Our laughter sounds exotic in that concrete street. He shakes his head, watching me. 'Eva, of course I'd like to see you again, but it's difficult. You have to understand – I didn't expect this now. It comes too late for me.' He looks away from me, assailed by a thought from outside.

'Why? You're not old.'

'No, I'm not. But I'm dying.'

I want to have misheard the word but it isn't possible. Its echo fades into the air. I want to start laughing again and I look into his face, hoping that I'll find mirth there. But what he's saying is real. 'You can't be.'

'Of course I can.' He taps the flat of his hand against his chest. 'My heart is worn out.'

I move towards him, standing close, and, without thinking, I put up my hand and touch his cheek. Deep inside him I feel a shudder, as though a breeze has moved through the leaves of a tree, but his eyes are untroubled. He reaches up and, taking hold of my hand, he presses it against his face. 'Of course, my dear. Friends. Of course.'

He holds my hand against his cheek a moment longer, then he leans down and kisses my forehead, so gently that I hardly feel his lips. I want to catch hold of his hand but I know that I mustn't. He turns and walks away. The street is monochrome and swept by a cutting wind. Other people weave around him, heading towards the station, or pushing to cross the road. At the corner he looks back and waves.

I'm gripped by a black panic. I must run after him and stop him, say those vital words I needed to say, whatever they were. But he's gone and I'm alone, gasping for breath. He's dying, dying. The word echoes in my head. I step back into the doorway of a building, my hands flailing, as I try to push images of that child away.

The child is far out on the beach. She wears a blue smocked dress and she's making patterns in the mud with her new ladybird Wellington boots. When she looks up, she sees that her father is far away, down towards the sea. A russet-coloured dog, which belongs to Mr Reynolds, the farmer, has followed them down the beach. It races on sprawling legs, barking and leaping to snap at flies. The sky is bronze and the wind pulls this way and that. The yellow clouds flap like sheets cracking on a line. In the distance thunder stirs. Gulls swoop overhead, screaming.

The child pulls at the end of her plaits, which are secured with see-through purple bobbles, then she runs to follow her father. He stands at the water's edge, where lines of grey lace froth and fade across the sand. The sun is setting over the sea, its rays divided like the spokes of a wheel, breaking down through the edges of the clouds. The child's father is held by the light, and the edges of him are turned fiery red. She stops still to watch him there, seeing his hair standing on end, his hands waving.

Then she runs towards him and he sweeps her up in his arms, holding her too tight. His eyes are bright as flames. The child grips at his jumper, feeling the softness of it in her hands. This is her favourite jumper – a grey turtleneck with a cable stitch running down the front. Over his shoulder she watches the sea roll up the beach towards them, slow, and then slide back. Next time will it come too close and suck up their legs? Her mother would be angry if she knew that they were out on the beach at the time when the tide turns.

Her father puts her down and then bends to talk to her. He's telling her about a place he went to once. It's a place called Mexico and it's on the other side of the globe, but it has a beach as well. Not like this one – a beach of turquoise and gold. And in that place, at certain times, stars come down to the earth. Is that what he's saying? The child can't hear properly because of the sea and the screaming of the gulls, but she loves the words anyway.

She says—couldn't you make that happen here? And her father says that perhaps it might be possible. Perhaps if they used her butterfly net then they might be able to catch a star.

And that place on the other side of the globe – is that where Aunt Amelia and Rob live? she asks. The letters which come from there have blue postmarks and parrot stamps.

No, her father says, not there. That's Rhodesia – another place very far away.

Can we go to Mexico? Can we go?

Her father is silent and his arms are still. The thunder growls, and the wind pulls at the child's dress. The sun is lost behind a cloud and the beach turns dark. We should go back, her father says. But the child doesn't want to go. A sudden squall of rain comes in from the sea, splattering across the sand. The dog runs close to them, crouches, barks and then dives away. Further up the beach it stops, watching them, barks again, then whines. The child stares back up the beach. The gate which leads to the lane is tiny in the distance.

The child's father is looking out over her shoulder, at the sea. The clouds hang low now and are the colour of pewter. The rain falls harder, dancing through the air, tossed this way and that by the wind. The child watches her father's eyes. Something far out at sea has taken hold of them and keeps them there. The child turns, trying to see what it is, but everything is lost behind a curtain of grey.

The sea draws breath. A line of water dashes towards them, and the child feels the pull of it around her new boots. Her father's shoes and the bottom of his trousers are soaked. A crack of thunder shakes the sky, a fork of lightning splits the horizon.

The child feels her father's hand gripping tight around her wrist. She's still looking back at the sea, but he's pulling her up the beach. Her boots flap and suck in the mud, and rain batters down onto her bare arms. She can't see the gate, or the lane, or the sea wall. But the dog is ahead of them, barking again and again. Her legs ache and it hurts to breathe.

She imagines the sea behind them. Like a great monster it will gather itself together. Black and slimy, with red eyes, it will gush up the beach, carrying them with it. The lane will be flooded, the gate ripped from its hinges, the trees pulled up by their roots. The black water is clinging to her legs. It will catch hold of her and her father, and fill their mouths with blackness.

Run, her father says. Run. He reaches down and lifts her up. His breath rasps in his throat and her swinging legs bump against him. She imagines saltwater filling their mouths, their noses and ears. Soon they will be swept down into the deep and her father will not be able to keep hold of her hand. She'll be wrenched away from him and swallowed in darkness.

Then suddenly she's at the gate and her mother is there with her face screwed up tight. Rain has plastered her hair across her cheek. She wears no hat or coat but a pair of binoculars swings from her shoulders. She's shouting at them but the child can't hear the words. The girl's father puts her down and her foot touches mud. One of her new ladybird boots has gone. She pulls at her father's hand. My boot. My boot.

I'll go back, her father says. No, no, her mother shouts.

Let me go with him. Let me go with him.

Her mother catches hold of her hand, tight, as her father runs back down the beach. The child pulls on the end of her arm, screaming, Let me go. Let me go. She kicks and thrashes, falling down into the mud. Her mother tries to pick her up, but still she punches and struggles, her head shaking back and forwards. She turns her head and bites into her mother's wrist, but although her mother cries out, she doesn't release her grip. The child kicks, her one boot smashing against her mother's shin. For a moment her face comes close to her mother's. She sees eyes set hard, and a mouth gripped shut.

Then her father is back beside them, holding her boot. Sobbing, the child takes it from him and he reaches down and picks her up. Together, they all go through the gate and hurry up the lane, heads bent against the weight of the rain. The strands of barbed wire which edge the lane rattle in the wind. Ahead of them, Marsh End House, redbrick and solid, stands up too high in the flat and battered landscape.

They cross the drive, which is half-underwater, then enter the house. The back door slams shut. Now the only sound is wet clothes dripping on to the tiled floor and the lid of a pan rattling on the hob. The child stares down at her dress and the one boot which she holds in her hand. Everything is caked brown with mud. Her mother is shouting at her father. For God's sake. You promised me, you promised me. You of all people. And look at her, just look.

The child is pressed against her mother's stiff mackintosh. But she wants to say, No, no. You don't understand. Because it isn't fear that is making her cry. Her father stands near the back door, quite still and silent – but he understands, he knows. She wants to be back out on the beach with sun breaking through the cloud and the tide turning.

From the kitchen the boiling pan rattles on its ring, and then, with a hiss, liquid spills across the top of the oven. The child's mother goes to turn the pan down and fetches a blanket from a cupboard under the stairs. She tugs off the child's muddy dress and wraps her in the scratchy blanket. The girl's father is still staring out through the panes of the back door towards the sea.

What are you doing? The mother's voice is stretched tight.

I'm waiting, the father says.

For what? There's nothing there.

Her father doesn't turn around.

Come away from the door. There's nothing there.

There is, the child says.

No, there isn't.

I saw it. I saw a monster.

Be quiet. The child's mother pulls the scratchy blanket too tightly around her. The child is still watching her father but her mother catches hold of her chin and forces her face towards her. Monsters? Don't be so stupid. There aren't any monsters. But the child knows her mother is lying.

The No Name Café, Moscow

November 1990

I met Jack every day, hurrying from the college to the No
Name Café. When I arrived, I'd wipe a circle in the
steamed–up glass of the window. And then I'd see him there,
and he'd always be writing in a blue notebook. A pen would
be gripped in his hand, and his tortoiseshell half–moon
glasses would be perched on the bridge of his nose.
Sometimes I'd just stand there and watch him for a while
before going in. I liked to see his thick fingers around that
slim, green pen. And I liked his stillness, and the way he
looked up occasionally, staring into the air, thinking.

With him, for the first time, I was not alone.

If the weather was more than normally bad, we'd sit in
that café for hours, talking and talking, until it seemed that
the words themselves were quite worn out. Often we talked
about my childhood, my father, the reasons why I couldn't
make decisions. Jack had theories on all of that. When he
asked me questions about myself he never let me get away
with easy answers. He could be harsh and critical if he
suspected any evasion or pretence. He would never say
anything directly against Rob but he made it clear that he
thought I was throwing my life away. 'When are you going

to stop playing roles in other people's movies,' he said, 'and decide for yourself what you want?'

He was extraordinarily well-read. He knew about medicine, religion, philosophy, astronomy, art, ancient history. But it wasn't his knowledge which impressed me, it was his ability to turn an idea around and see it in a totally new way. Frequently I was annoyed by him, but I indulged him because I understood that he had an urgent need to pass his ideas on to someone, before it was too late.

I was always trying, in a pathetic way, to find some means of impressing him. I told him about all the different places I'd lived in, and expounded the benefits of travel. But, despite having travelled far more widely than me, he wasn't convinced. 'Is it so interesting?' he'd say. 'Really, do you think that? I mean, isn't a tree in London as interesting as a tree in Moscow? You know, the desire to be free can be its own prison.' When he said that, it was as though someone had switched on a light inside my head.

On another occasion I talked to him about Rob's work. I supposed that he would be interested because he did care passionately about what was happening in Russia. But he said that he was too old for all of that. At his age he could only really put faith in the possibility of changes in individuals. Then he said, 'I suppose, on a personal level, that people get fascinated by situations like this because big problems can be so much easier to deal with than small ones.' I didn't reply because I didn't want to think about what he might mean.

On days when the weather was better, he showed me Moscow as no one else could have done. Before I met him, it had seemed to me like a city designed by Escher. Nothing joined together in the way I expected. Street-names, people's names, even the names of the Metro stops seemed to change all the time. If I asked directions, people turned away, frightened to be seen talking to a foreigner.

But with Jack it was different and I started to understand the city. Often we just wandered, making decisions about which street to walk down according to where a ray of sunlight might be found. On other occasions Jack took on the role of tour guide, taking me to the Tryetiakov Gallery, the Novodyevichii Convent, Tolstoi's House and Victory Park. He also took me to churches, many of which were newly reopened, their icons recently put back in place.

I loved the way he looked – that swept-back hair and slightly hooked nose. Those strange golden-green eyes with their dark lashes, and their suggestion of something exotic, powerful, ancient. Those smooth circles of blue at the side of his eyes where his glasses normally sat. I loved his otherness, the fact that I knew him, and I didn't. Both of us were clear from the beginning that our friendship couldn't last, and perhaps that was part of what gave it such intensity. We both felt as though we were being given something which we weren't really allowed. *Rented time* – that's what Jack called it.

A couple of times, when cold and hunger got the better of us, we sat in the sterile dining room of an Intourist hotel and had lunch. Even in those places the food was barely edible. I paid for those meals because Jack never had much money. And it wasn't just some delay in funds being transferred from the States. He really didn't have money. He'd come to Moscow because an American government aid programme had offered him some work. Usually they would never have considered him. He hadn't practised medicine for nearly twenty years and he'd written articles that were considered extreme. But American neurologists who can speak Russian are hard to find, he said, and so he'd got the job. But now it was at an end, and so was the money.

Occasionally a cheque for a few dollars arrived – royalty payments on books he'd written years before – but that was all. In Moscow he rented a room in the apartment of an elderly woman – Mrs Galina Pastukhova – who'd once worked for his family. She had a small dog called Kashtanka whose antics he described to me in rather too much detail. He didn't have a house back in the States, or any family. He had been married once but his wife had died more than twenty years ago. All he possessed was the day he was standing up in. He wanted no dealings with material things, no clutter, no distractions. It was a waste of time to ask him what he might do next month, or even next week, because he really never thought about such things.

He believed in all sorts of stuff that I thought cranky – past lives, astrology, faith healing and leylines. He also told me that having one of his molars taken out had cured the arthritis in his knee. It surprised me that someone so intelligent should believe such things, but I never said so. As a young man he'd experimented widely with drugs and he explained to me that the mind is a limiting mechanism which keeps us from seeing too much. Drugs get rid of those limitations, he said.

He was incredibly easily pleased. A packet of shortbread, a bunch of flowers, the colour of the paint on a particular door – those things made him happy. He enjoyed the fact that our birthdays were two days apart. I was more interested in the day in between. I never let him say anything about the age difference between us because I wouldn't allow it to have any importance. But it did have an effect on our friendship. Twenty-nine, sixty-four – that immutable equation. I had something he didn't have, and would never have again. I was powerful as I'd never been before. Our friendship was the only thing in my life which I knew to be truly mine.

30/16 Ulitsa Pravdy, Moscow

December 1990

Maya's note was written on mauve paper which smelt faintly of lavender. I found it lying on the kitchen table when I got back from an afternoon with Jack. How had it arrived there? Had Rob left it for me that morning? My name was written on the envelope in watery blue ink. The handwriting was unsteady, with a shaky flourish to the capital letters. I took off my coat, and one of my jumpers, then pulled the envelope open to find three scrawling lines covering the entire page. *Would be lovely to see you. Do come round any time.* I laid the note down on the table, vaguely hoping that it might just evaporate, but it lay there, solid and insistent.

I wanted to sit down and do nothing for a while, but since I'd been in Moscow I'd lost the ability to do that. My mind was churning around, replaying the conversations I'd had with Jack. I'd just spent an afternoon with him but still there were a hundred questions I wanted to ask him. I felt as though I was on the brink of understanding some vital idea which would unravel every mystery, but no matter how hard I tried, I couldn't quite fix that idea in my mind.

I started to tidy the kitchen and picked up a rubbish bag which needed taking downstairs. As I opened the door of the flat, I heard small feet tapping across the landing. It was the little girl from next door. The sound of her feet, and the pattern of her movements, had become familiar. Left foot, right foot, both feet together. The game she played was a kind of hop-scotch organized around a deep crack which ran across the concrete of the landing. She made her way along the length of that crack, jumping from one side to the other. Left foot, right foot, both feet together.

She stopped when she saw me, fixed me with her blank eyes, then went on. Her arms stuck out sideways because she wore so many layers of clothing. Around her, the landing was filled by a greenish glow from low-hanging striplights which stayed on all day and all night. A star-shaped fracture glittered in one of the panes of the landing window. Behind the glass, long icicles hung down. Left foot, right foot, both feet together.

I went back into the kitchen and found a tin of choco-lates that one of Rob's colleagues had brought over from New York. I picked out three and went back to the landing. The child's tiny, pinched hand reached for the chocolates. She stared at the coloured cellophane wrappers, then pushed them down deep into the pocket of her skirt. I'd given her chocolates before but I suspected that she didn't eat them. I think she thought them too precious for that. I tried a few words of Russian but she didn't seem to understand.

As I moved towards the stairs, a rising cry came from above and a splintering crash. The bag of rubbish slid from my hand. The little girl stood on her left leg, like a stork. I heard a door open downstairs and an elderly man came out, disturbed by the noises from above. I'd seen this old man often before, and his wife. Both in their eighties, they were known to be staunch Communists. His suit was always clean, the creases sharp. Sometimes he wore a chest full of medals.

She wore a buttercup-yellow cotton dress, a neat cardigan, a cloth tied on her head. The old man peered upstairs for a long moment, shook his head in contempt, then disappeared back inside his flat, shutting the door.

Around me, the whole building seemed to be turning in on itself. Did I hear shuffling, throats being cleared, doors closing? The little girl wobbled on that one leg, then ran away into her flat. From upstairs I heard a shout from Mrs Balashova and a grunt from her husband. Behind their voices a dull thump sounded. '*Nyet, nyet, nyet.*' Another thump and a bottle or glass breaking. I thought of bones splintering, a thick hand gripping hair and yanking it out.

I ran up the stairs. The door opened three inches inwards, then slammed shut again. A roar and a shuffle came from inside. '*Vsyo, khvatit, perestan'.*' That's it, that's enough. Stop. The door shuddered and started to open again. A hand appeared around the side, forcing it wider open. Mrs Balashova was trying to get out and her hand was about to be trapped. I flung my shoulder against the door but it didn't move one inch. I looked down at those hands gripped around the door. Small, pale fingers, but covered with dark hairs – the fingers of a man.

I stepped back from the door, and stared. It couldn't be Mr Balashov who was being hit. Men do not get hit by women. But as the door opened further it revealed a tired face with round glasses – the man I'd seen going up the stairs before, except now his glasses were skewed to one side. And under the line of his grey-brown hair was a new gash, vivid in the pallor of his face. Behind him stood a wall of floral material, topped by a balloon face and orange hair. A thick arm was locked around his neck. I needed to say something but I couldn't remember a word of Russian.

'What do you think you're doing?' My English voice

sounded ridiculous but it made the woman release her grip. Mr Balashov pulled away and headed for the stairs. For a moment I stood face to face with him, his eyes looking straight into mine. We seemed to stand there for a long time before he dodged past me. Mrs Balashova made a growling sound then slammed the door shut. The sound of her husband's footsteps faded in the stairwell. The silence around me was heavy after the struggle and shouting. I'd wanted to be heroic but instead I had the sense of having made some stupid mistake. As I walked back down the stairs, I noticed two smudged marks on the bottom step. In the harsh light I leant down to look at them. They were drops of blood from Mr Balashov's head.

I picked up the rubbish bag and went back into our flat. Maya's note was lying on the hall floor. When I looked at it again I didn't see mauve paper, instead I saw the eyes of Mr Balashov. They should have been full of fear and pain but instead I'd seen a look which was oddly familiar — was it excitement, even exhilaration? I folded Maya's letter up and went to the bathroom to deal with the hot tap. We always had a problem with it because it wouldn't turn off properly and, as a result, the bathroom was always full of steam. Still those eyes were in my mind. I whacked the heel of one of Rob's shoes against the tap, trying to get those eyes out of my head. I must phone Bill and Sarah, I thought. Surely they'll know where to find a plumber? I started to make some supper but the kitchen seemed too small and cramped. My mind was spinning round and round.

I put on my coat and went out. The night was so cold that, as I stepped out of our building, I gasped. Behind me, a voice started to shout. It was the one-armed *babushka* who sat in a curtained cubicle at the bottom of our stairs. It was her job to watch everyone in the building, but Rob supplied her with biscuits and stale pastries from his office, so she was always quite friendly to us. '*Dyevushka, ne vykhodi na ulitsu bez shapki.*' She was telling me that I mustn't go out without a hat.

Pulling a woollen beret out of my pocket, I stretched it down over my ears. I waved good night to her, then stumbled across the courtyard past the remains of a dismantled Lada. When I reached the two-storey-high arch which led out into the street, I looked back at the windows of our block. My mind turned around – questions, questions, questions. And Mr Balashov's eyes still staring inside my head.

10/38 Kutuzovskii Prospyekt, Moscow

December 1990

It shouldn't have been possible just to walk into Maya's building but it was. A man coming out held the door open for me, and then I crept past the floor lady as she snored gently behind her desk. The hall was the size of a tennis court with a grand chandelier and columns of dogmeat-coloured marble. I felt sure that until recently, this building must have been reserved for Party officials. An ancient lift was clanking upwards on a thick pulley but I thought that if I pressed the button I might wake the floor lady. So instead I took the wide marble stairs which led up beside the lift-shaft into darkness. A ray of light from a landing window touched on broken floor-tiles, a cracked marble step, the elaborate twists of a wrought-iron stair-rail. As I walked, I could hear my boots trudging on the steps and my breath beating in my ears. My hand searched the wall, touching dust, cracks, wiring, but never a light-switch.

When I reached the fourth floor, I stopped. On the landing above, light shone through an open door. I hesitated, went up to the level of the door, stopped and looked in. Pale blue wallpaper with gold stars — I remembered it from the night of the party. I moved closer and heard a rustling sound. I could see Maya's dyed black hair and the skirt of her long velvet dress. But a twist of blonde hair lay against her shoulder, and blood-coloured nails were pressed against her back. Feet interlocked, and I saw an angle of white cheek. I felt blood rise to my face, and I backed away, but in the darkness my boot struck against the stair-rail. I stumbled down the stairs, but then, hearing footsteps above, I turned back, making an inadequate pretence that I'd just arrived.

'Who's that?' An edge of panic sounded in Maya's voice.

'Sorry, sorry. I should have telephoned.' I stepped forward into the light.

'Oh Eva – my God. You scared me half to death.'

'Sorry, sorry. I'll go . . .'

'No, no. It doesn't matter. Not at all. Do come in.' Maya waved her hand in an extravagant gesture of welcome and I stepped into the hall. The blonde woman raised her hand to tidy her hair.

'Eva, you remember Estelle, don't you?'

Estelle turned around, as though she'd only just realized I was there. Her face was flushed and her lipstick smudged. She was pretending that she couldn't quite place me. 'Oh yes, of course.' She looked me up and down as though I was something that should be put out with the rubbish. 'Yes, perhaps I do remember. At the party. You work for some . . . charity?'

'It's not a charity, actually . . .'

'Sadly, Estelle's just going.' Maya gave another grand wave of her hand, this time to usher Estelle out of the door. But the woman wouldn't be hurried. She leant forward and planted a kiss close to Maya's mouth. As she whispered something in her ear, her red nails flickered against Maya's cheek. Then another long kiss, before she swept out of the flat, located the light-switch without any difficulty, and clattered away down the stairs.

'Really, I could come back another time.'

'Not at all.' Maya gave a dismissive shrug as she shut the door. 'You re-e-ally mustn't take any notice of Estelle.' She slid my coat from my shoulders and I took off my boots. On a table, a gold clock under a glass dome chimed seven. Beside it, a photograph showed a young man in a pin-stripe suit with a vicious smile. The sitting room was just as I remembered it – dusty, exotic, cluttered. I was sure I could still smell the cigarette smoke and stale alcohol left over from that night. What was it Rob had said – quaint? That was just the sort of thing he would say.

Maya led me close to a low lamp, and stared down into my face. 'Dre-e-adful,' she said. 'You look absolutely dr-e-adful.' It was true I hadn't slept properly for the last couple of weeks, and was as tense as a violin string, but I didn't think I looked that bad.

'It won't do at all. Harvey told me – living in some ghastly place, trying to save the world.' She steered me into the kitchen. 'Food. I think that's where we need to start.' Everything in the kitchen was coated with dust and grease, but my stomach leapt as I watched Maya's shaky hands piling food on to a tray. White bread rolls, Brie and thin slices of ham, a jar of mayonnaise, muffins, yoghurt and fruit. She made me a cup of coffee and poured me a fish-tank glass of vodka. 'Carry that tray,' she said, and I followed her back into the sitting room.

I spread butter on a white bread roll then filled it with mayonnaise, Brie and ham. Thank God for Stockman's or whatever foreign-currency shop she'd got it all from. While I ate, Maya complained about Russia. And all this was done in the name of equality, she said. But actually this was the least equal country you could ever find. A half-mile queue for petrol and Party officials could just cut in front of everyone else. In what other country would you find that? And everybody talking now about the Mafia. 'But there's been the Mafia for ye-e-ars,' she said. 'They just happened to be called the Communist Party.'

The flat was heated by huge radiators which stood like toast-racks under the windows, and I soon felt so cooked that I took off two jumpers and sat there in my T-shirt. Even then, my legs were too hot in their woollen tights. I felt embarrassed by my greed but couldn't resist a second bread roll, and then a third. I wondered if Maya had fed my father like this on his visits to London.

'Go on,' Maya said. 'Have as much as you want.' She didn't eat herself but lit a cigarette. The coffee turned out to be tepid but I drank it anyway. Maya had finished her rant about Russia and was telling me about her work. She was really retired, she said, but she still had links with some galleries.

'You've got some wonderful pictures.' I spoke through a mouthful of cake.

'So kind of you to say so, my dear, but I have to be honest – they're not ne-e-arly as good as they look. Of course, when I knew I was going to come back here, I thought perhaps I'd find some lost Kandinskii hidden in a cellar, and actually some interesting things a-a-re turning up. But nearly everything I'm shown is fake. But then sometimes, I can't stop myself, and I finish up buying the odd thing anyway. Because I do always ra-a-ther like fakes, don't you?'

'Yes, I like fakes as well.'

I didn't know why I'd said that. Was it even true? Maya gave my foot a prod with her walking stick and poured more vodka into my glass. 'I can't see you properly there.

Come and sit near me.' I positioned myself at the end of the sofa but still she beckoned me closer. As I edged towards her, she fixed me with those exaggerated eyes. 'So tell me – you're in lo-o-ve?'

The cup in my hand trembled on its saucer. I put it down on the table, dropped the teaspoon, fumbled around on the floor looking for it. Of course I wasn't in love, whatever was she talking about? Then I realized what she meant. 'Oh, Rob. Yes, of course. In love. Yes.' I placed the teaspoon back on the saucer. It seemed that the vodka was already ringing in my head. I took a deep breath, sat back in my chair, folded my hands. 'Yes, in fact you might remember Rob. His mother was my father's cousin.'

'Oh, Amelia? Oh, really? So he's the son. Oh, now I see. And she was married to – King Midas?'

'Yes, Guy Kingmuiden.'

'Oh yes, I remember. And she became involved in all that political trouble in Rhodesia, didn't she? And then went crazy and got herself killed.'

'Well, not exactly . . .'

'And Guy writes books now, doesn't he, on some obscure subject?'

'The origins of languages.'

Maya picked up the vodka bottle and poured herself a glass. 'I'm sorry,' she said. 'At the party I fear I said a-all the wrong things.'

'No, no. Not at all.'

'I just didn't understand that you hadn't heard from your father. And I didn't realize that you – well, I thought your mother would have talked to you.'

'She did talk. But only really to complain that he never sent any money.'

Maya took a long drag on her cigarette and shook her

head. 'Typical. Typical. That's crazy, my de-a-ar. Crazy. I mean, she could have sold the house at any time. And in total, the paintings would be worth half a million.'

My mouth opened and shut. My mother had always told me that only a few of his early paintings were any good.

'Half a million — at le-e-ast. And he was only re-e-ally at the beginning of his career. I mean now, if one wanted to sell them . . . He has been rather forgotten, but at the time . . . one can't imagine now the impact they had. All that enthusiasm he had for Mexico and the Mayan culture, and all of his ideas about the shaman, and the ancient astrologers. All of that came out in his paintings. Really, he was trying to touch on some other, unseen world. To have some communication with . . .' Maya shook her head and sighed. 'People must have written to your mother suggesting ideas for exhibitions. I'm sure I even wrote to her myself, ye-e-ars ago . . .'

I couldn't believe we were sitting here talking about my father. A key rattled at the front door and we heard ponderous footsteps in the hall. Harvey cleared his throat and entered the room. He was a solidly built American, open-faced, tanned, with silver-grey hair. It seemed as though he should be wearing a Stetson, cowboy boots, and guns on his belt. Russia — just another frontier to be conquered.

Maya introduced me although we'd met on the night of the party. His dry hand folded around mine. 'Well then, here you all are.' For a long moment he shuffled from one foot to the other, standing near to Maya, then he headed for the door, making some excuse about work.

'You know, I have one of your father's paintings,' Maya said. 'Would you like to see?' As she led me down the corridor, my head swayed from the vodka. She took me to the room where I'd first met Jack. It seemed to be her bedroom as well as her office, but there was no sign of Harvey there. On a table beside the bed, an ashtray was overflowing with cigarette ends, their smell mingled with a cloying scent of perfume. An emerald-green scarf lay draped across the end of the unmade bed.

Maya laid down her stick and shuffled a canvas out from the pile which was propped against a bookcase. Then she asked me to help her to turn it around and stand it against the wall. A vivid mass of clashing colours and jagged shapes confused my eyes. Then I began to see objects within it. I saw mouths, clouds, a man with a raised knife. This was Abraham poised to sacrifice his son. Amidst the tortured slashes of red and yellow, only the faces of Abraham and Isaac were clear. Abraham looked up towards the heavens, offering up the murder he was about to commit. So this was a picture painted by my father. To look at it seemed to me an invasion of his privacy. I felt suddenly tired and sat down on the crumpled bedcover.

'Of course, this one is quite untypical,' Maya said. 'It's one of the last paintings he ever did. Or at least I assume so, unless he's still painting now. It was shown in that last exhibition – early January 1967. He was turning back to Christian images at that time.'

Maya came to sit beside me. I didn't want to look at the painting because I couldn't imagine how the man who painted it could ever have lived at Marsh End House with my mother. My fingers fiddled with the fringe on the emerald-green scarf. Maya was lost in the painting, her face alight. 'Oh, I do so miss your father.' Tears brimmed in her eyes. 'It's such a shame that you can't remember. He was so-o full of life. And he was someone one could always talk to. You know, for me it was like . . .' She searched for the words.

'Like someone you knew before you were born.'

She turned to look at me, her eyes clicking open. 'Yes. Maybe like that.' She laid a hand on my arm. 'Oh, my de-e-ar, it is such a shame you never knew him. And he loved you so very dearly.'

I looked back at the picture and my head swirled with colour and vodka. Maya rested a hand on my shoulder. I looked down to see my fingers twisting the fringe on the emerald scarf. Maya curled a strand of my hair, then moved close to me, gathering up all of my hair in her hands and holding it back from my face. 'You should wear your hair tied back, you know. You shouldn't hide a face like that.' Embarrassed, I avoided her eyes although I could feel her breath on my face.

My hand stroked the fringe of the scarf. 'Try that on,' she said. 'I think it would be your colour.' She stood me in front of the mirror, and, folding the scarf into a triangle, she knotted it around my neck. The wool was tender against my skin and when I looked in the mirror I didn't look like my normal self at all. So my father had loved me. Of course he had.

A door slammed and Harvey cleared his throat. I stepped back from the mirror. 'I should go. I'm sure you want to spend some time with Harvey.'

'Oh no. Not at a-all. You shouldn't think that. Harvey likes me to have my female friends.'

I started to take the scarf off.

'Oh no,' Maya repeated. 'You must keep it. Have it as a pre-e-sent.' Her hands gathered the scarf up and rearranged it, bunching it closer to my neck. 'Better like this, I think. Yes, it re-e-ally suits you.' She leant forward and kissed my cheek. 'You should wear it for your friend Mr Flame.'

'Who?'

She didn't answer but watched me with raised eyebrows. 'He's not my friend. I hardly know him.'

'But of course. And he's much too old for you. He has quite a reputation with women, I'm told.'

'I'm going out with Rob.'

'Oh yes, so you are.' She considered me with narrowed eyes. 'But isn't it always nice to have other friends?' Again her hands adjusted the scarf. 'What I'm saying, my dear, is that you don't know the value of your own currency. You should spend it before it drops.'

I looked away, promising myself that I wouldn't let this conversation go any further. I shrugged my shoulders, examined my fingernails. 'So you know him well?'

'No, hardly at all. My family knew his, ma-a-ny years ago now. I think he left Moscow with his father when he was ten. His mother was expected to join them.' Maya shook her head and sighed. 'So many of those stories.' Her hand smoothed the bedspread. 'Of course, they do say he's part of the Intelligence Services.'

'What?'

'Well, it stands to re-e-ason, doesn't it? I mean, it's quite an advantage, wouldn't you say, to speak both English and Russian fluently? And then there's that fabricated name ... and he doesn't ever seem to give anyone his telephone number or his address.'

'Yes, but none of that means anything. It doesn't mean anything at all.'

'Perhaps. Perhaps not. Does it matter? We've all got our cover story, haven't we? A love affair with a spy – rather exciting, don't you think?'

Harvey clattered in the hall again. 'Oh, whatever does he want?' Maya said. 'Wait a minute. I'll be back.' I said that really I should go, but Maya wouldn't let me. 'Really, there's no need for you to leave,' she said, and shut the door on me firmly. I walked around the room. I'd eaten too much and now my stomach felt bloated. My mouth was dry because of the vodka. I thought of Jack standing in that room and of the way he'd manipulated my spine. We'd never spoken of that again, but at that moment the past had started to move forward into the present and now there was no way to stop it.

Maya didn't come back so I wandered over to her desk. Peacock feathers, stuck in a vase, drooped over piles of books. A green-painted cup full of pens stood next to a card-index box. An invitation to the opening of an exhibition in Paris was propped against it. Photographs of paintings lay half-pushed into envelopes. Underneath a book I could see a faded green cardboard file, with the flap open. Written in ink on a smudged label in that unsteady hand was a date – *1966*.

I eased the file out from under the book. Inside it were papers, and an envelope full of photographs. I looked back at the door then flicked through them. Some of the people in them looked familiar. Long collars, flared trousers, geometric patterns, flowing hair. I turned over a photograph which was crumpled and discoloured. Surely it showed a figure in a frockcoat? No, of course it didn't. I pushed the photograph closer to the light and bent down to stare at it. Yes, a frockcoat and a three-cornered hat. I'd been so sure that that image I'd seen in my head was *not* a real memory, and yet here was a photograph of exactly the same man.

The photograph wavered in my hand and I bent to stare at it again. It seemed as though it had been taken by accident. A bright patch of light ran down one side of it, and the frockcoated figure was in the background and half out of the photograph. Above were the latticed leaves of a tree and in the foreground an iron gate, standing open. Was that a monkey puzzle tree? And did that wrought-iron gate have a design like a spider's web? In the garden at Marsh End House we had a monkey puzzle tree and an iron gate, but this wasn't a photograph of our garden. Of course it wasn't.

I didn't even see Maya as she came back into the room. 'Ah yes, that file.' Her voice made it sound like nothing, but she reached out and took the photograph from me.

'Who is he?' I asked.

She stared down as though seeing the photograph for the first time. 'It must be your father, but it isn't very clear. It isn't one I took.' I looked towards the photograph again but she had placed it far back on the desk.

'I must go,' I said.

'But why go? It's late, and you don't look well. Perhaps you should stay here – wouldn't that be better?'

'No. No. I must go.'

'But Eva, re-e-ally – you should stay here. I insist. It would be better for you to go to bed now.'

Suddenly we were arguing as though it mattered. *You must go to bed now. You must go to bed.* She was insistent and I was tired and awash with vodka. And so I finished up in her spare room, putting on a white lace nightdress she found for me, while she telephoned Rob to explain that I wouldn't be back. She came to tuck me in, and kissed me good night – tenderly – so that I felt I was a child again. And then I was alone with the monkey puzzle tree and the iron gate with the design like a spider's web. *Eva, you must go to bed. You must go to bed.* But it wasn't Maya's voice which should have been saying those words.

12/20 rue de Lausanne, Geneva

October 1991

My hand unknots from the barrel of Jack's pen. I stare at the lake. Morning again. The sun is a stain of yellow in shades of grey. The days are relentless. They come at me like cars on a blind bend, their details sharp for a moment, before they speed away into the past. This business of writing has become as necessary to me as it once was to Jack. As words form on the paper, my grip on the day grows stronger.

I asked Jack once what he wrote in his endless blue notebooks. 'Just details,' he said, 'the exact way things are. If I do that accurately enough, then I find that everything else is somehow revealed.' I keep that in mind, but it isn't the same for me. No pattern emerges, no system of cause and effect. Everything remains blurred and meaningless. A sprawling mess of events tumbles towards this futureless flat. To make it into a story I would have to invent, which I could do, of course, with worrying ease. But I've already spent too much of my life in the Land of Makebelieve.

I get up from my desk and wander into the bedroom. For the last few days I've been wearing pyjamas, a self-pitying cardigan and my overcoat. It's cold and damp in this flat because I can't work out how to turn the central heating up. I need to go down and speak to the concierge, but even that level of human contact would be too much.

I brush my hair, pull on jeans and a jumper. This flat is bland and functional, but luxurious compared to most places I've lived. White light shines in through picture windows onto pale walls and parquet floors. The smell is of floor wax and new paint. In the sitting room, I step over suitcases, crates, piles of books. A dismantled wardrobe and some pictures are propped against the wall.

I pull my coat on again and go out to buy some food from the mini-supermarket at the corner. After Moscow, the lights in the shops here seem garish, and the music is an assault on my ears. I can't get used to the fact that there's no queue. The efficiency is offensive, the abundance vulgar. One whole wall is covered with chocolate bars. I hurry away as soon as I've made my purchases. When I get to the flat, I eat a bread roll and some tinned soup, then sit down at the table again.

I think back to that conversation with Jack. All that talk about detail – was that really what he thought? It was impossible to know. He said different things at different times. Once he even said that he considered writing to be a bad habit, and that he would have hoped, by his age, to have given it up. But when I accused him of being contradictory he wouldn't allow me that. He just said that any intelligent person should be capable of holding two or three conflicting ideas in their mind at any one time.

And then there was that day, not long after we first met. Nervous and brash, I stumbled into the café, full of clever and interesting things to say. But then, when I saw Jack, all the sentences drained from my head, and so I stood there with my mouth opening and shutting like a fish. Finally I pointed to his notebook and said, 'So what are you writing?'

He said nothing. And nothing and nothing. Why didn't the silence unnerve him? My mouth opened and shut. 'A love story perhaps?' As soon as the words were out, I curled up inside, wondering how I could have said them.

But Jack took the suggestion seriously. 'No. I wouldn't write a love story. In the modern age I'm not sure that such stories can really be made to work.'

'No, perhaps not.'

'Anyway, I've always thought those stories were the wrong way around. Love comes at the end, when really it's a beginning.' A bottle of water was open on the table and he motioned to me to sit down, and poured me a glass. He turned his head to one side, thinking. 'I suppose love stories used to rely on obstacles. Obstructive fathers, barriers of class, or race, or religion. But none of that exists any more. The obstacles lie within ourselves. So when love fails it's just a grubby tragedy of people's smallness.'

'Yes, I suppose you're right,' I said. 'No one wants to read about that.'

'No. Not if it *is* like that. But of course, it wouldn't have to be, would it?'

His fingers were clasped around my glass of water and he looked at me intently before he pushed it towards me. The sides of the glass were wet. I took care that our fingers didn't touch. He raised his glass to me, as though it contained champagne. I stared down at the black plastic surface of the table. But I moved my fingers on the glass, placing my thumb exactly where his thumb had been.

The No Name Café, Moscow

December 1990

It's the day after my evening with Maya. I go to the No Name Café and stand outside, wiping a circle on the window. I want to tell Jack what Maya said about my father; I want to describe that painting to him, to ask him about shamans and about astrologers in the ancient world. I stare through the window and Jack is there – but he's not alone. He's with a woman. Is that Valia or Anna or whatever her name was? Or is it one of the other women he sometimes mentions? Sunlight reflects on the window so I can't see clearly. Hands move, mouths open and shut, the woman laughs. I step back from the window. Phrases float back to me from my morning classes at the college, examples of how to use the negative. *They are not his friends. They should not be in our café. This should not be happening.*

I'm wearing Maya's emerald scarf and I twist it through my fingers. Of course, I've seen him talking to people before, but not like this. When I look again, his fingers have closed around that woman's arm. I raise my hands to shield my eyes and swallow several times. But then I know this isn't important. He can do what he likes. Our friendship isn't about possession. It's on a level far above that. If he wants some cheap Moscow blonde, then that's fine. I suppose she is more his age.

Through the window I see that she's getting up to go. And then there's another man, and I'm not sure whether he's with her or not. He's dressed in a ski-jacket, and a fur hat lies beside him on the table. That jacket suggests an American rather than a Russian. He hands a large white envelope to Jack and now he and the woman are moving towards the door. I step back under the porch of the next-door building until they've gone. I think of Maya and her comments about the Intelligence Service. She was wrong, of course. Totally wrong.

When I go into the café, Jack is just as he's always been. He bends to kiss me but, as a waitress dawdles past, I step out of his way. He suggests that I should sit down, and I do, but not before moving the chair further back. I'm tense and tired because I haven't slept properly for weeks. Jack suggests that we get something to eat. I say that I'm not really hungry although I am. He's determined that I should have something. He tells me about a church he wants to take me to see. It's called the Church of the Resurrection. We can get the Metro to Polianka and walk from there. 'Sounds nice,' I say, making my voice unenthusiastic.

At the next table a teenage Russian couple have pulled their chairs close. The boy wears a baseball cap and the girl has a smart Italian handbag. They must be Mafia children. The boy's hand moves up under her short pleated skirt. He kisses her and slides his other hand inside her jacket. Probably they live with their parents and have nowhere else to go. I try not to look at them but they're right in front of me. On the table are two coffee cups belonging to those people who were talking to Jack. That white envelope lies underneath Jack's book. In an ashtray a curl of smoke still rises from the stub of a cigarette which is stained with red lipstick.

I can't sit still. My hands fidget and the muscles of my shoulders are tight. No one comes to serve us so Jack goes to the counter. This café is a place which, in this new era of Soviet capitalism, has recently been taken over by a co-operative. As a result, you don't have to queue and the tables and chairs are made of new black chrome. Vases of plastic flowers decorate the tables. But the staff are still products of the old regime. They stand behind the counter, smoking and chatting. Occasionally one of them pushes an antiseptic-smelling mop across the concrete floor, or stands at the sink, washing up in brown water.

Usually most of the food on the menu isn't available, but if you offer dollars then it's surprising what turns up. Jack always gets what he wants because he knows how this works. No anger, no bribes, just some long story, preferably involving a tragedy in the family. Russia, he always says, has more regulations than any other country, but there's a way around everything. He comes back, shaking his head, and gives me some change. He tells me that he once saw a van which was meant to be delivering food to this café, but everything was being whisked away into a car belonging to one of the cooks. Capitalism is really wasted on the West, he says.

I nod my head and shrug. A thin curl of smoke still rises from that cigarette.

'So,' Jack says. 'What's the matter?'

'Nothing. Nothing.'

'Why don't you just tell me?'

I mumble something about feeling tired. He eyes me doubtfully. I know that if I don't tell him he'll start on some rant. 'All you're doing is relying on some secondhand emotion, some idea of what you should feel. We're living in a world of packaged emotion. All these films and books, telling us what our experience should be. It's almost impossible now for anyone to be authentic.' Blah–blah. That's what he always says.

'It's just – well, Maya said that . . . Well, that you work for the CIA or something like that.' My words fade out because I already know they're ridiculous.

Jack looks at me and starts to laugh. 'How she flatters me. Of course, the Neurology Departments of universities are crammed full of state secrets.' He laughs so much that he has to get out his handkerchief and blow his nose. 'That just goes to show that there's nothing so mysterious as someone with nothing to hide.'

The mop woman comes to our table with a tray.

'You mustn't worry about Maya,' Jack says.

'I know, but she made me angry. What has it got to do with her? I mean, it's not as though there's anything to talk about, is there?'

'Oh no,' he says. 'Nothing at all.' He raises an ironic eyebrow at me and stretches out his hand. I jump back as though he's bitten me. 'Eva,' he says. 'You need to slow down. Just slow down.'

He's right, of course, that's what I need to do. I tell him then that I can't sleep, and that my mind feels like a symphony orchestra playing in a cupboard, the sounds distorted, dangerous, frantic. Everything seems to link up, everything is connected, and I'm always within sight of some final explanation, but I never quite get there.

He listens to what I'm saying then he produces a book of poems from his bag. He'd been going to lend it to me, he says. He'd already introduced me to Maiakovskii and Mandelstam. Now, leaning close to me, he opens a collection of Anna Akhmatova and points out some of the poems he likes. He reads one or two, slowly and quietly, enjoying the words. It seems an odd thing to do, in the middle of a café, but it makes me feel calm.

I drink my coffee, which is gritty and has too much milk, and I thank him for reading, and for lending me the book. I don't know why I ever worried about what Maya said. People are just suspicious of him because they judge in conventional ways. He challenges people because he's different, and they just don't understand.

He touches Maya's scarf. 'That's a great colour. It suits you.' I know that he wants to take my hand. He's tried to do that before but I don't let him. It wouldn't be fair on Rob. But it isn't only that. I also feel quite sure that he isn't really attracted to me. He just flirts because that's how men of his generation relate to younger women. I even told him once, when he really pushed me, that when he tries to touch me it somehow degrades him. He gave me a long look when I said that, but didn't disagree.

We eat *shchi*, cabbage soup, and something which is called a salad Olivier but is really yesterday's vegetables covered in cheap mayonnaise. As we finish our meal, the couple at the next table lock their lips together, and their tongues search each other's mouths. The boy's hand strokes a patch of skin on the woman's hip between her jumper and skirt. I keep my eyes fixed on my empty plate. I know that Jack is enjoying my embarrassment and I hate him for it.

He goes to the counter to try to order some more coffee. A man pushes past our table and Jack's book falls to the floor. A brown envelope drops from inside it, and I reach down to pick up the envelope and the book. The envelope is empty so he must have been using it to mark his place. It's got an American stamp and, on the front, his name and address written in Cyrillic script. I look at the words, trying to decipher them. Which area of Moscow is that? I know that addresses in Russia are written with the name at the bottom, and the country at the top, but still I can't make sense of it. Jack is finishing his negotiations with the counter woman. Just as he turns, I push the empty envelope into my trouser pocket. As we drink our coffee, I feel its imaginary warmth against my leg.

By the time we reach the church, the sun has gone and our lips and fingertips are numb. The air is clouded by a fine mist, and it feels like evening although it's only three o'clock. We walk through industrial metal gates and across a courtyard. Jack tells me that, during the Second World War, the buildings surrounding the church were taken over by a factory which makes army uniforms. We walk past dirty windows, three metres high. A door swings open and we glimpse women crouched over sewing machines. A gentle rattle comes from the building and a smell of engine oil. Those women probably don't even know that the Cold War has ended, Jack says.

The church itself is dwarfed by the buildings around it. It has white walls, and several small domes which support a fragile lantern topped by a gold cross. A *babushka*, bent almost double, stands near the gate, with her hand stretched out. She stares at us as though she's never seen anything so extraordinary. I give her a rouble and we push through a curtain into the church. Dark and windowless, it is divided up into tiny rooms. The air is heavy with the smell of incense and the walls thick with gilt and jewelled panels. Jack shows me an icon of the Virgin Mary and one of the Crucifixion. He's told me before that icons are windows into Heaven, they represent the world we can't see. I stand there staring up at the golden-green halo of Christ, crossed by black thorns.

'This is the church I used to come to when I was a child,' Jack says. I think of him being forced out of his home, and his country, aged ten. And then losing his mother as well. He told me that, when he was in his teens, he found out that she had died in an asylum. That's what they did with anyone who tried to speak the truth, he said.

I wander past brass lamps, hanging down on chains, and pass through forests of thin candles. The churches here in Russia are quite different to any I've seen before. They consist of a number of linked rooms and I always wait to arrive at some central point but am never sure if I have. When I go back to look for Jack I find him sitting on a chair staring up at the Crucifixion icon. I know immediately that he's not well. As I approach him I hear him breathing deeply. His face is drained of colour. I've seen him like this before, but he never makes anything of it. Now, when I ask him if he's all right, he just says he needs to sit down for a while. He's explained about his illness. It's called dilated cardiomyopathy. He even wrote the words down for me. It's a condition which weakens the muscles of his heart and there is no cure.

'You should be taking pills,' I tell him.

We've been through this before but I don't get anywhere. He just doesn't seem to care, and I'm frustrated because I want to comfort and support him, but he doesn't seem to need that. Instead he just talks about death in a way that suggests it's a subject you could study through a correspondence course. He talks of choices, and decisions, as though death is something which can be done well, or badly.

'And for the people left behind?' I ask.

'Well, there's always a purpose in death, even if that purpose isn't immediately clear.'

He talks, then, about what it's like when you die. How

you merge into everything around you. How you finally arrive at the place you've been travelling towards. 'It's something you search for, and you never find it. And most of the time there's just nothing here, and you feel there never will be. But you can't stop searching.' I watch him staring up at the icons and I've never seen anyone look so happy. That feeling radiates off him, surrounding him in a warm haze. The thought comes to me that although I spent my whole childhood amongst people who supposedly believed in God, none of them actually seemed to have any real sense of Him, or at least not in the way that Jack does.

We sit on longer in the church and I'm drawn deeper into the silence, and into his calm. I feel every burden lifting from me. And I feel his presence there, and mine, and everything is all wrapped up together. I don't want the moment to break but the old lady comes into the church and beckons to us. As we stand near the curtain at the entrance I say, 'Aren't we lucky? Aren't we so lucky?'

'Yes,' he says. 'Rented time.'

I realize suddenly that I'm gripping his hand tightly in mine. I drop it and shake my head. And we're back in the courtyard with the long dusty windows and the smell of engine oil.

I'm so cold I've begun to feel warm. The lights from the factory windows shine out across the courtyard. As we walk past the textile factory, we see a room like a café, behind bars, and half-underground. Jack suggests that we find something hot to drink. I look at my watch. I promised I'd meet Rob at half six in Teatral'naia Ploshchad' near the Bol'shoi Theatre. He's got to drop off some papers at Sasha's flat, which is where the editorial work on the newspaper is done. Rob said he'd take me with him because I'm always asking to go. But it won't take three-quarters of an hour to get to the Bol'shoi.

The café doesn't look as though it's open to the public but Jack talks his way in, and insists that I should sit down while he queues. I point out that he's the one who's ill but he doesn't listen. I sit by high windows watching feet trampling past above me. The room is warm and my feet and fingers tingle painfully as blood flows back into them. A radio burbles behind the counter. Old men, crouched around a table, exchange glances and nod in my direction. Jack carries two cups of coffee to the table. He asks me what I'm thinking about.

'Just about my father.'

'Eva, what you should do is write to him.'

'But what if he doesn't get in touch? You know, the fact that he went away always makes me ask what kind of a person would I need to have been, to make him stay? And it makes me feel – I don't know – as if I don't really exist.'

'But whatever he decided, he had his own reasons. It doesn't really have anything to do with you. Whether he gets in touch with you or not, you'll still be the same person. It seems to me, if you want to live fully, you need to take the risk.'

'Maybe. You know, I think he had an affair with Maya.'

'Really?'

'Yes. And I was just thinking – it must have been so hard for him. He was Catholic and married, and then I suppose he met Maya and fell in love with her.'

Jack cups his hands around his coffee. 'Yes, if that's what happened, it must have been hard. There isn't much place in normal life for that kind of thing.'

'Isn't there? If people love each other, don't they find ways of being together?'

Jack looks at me with eyes full of pity. 'Oh really, Eva. What have you been reading? The truth is that the world crushes such feelings—' A voice booms from the radio and everyone turns to stare. One of the serving staff has turned it up. This is Radio Echo, one of Moscow's few independent stations. I can't understand the words and when I turn to Jack, he raises his hand to silence me. The report comes to an end and the waitress turns the radio down. She looks over at her colleagues who nod and shrug. Jack explains that Vilnius is the capital of Lithuania. I know, I say. Lithuania is negotiating to have its independence from the Soviet Union. I know that as well. Now it seems that Gorbachev won't let them go without a fight. After Christmas there'll be trouble.

'What − a war?'

'No, perhaps not that. But the situation is going to get more difficult. The Red Army will probably start by taking over the television station. Civilians will mount a protest and the Army will turn the guns on them.'

I remind Jack about my expired tourist visa. 'But it'll be all right,' I say. 'It's only two weeks now until I'm going back to England for Christmas. I'll get a new visa then.' But we both know that no amount of visas will do any good. I sit in silence, stirring my coffee. 'Jack, you know, it's not that I couldn't feel anything for you, it's that I might feel far too much.'

'Yes, I know. And that's one of the things I like about you. The feeling that if you ever did decide . . . I like that part of you which wants everything to be so grand and intense.'

'And you think that's something admirable in me, but it isn't.'

He shrugs and drinks the last of his coffee. 'People's best qualities tend also to be their worst failings.'

We sit in silence and Jack stares up at the feet walking
past above. He looks strained and tired, even his eyes have
lost their usual glint. 'You look sad,' I say.

'Yes, I am.'

'Why?'

'I suppose it's the waste.'

'Yes, it is a waste, isn't it? But I've got to do what I can
do. I'm no good at grand passions. They're not the right
thing for me.'

'Perhaps. But it isn't strong emotion which will kill you.
It's trying to live conventionally, that's what'll bring you
down. It's like the letter to your father. You won't send it
for fear of what you might feel. But you're dying of not
feeling anything.'

I don't have any answer to that. As we get up to go,
Jack says it'll be quicker for us to try to get a lift in a car,
rather than take the Metro. He flags a car down and nego-
tiates. We climb in and bump over potholes. The driver has
no windscreen wipers and moves his head continually so
he can see out through the smeared windscreen. He drops
us near the Moskvorechkii Most, I pay him, and we walk
on.

The streets are crowded with people hurrying home from
work. No stars are visible. As we cross the bridge, a freezing
wind batters against us. An occasional lorry passes, or a bus.
The bridge is illuminated by globe lights held high on
twisting stems. Jack stops for a moment to stare down at
the deserted river. Above us, the walls of the Kremlin are
floodlit. Further down the river, smoke rises from the power
station. I walk on and then look down. The river is frozen
except for a thin channel of black water which still flows
at the centre. I feel Jack beside me. 'Are you all right?' he
asks.

'No, I'm angry. Because we've got so little time.'

'Then why are you wasting it?'

Without warning, he bends down, pulls me to him, and kisses me on the lips. For a moment it's easy, so easy, and we could just go on and on. But suddenly I'm uncertain, and pull away. I expect him to keep a grip on me, but instead he moves a step back. I want to slap him, or tell him to keep his filthy hands off me. But by stepping back, he's deprived me of the opportunity to pretend that I was forced. I stand quite still, too close to him. He looks down at me, head slightly back, one eyebrow raised. He knows he's got me in his power. Both of us are tied up in longing, and hatred of that longing. We can't walk away because we both understand too well what this is. Finally I reach up and kiss him on the cheek. He stands motionless and doesn't yield. I turn away and hurry on across the bridge, without looking back.

Teatral'naia Ploshchad', Moscow

December 1990

I'm twenty-five minutes late to meet Rob. His Volga is parked with two wheels on the pavement. Brown clouds billow from its exhaust into the freezing air. I open the passenger door and climb in. I'm still shaking and I wipe at my face, and hair, as though some trace of Jack might be evident there. As I lean over to kiss Rob, I'm sure he'll taste that other kiss. 'Sorry I'm so late.'

'That's OK. It doesn't matter. Where were you?'

We set off, the wheels spinning in the ice-covered street. 'I met up with Jack. We had a cup of coffee, and I left with loads of time to spare, but then I got on the wrong Metro. You'd think I'd have stopped doing that by now.'

Rob is bent forward, watching the road. We drive out through Taganskaia Ploshchad', then turn off the main road and rattle and bump through narrower streets. If there are any road signs, it isn't possible to see them. I lick at my lips, trying to get rid of the taste of that kiss. I look across at Rob, hoping to see in him something I don't like. But he's just the same. He wears an old sheepskin jacket he's had for years. I know the warm smell of it, the exact size of the tear in one of the button holes. Surely if I love spending time with Jack then I must like Rob less? But it isn't as simple as that. Underneath me, springs stick up through the car seat, digging into the backs of my legs. I rearrange the cushion which covers them. 'I wondered if you mind me meeting up with Jack? I mean, I could not.'

The car wheels slide sideways on the ice and Rob jerks the steering wheel into the skid. 'Why would I mind? He seems like an interesting guy. And it's hardly likely you'd want to get inside his dusty old trousers, is it?'

'Of course not.' I try to laugh. He's right, of course, it's ridiculous. Jack is thirty-five years older than me. I'd never think of him like that. Flakes of snow whirl through the car headlights. I pull my coat more tightly around me, trying to stop the shivering. Rob has to keep his foot hard on the accelerator because, if he lets the car slow, then the engine cuts out.

'You know, your mother rang and she wants to speak to you,' he tells me. 'Perhaps you could come around to my office tomorrow and give her a call?'

'Yeah, maybe. I should at least tell her we've met Maya.'

'I don't really see why. I mean, it's not as though we're going to get to know her, is it?'

I knew he'd say that. I mustn't get to know Maya because that might upset my mother, and we must never do that. I think back to a conversation I had with Jack. I said to him that my mother had probably never talked to me about my father because she wanted to protect me. He said, 'Isn't it more likely she wants to protect herself?' And as soon as he said that, I knew it was true.

'I don't see why I shouldn't tell my mother about Maya.'

'I didn't say you shouldn't. It doesn't really matter.' At a junction we stop while a convoy of Army lorries rumble past. Their headlights sweep along the sides of buildings. It seems as though they've got no windows. As each one passes, I think it must be the last, but they keep on coming. Where can they all be going? It's probably better not to know.

Rob's foot moves up and down on the accelerator, as he looks across at me. 'You know, about Maya − I just always feel as though she contributed to the making of a myth. It was always her, and your father, and they were glamorous and interesting. And my mother as well.' The car engine dies and although Rob sticks his foot down flat, it cuts out. He swears and turns the key in the ignition. 'And no one took much notice of your mother. But she was the one who mended the clothes, and organized the dentist's appointments, and drove a hundred miles with my football boots when I'd forgotten them at the beginning of term.'

Finally the last truck disappears and we drive on, arriving in an area of tower blocks and half-made roads. Rob slows the car, and the headlights touch on construction work and straggling trees. I shift on my cushion and pull my coat more tightly around me. Of course, my mother is practical and good, and so is Rob. And they've tried so hard to recruit me into their camp. But what if the girl behind the cardboard cut-outs just isn't like that?

Rob stops the car outside a tower block. I try to shut the door but it's never worked properly and now it won't close. Rob comes to help me and his hand brushes against mine but I move away. 'Eva, listen, you do what you want. All I'm asking is that you take care of your mother. Every time she rings I have to invent some story about why you haven't called. And I don't like having to lie to her. She deserves better than that. She's made a lot of sacrifices for you. You've got a responsibility towards her.'

'I don't see why.'

Rob's voice is suddenly acidic. 'I would have thought that

was obvious. If someone cares for you, then you have to respect that, even if you've stopped caring for them.' He strides away towards the block of flats opposite. I follow him, trailing through mud and ice. Rob keys in a code to open the door and we push the button for the lift. The hallway smells of piss, and the pages of a porn magazine are screwed up on the floor. Usually Rob would joke about a place like this. 'Not too much *glasnost* here,' he'd say. But he's not going to joke now.

We take the lift to the tenth floor. Sasha's flat is dark, hot and cramped. It smells of cabbage and pickled herring. A glimpse of the kitchen reveals a string vest and underpants strung up above the sink. A bed in the sitting room means there's hardly space to stand. The furniture is brown chipboard, standard Soviet issue. I've been to flats like this before, but still it shocks me to find First World people living in Third World conditions. Most of the tenants who inhabit this building are better educated and more intelligent than me but they're living in one third of a room and sharing a bathroom with six other people.

The only evidence of the newspaper is a bedroom filled by two crooked tables and three antiquated typewriters. I know that the paper is printed at night in a factory in the south of the city. The supervisor of the factory can be bribed to open the place up at night. It's not illegal to produce an independent newspaper, but it's certain that everyone involved in the newspaper is being watched. The aim is to produce the newspaper in Voronezh and Nizhnii Novgorod as well, but that's more difficult. The people there are unreliable, no one cares about politics and it's difficult to find printing facilities. The truth is that, even in Moscow, the newspaper is usually only eight pages long and printed in fuzzy black and white on paper as thin as tissue. Most of it is taken up with advertising. But Rob sees it as an important start, and I suppose it is.

Under the law the newspaper has to be sponsored by an enterprise so it's technically managed by Vladimir who's the boss of a meat factory. He's fat, with small hands and calculating eyes. But I like him because, having spent some time in Cuba, he speaks Spanish, and so I can understand him. I'd like to talk to him now but he's buried in conversation with Rob and doesn't even see me.

I move towards the bedroom, trying to keep out of the way. Sasha is on the telephone. Here he's not the same person as the guitar player who comes to visit our flat. He's serious and committed, issuing instructions. Behind him, a window fills nearly the whole wall. I understand that he's talking about sending faxes. A journalist once said to me that fax machines were the main cause of the collapse of the Berlin Wall. Sasha puts the telephone down.

'You know, I can always fax something,' I say. 'There's a machine at my college.'

For the first time Sasha is looking straight at me. 'Do zey also have a photocopier? When would it be possible for you to use the machines?' But as Rob comes into the room, Sasha's face changes. He knows that Rob won't want me to get involved.

'It's no problem,' I say. 'All the teachers photocopy sections of textbooks so I can always use that as an excuse.'

'Thanks,' Rob says. 'But I don't think there's any need.'

'Yes, probably it's not really necessary,' Sasha says.

But then Vladimir comes and stands near the door, looking me up and down. 'But we are always needing more copies.' He speaks to me in Spanish and I explain about the college. And so it is agreed. But even as we say goodbye, and go down in the lift, I can feel Rob's disapproval. In the car he starts to tell me that I shouldn't photocopy anything. 'You'll get yourself into trouble, Eva. You shouldn't even be working. You don't have a proper visa.' We've had this conversation before and I know how it goes. We don't need the money. You don't understand the risk. That boss of yours – he's a complete crook. Blah-blah.

'Yes,' I say, 'but that's exactly the point. Because Mr Baloni is frightened of the authorities he's hardly going to report me for not having a visa, is he?' Usually I get worried by this kind of conversation, and try to change the subject, but now I just insist that I'm going to do what I want.

When we get back to the flat, Rob turns on the television and disappears into the bedroom. Tomorrow he's going to Kiev for three days and he's got to pack. I sit on the bed although I sense he doesn't want me there. Rob and I have never really had an argument before. I wonder now if the girl behind the cardboard cut-outs actually likes to argue. 'Have you seen this scarf?' I say. 'Maya gave it to me.'

Rob gives a vague nod in the direction of the scarf while making it clear that he doesn't have time to bother with scarves.

'It was interesting, actually. Talking to Maya.'

'Oh yes? Why? What did she say?'

'Nothing special. I just asked her a few things. Sometimes I'm curious about things in the past, aren't you?'

Rob is laying out shirts and socks, and a jacket. 'No, not really. I mean, of course, you and I come from a fucked-up family. My mum is dead, your dad cleared off to Mexico. But so what? The great thing about the past is that it's past.'

Of course he would think that. He's the man of action, the man who believes in the future, and I'm the silly little girl who sits around asking existential questions. Except that now I'm fed up with apologizing for the way I am. I've got a right to ask what I like. That's what Jack says.

'I'm not sure we really need the Montezuma Mystery all over again, do we?' Rob says. That's a reference to some childhood game I can't even remember. When Rob mentions that, I'm meant to laugh and admit that I've got quite a capacity for conspiracy theories, and inventing mysteries which don't exist.

'I mean, you understand that, don't you, Eva?' Rob says. I nod and move back into the sitting room. That phrase is used so often in our relationship – *you understand*. And I've always thought we say that because, having known each other since childhood, there's not much need for us to talk. But now I doubt whether either of us really understands anything at all. And I start to wonder vaguely how relationships end. How did my father finish up leaving for Mexico? Did he just spend more and more time in London with Maya? Or did my mother come home to find a note on the kitchen table, and the wardrobe half-empty?

On television there's a South American soap opera dubbed into Russian. I recognize it from when I lived in Lima. Suddenly I long to be back there – living in a room on my own, in a country full of colour and light, a place where I could at least understand the language. I find a pad of writing paper and sit down in the black swivel armchair with it resting on my knee. I'm going to write to my father, that's what I'm going to do. I haven't got his address but I can get it when I go home at Christmas.

The piece of paper is large and empty. No words arrive to take possession of it. I thought I had questions to ask but now I can't remember what they were. I put the point of the pen on to the paper and a black circle spreads around it. I look through to the bedroom and see Rob standing by the bed. Perhaps he was right. What exactly was the question?

In the attic bedroom the child stands at the window and watches rain gurgle in the gutter below. The branches of trees roll in the wind and the drive is thick with fallen leaves. A car pulls in through the gate and Father James appears in his black mackintosh, flapping towards the house like a crow. The child hears Rob's voice and goes to sit beside him as he opens the tin trunk which came from under her mother's bed. It contains maps, and ships' timetables from 1912 printed on fragile paper. Black-and-white photographs in an album show men sitting on horses in front of a white church with a bell-tower. Other photographs show stone carvings of monsters with eight arms, and pyramids covered in thick jungle. A book tells the story of Hernan Cortés and the conquistadores, of the Aztec priest and ruler, Montezuma.

All the things that are in that box are clues to solving a mystery. Some months ago, an Aztec princess was taken hostage by the conquistadores who've come to conquer Mexico. They've hidden her deep in the jungle and no one can find her. But now that the children have got this box, they'll be able to find out who kidnapped her, and follow their route into the jungle. The child loves this story. Even the words are exciting – Montezuma, conquistadores, Aztec.

Rob takes a map from the box, explaining that this will help them plan their journey. This room used to belong to the child's father when he was a boy. Above them, model aeroplanes hang from beams by invisible threads. A rag doll with a sagging head and black woollen hair sits on the mantelpiece. The grate is full of pine-cones, and on the windowsill there's a transparent dome which you can shake to make the snow fly around, and inside it two figures skate, their arms linked.

The child is happy because Rob has come to stay for the whole of his half-term. His parents were meant to come back from Rhodesia but then they couldn't make it. All most upsetting and disappointing, her mother says. Such a shame they couldn't come. The situation in Rhodesia is so difficult at the moment. The child repeats these words but secretly she's glad they didn't come.

Rob's finger moves over the map. Their journey through the jungle will be fraught with danger — snakes, caimans, conquistadores, and a lake full of piranhas. An army will be needed, so Rob lines up plastic soldiers on the floor. These soldiers will need tents to sleep in so the child hangs sheets between the beds. But there are too many soldiers and only one sheet, so she goes down to her bedroom to strip her bed. As she enters the bedroom, with its pink rocking-horse wallpaper, she hears her mother's footsteps rattle across the tiled floor below.

She turns back and stares down into the hall. Father James is speaking, his voice deliberately calm. Her hands curl over the rounded spindles of the banister. Words rustle upwards, and she cranes her neck, trying to hear. Amnesia-cat-teaser-amnesia-cat-teaser. Her father is on the phone again. He's been calling people for the last three days, and banging the doors open and shut. Once he was even on the telephone when everyone else was asleep in bed. More words she can't hear. Glove-misting-dove-hissing? She moves closer to the top of the stairs. Rob is behind her. He's found a biscuit tin which makes an Indian drum. Bang, bang, bang. He marches the child back upstairs. Glove-misting-dove-hissing? You must put your foot down exactly at the moment when the drum bangs.

Rob looks at the map again and they've reached the piranha lake. It stretches across the whole floor of the room and they'll have to get around it, there's no other way. They jump from bed to bed, then climb over the bedside table onto the chest of drawers. The child follows Rob, as they practise the journey again and again. It's easy to bounce from one bed to another, to wobble along the back of the chest of drawers. But each time the child swings down from the top of the glass-fronted cabinet to the armchair, she nearly slips. And she feels the piranha close to the surface, waiting for her to fall. They can eat every bit of your flesh in less than a minute, and only your bones are left.

The rain has stopped and Rob says that they need to go to the farm. Mr Reynolds, the farmer, is one of the conquistadores and he was involved in the kidnapping. In his office there's a cupboard with a gun in it, and a bag with a red stain hangs on the door. They take a magnifying glass and a pot of flour to dust for fingerprints. As the child leaves the house, her father is talking on the phone, and he grips the receiver so hard that his hands are white.

In the farmyard they spy on Mr Reynolds round his office door. They need him to leave so that they can investigate that bag further, but he stays where he is, writing figures in a book, so they stick their hands through the bars where the cows are and feel sandpaper tongues nuzzling over their fingers. As they sneak back towards Mr Reynolds's office, he suddenly appears. They dash for the tractor shed, but he's seen them. They hear him shouting, but just in time, Rob finds a door at the back of the shed which leads out into the lane. They dive into the woods opposite and hide deep in the trees. And there they find more clues — symbols carved into the trunk of a tree, pleas for help from the captive princess. And a campfire and pieces of soggy bread. The princess is somewhere not far away, and Mr Reynolds is holding her captive.

When they come out of the wood, the sky has turned the colour of pewter and the rain comes down in gusts. They need to get some supplies and make a camp for the night. Tomorrow they'll start their search again. They set off for home, passing the entrance to Wyvelston Hall and the gate which leads through the pinewoods to the house. As they pass the boatyard, a car pulls out of the gate and they run and hide in the laurel hedges which line the drive.

When they open the door to the house, everything is silent. The telephone doesn't ring, the doors don't open and shut. None of the lights are on and the child wonders if her parents have gone out. But they wouldn't have done that. In the kitchen the table is empty. For the last few days no one has cooked sausages, or fish fingers, or scrambled eggs, but sandwiches have always been left on the table.

The child listens. Someone is in the house. A tiny, tight sound, like a mouse scraping, comes from the sitting room. The child's hand grips the brass handle and eases the door open. No flames flicker in the grate. Evening light slants through the French windows, making a pattern of squares on the carpet. That sound comes again, but it isn't like a mouse scraping. It's a wet sound which comes in jerks and gasps. The child notices that one of the cushions is missing from the sofa. You must never take the cushions off the sofa. You must not use them to bounce on, or build dens with, or do head-stands on. You must not move them at all.

A foot lies on the floor between the sofa and the armchair. The child cranes her neck so that she can see. Her father is lying on the floor, curled up, his head pressed into the missing sofa cushion. His glasses have fallen off and lie on the carpet. A shawl – red and gold and orange in a pattern like question marks – is scrunched up against his face. He's got it pulled in so close to him that not one corner sticks out, not even a strand of the fringe. The child's mother kneels close to him and they're both quite still. And suddenly those words seep from the walls. Amnesia-cat-teaser-Rhodesia. Glove-misting-dove-hissing-gone-missing. All most upsetting and disappointing. Such a shame they couldn't come. The situation in Rhodesia is so difficult at the moment.

A hand reaches over the child's shoulder and the door closes in her face. *The child looks up expecting to see Rob. But instead she's looking at bones and staring eyes. The piranha fish have eaten all the flesh off him. The child puts her hands out to him but he's moving towards the kitchen, head down. He stands at the kitchen sink, and it's full of dirty pots, and he's leaning over them, making a choking sound. Then his hands grip the taps and water spurts everywhere. He drops down beside the sink — his hands, face, shirt soaked. I must go and get the grown-ups, the child thinks. But then she remembers that there aren't any grown-ups any more. They're making that sound, which they shouldn't make. And they've put the sofa cushions on the floor which they shouldn't do. Not even for dens or handstands.*

The telephone rings and they hear the child's mother go to answer it. This is not the same as the telephone calls before. The mother's voice is dull and she says sorry several times. Then the receiver goes down and she flames into the kitchen, shouting. What have you been doing? You're not to go playing in the sheds at the farm. Do you understand me? Her face is all squeezed up and her eyes are full of red veins. I've told you before. A spike could fall down and go right through you. Or a blade could drop and cut off your hands.

The child starts to explain. We have to go to the farm. Mr Reynolds is a kidnapper. He's got a bag with a bloodstain on. And in the woods there are marks on the trees which are pleas for help.

No, no, no! The child's mother grips her by the shoulders and shakes her. Don't be so stupid. Of course Mr Reynolds isn't a kidnapper. All these silly things you invent and you just don't know when to stop.

But it's true! You don't understand. There are pieces of bread, and a fire where a camp was. And so we know that this princess is somewhere close. And because of you, she's never going to be found. And she's going to die there in the woods, all on her own.

Stop this! Stop it now! Perhaps there are fires and bags and *bread and I don't know what. But there isn't any mystery. You have to understand – there are perfectly reasonable explanations for all of these things.*

Marsh End House, Malthouse, Norfolk

Christmas, 1990

Nothing has changed here but everything has. I lie in bed and stare at the pink rocking horses which prance on the wallpaper, the line of teddies on the shelf, and the green frog stickers on the chest of drawers. I'm seeing this house as Jack would see it, and I'm explaining to him what my life was like when I lived here all the time. The daily journey to school in Sheringham and back. Mass on Sundays, a walk on the marsh. Boredom stretching from one horizon to the other. Long afternoons spent lying in this bed, after an asthma attack. And all the time my mother telling me how lucky I was, because we lived near the sea, except there wasn't a beach, or any cafés, or a pier, or candy floss. Just mud and caravan parks, a boatyard and a smell of rotting fish.

I cough and my throat stings. My head is heavy and I feel sweat under my hair. Even before I left Moscow I was ill, and since I got home two days ago, I've been in bed, sleeping, reading and listening to the radio. The news is all about the fall of Mrs Thatcher and the war in the Gulf. That's what is going on in the real world. Except for me the real world is Moscow and Jack. My mother slides into the room and comes to stand beside me. 'Do you feel any better?' She straightens my sheets and blankets, tucks them in. She's going to refill my hot-water bottle and fetch some aspirin. Perhaps she should call Dr Evans? No, I don't need a doctor and I don't need aspirin.

She's just going to tidy up a few things, then she'll sit with me while she does some sewing. The truth is that she's enjoying all of this. She draws the curtains, then picks up a lavender-coloured cardigan which lies in a heap on the floor. 'Oh I like that,' she says, as she puts it on a chair. She asks me questions about Moscow, and tries to sound enthusiastic, but deep down she distrusts any place east of Berlin. She herself is Hungarian, although she never mentions it. All I know is that two years before she met my father she walked ten miles across a frozen lake at night to get out of Hungary. She carried with her one suitcase. Now the only evidence of her nationality is the Hungarian Bible next to her bed, a china bell on the bedroom mantelpiece, and the kind of blind patriotism which only immigrants ever have.

'Well, of course, I think it's marvellous what Rob's doing,' she says. 'Because somebody's got to try. But I fear it won't do any good. You can't really do anything about the Russians.'

I start to explain why it's different now, but my throat rasps and I cough. She reaches for a glass of water. 'That cough is terrible. I hope it doesn't make your asthma worse.'

'Mum, I don't have asthma.'

'Well, that's certainly good news, isn't it? I do worry. It's so difficult to call. Even if I ring Rob's office, I sometimes have to dial twenty times to get through. What would happen if you became really ill in Moscow? I'm sure that if Rob could see some future in all this he'd come back to England.' She gathers up papers, and taps the edges of them down on to the desk, making them into a neat pile.

Maya says that my mother used to be beautiful. It's true

that she's got high cheekbones, bone-china skin and yielding eyes, but she looks years older than she is. Partly it's the 1970s orange and brown cotton smock and leather boots with chunky heels. Her philosophy is: why go and buy new clothes when the ones you've got are perfectly good? And those beads – almost certainly made by some African co-operative. I always look at her and think, Go on, buy a luxurious red coat and sleek suede boots, eat a big cream cake, then spend the rest of the day watching bad television. But it's never going to happen.

'Such a shame Rob didn't come for Christmas, but I suppose his father needs him.' She pours me a glass of lemon barley water from a jug on the bedside table. Of course, I haven't told her that I didn't invite Rob for Christmas. He kept waiting for me to do that and, when I said nothing, he invited me to Nice to stay with his father. But that wasn't possible because I needed to pass through London to get my visa, and so we decided to spend Christmas apart. Just one of those logistical inconveniences, nothing more than that.

My mother opens her sewing box and places the chair from my desk closer to the bed. 'Why is there a problem with Rob?' she asks. 'I don't think you could hope for anyone better. He's always so positive about everything.'

On the chest of drawers, the toadstool night-light is still there, although it hasn't been used in years. And the Bluebeard book still lies on the shelf. I don't have to open it to see the pictures of the castle with the fountains and peacocks and chandeliers. I think of my father's hands, turning the pages, passing through that speckled light.

'Mum, you know, I've been meaning to tell you. In Moscow I met Maya.'

My mother is sorting through her workbox, trying to

find the right colour cotton. Her head is bent down and
for a moment her hands are still, then she carries on searching.
She takes out three different reels of thread and lays them
on her knee. When she looks up, she makes sure her face
has no expression at all. 'Maya? In Moscow? How strange.
I never thought she'd go back.'

I explain about Harvey.

'But I thought her husband was French?'

That was her first husband, I say.

'Ah yes, I see. So that marriage didn't last?'

'Obviously not.'

'She used to drink. Does she still?'

'Yes, I think perhaps she does.' My mother's hands pull
at pieces of thread, laying them against the cream material
she's working on. Rob had said about Maya, Well, it's not
as though we're going to get to know her, is it? But during
the two weeks before I left Moscow, I'd spent every evening
at her flat. That lavender-coloured cardigan my mother had
just picked up was a present she'd given me, something she
didn't wear any more. A ballerina-style cardigan, it crossed
over low at the front. 'Oh, I do so like to corrupt a nice
Catholic girl.' That's what she said, as I tried it on.

'You didn't get on with Maya?' I ask.

'Oh no, I wouldn't say that. She was charming – as people
who've been spoilt so often are. And she was terribly exotic
for Norfolk, what with those clothes, and speaking four or
five languages.' My mother unwound cotton from a reel and
took a needle from a felt case.

'And then?'

'Well, nothing really. Except – well, she did interfere. Such
fun to lead other people's lives vicariously, encouraging them
to take risks when you've no intention of taking any yourself.'

'And she wasn't married at that time?'

'No, no.'

'But she was thirty-six?'

'Well yes, but Maya was strange like that.'

I think of Estelle and the way she always stands too close to Maya. She came around to Maya's flat once just a couple of days before I left Moscow. Filling the whole space with her insistent voice, her shiny nail varnish and swinging fur coat, she ignored me completely. I said I'd go, but Maya wouldn't let me. And the voyeur in me did want to stay. Harvey was away. I wondered if Estelle would spend the night at the flat and what would happen if she did.

'Strange in what way?'

'Restless. She could never settle for anything.'

My mother holds a strand of thread up to the light, then lays it flat on the material. Perhaps she'll go down and get me some supper, she says. Would I like a bowl of soup? A sandwich? Some stewed fruit and custard?

'You know, I talk to Maya about my father.'

The silence is tight and I hear my own breath.

'Oh yes?' Cottons drop from my mother's knee and she leans down to pick them up.

'Why do you and I never talk about him?'

My mother shrugs. 'Well, you've never really asked.' I wait for her to say that my father never sent any money. Or that only his early paintings were really any good. Instead she unwinds cotton from a reel. This is the moment. I can ask whatever I want. Why did he leave? Maya had an affair with him, didn't she? That's what happened, isn't it? But the words won't form. I think of Jack. I do have a right to know this. It's not necessarily about some big problem, he said. It's just a question of getting things clear in your mind. Sometimes we don't see the present clearly because it's distorted by the lens of the past.

'I loved him, of course.' Those words sound so alien that I find myself looking around the room as though trying to identify some speaker other than my mother. She's never said anything like that before. Now she's staring at some invisible point far up the wall. 'Isn't that the most important thing?' Her words sound too naked. Suddenly I don't want her to say anything more, but now she's started, her words come easily. Sitting with her hands folded, she tells me about the day she met him.

An April day, she says, showers of rain, bursts of sun, then sudden battering wind. She was working in Soho then and her sewing machine was in the window of the shop. Outside, paper bags blew around and a dustbin lid rolled down the street like a wheel. And then this man appeared, dodging the dustbin lid, and crashing in through the door of the shop. He'd got a bad cold, a gaping hole in the knee of his trousers, and an interview for a teaching job in twenty minutes. She sewed up his trousers while he stood beside her in his long shirt and socks. Miraculous, he said, miraculous, when he put his trousers back on, because he couldn't even see where the hole had been. Then he bent over and kissed her, and the men who worked at the back of the shop whistled, and everyone laughed, and she just wanted to hide under the table.

When she left work that evening he was waiting for her, and took her out for a cup of tea. They shared an iced bun and a piece of apple tart. And then she just didn't know how, but it was impossible to say no, and he wouldn't listen to her, and so she found herself on the last train to Norwich. When they got back to Marsh End House, it had rained so much that the porch was six inches underwater. My father picked her up and carried her over the threshold. Three weeks later they were married.

As she finishes telling me this, her head is tipped back, and I suspect that she's trying not to let tears fall. I feel the world she's created fading away and I want to keep hold of it. I know now that I won't ask her any of those questions. I watch her as she stands up, and moves to the door. She says that I need to put the light out and go to sleep.

'Mum, don't you ever wish he'd come back?'

'Yes,' she says. 'Every day.'

After my mother has gone, I lie awake and think of the day when I went to Tsaritsyno with Jack. He asked me then whether, in my everyday life, I'd ever had a sense of my life as spectacular. And now memories come back to me of when I was eighteen – those few short months when anything seemed possible, followed too soon by a perilous descent into darkness.

I see myself propped on the sofa in the sitting room of this house. I've got a bandage on my arm from the hospital and packets of pills lie on the table. The application forms lie beside them. My mother comes in with a cup of tea, and after she's put it down, she rubs at her hands uncertainly. Her face is the colour of fear. 'Eva, dear, I know it's difficult. Of course, you should really go up to bed and rest. But the deadline is tomorrow. I could try to ring and see if there's any way it can be extended . . .'

I look down at my trailing patchwork skirt, fingerless gloves and jumper down to my knees. A trilby hat, and a long scarf in stripes of brown and green, lie beside me. I pick up the scarf and twist it in my hands. Mr Raven used to have a scarf like this, except his had wider stripes, and no tassels. I look over at the forms with their black lines and boxes. 'Mum, I don't need to fill those in. I've already decided.'

'Yes, I know, dear. But what if you change your mind?'

My arm aches where the nurse put a drip into it. She dug around in my arm again and again because she couldn't find a vein. I think back to the day four months before, when I first bought my patchwork skirt, my scarf and my hat. They were the best clothes I'd ever had. They made me brave enough to do anything. In those clothes I could become one of the girls hanging around the Clock Tower, and I could smoke dope and say how we-eird everything was, and how it made me feel like I was flying, and how everything looked technicolour.

And I could lose my virginity to a man in the park, who had a raincoat and a Highland terrier. And I never even asked his name, just pulled my knickers over my clumpy shoes and lay down in the grass, while the dog watched with a look of hairy disbelief on his face. And in those clothes, if I got sent to see Father James, or the headmistress, I didn't care what either of them said. *You've always done so well at school, why throw it all away? You must think of your mother. Things have not been easy for her, she's done her best in a difficult situation.*

I watch my mother as she stokes up the fire and adds another log. Despite all her efforts the room is still cold. She pulls up a chair, sits down beside me and pushes the cup of tea towards me. Mascara is smudged on her cheeks from when she was crying at the hospital. She looks through those forms, as though she doesn't know perfectly well what they say. 'How about geography? Or history? You've always been good at that. Or Development Studies? Rob is really enjoying his course.' She's been going on like this now for weeks.

The ambulance came to the school this afternoon because I couldn't breathe. At the hospital they kept saying, 'What happened? How did it start?' I couldn't say that I'd just been waiting too long. Over six weeks. And perhaps the letter had got lost in the post. Or perhaps he and his girlfriend were just too busy setting up their new flat. But then – in the middle of double geography – the idea came to me that perhaps he never would get in touch. Perhaps I would never see him again.

But he had liked me, he definitely had. He said that my work was the most promising in the class. And when I was the model in the life-class, he said I was easy to draw because I was well-proportioned, and had good bones. And when he looked at the picture Liza Grant had drawn of me, he said, 'But you haven't made her look pretty – she's much prettier than that.'

And it was because of him that I'd decided to become an artist. The school hadn't wanted me to do art in the sixth form. Art was for people who couldn't do real subjects. I could carry on for a year if I wanted, but after that I should concentrate on a place at a good university. But then Mr Raven arrived and I knew I would become an artist. I spent hours after school in the art room, I borrowed piles of books from the library, I persuaded my mother to take me to London to the Royal Academy, the National, the Tate. My father had been an artist, so why not? I wanted to know about his paintings, but when I asked my mother she said yet again that only the early paintings were any good. I found a box under her bed but it didn't have paintings in. There didn't seem to be any way of finding out anything more.

My mother lays the forms down on the table and reads the details on the pills. 'You need to have another one of these in an hour.' She goes to the fire again, trying to stoke some life into it. When she lays down the poker her shoulders go up and then collapse with a sigh. 'Eva, I don't know what you think, but I don't want you to go and see that Doctor Gurtmann again. I blame all of this on him.'

I'd always had asthma, but over the last year it had got worse, so the school had sent me to see Dr Gurtmann, who was some kind of specialist. My mother had insisted there wasn't any need. I'd been to see Dr Evans, a man with an excellent reputation, and he'd said it was simply a question of rest. But the asthma kept on getting worse. When the headmistress asked me whether there was anything I wanted to discuss, I couldn't say, 'It was all your fault. You let Mr Raven leave, you let him take another job.'

Finally, when I did go and see Dr Gurtmann, he told me that my problem wasn't asthma. I was furious and sure he was wrong. How dare he accuse me of making things up? I wouldn't let him take my asthma away from me. And I couldn't allow my mother's judgement to be questioned in that way. He asked me a lot of questions. *Do you suffer from headaches? Have you had problems with your eyesight? Abnormally bad period pains? Why are you so thin?*

His office was furnished with thick cream carpets, shiny pine, Hessian wall hangings and tactfully positioned boxes of tissues. A bronze of a naked woman with her legs splayed stood on a side table. 'What did you feel like when your father left?' he asked. I said that it was upsetting for my mother because she was Catholic and so she didn't believe in divorce. 'And what did you feel about it?' he said. I said that my mother had never really had many friends. 'Yes, and what did you feel?' My mother couldn't start another life after he'd left. His voice was suddenly loud. 'And you?' he said. 'You?' I looked at him and wondered what he was talking about.

I reach out for the mug of tea with my good arm. 'I think you're right,' I say. 'I don't think I should go and see him again.'

'Yes. It's really too far to drive. You know, if you're feeling too tired I can fill these forms in for you. It doesn't matter, as long as you sign them.' She's got the pen in her hand but I shake my head.

Earlier in the day, when I couldn't breathe, I'd seen this child. A child standing on a path in a wood, staring at a gate. And it wasn't a memory or a dream. It was as though the past had stepped forward into the present. It was vivid, every detail sharp. I think of Mr Raven. I want to lay my head on his shoulder and tell him what's happened. I look down again at my skirt and jumper. Really I look ridiculous. Of course I won't become an artist. I've never been any good. Mr Raven said I was, but he was a liar. He lied about everything.

I look at my mother as she reaches for the poker again. That stain of mascara is still smeared on her cheek. This afternoon at the hospital, a nurse brought her a cup of tea and held her hand because she was crying so much. I reach out and pick up the application form. Art is frivolous anyway. Why paint pictures when so many people are dying of starvation? Rob told me that in some countries, a child dies every eight seconds due to lack of clean drinking-water. I start to fill out the form.

Marsh End House, Malthouse, Norfolk

Christmas, 1990

My mother has gone out to Evensong. I get out of bed, put on a dressing-gown and wander through the house, rediscovering its particular sense of unease. The doors, staircase and window-frames are all made of the same dark wood which never changes colour, no matter what the light. In the back corridor, patches of mildew rise above the skirting boards and the parquet in the sitting room is warped. Stained glass in the front door, and in the bay windows, creates faded spectrums of light. Books, which no one has opened in years, line the sitting-room walls. It seems to me that the rooms should smell of pipe smoke although, in fact, they don't. I wonder what it must have been like for my mother when she came here with my father that first night. A man with too much past, and a woman with too little.

The hall is decorated with holly and loops of tinsel hang over the doors. I idle up the front stairs, cross the landing, and open the door to the guest room. It waits in sparse and dusty anticipation for the guests who never come. In my mother's bedroom the wallpaper is patterned with thick-stemmed pink roses. The wardrobe and chest of drawers are tall, dark and polished. I walk over to the window. I still can't get over how small England looks. Everything is quaint, clean and brightly coloured. Even the sky seems cosy and well-organized.

In the garden the monkey puzzle tree is shrouded in frost. That wrought-iron gate with the cobweb pattern which leads out to the lane has been left open. I think back to that photograph at Maya's flat. The shadowy figure in the frockcoat, the tree in the background. That photograph wasn't taken here because the tree is on the other side of the garden. My eyes turn back to the gate. My mother will be worried when she finds that it's open. She likes to keep it shut, although no one ever comes to the house that way.

I feel much better today, the sore throat and headache have gone. Tomorrow I'm going to London and then back to Moscow. Whenever I come here it's the same. I tell myself that I'm desperate to get away but, as the moment of departure draws near, a hollow feeling gathers in my stomach. That endless sense of missed opportunity. I turn away from the window, kneel down and feel under the bed. The two boxes are still there – the tin trunk which provided the inspiration for the Montezuma Mystery and the cardboard box containing those few remnants of my father. When I opened it more than ten years ago, it didn't seem strange that one box is all that remains of him. Now I'm not so sure. People don't disappear and leave so little trace.

The contents of the box are no more interesting than they used to be. A slide rule, a medal on a green ribbon, a leather case containing screwdrivers, an ivory paper-knife. I look at some papers in a cardboard file and then lay them to one side. In an album I find photographs which look similar to the pictures I found in Maya's flat. The same over-bright colours, the same thick fringes and long collars. Flicking through them I find several of Maya. In one she's sitting on a rug with my father. He's got his arm around her waist. I'd forgotten how attractive she was. That manic smile, those teeth which are a little too long, a scarf in her hair, a white lace dress.

There's also a photograph of me, looking exactly like that child who stands on the moonlit path. I'm at the top of the staircase in this house, shock-headed and with thin legs. In my hand I'm carrying a stick and I'm wearing a red tunic and bar shoes which are too big. I hesitate at the top of the stairs. My eyes are brimming full of expectation. As I look at that photograph I remember that costume. It was one of several I had in my dressing-up box but I wore it more than any other. The little red devil. Yes, that's who I was. My mother must have made that costume. But when was that photograph taken?

I pull out the tin trunk and open that as well. Folded on top of the files and books is Aunt Amelia's shawl with its Paisley pattern of question marks. I haven't looked in this trunk since that autumn day of telephone calls and sofa cushions. All through my childhood Amelia was never mentioned. She was my father's cousin, and since he had ceased to exist, then she was banished as well. To this day I don't really know exactly what happened to her. I did once ask and my mother said that, as a diplomat's wife, Amelia shouldn't have become involved in politics. Independence had been declared in Rhodesia, it was a dangerous time. That's what she said, and then briskly changed the subject. I suppose Rob must know more but he pretends to take no interest. I gather the shawl up to my face, as my father did on that autumn day. It smells of old tin trunk, nothing more. Maya had gone away and then he lost Amelia as well? Was that why he left?

I turn back to the cardboard box and unearth from the

bottom spiral-bound calendars, stacked in piles. I was six when he left – in 1966 or 1967? I sort through the pile, pick out 1967 and flick through the pages. Early January is crowded with entries. *Exhibition. Boltons, two crates of wine, a barrel of beer, six bottles of champagne. 6 January – 15.30 Hislops and Carrs. 17.02 Rachel and Edith.* A scattering of telephone numbers. Then, after that, three more entries, all crossed out, then the calendar is empty until September and my mother's hand – *Eva school.*

I open the 1966 diary. Entries appear on every page in both hands. I flick through the pages – *school starts, Eva dentist,* then *Cornwall* with a line which runs on over the next two pages. So we went for a three-week holiday and I have no memory of it. Perhaps most people can't remember much. At the beginning of November, I find half-term marked and the names – *Amelia, Guy, Rob.* Except only Rob ever came.

I open the 1967 diary again and look at those blank pages between mid-January and September. So he left sometime early in 1967 but that was more than two months after Amelia's death. What happened in those two months? I look through piles of bills, files and old newspaper cuttings. Underneath them is an envelope. I remember this envelope, it contains the separation papers. The paper is cream, the postmark red, and the address of the solicitors is printed on the back. *Hammond & Jones, 55 Red Lion Square, London WCI.* I tear out that section of the envelope and lay the address down with the cardboard file.

I unfold the papers and start to look through them, but I already know they don't contain anything of interest. My eyes brush over a few paragraphs – arrangements about the house, the bank account. I'm about to push the papers back into the envelope, when some pages drop to the floor. Held together by a staple, they are photocopies, and the person who made them didn't put the originals straight on the machine, so the words are tilted to one side. *That Theo Adam Curren . . .* The document is a court order. *Resident of 54 Redesdale Street, London SW3 . . .* Just another part of the separation papers. Then my eyes slow. I read the words once and then again. *Shall be forbidden from any contact with his daughter, Eva Lucy Curren . . .* The papers are dated November 1966.

I try to put the papers back into the envelope but they won't go. One page sticks out. I realign them, try again. But I've got them at the wrong angle. I force them and the envelope tears. I ram the papers and the envelope together, my knuckles smashing against each other. And then suddenly I'm sure that the window must have come open because I can smell the garden, frost, pine trees.

The child is with her father and she kneels on the kitchen table. It's a bright evening and the room is yellow. The kitchen windows hang open and she can see tall sunflowers outside nodding in their pots. Her father holds a spoon covered in honey and the child watches a strand of gold dribble down from the spoon. Although it's teatime, the sun outside is so hot that it makes her want to yawn. Her father twists the spoon, watching the honey slide across the back of it. The child puts her finger into the stream of honey and tastes it. The spoon wobbles and honey spills on to the table.

Her father laughs and passes the spoon to her. She tries to hold it steady over the pot but the air is so hot that she can't concentrate and soon there's honey dribbling all over the table. The child and her father laugh. He finds another spoon, and together they start to draw patterns across the table. The honey makes intricate squiggles as they swing their spoons back and forwards. The child rubs the back of her spoon across the surface of the table, merging the squiggles together into one golden pool. The honey smells of summer and flowers. Her father flies his spoon through the air, trailing a thread after it. He's talking about the country where the beach is.

I could show you a map, he says, and their spoons drop back into the honey pot. Her father takes an atlas down from a shelf and opens it on his knee. He tells the child that her great-grandfather went to Mexico and never came back. The pages of the atlas are a patchwork of pale blue, pink and green. The names are written at crooked angles. The child licks at her fingers and watches her father's hand moving over the page. Mexico is a fat, pink country with a long tail, and it is very far away.

Further than London?

Yes, much further.

The child leans down to look at the page more closely.

I'm wondering, her father says, whether you might like to go there?

The child looks up at him. Then she jumps up and down, and swings on her father's shoulder. So when will we go? When?

The back door opens and then shuts. The child's mother comes in and sees the honey spread on the table. Her head goes back like a horse refusing a fence. What are you doing? What are you doing? Her face crinkles up in lines. She gets a cloth and wipes up the honey. Moving back and forth between the table and the sink, she rinses the cloth, wrings it out, then scrubs as though she wants to wipe the whole table away. She sighs and mops at her forehead with her apron. Then the atlas is put away, and knives and forks appear on the table. The oven door opens with a gush of heat.

Daddy and I are going to go to a place where stars come down to earth.

Her mother turns to look at her but says nothing. The child pulls herself closer to her father. She looks up at the shelf where the atlas is. Where is that place? Show me where it is. She feels her father's hand in her hair but he doesn't get the atlas down. He's staring across the kitchen at her mother. The child gets a chair and tries to reach up to the shelf.

No, get down from there, please. Supper is ready.

The child's mother pulls her down. The child sits between her parents as supper is served. She says she doesn't want green beans but her mother says she must have some. Outside, the sun is getting hotter and hotter. It's hard to eat or even to breathe. The sunflowers at the window look weary. The chicken casserole steams on the table. She looks up at her parents and their faces are closed tight. Her mother clatters chicken down on to her plate. The silence feels like a great mouth opening ready to swallow them. The child stares down at her plate and sees that the green beans are moving.

Perhaps I'll just go to Mexico for the weekend, she says.

Yes, her father says. Quite right. Back in time for school on Monday.

By the stove, the dog howls. Despite the heat, the child shivers. The green beans are standing up on end now. She pushes them away but her mother tells her to behave and pulls the plate back towards her. The green beans are dancing a devilish jig. The child is up from her seat, her chair tips over, she presses herself against the sideboard. She screams and screams and still the beans dance, faster and faster. Her father picks up the plate and tips the beans into the bin. He takes the child into the sitting room and holds her tight, sitting beside her in the big armchair. Together they make up rhymes – bean-greens-dancing-stop. Lean-seams-dancing-pop. Pop-seams-prancing-lean.

When her father goes back into the kitchen, she hears her mother talking. I don't understand what's the matter with her.

The beans were screaming.

No, I mean, what's really the matter with her.

Well, I expect if she says the beans were screaming, they must have been.

Theo, Theo, for pity's sake.

The child lies on the sofa. Her father comes and asks her if she wants to go up to bed. She's frightened to go so he brings her nightdress downstairs and makes a bed for her there. Outside, the sun is fading but the heat still clings to her. Voices rise and fall with the jangle of pots being cleared from the table. The child drifts towards sleep, then wakes to hear those same voices snarling like fighting dogs. The room is half-dark, the child goes to the kitchen door and eases it open a crack. Her bare feet curl on the carpet. The kitchen light shines low over the table. She sees her mother but not her father. Her hands press over her ears so she can't hear. Her mother's face is hard and white. An envelope lies on the table. It has a red postmark and an address printed in red on the back. The diamond engagement ring on her mother's finger catches the light as she pushes this envelope across the table. Her father's hand appears pushing the papers back. The child shuts her eyes so she can't see his face. Inside the dustbin the green beans still dance.

I'm sitting on the stairs when my mother opens the front door. She's got her smart shoes on and she wipes them on the mat. She's singing a little tune to herself, in the way she sometimes does. I wonder now if this tune-singing is how she convinces herself that she's happy? She takes two steps across the patterned tiles of the hall and then stops. The light is dim but she's seen me. She moves forward, ready to make some cheerful greeting, then her eyes fix on the papers lying across my knees. I've left the cardboard file and the solicitor's address in my bedroom, but I turn the slanting photocopy towards her. 'He wanted to take me with him.'

For a moment she thinks of rushing forward and offering

comfort, she considers hurrying me away to bed and filling me up with aspirin. But she knows now that neither will work. Instead she lays her gloves down on the telephone table, takes off her coat, brushes at it with her hand, then hangs it on the hooks next to the sitting-room door. She sighs over a scarf which has fallen to the floor. As she bends down to pick it up her hair swings forward, covering her face.

'You sent him away. Why?'

She hangs the scarf back on its hook.

'Eva, if you look at those papers you'll find they were never signed.'

I turn to the third page and find the place where the signature should be. Dots file across the page, but above them the paper is empty. For a moment I feel defeated. Of course, she's right. Why didn't I look at that before? My eyes turn to her face. She looks so determinedly innocent but behind her eyes there's a glimmer of triumph. She thinks she's going to put a stop to this conversation.

'Why don't you come and sit down? We can have a cup of tea.'

I hold the papers out to her, trying to force her to see what I'm asking.

'Eva, you must understand. I was placed in a difficult situation.'

'What situation?'

My mother moves to the telephone table and reorganizes the papers there.

'Was it because of Amelia's death? Was he upset about that?'

'Yes. He was certainly badly damaged by that. Yes, of course.'

'And then?'

My mother picks up her leather gloves from the hall table, straightens out the fingers, and puts them away in the drawer. 'I was thinking we might have cauliflower cheese for supper, would you like that?'

'Why did he leave?' My voice is suddenly loud.

'Oh Eva, really. Why must you go on and on?' She walks to the bottom of the stairs and stares up to where I sit. Both of us are shaky, drunk on the strangeness of this. Around us the house stirs. It's as though windows, long closed, are being opened. Inside me, a strange excitement surges. My mother wants to shout at me that there isn't any mystery, that I mustn't be hysterical. But I'm not six years old any more.

'Sometimes you marry someone and they turn into another person,' she says.

'What other person?'

'Eva, I don't know. He just – he became very extreme. He wanted to know things you can't possibly know.'

'Things like what?'

'I don't know. He had all these odd ideas about the Mayan culture, and shamans, and the planet Venus. He talked about meeting God, or something. But all he really wanted was some peace of mind.'

'And he wanted his freedom?'

'Freedom?' My mother's mouth moves around that word as though it tastes bitter. She raises a hand to push her hair back from her face. She's staring upwards at nothing. Her hand waves in a dismissive gesture. 'That's what everyone said. "Just leave him alone, give him his freedom".'

She turns and walks towards the door into the back corridor. I think that she'll just go into the kitchen and leave me alone here. But she stops at the door, her head drops, and she rests her hand against the frame. I mustn't start to feel sorry for her. She should have let me go with him. And ever since, she's been fighting with me. Trying to make me into the kind of small person she is, trying to stop me becoming like him. But it just isn't going to work any more. I am no longer the Good Girl. I am not like my mother. He wanted me. She even had to get papers to stop him taking me.

Slowly I stand up. Those careful Christmas decorations – the sprigs of holly tied in bunches, the looping tinsel – suddenly seem unbearably mournful. Like so much else in this house, they suggest some other life, which lies within reach, but is never grasped. Perhaps the life he took with him when he left? I have to stop myself going towards my mother, laying a hand on her arm.

'Mum, I've been thinking. Perhaps I'll go to London tonight. It's just – I've got rather a lot of shopping to do. You know, things to take back to Moscow. And I've also got to pick my visa up.'

'Is that what you want?'

'I just think it would be easier.'

We discuss the time of the train and the fact that I should get a cab from the station. And do I have the key to the flat? And do I need to ring Uncle Guy to tell him I'm going to stay there? She goes to the kitchen to check the time of the train and make me a sandwich. Upstairs, I push things into my bag. I'm suddenly desperate to get away. I feel pity for my father. Him and me. We can never be what she wants us to be. I know now what he felt. People my mother loves do seem to feel a need to leave the country.

I push a child's jumper, coat and skirt into my case. They're old clothes which used to belong to me and I'm going to give them to the hopscotch girl. I look at those crooked photocopies again. 54 Redesdale Street, London SW3. Whose address is that? I take the cardboard folder with me and I put the letter I've written to my father in my coat pocket. It's enclosed inside another envelope which is addressed to the solicitors at 55 Red Lion Square. I'm going to write a separate note asking them to send the letter on.

As we drive to the station, my mother says, 'I think you're right, it's much better this way. You'd have been so rushed tomorrow.' As the car rolls on under the dark dome of sky, she maintains a stream of chatter. Messages for Rob, advice about my health, when will I next be home? In my head I'm already back in Moscow and I'm talking to Jack in the No Name Café. He said he wasn't sure about his plans but I know that he'll be there, waiting for me. At the station my mother comes with me on to the platform, carrying my bags, asking, have I got this, have I got that? I check that the letter is still in the pocket of my coat. I wait until the train is pulling in before I speak. 'I've decided I'm going to write to him.'

'Oh Eva, no. Please. Don't do that. All you'll do is hurt yourself. Endless people have tried to get in touch with him but he never replies to any letters, never has. You've got Rob. You've got your chance of happiness. Don't let him spoil that.' She lays a hand on my arm. 'Listen, dear. Please don't let this come between us. We've always got on so well, haven't we?'

Despite myself I kiss her goodbye and tell her not to worry. As the train pulls out I watch her growing small on the station platform, in her neat little coat, and her smart shoes. I think of her driving back on her own to that dark and uneasy house. The carriage of the train is almost empty. I put my two bags down on a seat and my coat on top of them. Then I sit down at the window. I see my face reflected in the glass, surrounded by lights. Turning my head away, I push my face down into my coat, suddenly hating myself. But still, when I arrive in London, I will post that letter.

The No Name Café, Moscow

January 1991

I stand at the window of the No Name Café and wipe a circle in the steamed-up glass, but Jack isn't there. My eyes move from table to table. I go into the café and walk the length of it. Once, twice, three times. The woman with the headscarf mops the floor, a couple kiss in the corner, two businessmen look through papers laid out on their table. But I don't see any of that, I only see the place where Jack should be.

This is the third day now. He knows this is the time I finish work, he said he'd be here the day I got back. In the street the cold is vicious. Layers of ice have built up on pavements, above windows, along pipes. The roads are cracking open, the kerbstones splitting apart. I wear two alpaca jumpers which I bought in South America and two pairs of gloves. I've borrowed an old fur hat of Rob's and I tie my scarf across my nose and mouth. With Jack gone, the whole of Moscow is depopulated.

I think of the Church of the Resurrection – that's where he'll be. I travel down the long wooden escalators into the Metro and take the train to Polianka. As I hurry through the walkways, I'm sure I see his golden-grey head moving away from me, the tail of his coat flick as he disappears through a swinging glass door. When I get to the church, the metal gates of the factory are shut up. The church looks insubstantial in the bronze light. I walk away, digging in my pockets for a handkerchief.

It's not as though I care that much. I really don't. I just want to understand why he's doing this to me. I was meant to be like Valia or Anna or whatever her name was. He wanted to kiss me, to fuck me. He wanted a holiday romance perhaps.

I walk back to the Metro, trying to work out how I can find him. That job which first brought him to Moscow? It was something to do with a team of neurologists, an American aid programme, advice on restructuring Soviet mental hospitals. But he never told me exactly who he worked with, or where.

When I get back to the flat the telephone is ringing, but when I pick up the receiver, the line goes dead. Rob won't be back until late. Last night he wasn't back until two o'clock. He told me then, as we lay in the darkness, that in Vilnius crowds of civilians have erected barricades to defend their elected parliament. But Gorbachev has warned them that they need to restore the Soviet constitution.

I open that cardboard file I took from the box under my mother's bed. My father's handwriting is distorted and jumbled, but it seems to contain notes he was making from a book. The language is a mixture of Spanish and English. Something about Mexico? About astronomy? Maya had mentioned shamanism, my mother had mentioned mysticism. I think of that day on the beach and his promise of stars which came down to the earth. I wonder now whether that was just a game. I want to talk to Jack, he's the only person who might understand.

I long for someone, anyone. The man downstairs with

the Communist medals greets me when he sees me on the stairs but when I try to talk to him he can't understand what I'm saying. I don't know whether that's my Russian or his hearing. Maya is still away in America. I pick up one of my mother's kitten and puppy cards. For a moment I think that tomorrow I'll go to Rob's office and phone her, but, of course, I won't. I don't know who she is any more. I see her as in that flicker of memory. The cartwheel summer. Her feet on a sky of green lawn, her head dangling down into vivid blue, her frown changed into a smile.

I pick up a copy of the *Moscow News*. The front page shows a photograph of a man in a fur hat standing amidst silver birch trees. He's from an organization which has been formed to look for bodies buried during Stalin's Terror. Twenty million died, the newspaper article says. Hundreds of mass graves may lie hidden in the forests around Moscow. I stare out of the window and wonder if the graves may be closer than that. I think of bones under the mud of our courtyard, skeletons barely concealed in the woods of Fili Park.

I open the drawer of my bedside table and take out my small collection of memories, the story of Jack and my friendship. Two poetry books he lent me, the ticket from a gallery we visited, a pencil stub which belonged to him, and a handkerchief. For a moment I see this situation as though I'm not part of it and I know myself to be pathetic. He's old, I tell myself, and a failure, and cranky, and dogmatic. And there was always something about him I didn't trust.

But still it feels like a phone call cut off in the middle of a sentence, and I am left alone, the receiver gripped in my hand, pressing at the knob again and again, hearing only a continuous beep where a voice should be. *Are you there?*

Are you there? But the line is dead. I think I know now what was behind all those cardboard cut-outs. Nothing at all.

I get out that envelope which I like to think Jack gave to me, and find the street map of Moscow. He lives in the south of the city, that's what he said. I decipher the address – Sibirskii Pereulok 1/8, fourth floor. I've imagined his flat so many times that I'll be able to find it immediately. It's in an imperial building in a tree-lined street just near the Tryetiakov Gallery. The windows of his room are long and open onto a curly iron balcony. In the evenings he sits near those windows, reading or listening to music. But Sibirskii Pereulok isn't anywhere near the Gallery. I search for it all over the bottom half of the map, trying to match one set of Cyrillic letters to another. The lids of my eyes feel swollen, all the streets merge together. He lives in a place which doesn't exist.

Three more days pass, their moments grinding past so slowly that I sometimes press my watch to my ear to hear its tick. The Russians celebrate Christmas on 6 January, and so for three days everything is closed. Rob and I are invited to a dinner by his Russian friends. On the way there, we see candles and home-made lanterns being carried around a church. This is the first time for seventy years that the churches here have been able to celebrate Christmas. At the dinner I am the Good Girlfriend and sit in the corner of a cramped flat, eating some porridge-like substance and smiling until the muscles in my face ache. I know that Rob and I are living through something extraordinary here, but I'm imprisoned in my own head.

Rob discovers that someone has been sleeping in our car. We discuss whether we should try to get the lock fixed and decide against it. Sarah calls to tell me that outside their building a man was killed by a falling stalactite which dropped from the edge of a roof and split him in half, as a log is split by an axe. One of my Russian friends at the college tells me that she's going to take her children to McDonald's at least once a month. Even if you have to queue out into the street, it's worth it because of all the vitamins in the food.

I move through the shuddering city like an amputee – unstable and awkward, dragging around the bloody stump of a lost leg. My eyes sift the streets. Jack is everywhere and nowhere. In the No Name Café I sit opposite his empty chair. I go back to Tsaritsyno and sit in the ruined Palladian pavilion and walk through the skeleton of the palace.

I start back at the college and we're studying the continuous present tense. *He is waiting for me at the café today. He is in Leningrad but he never told me. He is a spy and he's been deported. He is too ill to get out of bed and no one is there to look after him. He is with some other woman.* Sometimes the office phone rings, and I stop in mid-sentence and gaze at the door, waiting for someone to come and tell me that the call is for me. When I look back at my students, I find them staring in confusion. I look down at my book, and I can't remember where I was, so I say, 'Right, I think we've all understood that, let's move on.'

But time doesn't move on. I need to find a map which covers areas beyond the city centre but not many exist, and the ones that do are out of date, or inaccurate. That's what this country is like – even the lay-out of the city is a secret. Eventually Mr Baloni lends me a map which covers the whole area south of the river. At home I lay it out on the floor and move a lamp so I can see it clearly. Eventually I locate his street. It's south of the Dobryninskaia Metro, an area I've never been to before.

Just as I finish folding up the map Rob comes back. 'You do look awful,' he says.

'It's just that bug I had at Christmas,' I tell him. 'It keeps coming back.'

'Sleep,' he says, 'that's the only thing.' And he makes me go to bed and brings me a cup of tea. Later he comes to say goodbye because he's going out. After he's gone I lie in bed listening to the howls of stray dogs, and the sound of someone trying to start a car in the courtyard below. The engine whines and falters, whines and falters. I get up, wander through the flat, then pull on my clothes and my coat and go out.

A full moon hangs over the vast Phillips sign, written in Russian, which sits on top of a tower block. I take the Metro to Dobryninskaia and come up into a narrow square which is poorly lit. I consult the map and Jack's envelope. A trolley bus splashes and crackles through the ice, heading north up the long road towards the centre. I cross the road, and set off in the opposite direction along a wide street called Liusinovskaia Bol'shaia. Streetlights shine through the mesh of leafless trees. People queue at a kiosk. The blocks here are low-rise, flat-fronted and painted pale green. Lights come on at windows, revealing pot plants, net curtains, flickering television screens.

The map seems to be wrong. The ordered pattern of the streets has broken down. Highways link blocks of flats and stretches of worn grass. There are no signs anywhere. It starts to snow and the map gets soggy. An old man emerges from a building and I try to ask him. His face is a mass of swollen red veins. Waving a hand, he stumbles and nearly falls. I drift deep into a forest of tower blocks. No street lighting, no roads – just dirt tracks and half-finished construction work. I speak to a man who wears shoes, but no socks, and is siphoning something out of a car. He's never heard of the street where Jack lives. I slip and tear open the knee of my trousers. I look down and see blood but I'm so cold that I feel no pain. Ahead of me, three figures are crouched around a fire. I move towards them holding my hands out towards the warmth. A man edges half of a rotting armchair into the flames. I speak to a woman who is small and thin as a child and she points me back towards the main road.

Then suddenly I'm at the corner of his street. I find his block and go to the door. It's upholstered in black leather and has a peephole. I cross the road, standing back from the building so I can see better. It's the same as all the others, a tall modern building surrounded by mud and twisted trees. Swings and slides in a children's playground are black and spiky in the furred grey of the night. Lights are on in some of the windows and I count up to the fourth floor. So that's where he lives. It seems impossible. Nothing marks that floor out from any other. It's all too small and ordinary, too random. On the fourth floor, two windows are alight. In one a pair of trousers swings from a coat hanger. There is something shameful in those trousers.

A shadow moves at the other window. So he is there. I wait for that shadow to move again but it doesn't. As I walk back towards the Metro, a figure walks ahead of me. It looks like Jack. I move forward, trying to see more clearly. For a moment, the man is illuminated under a streetlight, pulling his scarf tighter. I know it's him because of the length of his stride, the cut of his coat. That shadow at the window of the flat must have been someone else. My heart turns inside me, wide as a fairground wheel. I start to run but then I stop. What if he doesn't want to see me? I walk on, keeping close into the sides of buildings. I catch glimpses of him as he steps through squares of light which fall from windows. He carries nothing in his hands but one of his pockets is weighed down. Jack always has a book with him and it's always in that same pocket.

He reaches the end of the street and turns left. I move as though attached to him by an unseen thread. He approaches the Metro and I hurry to catch up. If I don't speak to him now then he'll be lost in the crowds disappearing underground. He's stopped at a kiosk and is reaching into his pocket for his wallet. He pays for something, slips it into his pocket and then moves on. I walk up to him and say his name but he doesn't hear me. I move closer and lay my hand on the sleeve of his coat. He turns and I look into his face. He stares down at me and he doesn't know who I am. I'm saying his name – Jack? Jack? But he doesn't recognize me. And then I realize. This isn't Jack. It's some man with thin and bristly hair whose coat isn't even the right colour. I look down at my hand gripping the sleeve of the wrong-coloured coat. The man jerks his arm away and walks on.

The next day, when I get back from the college, I find Mr Balashov, our neighbour from upstairs, sitting on the stairs with his head in his hands. I say good evening to him and he babbles at me, pointing up the stairs, using his hands to indicate a key turning. His face is damp and distorted. It seems his wife has locked him out of the flat. As he's telling me this, I'm rubbing my hands together and wriggling my frozen toes. Outside it must be minus fifteen, or perhaps even colder. The hopscotch girl appears from her den under the stairs. She's wearing the clothes I gave her and walks with a touch of pride, although the skirt hangs down far below her knees and the sleeves of the coat are rolled up.

Mr Balashov is babbling again, complaining about his wife. He's got to leave, he can't stand it, but where can he go? He's standing with his feet close to that crack. Surely more concrete has chipped away from the sides of it? Above us, the strip-lights buzz. Ice has cracked open one of the windows on the landing and someone has tried to plug the crack with cardboard, without much success. I'll either have to shut the door on Mr Balashov or invite him in. I settle on the latter and usher him and the hopscotch girl into the sitting room. Mr Balashov sits in the black swivel armchair near the television. The hopscotch girl hangs back, half-hiding behind the side of the bookcase.

I stare at the telephone, wondering whether it might have rung while I was at the college. Maybe Jack is trying to ring but he never finds me here? I go to fetch milk for the child, vodka for Mr Balashov, tea for myself. I'm glad to have visitors, any visitors. While I'm in the kitchen Mr Balashov tells me that his wife shouts at him all the time. Does he think I'm not aware of that? And she makes him do all the cooking and cleaning, she won't let him eat, she hardly even lets him sit down. I nod at him through the door while I'm waiting for the kettle to boil. Some part of me finds Mr Balashov comic – the old sitcom caricature of the henpecked husband – but when I look closely at him there's nothing funny about the state he's in.

He seems to be telling me that his wife is ill. He points to his abdomen, makes a circle with his hands, trying to explain. I'd like to say that someone who can draw blood from another person can't be that ill. I give him vodka and hand a cup of milk to the little girl. Mr Balashov is talking again about how he must leave. I sit down beside him and nod sympathetically. After a while I join in. 'Yes, it's very difficult,' I say, 'when someone behaves badly to you. You think that they care but they don't. You can't understand, and it hurts, it really hurts. You don't know if they've gone away, or they're sick, or they're disappointed in you.' In a way it's easier to have a conversation with someone who doesn't speak your language. Perhaps that's what I've been doing all my life.

The bell rings and for a mad moment I think it might be Jack. But instead I find Sasha on the doorstep. He's wearing a new black leather jacket and carrying a plastic bottle and a small paper package. He's come round several times since Christmas and he always asks for Rob, but he comes when he knows Rob isn't here. Each time he's asked me to send a fax, or photocopy some papers. I know now that he wants to check if I've sent a fax which he gave me three days ago, but I wait for him to ask. He accepts a glass of vodka and we discuss *Bleak House* and *Great Expectations*. It's only after we've discussed both in some detail, that Sasha mentions the fax. I give it to him and he produces a document which he needs photocopying.

I'm glad he wants photocopying because that's easier than faxes. The faxes have to go to Nizhnii Novgorod and Voronezh, and sometimes I have to dial ten or twenty times before they go through. Fortunately Mr Baloni is unlikely to ask what I'm doing as he's seldom around. He's got a twenty-year-old Russian girlfriend, having ditched his wife and three children in Tuscany. Is her name Irina or Raisa? Anyway, she wants a flat in some new condominium on the Leninskii Prospyekt so he's busy with the negotiations.

Mr Balashov switches the television on. The bottle of vodka in our fridge has run out but Sasha produces his plastic bottle. Home-made vodka. I'm nervous of drinking it because it might contain meths. Sasha opens the paper package and produces bread, hardboiled eggs and cake. His uncle works at the Hotel Smolenskaia and the food has come from there. He always tells Rob and me that it's the leftovers, but we know it's stolen. In this city, honesty is a luxury most people can't afford.

The little girl has fallen asleep, her head propped against the bookcase. Her mouth is open and a thin line of dribble runs down from the side of it. I move her head gently, and prop a pillow against the bookcase to make her more comfortable. On the television, a man in a glittery suit struts on a stage. He's a hypnotist and a psychic. People here believe in all that. The city is full of fortune-tellers, astrologers, witches, clairvoyants, mediums, Mormons and Hari Krishnas. A Russian woman who works at my college tells me about spaceships seen over Gorkii Park and aliens landing in the Luzhniki Stadium. Jack says that people believe in incredible stories when the real ones are too hard to accept.

On the screen, the glittery-suit man has hypnotised a man from the audience and is making him dance around the stage like a ballerina. I remember the tone of derision in Jack's voice when he talked about these programmes. I pointed out to him that some of his beliefs are far-fetched, but he was quick to tell me that there's all the difference in the world between his ideas and this kind of populist rubbish.

Just as the programme finishes, a shout sounds outside the door. Mr Balashov is out of the door like ice off a hot-plate. I follow him out on to the landing. His wife fills the width of the stairs, wearing a tight dress made of red stretchy satin and a green woollen coat. The dress comes down to her puckered knees, which are far apart, cushioned by flesh. Her make-up, beneath the dried-out orange hair, is garish. Without a word or a movement, she somehow sweeps her husband away up the stairs. I imagine her like quicksand, sucking him in, his arms and legs flailing, until there's nothing left, and only his glasses remain, dropped where he stood.

I go back into the flat and sit at the kitchen table, talking to Sasha, my head fuzzy with drink. He leans close to hear what I'm saying and bangs at his ear with the palm of his hand. I think he does that due to a problem with his hearing. Occasionally he smiles, revealing stained and crooked teeth. His conversation veers from the mundane to the philosophical. 'The best shop to buy milk is in Begovaia Ulitsa, close to ze cemetery. Of course, you must visit ze Danilov Monastery. Just go to ze Shabolovskaia Metro and zen take any bus along Serpukhovskii. And do you believe in God? And what, in your opinion, is ze true nature of love?' The hopscotch girl sniffles in her sleep and snuggles close to the pillow. Sasha insists on pouring me vodka from his plastic bottle. Why not? I don't really care if I get poisoned.

Sasha is worried about Rob. As he speaks, the birthmark on his face burns red. 'You know he does not having any proper contract. Zat man Herr Mecker has a new BMW which is imported from Germany. And he don't speaking any Russian and do not any work. Rob should make zem give him same or find some different job.' I try to explain that Rob isn't interested in money. Sasha shakes his head in disgust. 'But you are from the West. How is it zat I am explaining to you capitalism?' I tell him that capitalist societies aren't all about money. But Sasha isn't having any of that. I wonder what he'd say if he knew that Rob's father sometimes sends cheques for three thousand pounds, which Rob rips up and scatters in the bin.

Later, he tells me about his childhood. He was taken to an orphanage when he was five after both of his parents were arrested. 'Cold,' he said. 'Always very cold. On Sundays zey sometimes light a fire. I always long for zem to light a fire.'

The Lady with a Hundred Relatives comes looking for the child, shakes her awake, and pulls her yawning out of the door. Sasha says that he must go as well and I look at my watch. Two o'clock. However will I get to work tomorrow? At the door, unsteady on his feet, Sasha lays a hand on my shoulder. 'I'm very happy now zat I know you. Before, I wasn't kind to you. You were kind to me, but I didn't . . .' He spreads his hands wide as though waiting for words to drop into them. 'You know, for me it is difficult. When people are kind I sometimes not even notice. I have not . . . any shelf where I can put zat.' I watch him go, his long legs tumbling away from him down the stairs.

I go to bed and lie awake under the five-armed light. I realize that Sasha has almost become a friend. I don't usually do friends. I remember talking to Jack about that. It was when I said that I like to travel, to move on. And he said, 'What, before someone notices?' And I said yes, because it is like that.

From outside, a bang sounds – a car exhaust, or a gunshot? I can't sleep. For some reason that odd phrase of Sasha's twists and turns in my head. *I have not any shelf where I can put that.*

10/38 Kutuzovskii Prospyekt, Moscow

January 1991

Maya lounges on her blue-green sofa, her hand cast idly to one side, a cigarette propped between two fingers. Clothes, books and tins of food from her four matching suitcases are spread around the sitting room. As always, the blinds are pulled down and the air is stagnant. 'Why e-e-ver did I come back?' A channel has been cut into the wall by the fireplace, and a thin coating of plaster dust lies across the room. 'They've just come in and done this,' she says, 'without a letter or any notification – and what can you say, because they own the place?'

She leans over and pours herself Chardonnay from a bottle on the table. Harvey has said that soon they'll have to move somewhere else, to a flat with proper security. The Mafia are everywhere, really e-e-everywhere, and so many people have been murdered. The country has become corrupt and dirty. The people lie and are idle. I sit listening, marvelling at how people get away with racism when they're talking about their own country.

'But whe-e-re else can I go?' Maya says. 'I've lived in so many countries, I no longer know where home is.'

'But you've got good friends, haven't you? Like Estelle and . . . ?' I can't think of any others. Maya is anyway dismissive of Estelle. Consolations and compromises, she sighs. Consolations and compromises. She's determined to feed me although I'm not really hungry. Heading for the kitchen, she pokes at things with her stick as though she's blind. 'No, no. You stay there,' she says as I get up to help.

I examine a pile of books on the low table in front of me. *Memoirs of a British Agent*, *Europe in the Russian Mirror*, *Baedeker's Russia 1914*. I know that Maya will have read these books from cover to cover and will remember their contents. And yet she never goes out of this flat.

Something smashes in the kitchen and Maya swears in French. Rob and I were meant to be spending this evening with Bill and Sarah, but Rob had to cancel because of some problem with the newspaper. When I rang Sarah to explain that, she pressed me to come on my own. 'It's so hard for you,' she said, 'with Rob always working. I really don't know how you put up with it.' I suspect that she was talking about herself. Rob tells me that she's more insistent than ever that she's leaving here by the summer, with or without Bill.

Maya brings bread, ham, and chocolate cake, but I eat only a few mouthfuls. 'Smoked salmon?' she says, poking her stick into one of the suitcases. 'I brought it back from the States.' I long to tell Maya about Jack, or to ask her about those papers I found under my mother's bed, but she's talking about her son from her first marriage. He's the one in the photograph on the hall table, with the shark-like car, pin-stripe suit and vicious smile. She's told me before that he's a Wall Street broker and earns a million a year. Playing slot machines, she says, that's all it really is.

But now she tells a different story. 'Addiction.' She sucks on her cigarette, drawing smoke deep into her lungs. 'It's ri-i-fe in that world, of course. And when I saw him this time . . .' She sighs, her head goes back, her eyes click shut then open again. 'You know, they never tell you the truth about drug addicts. They never tell you how wonderful drugs can make you feel. He tells me that – about how the world becomes beautiful, perfect. How you feel as though you can do a-a-nything. And then the question is – how do you tell someone to give up pleasure like that?'

She shrugs, not expecting an answer. Outside, the wind howls and rain smashes like pebbles against the windows. Maya leans closer to me, then she takes my face in her icy hands and stares into my eyes. I'm trying not to look at her. 'Loss,' she says. 'You and me both.' She lets go of my face but keeps her eyes fixed on me. The rain patters at the window again, and I hear the shuffles and clicks of the flats around us.

'Jack, I suppose?' she says.

'Yes. It's just – I haven't heard from him.'

Maya suggests that perhaps he's gone away.

'No. I think he's here.'

'Have you called him?'

I hesitate. 'Yes, but he hasn't got back to me.'

'Oh my dear, I'm sorry.'

'It doesn't matter. He was only a friend.' Maya asks me to get her some vodka. In the kitchen, I pour a splash into her glass, then top it up with water.

'It's hard,' Maya says, taking the glass. 'And sad, ve-e-ry sad. Probably I should tell you that some good will come of it. The strongest metals are cast in the fire of pain, and all that. But re-e-ally that's all rubbish. Loss is what it says it is. And it happens again and again, it chips away at you until you're less and less. If the pains were new pains they'd be easier to bear. But things go in circles and you pass the same point again and again.'

Maya is quite still, staring into nothing. Her stillness, her sadness, are like a presence in the room, as distinctive as the scent of lavender, or the taste of olives. The thought comes to me that Maya has a talent for sadness. She just lets it be what it is. In the world I come from, people always say, Come on, cheer up, you must be positive, count your blessings, look on the bright side. But actually why does anyone do that? Why don't they just sit in silence, as Maya does, and say it's sad, it's just very sad.

My head slides down against her shoulder. She runs her hands through my hair.

'Eva, you know, if someone doesn't speak to you, then often that doesn't mean they don't care, it means they care too much.'

It's late and the rain still breaks on the windows like gunfire. Maya insists that I should stay, so I ring Rob on Sasha's number to let him know. She takes me to the room where I first talked to Jack. I feel his absence there. The chair where he doesn't sit, the wall where his shadow fails to appear. Maya takes a lace nightdress from a drawer. 'So strange,' she says. 'All these cheap images of romance. Then the re-e-al thing can be so unexpected, so improbable, we simply don't recognize it.'

I stand by the bed, staring at her. Of course, she must be right. That's what it is. I'm in love with him. I feel a weight lifting from me. The idea seems bizarre, incredible, even faintly disgusting, but I enjoy the fact that it's concrete, absolute, beyond any question. I'm in love with him. I put on the lace nightdress and get into bed. Maya sits down beside me, finishing her glass.

'I suppose it must have been like that for you with . . .' I want to ask her about my father, but I can't say the words. 'I mean — with your first husband?'

'Oh no,' she says. 'Not him. No.'

I think of those photographs – my father with his arm around her waist. That toothy smile, and the scarf in her hair. He kept going to London to see her when my mother wanted him to stay at home. She understood his paintings, and wanted him to be successful, whereas my mother thought he shouldn't be interested in any of that. And then one day my mother found out, and she was so angry she talked to the lawyers about a court order. That's how it was. 'You know, Maya, I was trying to remember – where did you live in London?

'Chelsea.'

'Somewhere near the river?'

'Redesdale Street.'

And that was where he went to when he first moved out, except Maya wasn't there then because she'd already moved to Rome. Did he plan to go and join her? And if so, then why did he go to Mexico instead? Maya is brushing cigarette ash off her skirt. She looks at me, shakes her head, shrugs.

'You know, you don't have to worry,' I say. 'I'm sure it wasn't your fault.'

Her head jerks and then steadies. Her eyes are fixed on me but deep inside them I can feel fear. 'You know?'

For a moment we're so close that our minds are touching. I feel a rush of relief because now we're going to understand each other. I start to lean forward, wanting to stretch out my hands to her. Her eyes watch me, her head is back, her lips are slightly parted. Then suddenly she's looking down, her hands rustling in panic beside the bed. 'You know,' she says in a rush. 'I've got a surprise for you, a Christmas present.'

But I don't want a present. I want to know what she was going to say. I want to be back in that moment when our minds touched against each other. Instead I'm holding a bag in my hand and she's telling me that I should open it up, taking another swig of vodka, starting to tell me the story of where she bought the present, how she's sure it's ju-u-st the right thing for me.

The child is standing on a chair, boiling milk to make cocoa for her father. He's got flu but he'll be better soon. He's been sitting in a chair in the sitting room all day, and his face looks collapsed. He doesn't use his telescope any more, or paint, or read his star books.

Mrs Reynolds from the farm has been helping to look after him. She comes every morning, bringing a shepherd's pie for lunch wrapped in a checked tea-towel. The child can see her father through the sitting-room door. He shivers and she decides that she should go and get his book for him. He left it upstairs but he might want to read it again now.

Her mother is in the hall, talking on the telephone to someone about an exhibition which might take place in the New Year. It's not a question of the work, she's saying. He's just not that well at the moment. I don't know whether it's a good idea. We should leave it a while before we make a decision. Well, I'm sorry, but I've got to put his health first.

The child takes the milk off the electric ring and goes up the back stairs. She longs for Rob, and the biscuit-tin drum, and the plastic soldiers and the tent made out of sheets, but Rob has gone back to school. As the child goes out of the door, she sees her father entering the kitchen. He shuffles and his shoulders are slumped. He isn't meant to walk around. If she hurries for the book then maybe she'll be able to persuade him to sit down again.

She's halfway down the stairs, carrying the book, before she realizes. The smell is charred, metallic, a hint of roast meat. The book drops from her hands and falls away down the stairs, opening and closing as it goes. She jumps after it and pushes the kitchen door wide open. Her father has mislaid his hand. It's spread out on the angry red surface of the electric ring. In the hall the child's mother rattles the phone back onto the hook. As she rushes into the kitchen she's keening like a trapped animal. The child looks at the hand. Her father looks at it as well. The white sides of it are merging with the hot-plate, turning red. A smell of burnt wool rises around them. The cuff of his shirt and jumper are alight. Her mother pulls his hand off the hot-plate.

Her father shrugs, smiles, blusters. He wipes his flaming hand on his trouser leg, whistles silently. Her mother rushes at cupboards, fumbles over bandages and lint. The child grabs antiseptic cream from the drawer by the sink. Her mother starts to ring 999 and then puts the phone down. The panic dies. Because the truth is that it doesn't really matter. After all, he doesn't seem to mind. Finally it's only like the toast got burnt.

The child's father goes back to the sitting room and hunches up in his chair. Her mother sits at the kitchen table, her face blanched. This can't be the right way, she says. The child sits next to her father and makes up words for him. Bean-greens-dancing-stop. Lean-seams-dancing-pop. Pop-seams-prancing-lean. Her father tries to play the game but his mind isn't with her. She keeps on — lean-seams-dancing-pop. Bean-greens-dancing-stop. The words make it easy not to think. She knows now that there's a sound worse than a scream of pain — and that's the silence where the scream should have been.

30/16 Ulitsa Pravdy, Moscow

January 1991

It's Sunday morning, and Rob is still in his pyjamas, reading the newspaper in bed. I've been back from Maya's for half an hour and although I'm exhausted I can't keep still. Rob lays the newspaper aside, heads for the bathroom, stops. 'Listen, sorry. I forgot to tell you. Bad news. Your mum called on Friday and she's been made redundant.'

'Redundant?' My mother doesn't get made redundant, she's worked at the same school for over twenty years. 'Oh my God. So what will she do?'

Rob tells me that on the phone she sounded positive. After all, she's still got her own work. But Rob and I both know that the market for that is limited. The dresses she makes are hand-embroidered and worth thousands of pounds. Sometimes orders come from specialist London shops, sometimes they don't. 'I think it isn't really the job she minds about,' Rob says. 'It's just that apparently the school took the decision last summer, but then didn't tell her until she went back for the beginning of the term. That's what always gets to people – not what's happened but the fact of not being told.'

A crash comes from upstairs. Rob and I stare upwards, preparing ourselves for more thumps and bangs, but no other sound comes. 'I think for once they really just dropped something,' Rob says. He heads for the bathroom, a towel wrapped around his waist. I sit on the edge of the bath and watch him shave. Steam rises in clouds from the defective bath tap. The mirror is propped above the sink so he has to bend down to look in it. I tell him about my evening with Mr Balashov and ask if there isn't something we can do. Rob doesn't think we should get involved. 'You know, if he really wanted to go, he would. In those relationships there's usually some kind of dependency.'

'Perhaps – but what exactly? I mean, why does anyone stay in a relationship that's making them unhappy?' My eyes meet Rob's on the surface of the mirror. He reaches over, clicks the switch on the radio, and tunes in to one station after another, trying to find the latest news from Vilnius. Shaving foam drips from his razor into the sink. Why is he so interested in events thousands of miles away when he couldn't care less about Mr Balashov? Perhaps causes make people callous, I think.

I wander back to the bedroom and lie down. The sheets and pillows are still warm from Rob. Today is refusing to happen. I should try to fix the light in the kitchen or rearrange some of the junk our landlord left on the balcony. Or go for a walk in Fili Park, take the tram to the Rizhskii market. Rob and I should have arranged to go away somewhere for the weekend. That's what I'd really like, but it isn't possible because I don't have a visa. And even if I had one then it'd still be difficult to get a train ticket, a hotel booking, an invitation. It's not surprising that many people in this country seem deranged. If you're never able to just jump on a train when you want to, then of course you finish up like that.

'Are you OK?' Rob switches the radio off and comes to sit down on the bed. 'I'm sorry,' he says, putting out his hand to me. 'I know I haven't been around much. It's going to be easier now, I think – although, having said that, I've got to see Sasha at four today.'

'That's OK. You go. I don't mind.'

He leans to kiss me, and my hand touches the skin of his neck. I pull him to me, kiss him again and wonder why it is that he and I never seem to find time to make love. As Rob puts on his clothes, he's looking at the bag which contains Maya's Christmas present. 'What's that?' I tell him, and he wants to see. He's only taking an interest because he's worried about me, but I show him the blouse, feeling embarrassed by its translucent luxury.

'Put it on,' he says.

'No, it's not really me.'

'Go on.'

I pull off my jumper and T-shirt and put the blouse on. The material is fragile and crinkles against my skin. Rob watches me, as his hands tighten the laces of his shoes. 'I like that. Very smart.'

'Nah.'

He tells me there are muffins in the kitchen, he was given them yesterday by someone visiting from America, and he suggests we should warm them up for breakfast. In the kitchen he switches on the oven and puts water to boil. 'This morning we might even have an overhead light in the kitchen,' he says. He's got a bulb from the office so now he's just got to get the remains of that other bulb out. He pulls up a chair even though he can nearly reach the bulb.

'So did you have a good time with Maya last night?'

'Yes, fine.' I've never told him about the papers I found at home, or the conversations I had with my mother, and

I know that now I shouldn't say anything to him about Maya. It won't do any good and we're enjoying this morning, so I shouldn't spoil it. 'But I was wondering – do you think my father might have had an affair with Maya?'

Rob looks down at me and shakes his head. 'No. No. Your father wouldn't have had an affair. Maya, perhaps, but not your father.'

'But we always think people wouldn't do that – and sometimes we're wrong. Because, you know, my father used to stay at her flat in London after your—'

Rob snatches his hand back from the broken bulb. 'Bugger.' He steps down from the chair and shakes his hand up and down, wincing. 'It's hot. The switch must have been on.' He turns the tap on, but the sink is full of yesterday's pots and water splashes everywhere. I'm moving towards him and then I stop. Because just for an instant he's ten years old, and we're at Marsh End House, and he's got water all down his shirt, and he's crouching by the sink, with water spouting everywhere. I reach over, turn the tap down and pull some of the pots out of the sink. He puts his hand under the cold water but he won't look at me. 'It's fine,' he says. 'It's nothing.'

I put my arms around him, asking if it still hurts, but he moves away. 'It's nothing. Really, nothing.' He stops the taps, dries his hands, then takes the muffins from their packet and makes the tea. He's angry with himself because he isn't the kind of man who makes a mistake like that. His burnt hand jerks away as he accidentally touches the cupboard door. In my mind that picture keeps coming back of him, ten years old, and frightened, with water down his shirt. But he won't let me pour the tea or get the milk from the fridge, he's determined about that. 'Sit down. I'm OK. I'm getting breakfast.'

We sit at the table, our knees close together. The muffins

are several days old, and crumbly, but they still taste good. Rob is purposefully good-humoured. I watch a red blister forming on the pad of his thumb. He never really said much about Christmas with his father but now he starts to fill in the details. 'I got there and he'd done nothing. Nothing. Not one sprig of holly, not even a candle. So I said, "Dad, this Christmas business, I agree there's no need to make a big thing out of it, but should I at least buy us a turkey?" Then suddenly he has this huge fit of guilt. "Christmas, yes, Christmas. Of course." So he books us into the flashiest restaurant you've ever seen, and it's all truffles, foie gras, string quartets. And all I wanted was a turkey.'

Rob winces as he tries to undo the lid on a pot of jam. Again the boy, the water, the sink. I stretch out my hand but the lid is off. 'And of course the conversation is always the same,' Rob says. '"Shouldn't a young man like you be doing the exams for the Foreign Office?"' Rob does a good imitation of his father's heavy-smoker voice.

From the sitting room the phone rings. I go to answer it and my head is so full of the blisters and the splashing tap that I don't even think of Jack. So when I hear his voice my head lurches forward like vertigo. He asks me how I am. Fine, fine. He knows from my voice that I'm not alone. He asks me if I want to meet up some time. When? Maybe today, he says. And I'm thinking, How dare you ring up on a Sunday and demand to see me right away? And how dare you behave as though it's normal just to disappear and then turn up again?

But I say, 'Today? Well, yes, we could do.' And so it's agreed. We'll meet at the Polianka Metro at four. I try to put the receiver down, but I keep getting it the wrong way round, and it clatters against the phone again and again. I'm still wearing that ridiculous blouse and I look down at the sleeve, seeing my arm through the translucent material. I wonder if Maya used to wear a blouse like this when my father came to visit her in London?

'So who was that on the phone?' Rob asks.

'Just a friend from college. I said I might meet up with her later – since you'll be out. I won't go for long. I'll probably be back around six.'

'OK. I'll be back around the same time. So then I'll cook some supper. Carrots in a frying pan, perhaps?' He's still finishing his muffin, but stretches out his hand and touches my arm. Another blister has formed on the side of his index finger. I stand beside him and pull his head towards me, holding him against me. 'Yes, carrots in a frying pan. Why ever not?'

Jack is less than I remembered him. When I see him standing near the entrance to the Metro, it takes a moment for me to align the image I had in my head with the reality before me. Wasn't he taller? More vivid? I let him kiss my cheek. I want to be vile to him, but I know that I'm not going to manage it. All those eloquent, vicious speeches I prepared over the last two weeks shrivel in my throat.

For days it has been too cold for snow but now the temperature has lifted and the air is muffled. Snow falls in huge, slow-moving flakes. People trudge past with their heads down. Darkness is already gathering and along the streets, lights come on.

Jack and I shelter under the overhang of a building and talk about where we should go, but we both know that on Sunday everywhere is closed. Jack suggests that we take the Metro back towards the centre. At least there we may find somewhere to sit down. I don't mind what we do. All I can think of is how to make this time last. When we turn back to the Metro, a crowd has gathered. Jack approaches a man to ask what is going on but the man looks at him in fear and turns away. He speaks to a *babushka* with a black shawl around her head. 'A power failure,' he tells me. 'Or perhaps some problem due to ice.' I'd thought that the Metro never broke down.

We stand together in the street, snow gathering on the shoulders of our coats. 'What can I do? I said I'd be back by six. I'll have to start walking.'

Jack is close to me, his eyelids full of snow. 'You can't walk. You'll get frozen.' Across the street a trolley bus pulls up and crowds of people fight to get on. Most of them are turned away. A car passes but it's as full as the bus. Jack turns to me, wiping snow from his face. 'You could come back to my place. It's about a mile from here.' His voice is apologetic.

'No, I can't do that. I've got to get back.' I'm gripped by a sudden fit of temper. Like a child, I might stamp my foot, or shout. I don't want Jack to have this victory. It's the fault of the snow, the stupid, stupid snow. I don't want to go to his flat. I want to go to the No Name Café, and I want to sit there talking, and I want it all just to go on as it was before.

'Come on.' Jack puts his hand out and pulls up the collar of my coat. I brush his hand aside and walk behind him as he sets off. When I look up, the shapes of buildings are lost in whiteness. My boots are soon soaked, and my hands are numb although they're pushed into the pockets of my coat.

Ahead of us, a lorry pulls in close to the pavement and stops. Two men jump down and undo a piece of tarpaulin at the back. They shout words I can't understand and two or three people gather. A light inside the back of the lorry shines out into the falling snow. In typical Russian style, people begin to form a queue even before they can see what might be available. Jack pushes forward to see what's going on. The lorry is stacked with crates of oranges and the two men start to weigh them out. I've only ever seen oranges in Moscow once before, and that was in a hard-currency shop. The oranges drop, flame-coloured spheres, into reaching fingers. People are laughing as they turn them in their hands.

Jack says shouldn't we buy some oranges, but I don't want to bother. He takes no notice of me, pushes forward and holds out a note. Suddenly we're showered by fiery oranges. We don't have a bag to put them in, so we push them into our pockets, our jumpers, the lining of my coat. We turn away, fat with oranges, and despite myself, I can't help smiling at Jack.

'I know,' he says. 'I know, I'm sorry. But at least if we go to my place then you'll be able to call.'

We walk on, the oranges jostling against us. The snow is getting deeper and the wind starts to blow. Above us the sky swirls and snow comes straight at us, gathering on the front of our coats, turning our faces to ice. We cross the Dobryninskaia junction, although it's hard to recognize it, and head south along Liusinovskaia Bol'shaia. Walking with Jack the route seems easy – just one left turn off the main road.

When we reach his building I stand behind him as he keys in the code. I watch his fingers – 4660. I repeat that number to myself several times. The door clicks open and we enter a high-ceilinged hall. Ahead of us are concrete stairs, beside them a broken pram and scattered newspapers. The lower half of the walls is covered in green tiles. The air is sharp with the smell of rubbish bags and bleach. As we climb unlit stairs, I grip the metal banister and stare up through twisting rails. High above, a flat glass roof, dirty and green, is divided by a metal grid. Light from the snow, falling through it, fills the hall with an underwater stillness.

We reach another steel door and Jack puts a key into the lock. We step into darkness and a smell of vinegar. Jack turns on a light, revealing a high-ceilinged corridor, narrow and white, without any pictures. Jack takes off his shoes and I do the same. A small woolly dog lies in a basket, wriggling and snuffling. Jack tells me that this is Kashtanka. He allows the dog to lick his hand, then he picks it up, stares into its eyes, snuggles its woolly head against him. To me, Kashtanka looks like a mouldy sort of dog, but I like Jack's affection for him. Two or three pairs of worn sheepskin slippers lie near the door and Jack pushes a pair towards me. I say that I don't need slippers but he tells me I'll catch cold. As I push my feet into them, I wonder who else might have worn these slippers. Anna or Valia or whatever her name is? Through a half-open door I see a twin-tub washing machine and a mangle. We push past a curtain which hangs from a piece of cord.

Jack ushers me into a darkened room and fumbles for the switch. The room wakes suddenly, flooded by light from a standard lamp with a yellow shade. So this is the place where Jack gets up in the morning, where he sits, where he works. The room is large and bare. It's like a boarding school or a guest-house, but there's nothing squalid or dreary about it. A vase on the desk is full of catkins. Each object in the room seems loved and precious and has been positioned with care. Against the wall, a gate-leg table is covered in books and papers. A cheap oriental rug covers the brown painted floor. One corner of the room has been divided off to make a kitchen, but the partition wall doesn't reach up to the ceiling. A double bed is neatly made, a white sheet, poking up above the blanket, is pulled flat. 'It's a good room,'

I say, but in truth, I'm shocked by how naked his life is.
Other foreigners in Moscow own property somewhere else,
or go back to families with proper lives. For Jack, this is
really everything.

'Can you stay here permanently?' I ask.

'No, unfortunately not.'

'So what will you do when you have to go?'

'Something will come up. Someone I know has a *dacha*
in Malakhovka. Anyway, I have to go to Leningrad in a
couple of months and I may stay there.'

Is that where he's been since Christmas? A grey metal
heater stands against one wall and Jack pulls two chairs
towards it. We unload the oranges and Jack hangs my coat
up near the heater. I look at my watch and it's a quarter
to five. Jack takes me back along the corridor to where
the telephone stands on a table. I call Rob at home but
there's no answer. I telephone him at Sasha's flat – again,
no answer.

'I'll make us some tea,' Jack says. He disappears into the
partition kitchen. I wander over to the bookcase and note
the academic-looking tomes about psychology, myths and
medicine, and try not to see the cranky-looking paperbacks
about astrology, past lives and faith healing. Press cuttings
and political magazines are organized in a neat pile. Next
to them is a stack of blue notebooks and on top an Aeroflot
ticket. Destination – Vilnius, Lithuania.

A sea shell lies on his desk, and a small wooden box with
an ivory clasp. I check that Jack isn't looking, then raise the
lid. Inside are syringes and needles, in transparent packages,
and tiny bottles standing in a row. Perhaps he has started
taking medication for his heart? China clinks behind the
screen and I push the lid of the box back down. I turn to
find Jack carrying a tray with a pot of tea, cups and saucers,

a jug of milk, a bowl of sugar. He's also brought a plate, a knife and two oranges.

He sees me looking at a glass case on the mantelpiece which contains a teapot and two small teacups. Their edges are rimmed with gold and they're made of china so fine it's almost transparent. Beside the case is a black-and-white photograph in a frame. It shows a house in the country, like a large Swiss chalet. In front of it is a horse and cart, women in long skirts, men in hats, and one small child. Jack puts the tray down, stands beside me and points out his mother. 'This was taken only a year before we left. Strange, isn't it, to see us all gathered there . . .'

He turns away and begins to peel one of the oranges. 'You're still cold,' he says, as I sit on the chair near the heater. I'm not cold, but I'm shivering. 'I like that blouse,' he says, and he touches the sleeve, rubbing the material between his raw fingers. Was it only a few hours ago that Rob said the same? It seems to me ridiculous that there has to be this separation between the two of them. They're people who'd probably get on quite well together, who'd agree about most things. I look back at his desk – that wooden box, the ticket to Vilnius. 'Jack, you know I was worried when you didn't call.'

'I'm sorry about that.' His hands work with the knife, easing the peel off the orange, then he looks across at me. 'The truth is, my dear, that I thought – hoped – that I was finished with all this. But it seems that isn't the case. You know, in three months I'll be sixty-five. I hadn't really expected to last that long and I feel this rented time I've had coming to an end. There are other things I should be doing – and the same is true for you. But then – well, I suppose I'm just shocked by the extent to which you affect me.'

I get up and move away from him towards the window. Outside, the snow glitters in the light from the window. In the distance, cars and trolley buses creep along the main road. The snow is nearly six inches deep. I turn back to look at him, still holding the orange knife in his hand. So he's the wicked old philanderer who suddenly found himself in too deep. He wanted another Anna or Svetlana, a good-time girl, but instead he's finished up trying to save me. I'm starting to love him a little less, now that I have him in my power.

'Jack, you have to understand. I can't do this – not unless I leave Rob.'

'And your own life counts for nothing, I suppose?'

I don't answer him. I'd like to start a conversation about how we're both powerless in this, how we're being over-whelmed by a force beyond our control, but he would never let me get away with that. I stand with my back to the window, thinking that I should leave, and knowing that I won't. He's filled with an urgent physical yearning for me, I know that. I've seen it in men before and it makes me curious, and perhaps a little jealous.

He comes towards me and puts up his hand to touch my face. 'Tell me,' he says, 'what's the fear? Is it because you're so sure there's something wrong with you? I don't believe that. There may be something wrong with some of the people around you, but there isn't much wrong with you.'

'Jack, if you start this, you'll be sorry.'

He bends down and kisses my lips, gently. 'You think all men leave? Is that it? Sometimes you have to believe that there could be an exception to the rule, or nothing can ever change.' He picks up my hair and runs his fingers gently over the knobs of my spine, and then places his hands either side of them, feeling his way down my back, as he did at Maya's party.

He touches a muscle and, for one second, I glimpse the child on the sandy path in the stripes of moonlight. 'I have to go,' I say. 'I'm sure the Metro will be open.' I reach for my coat and scarf and pull them on. My limbs are fluttering and weightless, my lips feel swollen where he kissed them. I must leave now, for him as well as for me. What I want is to be friends with him, but he's not going to agree to that. I remember the old seaside postcard joke – men talk to women so they can go to bed with them, women go to bed with men so they can talk to them. There may be truth in that. At the door I look back and see that he's turned away, his head bent down.

'I'm sorry,' I say. 'But I can't.'

'You don't have to apologize. I know I've got nothing to offer you.'

I think how cheap he is, playing the sympathy card, and I gather my coat around me ready to leave. But instead I allow myself one last look at the makeshift room, and see his bent head, and that grey polo-neck jumper he wears, which is so neatly darned at the elbow. And I know that he's going to die, and who will be with him then? None of those cheap Moscow women, I'm sure of that. And on the mantelpiece, in that glass box, those china cups glisten, and next to them the photograph of the people who had no idea that disaster was about to engulf them.

I move towards him and he stirs. He takes hold of my hand and places it against his lips, kissing the palm. I rest my head lightly against his shoulder, and he gathers me to him, so I can feel the rise and fall of his breath. Then he takes off my coat, undoes my scarf, leans down and kisses my neck. He pulls me to him and I dissolve into his body, his hands holding the back of my head. He draws me down onto his knee and undoes the top buttons of Maya's blouse.

The clasp of my bra seems ridiculously small in his hands. He can't make the clasp work because he's shaking. I undo it and watch as he reaches out to cup my breast. He bends down and I feel his lips touch me. I push my cheek against his hair. His hand moves across my back and I kiss him then, surprised by how natural it seems, how easy. I feel him touch the inside of my thigh and I press my lips against his.

A door slams and a voice rustles. We sit in stillness and hear the turn of a key and footsteps in the hall. 'Who's that?' I start to pull my jumper down but Jack says it's just a neighbour from upstairs, and that she won't come in.

'But Mrs Pastukhova might come back.'

'No, no one will disturb us.'

I feel his hand on my thigh again. 'Jack, I can't . . . Please, not here.'

He nods, kisses my neck and straightens my blouse. 'I know. You're right. Not here.' His hand runs up and down my ribcage, his lips brush my forehead and he puts my jumper back in place. 'Not here. But stay – just for a while.' He puts out his hand and I follow him to the bed. We lie down together. I know that he wants to kiss me again, but he doesn't. My head is against his chest and I can feel the beating of his heart – a wind-up watch, its spring steadily uncurling, ticking out its time. And Rob's contract may not be renewed, and Jack will go away to Leningrad in two months' time. And there's nowhere we can go to be together. We've become like all those Russian couples kissing in the Metro, or gripped together next to the hot-air vents. It's only a question of logistics now. Only where and when, not if or what.

We lie together on that bed sharing the silence for half an hour, perhaps more. Then Jack gets up and makes fresh tea, and we drink that, and eat the oranges, sitting close on the bed, the juice running down our chins. I tell him then about the court order. He's sceptical that anyone would go so far just because of an adulterous relationship, but that's because he doesn't know the world I lived in as a child. I also tell him about the letter I wrote to my father. 'You know, when the school sent me to see that Doctor Gurtmann, he said that I must feel angry with my father, and my mother says the same – but they're wrong. I've never felt anger. But what I did feel was the desire to comfort him. I knew that things were going badly wrong for him and I did nothing.'

'Eva, you can't blame yourself for that. Nothing is ever the fault of a child.'

The snow at the window has stopped. 'I have to go.' He helps me put on my coat and scarf, and then walks to the Paveletskaia Metro with me. The streets are silent and bright as day. Our feet sink down deep. A snow plough rattles past. The wind blows, stirring up an ice-flecked dust.

'So what will we do?' I say.

'I'll work something out. And I'll call you. Soon.'

He kisses me goodbye and I look up at him. 'This will be a disaster – you know that, don't you?'

'Probably. But a brave disaster.'

As I arrive back at Byelorusskaia, I prepare my story for Rob. *Sorry, so sorry I'm late. I met up with my friend from college and took the Metro back as far as Borovitskaia, but then the snow came and the Metro stopped working. But fortunately I was near the flat of another colleague and so I sheltered there for a couple of hours.* The important thing is not to explain too much. I can feel how the lies will pirouette off my tongue.

As I walk up the stairs and pass the window with the star-shaped fracture, I can smell Jack in my hair. Rob will surely smell it too. I step over the landing crack and open the front door. Immediately I know that something is wrong. When I walk into the sitting room, Rob doesn't even turn around. He's standing in front of the television with Vladimir and Sasha. Their sunless faces and red eyes don't move from the screen. A man I don't know is talking on the phone. 'The Soviet army has stormed the television building in Vilnius,' Rob says. 'This morning they seized the main printing works and the defence headquarters. People are being shot or crushed beneath the tanks.'

'But it's a freely elected government there.'

'Not any more. Some Soviet-led Committee for National Salvation has taken power.' On the television screen, fuzzy black-and-white figures move across a grass bank below a high wall. Gunfire sounds and a tank appears. Those figures, no more than flecks of black on the screen, are hemmed in between the grass bank and the guns. The turret of a tank swivels towards them. Shots sound again and a flash lights the sky. Vladimir speaks to me in Spanish. He says, 'Only three days ago Gorbachev promised that he wouldn't use force, he said there'd be a negotiated solution.'

Sasha tells me that Rolandas Jursenas is trapped inside the building. He's a Lithuanian journalist who came to supper here once, not long after I arrived. I slip away through the watching faces and into the bedroom, then stand with my face gripped in my hands. In the sitting room the news report finishes. Sasha is arguing with Rob. 'Gorbachev isn't responsible for this. This is hard-liners in the military.'

'Well, that may be the case, but if Gorbachev has no control over the military, then why is anybody bothering to talk to him?' Discussions continue in Russian, arrangements about the newspaper, who will ring who and when. I hear the front door open and muttered farewells.

When Rob comes into the bedroom, I'm sitting on the

bed, still wearing my coat. I wonder if Jack has heard this news and what he'll think about it. He often pretends not to care what happens in Russia but I know that it does matter to him – more perhaps than anything else.

'Did they find out anything about Rolandas?' I ask.

'No. The phone lines are down. My guess is that he's dead.'

'Do you think so?'

'Yes.'

'The West won't intervene to stop this, will they?'

'No, no chance. They're too busy in the Gulf, protecting oil supplies. Look at Hungary in fifty-six, Prague in sixty-eight, Poland in eighty-one. It's the same all over again. They might cut food aid but that's as far as they'll go.'

'And that just means that poor people will starve.'

'Yes. And I think the violence is certain to spread. Apparently, two thousand troops have just been sent to force Estonians to enlist in the Soviet army.' He sits down beside me. 'You know, if this situation gets worse you shouldn't stay here.'

'Rob, I don't care what happens. I'm going to stay with you.'

I hate myself for that, but Rob bends down and hugs me, and when I hug him back, I mean it. I try to focus on Vilnius, the black stick figures on the grass bank, the high wall, the tank moving in towards them. But my mind is with Jack. I remember when we heard that news report in the café. He said then that this would happen soon after Christmas. How had he predicted it so accurately? I take care not to think about that Aeroflot ticket on his desk.

When Rob comes to bed we're both sleepless and lie looking up at the curtainless window. I turn over and wrap my arms around him. 'So what happened to you?' he says.

'In the storm?' I tell him my story and I want him to challenge me, to say, That isn't true. But he doesn't and I curse him because he's making this too easy. He should be stopping me. I lie there wishing that I could tell him everything. I want to say, I'm going to do something terrible. I can't stop myself. Please forgive me, please.

12/20 rue de Lausanne, Geneva

September 1991

The body has its own memory. In the deep Geneva nights, I turn in bed and a movement of my spine brings back an echo of his touch. I wake prickling with sweat, calling his name. I feel his lips against mine. His words muffle deep against my eardrum and his imagined finger rests on my collar bone. My body is formless now that it no longer rests between his hands.

I cannot stay in bed. I am drawn to his desk, to his pen. He had his theories about words, now I have mine. I write in defiance of time. In that Moscow hotel room, nothing remains. Even in the particles of dust under the chest of drawers, not one of our cells survives. The hand of time smoothes out every crease. But our fingers did lie laced together on that bed, our breath did unsettle the air of that room. I write to insist on that.

Around me, boxes remain unpacked, a pile of unopened post lies on the sofa. Coffee cups are lined up along the side of the desk, and a bowl contains the dregs of tinned tomato soup. I look at my watch — one o'clock in the morning. Outside, car headlights flicker along the road. Beyond that there is blackness — no sign of the lake. A starless, moonless night.

I let my hand go and see where it will lead. Words work their way up my spine, rising like damp. They come from the heart, from the liver, from the soles of my feet. The story is already there, it's just a case of chiselling it out. I cut and polish, positioning words so they catch the light. But still none of this expresses exactly how it was. I don't want to write about that time, I want to write the time itself.

The Hotel Universitet, Moscow

January 1991

It shouldn't have been possible for us to go there. In Moscow you can't just walk into a hotel and book a room, but somehow Jack organized it. A 1960s tower block near the Rizhskii Vokzal, the foyer was a place of dusty rubber plants, black leather sofas and watching eyes. We always had the same room – high up above the city, silent and light. Number 815.

I see us there now, walking along a red-carpeted corridor towards that room. The floor lady has a gold-tipped tooth and sits under pictures of Lenin and muscular Soviet workers. We open the door on to that nondescript room – narrow and high – with bubbly wallpaper, which peels along the seams and is covered over by cream paint. A mirror shines on the wardrobe door, light falls through the window on to the sheets, in the bathroom a tap drips.

That first day we were both so shy, and I hadn't thought he'd be like that, because I'd seen him with other women – the easy way he laid his hand on their shoulder, whispered to them, laughed. But there was always a certain formality in the way he behaved to me. It wasn't at all like you see it in films. He didn't push me back against the wall, press his lips furiously against my mouth, struggle to get my clothes off. Instead, he took off his coat and hung it in the wardrobe. I took off mine as well, and put it down on a red velvet armchair, with a sagging gold fringe. Carefully I straightened the sleeve of my coat and brushed a patch of dust from the collar. Then I went to look at the only picture in the room, a landscape which hung crooked beside the door. It was painted in thick oils, the perspective twisted, the colours brash. It showed a man and a woman walking away along a road which narrowed into the far distance.

Jack drew the thin curtains half-shut over the lace blinds, sat down on the bed and put out his hands to me. I sat down beside him, watched him undo the laces of his shoes and thought, Whatever am I doing here? The feeling was one of shock, disbelief, mild hysteria. *Surely this won't really happen?*

He said he wondered if I'd be hungry because he'd brought us some bread, apples and vodka. In the bathroom he found a tooth mug and we drank from it together. We lay down on the bed and kissed uncertainly. Then I stood up, took off my boots, socks, thick tights. The buckle of his watch clicked on the glass of the bedside table. I took off my bra and my pants, and turned to him. He was sitting on the bed, quite naked. I moved towards him and he drew me close, so that I stood between his legs. He reached up, undid the crucifix around my neck and put it on the bedside table. In the half-light, his face was hidden but I looked down at the thickness of his grey hair, and the shadows of his eyes.

He placed his hands on my hips and looked up at me. Leaning forward, he kissed my stomach, gently. 'Beautiful.' From his voice I knew that he was close to tears and I was embarrassed. We lay down on the bed and he kissed my breasts. 'You're very white.'

'I do get brown sometimes.'

'Don't.' His hands moved over my body and it was as though he was creating me, forming me. My flesh was like clay and from it he made the curve of my hip, the line of my thighs. He moved my legs apart and dropped his head between them. I felt his tongue touch me, and the feeling went up through my body, arching my back and stopping my breath. For a long moment he kissed me there. I was trembling, watching my own body moving, seeing the top of his head. When he kissed my lips again, he stopped for a moment to look at me. His golden eyes held me in their light. I'd never looked at anyone as I looked at him then.

His hand touched between my legs. He lay beside me and I watched his wrist moving. The world had shrunk to the size of that room. I felt stiffness drain from me, and I nestled close to him, my head against his shoulders. Then suddenly it broke upon me and I turned my head to press against him, and felt the spasms again and again, and then held him close, my face against the grey hair of his chest, before I leaned down to take him in my mouth.

Room 815 – for two months, all my life happened there. Love without a future is so very easy. My mind was numb, I was lost in the physical, I never slept. My breasts were sore, I ached inside, my legs were shaky, I was hungry an hour after I'd eaten. I was fired by a burning energy. Problems dissolved before I even approached them. Everything was connected, and it all made sense. I balanced somewhere far up high, defying gravity. Objects insisted on their presence, lights dazzled, colours clashed, the air itself was unstable. I was capable of grasping the globe in my arms. The veil between heaven and earth was perilously thin.

Making love – I'd heard those words before but I'd never really known what they meant. With him there was nothing to lose. He was entirely open, completely without shame. In that hotel room I took off my skin, as well as my clothes.

I wanted to be his, and his, and his. I wanted to become him. We shared such tenderness, such a desire to soothe. And I couldn't understand it because I'd never wanted a sexual relationship with him, and I'd never thought of myself as someone much interested in sex.

And yet there I was, ambushed by desire, a sexual woman against my will. I wore high-heeled shoes which Maya lent me. They were too big, and slipped and slid on the ice-cracked pavements, but I wore them anyway. My body felt skinless beneath my clothes. I was as big and brazen as Mrs Balashova. I put my hair up in a high ponytail and wore a low-cut top. Was this sexual woman the latest cardboard cut-out? Or was she the real person behind all those two-dimensional dolls? I worried, of course, that Rob might see the difference in me and become suspicious, but he never said anything. He didn't see because he was determined not to see.

I felt loved. A trite little phrase. I mean so much more than that. I felt it in my body. Going through me like a shock, touching places never touched before. I couldn't understand how I had lived in a world where I was apparently so much loved, and yet I'd never really felt that before. Rob loved me, my mother loved me. Other men, briefly, had claimed to love me, and I was sure that I was passionate about them, but still I'd never felt anything like this before.

Whatever that feeling was, other people were aware of it too. When Jack and I were together, it rose off our skin like a scent. Even when I was alone, people knew. Mr Baloni at the college made a clumsy pass at me. Even the hopscotch girl stopped for a moment, standing on one foot, and let her face break into a smile, as I came up the stairs.

I knew that Jack didn't love me as I loved him, but he let me love and that was enough. One afternoon, as we lay in that hotel room, watching flakes of snow drifting down at the window, I turned to him and said, 'Oh, we are such actors, aren't we?' He gave me a long look, then started to laugh. And I knew he liked me more than ever because I'd said that.

We didn't always make love, sometimes he was too tired. I never minded that. It was enough to lie there, feeling our bodies close together, the sounds of them echoing one against the other. Despite his thinness, his body was strangely yielding. The passage of time was recorded on his skin. A childhood scar above the line of his left eyebrow, red veins from raw winters, a line of stitches across one knee, shadows the colour of bruises beneath his eyes. Was it my imagination or did those shadows deepen as the days ticked by?

Once I stayed with him in that room all night when Rob was away. In the morning I lay with my head propped against the foot of the bed and held one of his feet in my hands. White skin, straight toes, high arches, each bone clearly delineated. 'You know we talked about places you can remember which seemed absolutely perfect?' I said. 'Where is like that for you?' And he told me about a small town in Provence called La Coste, which he'd visited once with his wife. By chance I knew the place. I'd cycled through there one university holiday, and stayed a couple of nights.

'We'll go there together,' I said, and that became a game we played often, imagining how it would be. A room high up, looking down over the crooked roofs of the town, the sleeping yellow stones, the fields purple with lavender. The room would be in an old house with shuttered windows, and we'd have a key to lock the door. In the cool of the mornings we'd wake and open the shutters and look down at the fields below, covered in mist.

That hotel room was our secret and no one knew –

except for Maya. I never told her but there was no need. The first time I went there, I visited her flat straight afterwards. As soon as I walked in the door she came towards me and sniffed the air. 'I can smell it on you,' she said, and we both started to laugh. I never asked whether it was him she could smell, or the sex, or the deception.

After that, I often went to her flat after I'd been with Jack. She made me round after round of hot buttered toast, or scrambled egg and smoked salmon, followed by slabs of chocolate cake. After I'd eaten she made me sit close to her on the sofa. Sometimes I went to sleep there and woke to find her fingers stroking my arm.

One evening, as I sat at her kitchen table, spreading butter on a third slice of toast, I tried to put it into words. 'It's like burning up all of your life in one afternoon. And you're just desperately trying to hold on to that feeling . . .' Tears suddenly poured down my face. I didn't know whether I was happy or sad, but I pushed my plate back, laid my head down on the table, and sobbed. When I looked up at Maya, her face was tight with fear. And I heard the words she didn't say. *Oh my dear, do be careful.* She'd seen all this somewhere before.

Far in the background, the shell of my old life remained uncracked. I made supper for Rob, sent faxes for Sasha, bought a doll in a *Beryozka* shop for the hopscotch girl, tried to persuade Mr Balashov to move out, hit back, broker a peace. The line of my mother's puppy-dog cards stretched right across the windowsill. In my mind I taunted her, *Look, I've turned into the person you never wanted me to be.*

As March came I waited to hear about Rob's contract but days passed and no news came. I knew that if it wasn't signed we'd leave Moscow soon. Rob was too proud to say anything much, but I knew he was angry about the delays. Every day as I walked into our building I waited for the one-armed *babushka* at the bottom of our stairs to hand me a letter from my father, but I didn't worry when she told me, yet again, that no letter had arrived. He'd write back to me. It was only a question of time. At the college I taught my students the conditional tense. *If I were a doctor, then I'd find a cure. If we were free, we'd go to the South of France now. If I worked for the Democracy Foundation, I'd sign Rob's contract immediately.*

All day, every day, I worried that Rob would find out. I imagined him following me to the hotel. If I heard a movement in the corridor I knew it was him. I sometimes checked three times that the door of Room 815 was locked. In my head I was ready with alibis and explanations to account for everything I did. *Yes, I did pop into that hotel, a woman I teach works there. Jack, yes, I do have lunch with him from time to time.* I worried that Rob would meet one of my colleagues and make a comment about the time we supposedly spent together. Every time he started a conversation I thought, Is this it? This time will he accuse me? Some part of me may even have wanted that. Dread, perhaps, always consists of longing as well as fear.

I knew that I shouldn't have been able to enjoy happiness bought at someone else's expense. But, although I was frightened of being caught, I never really felt guilty. That part of me which should have felt guilt just wasn't there. I knew that Jack didn't like the situation any more than I did. I told him once that I felt guilty about my lack of guilt. He said, 'Perhaps you can't imagine how he might hurt because you don't feel it yourself. Inflicting pain is always about a failure of imagination.'

★　　　★　　　★

Around us, Moscow was clenched tight against the cold. Supplies of everything were running out – food, fuel, medical supplies. Every day my Russian colleagues at the college had a new story of contaminated food – engine oil in chicken, cleaning fluid injected into apples, fish full of mercury, radioactive carrots. Queues extended out into the streets. For most people it was impossible to buy meat, or soap powder. Washing machines and light bulbs were permanently unavailable. My colleagues explained that light bulbs used to be made in Estonia, washing machines in Armenia. Now those countries wouldn't send anything to Russia unless the Russians sent them food.

For days sleet spluttered down and the pavements were awash with freezing water. Even at midday the sky was twilight grey. There was talk of armed resistance, an uprising, a coup, but it was hard to imagine how anyone would find the energy for it. At street corners people stood holding one item for sale – a worn pair of boots, the gearstick from a car, a chipped china vase. They stayed there through rain and snow, as still as statues, their faces expressionless. Many of them were university lecturers, researchers or nurses.

It seemed to me disgusting that Jack and I should live so fully in the midst of such misery. We were taking pleasure when pleasure was not on offer. I longed to do something to help, but I was as powerless as everyone else. Money wasn't the problem, it was the lack of anything to spend it on.

One day, on the way home, I saw a woman in tears in the street. A queue was breaking up and I knew she'd found no food. Although I had no more cash on me, I stopped and handed her a bag of shopping I'd bought for hard currency earlier in the day. The woman looked at me blankly and then peered into the bag. Gripping my hand in her grizzled paw she said in Russian, *God be thanked*. I walked away feeling cheap, knowing that I'd only really helped her so that later, at some moment of final judgement, I'd be able to say, Yes, I did try to help, I really did.

One day, Rob and I met Jack in the street. It was a Saturday and for once a pale sun shone in the sky. We were walking along the Novyi Arbat through scattered stalls selling pirated tapes, tins of caviar, fur hats and pictures of the Kremlin. A woman knelt on a blanket amidst a collection of amber, Russian dolls, peasant scarves. A man with one arm was selling Western and Cuban cigarettes, glasses in their factory crates, and a brand new car axle, presumably stolen from a production line. I looked up and saw Jack from a distance, idling along, and for a moment I panicked. I must create a distraction, steer Rob in the other direction. But I didn't know how to do it, and Jack continued to walk towards us.

When he saw us, he looked up and smiled. Nothing in his face suggested that I was more than a casual acquaintance. We exchanged a few words about the weather. I nodded and smiled and felt my face flaming red. But Jack was quite at ease. I fiddled with my gloves, stared away down the street. Rob asked him whether he was still doing his mental-health work and he said no, he wasn't, he was busy with some research. He'd never mentioned research to me.

As we parted, Jack said, 'Give me a call, and perhaps we'll have lunch.' His act was so convincing that I began to wonder if it was an act. Perhaps those hotel afternoons were something in my head? As he turned to go, strolling on down the street, I couldn't stop myself from staring after him. He didn't look back. Rob and I walked on, but I felt suddenly shaky and sick. It was like when I followed that figure through the streets, and I was so sure it was Jack. But it was someone I didn't know at all.

My birthday: 8 March. An empty bottle of *shampanskoye* stands on the bedside table in Room 815. The sheets are twisted up and the bedcover has fallen to the floor. I pick up my watch from the bedside table and find that it's five thirty. I need to be back by six. Jack told me earlier that he had a present for me and now, as I sit on the bed, he hands me a small package wrapped in brown paper. On the front he's stuck a white card which he's edged with a pattern of loops and chains, drawn with his fountain pen. He's written my name, the date, and *Happy Birthday*. I peel the paper away and find a book of Maiakovskii poems in Russian with English translations beside them. He must have asked someone to send it from America.

I give him a thank you kiss and hand him my present. I'd wanted to wait and give it to him on his birthday, but I won't see him then, and next week seems too late. It's a tin of shortbread which I bought for him in England. The tin has a tartan pattern, and a red ribbon is tied around it. On the front is a picture of a Scottish piper. I found it difficult to choose a present for someone who possessed so little. I'm glad the shortbread will be transient. I couldn't think of anything which would be worthy to sit among that worthless collection of objects, arranged with such care, in that rented room of his. He wants to open the shortbread and give me a piece, but I won't let him.

'You know, next week I have to go to Leningrad.' He says it just like that, as his fingers fumble with the button on the cuff of his shirt. My tights continue to slide up my legs. I put my foot into Maya's high heels and wonder what

I'm doing wearing such stupid shoes. I must look a fool in them.

'Oh yes? And when will you be back?'

'I don't know. Perhaps two or three months.'

I had thought if he went away it'd be for a week or two at the most. If Rob's contract doesn't get renewed then I won't be here when he gets back. I finish dressing, concentrating on buttons, collars, cuffs. In the wardrobe mirror I can see his reflection, but he's taking care not to look at me. I walk to the window, where net curtains hang from a wire. The sill is covered by a layer of dust, like the skin of a mouse. Outside, the sky is like unmarked paper. Any time of day, any time of year. So the turn has come, as I always knew it would. I think of Dr Gurtmann in his shiny pine room, with its hessian wall hangings and boxes of tissues. *How would you describe your relationship with your mother? Do you have any friends of your own age? Do you suffer from nightmares, headaches, period pains?*

'So when exactly are you going?'

'Monday.'

'What? This coming Monday?' I sit down on the bed and feel a sob rising in my throat. But then I look over at him, and his eyes touch mine, and I know he won't really go. Or perhaps he'll go for a week, then come back. This is all to do with his birthday, I'm sure of that.

'So I'll still see you next Monday?' I try to make my voice casual.

'That may be difficult. My train is at five.'

'Well then, let's have lunch.'

He picks up his watch from the bedside table. 'Yes, fine. Lunch – why not? But we should meet somewhere not far from the station. Perhaps the Lubianka Metro? We can have some lunch somewhere there and then I'll be on the right line for the train.'

Lunch. That's what he says but when I see him, we'll
finish up coming here, and he'll never get that train, I'm
sure of that. I button up my coat and pick up my bag. We
argue, then, about who's going to pay for the room. He
always wants to pay because, for the last couple of months,
he's had some money. But I always press him to let me do
it and sometimes he agrees. He doesn't like taking money
from me, and usually I don't like to see the awkward way
he pushes my money into his pocket, but today I insist that
I'm paying and I don't care how he feels.

We step out into the corridor and Jack turns out the
light. The room dissolves into a confusion of flickering
shadows. We walk along the red carpet, over the squeaking
boards. The floor lady sits at her desk with her pictures of
Lenin and his Soviet workers. She takes the key from us,
and nods. Her face registers nothing. We go down in the
clanking lift and I stand beside him at the desk while Jack
pays. I look at my watch again and see that it's past six
o'clock. I imagine Rob at home waiting for me. This evening
Maya and Harvey have invited us to go out with them to
celebrate my birthday. A beige shoe appears on the brown
patterned carpet, then the swinging edge of a fur coat. Red
nails flash near the desk. I turn to hide my face. The shoe
shifts on the carpet. I taste panic in my mouth. I hurry past
slot machines towards the revolving doors. Outside, the door
is blocked by security guards and taxi drivers. My high-heels
splash and stumble through a gutter swollen with ice and
frozen water. It's been raining and light flashes on every
surface.

'Eva, what are you doing? What's the matter?' Jack is
beside me.

'That woman . . . she saw us.' My hand is gripped to my
mouth.

'Eva, calm down. Just calm down.' He shakes at my arm, looks into my eyes. 'It doesn't matter. We could've been drinking in the bar.'

'No, no . . .' Why doesn't he understand? 'She's a friend of Maya's. She wears a fur coat and her hair is blonde.'

'There wasn't any woman like that.'

He watches me with worried eyes and I know that some part of him wants to walk away and leave me here. I'd like to walk away from myself as well. I can't breathe, and on the edge of my mind I begin to see the child. 'Come on,' he says. 'Let's walk. You need to sit down somewhere.' But I don't want to go with him. I don't know who he is any more. Wherever we go, Estelle will follow us. Every window in Moscow is full of eyes. I pull away from him and hurry towards the Metro. His voice calls but I don't look back. Suddenly I long to be at home, with Rob, eating supper at the kitchen table with our knees close. In the depths of the Metro I find a bench and sink down, my head gripped in my hands.

The child sits on a metal chair in a wide corridor lined with doors. It smells of cut knees and plasters. High above, strip-lights hang down on chains. At the end of the corridor a nurse with a starched cap is writing in a book. The child rearranges the skirt of her dress again and again, trying to keep the creases out of it. In her hand she has a bunch of holly, heavy with red berries. Tinfoil is wrapped around the stalks. Today her father might come home, and then it's Christmas, and after that an exhibition. Then after an exhibition there's always a party. Her mother doesn't want any of that. She never wants anything except pills for her headaches or a handkerchief for her cold.

The nurse sails down the corridor and tells the child that she can go in now. She points at a door straight ahead. The child gets up, straightens her dress, holds the holly with both hands as though she's a bridesmaid. She steps through the door and into a white room where a man lies on an iron bed. The room has a ceiling miles high, and a long window with a slatted blind. The child moves towards the bed but the man lying there isn't her father. Surely the nurse pointed towards this room? She goes back out into the corridor and stands there, uncertain. The nurse has gone, the corridor is empty. The stems of the holly have made a mark on her dress. She creeps towards the next room and peers in. This room has the same white bed, the same high window. A man is lying on the floor, wearing pyjamas, curled up like a baby, sucking his thumb.

No, no, dear. Not this room. Come along. Next door. The child is steered back to the room where she was before. The holly is falling out of the tinfoil, and she's got to keep it together and not let any more marks get on her dress. She looks back but the nurse has gone again. She moves towards the bed. The person there is a black-and-white drawing of her father, an outline. The shading needs to be put in, to give him a proper shape. She longs to have some of her father's paints so she can start to put the colour in. The man in the bed is staring up at the slatted blind. She moves closer to him. His head turns and he asks her for a glass of water. She lays the holly down, goes to the sink in the corner of the room, and takes a glass in both hands. She kneels on a chair and turns on the tap. She stands the glass between the taps while she turns the water off, then she goes back to the bed. The man takes the glass from her, raises his head, drinks and then hands the glass back to her. If he was really her father he would smile and pull her to him, kissing her cheek.

Who do you think that kind girl was who went to fetch the water? The man whispers these words. The child smiles, trying to play the game.

I don't know, she says. Didn't you know her?

No.

Do you think the girl who fetched the water was me?

It's possible. Do you think we should ask her?

The child wriggles and laughs, but she doesn't look at the man's face. He's staring at the blind and he waves a hand towards it. Of course, he never likes curtains or blinds closed, not even in the middle of the night. The child moves the chair from the sink and, standing on it, she pulls at the cord until the blind opens. A ragged three-quarter moon appears and a sprinkling of stars. Suddenly the man turns into her father. He has light and colour. He stares up at the window, the night sky, the ragged moon. The child goes to fetch her bunch of holly, she takes the tinfoil off the stalks and pushes them down into the glass. She asks her father whether the water in the glass will be enough and he says he's sure it will. So many berries on the holly, he says, and so very red.

The nurse comes in, smiles at the child, then reaches out for the cord. As the blind drops the child turns. Why doesn't the nurse know that she shouldn't have closed the blind? But the nurse has gone and the blind is down. She looks at her father and sees his face tighten. He's turning back into the outline man. A low groan comes from between his lips. He stretches out his arm and the child tries to take hold of it, but he's banging it up and down on the edge of the bed.

The child climbs up on the chair and pulls at the blind but she can't make it work. Behind her she hears the groaning, and sees the arm going up and down. Her father starts to shout and the child struggles with the cord. The nurse comes back and tells the child to get down from the chair. The child tugs at the cord. The nurse grabs her but she kicks and struggles. She has to get the blind up, her father needs to see outside. Her head is pressed against white cotton, but the toggle of the blind is still gripped in her hand. She wraps her body around it. The room is full of shouting and a sound like a dog howling.

*A smell of fresh laundry and antiseptic smothers her. She fights to get
away from the white cotton. She sees a syringe in a kidney-shaped
bowl. Suddenly the blind moves halfway up and the shouting stops.*

*But her fingers are being prised away from the cord one by one.
They will shut the blind again if she doesn't keep hold of the cord.
She catches at it again and pulls. With a crash the blind comes
away from the wall and collapses, hitting her on the head, show-
ering her with dust and plaster. The child looks up and sees a
glimpse of that ragged-edged moon. The glass with the holly is
smashed on the floor. But the howling has stopped. She's pulled
out into the corridor. Her mother is there, and next to her is a
priest. He has hair like flames coming out of his head.*

Eva, Eva, what are you doing?

*She wants to go back into the room to pick the holly up, but
her mother's arms are tight around her. She tries to tell them about
the blind, how it mustn't be pulled down, but no one listens. They
don't understand. The nurses, and the priest and her mother – none
of them understand. Her mother clings to her, smothering her, pulling
her away from her father's room. It's time to go home now, they've
got to go home. She mustn't worry, everything is going to be all
right. Please, please, don't let them put the blind back up.*

30/16 Ulitsa Pravdy, Moscow

8 March 1991

When I get home Rob isn't back, but a letter is lying on the kitchen table. On the back it has the address of my father's solicitors printed in red. I sit down at the table and stare at it. I get up and walk to the window, look down into the courtyard, go back to the table. I pick the letter up and turn it over again and again, examining the two addresses, the postmark.

So this is it. My mother said he'd never write, but she was wrong. Now that I need him he has come. I hold the envelope against me. From far below I hear the thread of a melody, one slow note after another, like a music box winding down. I push my finger under the flap, feel the paper unsticking. I know it'll contain a brief letter from the solicitors and then, inside it, a letter from my father. My fingers stumble on the stiff paper. I wait for that other letter to fall out. I check inside the envelope. Nothing. The words on the solicitors' letter blur in front of my eyes. My letter has been forwarded, they say, but no response has been received. The address they used may be out of date. It is their belief that my father is still in Mexico, and enquiries will be made.

My hands are numb as I fold the letter away. I feel him fading from me. I imagine my letter, pinned down beneath the timbers of a blown-down shack on a turquoise beach. The corner of it flaps in the wind. The ink has washed from the letter, leaving only a watery purple stain. But he will get in touch with me, I know he will. I look up to see Rob at the kitchen door although I didn't hear him come in. For a moment he stops and looks at the letter. Those notes still sound from below, slower and slower. Rob steps forward, wraps me in his arms, and we kiss awkwardly. 'Brrrrh,' he shudders, but the kitchen isn't cold.

He starts to open his backpack. 'Happy Birthday again.' He told me this morning he had a present for me but that he'd left it at the office. He's digging around now, trying to find it. As he puts his pack on the table, he pushes papers to one side, deftly shuffling my father's letter under my Russian dictionary. 'Here we are.' He hands me a flat package, wrapped in used Christmas paper, then looks at his watch. 'OK, so we've got an hour before meeting Maya.' He drops his coat on a chair, gets out glasses and a bottle of vodka.

I sit next to him at the table, our knees touching, and we drink. Dribbles of condensation run down the outside of the vodka bottle. A corner of my father's letter still sticks out from under that dictionary. Rob is waiting for me to undo the package but I don't want to start, because I already know what's inside. From below, those slow notes continue to press against us. I am a person coming to the boil. My cheeks burn where Jack's stubbly chin grazed my skin.

My fingers become thick as sausages as I try to undo the paper. I rip at it, blood pumping in my ears. The paper comes away. Inside is the same book of Maiakovskii poems. I balance it in my hands and conjure a smile. 'Thank you. Thanks so much. That's just what I wanted. I'd have bought

it for myself.' I feel that other copy of the book in my coat
pocket. One man, another man. Why does the difference
matter so much? I don't know, but it does.

In the basement restaurant of the Hotel Smolenskaia, glass
balls made of tiny mirrors hang from the ceiling. As they
turn, they spread glittering light. The tables and chairs are
metal and Formica, the curtains patterned in circles of brown
and orange. European businessmen sit beside Arab diplomats
and Russian girls with high cheekbones and dangerous eyes.
In one corner a man tinkles the keys of an electric organ
and women in tinsel skirts prepare to dance. This is the
world of people who aren't in love, and I envy them.

As always, there's a problem with the table booking. The
waiter seems to have no knowledge of the reservation Harvey
made. It's suggested that we should share a table with another
group. Rob intervenes and eventually they show us to a
table set for six. 'Oh yes,' Maya says. 'I forgot to mention,
Estelle and Manfred are coming as well.' Maya fusses with
her cigarettes and her shawl so she doesn't have to look at
me. In my head red nails flash and the hem of a fur coat
ripples.

An English family with two children come to sit at the
table next to us. I can hear fragments of their conversation
. . . *High Street Kensington, blossom in the garden, Granny for
the weekend*. I feel a sudden longing for home. Rob and
Harvey are talking about the referendum that will take place
a week on Sunday. It's the first-ever Soviet referendum, and
it seeks support for a new Union Treaty. Harvey says that
Gorbachev is going the way of every other Russian leader
– a few attempts at reform, which soon lead to violence,
justifying a return to the traditional methods of police rule.
Rob says it'll be different this time. Gorbachev will get

support for the Treaty but the referendum will also strengthen Yeltsin's hand.

Estelle and Manfred arrive. She isn't wearing a fur coat and her fingernails are no particular shade of red. I've never met Manfred before, but he turns out to be a German version of Harvey, except he works in telecoms rather than oil. The food was already on the table before we sat down – slices of cold meat, beetroot and a slab of butter. The electric organ starts to play.

Maya produces a bag from beside her chair. 'A birthday present for you.' She hands me a purple box tied with a gold ribbon. I push back my chair so I can open it. Inside layers of tissue, I find a coat, made of grey velvet with a fitted top and a wide skirt. Like a military uniform it has gold buttons, black braid on the shoulders, and wide cuffs. At the back, a horizontal panel and two gold buttons mark the waist. 'I bought it in New York,' Maya says. For a moment I imagine myself in Room 815, spinning around on one foot, showing the coat to Jack. Then I remember he won't be here.

'It'll probably be too long,' Maya says. 'And it's not made for these winters, but you can wear it in the spring, if spring ev-e-er arrives.'

'It's beautiful,' I say. 'Thank you.'

Estelle glances at the coat with sour eyes. She complains to Maya about the pot-holes in the roads, and how they've damaged the wheel of her car. A group of fat men wearing gold jewellery arrive at the next table. Drunkenly they leer at the dancing girls who loll near the organ. To the side of the room a man stands against the wall, watching. A bulge under his jacket suggests a gun. This is the first time I've seen people who look so obviously like the Mafia. A second plate of food appears, with green beans stacked at one side.

Rob sees me eyeing the beans and, with one deft movement, he moves them from my plate onto his.

Estelle turns towards me, raising her eyebrows and lighting a cigarette. 'You know, I'm just thinking, I saw you somewhere recently but I can't remember where.' My hands tighten on my knife and fork. I look up at Rob, still talking to Harvey and Manfred, and he has no idea how close we are to the edge. For a moment I'm reminded of myself as a child, far out on the mud beach with my father. The storm is about to break, the tide is turning. But I don't know that the sea monster is close, and that soon there'll be no more days with the sun spreading its rays like the spokes of a wheel.

Estelle is waiting for my response, but I turn to Harvey and start to talk about the referendum. How can it possibly have any validity? Six of the Republics are refusing to participate and all the radicals will certainly refuse to vote. I talk louder and louder but I can still hear Estelle's voice. 'What's his name? John Flame? Well, anyway, I was told that he's wanted in America in connection with setting up some cult.'

'Trading drugs,' Manfred says. 'I'm sure that's what he does.'

My mind veers away from an image of that wooden box with its ivory clasp. I feel my skin tighten. The smallest touch of my hand unbalances the glass of water. The tablecloth is soaked, the glass spins over the side of the table and smashes on to the floor. I stand up and reach for a napkin. 'Never mind,' Maya says. 'Ne-e-ver mind.' A waiter arrives and I think he's going to clear up the water, but instead he asks to speak to Rob. I turn to Harvey, determined not to let the conversation about Jack start again. 'Did you hear that the body of a man has been found in the river and they think it's definitely a Mafia killing?'

'Yes,' Harvey says. 'I certainly did hear that.'

Strange, really, because I just made that up.

'We've all got to be very careful,' Harvey said. 'The security situation is worse all the time. I'm just glad we're at least in a building which is secure.'

'But is it?' I say, looking over at Estelle. 'Because, you know, I'd hate to worry you, Harvey, but the very first time I went to your building, I just walked straight in without ringing any bell.'

I'm surprised that I dare to say this but what do I have to lose? I look over at Maya and her smile is both grim and amused. Estelle knocks ash from the end of her cigarette, her finger banging up and down. Rob comes back to the table and puts his hand on my shoulder. I jump at his touch. He bends down and speaks in a low voice. 'Listen, I've got to go. Sasha has been arrested.'

'Why? Why has he been arrested?'

'I don't know. It isn't clear. But it seems a bit of a co-incidence that it should happen at the time of this referendum.'

'Let me come with you.' I find myself clinging to his hand.

'No. It won't help. Don't worry. Please don't worry.'

Maya and Harvey can't believe Rob is going. 'You won't be able to do anything tonight,' they say. 'Surely you're not going to leave Eva alone on her birthday?' But Rob is insistent and I tell him to go. I think of a book I've been reading about Soviet prisons – the people kept for months in holes in the ground, the electric sticks, whips and meat-grinders. I never thought anyone we knew would get arrested. I watch Rob as he walks away, shuffling between the tables.

'And, you know, John Flame always says that he worked at Berkeley in the sixties but that's when my father was there and he can't remember him,' Estelle says. 'I think Manfred's right. Drugs – that's the only explanation.'

'That's not true. It's not true.' My voice is too loud. 'How can you judge someone in such a cheap way? Just because he doesn't want to live like other people – just because he doesn't want to live in a world of lies and triviality – just because . . . then you think he's a criminal.' The electric organ music tinkles on, and the sound of other voices rumbles around us, but our table is silent.

Maya leans over and puts her hand on my arm. 'Eva, dear, would you mind going to get my shawl for me? I left it with the doorman. Here's the ticket.'

I stand up unsteadily, and walk away through the tables, my face smarting. It feels like everyone is watching me. The perspectives of the room seem oddly distorted, as though I'm looking at it in a convex mirror. The glass doors, the metal window frames, are elongated and bowed. I arrive at the bottom of the marble and stainless steel stairs and ask the doorman for my coat.

I hear the swing door open behind me. 'Eva, are you all right? Why don't you sit down a moment?'

'I don't need to sit down.'

'Eva, dear, there's no need to shout.'

The doorman hands me my coat and I start to put it on. Maya reaches for my arm. 'Eva, I'm worried about you. You're losing your way.'

'On the contrary, I'm finding it. You know, very soon Jack and I are going to go away from here. That's what we've decided.' As I say that, I'm filled with lightness, a sense of relief. Words so concise, so absolute. Such luxury to find life narrowed down to a single purpose. I can just walk out of this situation and leave everything behind. Wounds heal, the grass grows back. On Monday I'll board the train with Jack,

I'll shed my life as a snake sheds its skin. And then I'll be in his world – a rented room, enough money for bread and milk, shortbread biscuits, a vase of catkins. We'll go to Leningrad and then the South of France, and on the way we'll stop in Paris and find a doctor who can give Jack pills. It's really as simple as that.

'Eva, you're crazy. There can't be any future in it. You know that.'

'Maybe. Maybe not. But if it's a failure it'll be a brave one.'

Maya's eyes are stretched open, her mouth slack. 'Eva, please stay. Please. You must come back with me.' I turn away from her and hurry up the marble stairs. For a moment I look down and see her below me, her hands stretched up to me, her face crumpled. I wonder now why she didn't go to Mexico with my father. She was in love with him, so why did she go away to Rome six months before he left? I don't know, but my suspicion is that her nerve failed her. And what I do know is that I'm not going to finish up like her. In my mind it's already Monday and I'm on the train with Jack. He and I are sitting side by side, feeling the rhythm of the train, watching at the window as the tower blocks of Moscow fade into the past.

The child stands in the corner of the kitchen, by the shelves built into the old fireplace. The carpet in the front hall has been rolled up, the dining-room table pushed back against the wall. Two armchairs have been lifted up the stairs into the back bedroom. Boxes of glasses are stacked in the back corridor. The child wanders towards the door. A hand closes on her arm.

Just stay here, dear. There's a good girl. Your mother is busy.

Mrs Reynolds and her friend Mrs Gooden have come to help

for the party. They wear white aprons, the strings lost in the folds of their waists. Mrs Reynolds's face shines with sweat. At the kitchen sink Mrs Gooden is up to her elbows in soapy water. They talk about the cold. That's what everyone talks about at the moment. Minus ten, it was, last night. Some of the creeks on the marsh are frozen, even though they're saltwater. Mrs Gooden has only ever known one freeze like this before and that was when she was a girl. The room smells of pastry, cloves and ginger. Mrs Reynolds grates the zest from lemons. On the table, cut flowers are laid out, their stems weeping on to newspaper.

The child moves back to the fireplace shelves. They're crowded with bottles containing herbs and spices. The child starts to put the bottles upside down, balancing each one on its lid. Later she'll show the bottles to her father, he likes things upside down. He came back from London earlier in the day. Yesterday was the start of his exhibition and the telephone has been ringing all day. She wants to see her father now but she's not allowed to disturb him. He's very tired and busy as well. He must rest or he'll get ill again like last time, when he had to go into hospital with pneumonia. As the child balances another bottle her mother comes into the kitchen. Come on now, Eva, time for bed.

The child pushes the upside-down bottles together so that they stand in a line.

What are you doing with those bottles? Stop it. Stop it immediately. Her mother snatches a bottle from her. Come on now. Time for bed.

The child turns another bottle upside down. No. I'm not going. I'm staying here.

Eva. Do what I'm telling you right now.

Come now, Mrs Reynolds says to the child's mother. Don't upset yourself. Eva, you stay down here with me for five more minutes and I'll find a treat for you. Then I'll take you up and help you get in bed, how about that?

*The child escapes from her mother into Mrs Reynolds's apron.
She's steered into the back kitchen. The window there is thick with
ice. Mrs Reynolds opens the chest freezer. In the corner of the room,
lying on the ironing board, is a long skirt made of heavy silk. A
wide straw hat lies on top of it, and a pale chiffon scarf which falls
down over the side of the board. On the floor are shoes with pointed
toes, stitched with flowers. The child walks towards those shoes but
Mrs Reynolds catches hold of her, gives her a red ice lolly, and
helps her peel off the paper.*

*The child sits on the kitchen table, shivering, her tongue sticking
on the lolly. Mrs Reynolds rolls up the sleeves of the child's jumper
and the white T-shirt she wears underneath. The child decides that
she's going to stay downstairs for the party. In her dressing-up box
she's got all sorts of good costumes. She could be a princess, or a
fairy, but she prefers her red devil costume with the forked stick
and horns on a piece of elastic. Soon she'll go upstairs and put
that on.*

*Mrs Reynolds is standing next to the sink sieving icing sugar
on to mince pies. Occasionally she turns and mutters something to
Mrs Gooden, who is washing up. They think the child doesn't
understand but she does. She picks out a word and makes it into
a rhyme for them. Problem-goblin-toppling-hobbling. And she tells
them about the place in Mexico where she might go with her father,
but only for the weekend. Mrs Reynolds and Mrs Gooden stand
together, their heads close, whispering. The child swings her feet
against the back of a kitchen chair, kicking at it. Left foot, right
foot, left foot. A trickle of red from the lolly runs down over her
hand and on to her wrist. Problem-goblin-toppling-hobbling. Her
feet bang against the back of the chair in time with the words, their
sound filling her head.*

Garlic-obsessions-rabbit-processions-garbage-lessons.

Eva, dear, do stop that noise, please.

The red lolly drips down on to the white sleeve of her T-

shirt. Right, left, right. Her foot bangs against the chair. Garlic-obsessions-rabbit-processions-garbage-lesson-manic-depression. The toe of her shoe catches on the back of the chair. Mrs Reynolds's sieve stops still above the mince pies. Mrs Gooden turns to look at the child, and her eyes move upwards as though she's frightened the ceiling might fall on her. The child looks at the red lolly dripping on her sleeve. She kicks at the chair, but gently now. Left, right, left. Garlic-obsessions-rabbit-processions-garbage-lesson. Manic-depression. On her white T-shirt, the red stain spreads and spreads.

30/16 Ulitsa Pravdy, Moscow

12 March 1991

I stand near the sitting-room window and look down into the courtyard. A weak sun hides behind a veil of grey. In the mud below, a young man perches on duckboards, examining the wheel of a Lada. Today I am leaving here. In my bag I've got fifty dollars, a plastic envelope containing travellers' cheques, an extra jumper, some underwear and a sponge bag. Jack telephoned last night to say he can't meet me until 3.30 but we'll still have time for a snack before the train.

One of my cardigans hangs on the back of a chair, and unwashed pots crowd the sink. I close the door on them, and on the various cardboard cut-outs who have occupied this flat. Today is the beginning of my real life. As I walk to the Metro, it surprises me that the people in the street don't seem to know what is going to happen. The station is more crowded than I've ever seen it. The first train is full, and when the second comes I have to put my head down and elbow my way in. I'm pressed up against a mother holding a tiny baby with a wizened face. She wears a veil, her eyes are shut and she sways with the motion of the train.

At Chekhovskaia, the Metro stops, an announcement

echoes through the station and everyone jostles out of the carriage, unfolding cramped limbs. It's only one stop from here to Lubianka so it won't take long to walk. As I emerge from the Metro, crowds line the streets, music plays and car horns hoot. The air smells of sweets and fried food. I remember now that I read in the *Moscow News* that as many as 100,000 people are expected to march through the streets today, all of them intent on voting against Gorbachev's proposed Union Treaty.

I turn a corner and set off downhill, heading towards Manyezh Ploshchad', but the way is blocked. Rows of police stand five deep, armed with truncheons and riot shields. Lorries, tanks and armoured personnel-carriers are lined up in side streets. Protesters shout and jeer at the police but still the atmosphere is more like a carnival than a political demonstration. The protesters carry pre-revolutionary flags without the hammer and sickle, or banners with slogans and pictures of Yeltsin. I feel as though I haven't seen the sun for weeks, maybe months, but now it glints on windows, the façades of buildings, the bonnets of cars.

I reach Lubianka and stare up for a moment at the vast façade of the KGB headquarters, a place where thousands died without even a proper trial. One of my Russian colleagues told me once that blood used to run out of the drains of this building and into the street. I think of Sasha. It's four days now since he was arrested and no one has been able to discover what he's supposed to have done. Rob has been to ask several times, but he never gets an answer. Bill has spoken to the American Embassy to see if they can find out anything. I take care not to let a picture of Sasha form in my mind.

I find Jack near the entrance to the Metro, reading

posters displayed in a glass case on a wall. The bottoms of his trousers are splattered with mud, and his shoes are dirty. He carries two small suitcases, both are battered and brown, one has a broken strap. When he turns around, I see the shadow of illness in his body. It's there in the hunch of his shoulders, and the way he moves – tenderly, as though the pavement might burn his feet, or the wind sting his skin.

We walk up Miasnitskaia Ulitsa, heading away from the crowds, searching for a place to eat. We talk about the demonstration. I say that, in one way or another, the reform process is certain to continue now because the population is firmly behind it. Jack is doubtful. For every one person marching here, he says, there are hundreds more who feel nostalgia for the old ways. And Moscow is quite different from the rest of the country. Protesters walk past us with buckets and people throw in coins and grubby banknotes. Jack tells me that the money will be used to help the coal miners in Western Siberia who are on strike, demanding the resignation of Gorbachev. I ask Jack whether the police will try to clear the protesters off the streets. He says the worst they might do is use water cannons or tear gas. Gunning people down in the Baltic States is one thing, the streets of Moscow are a different matter.

We stop at a café which must be newly opened. The tablecloths are red-and-white gingham and the seats of the chairs have been covered in red plastic. We sit down at a table near the window. The only other customer is an exotic young man with a handlebar moustache. He wears a striped suit and is accompanied by two wolf-like dogs with sparkling collars. I stretch my hand across the table to touch Jack's fingers. His thumb brushes against mine but he's looking around for someone to serve us. The waiter comes and Jack says he doesn't want to eat, but orders a coffee. I say perhaps I won't eat either but Jack insists, so I order *bitochki* and a cup of tea.

I want to tell him about those words I'd heard as the toe of the child's shoe banged against the chair. I want to say, 'What was there in my father is there in me as well, isn't it?' And I want to hear him say that that isn't true. But those words frighten me so much that I can't even begin to form them in my mouth. Through the window we watch the protesters filing past. People sing and blow whistles, flags wave and a child riding on a man's shoulders grips the string of a rabbit-shaped balloon. Across the road, a newly restored gold dome stands sober above the crowd. The waiter arrives with our drinks. The stripe-suited man is feeding pieces of bread to his dogs.

'So we're leaving at five?' I say.

'Eva, I'm not taking you with me. You know that.'

I sit in silence, waiting for those words to retreat. It's as though I've been stabbed. Pain digs in deep under my ribs. I feel blood seep from the wound, its warmth spreading on my clothes. The pulse is fading from my fingertips and toes. I stare at my hand as it lies on the table, close to his. I don't understand why the stripe-suited man, wiping his moustache with a napkin, doesn't seem to know what is happening. The waiter arrives with my meatballs. Surely he can see the blood running from me? But he places the plate in front of me and retreats. Outside, the carnival music plays. I stare down at a gravy stain on the tablecloth, then pick up my knife and poke at the meatballs in their pool of watery sauce. Out of the side of my eye, I see a blade of sunlight on the façade of the church. Later, that's what I'll remember, I think.

Jack is talking but I can't hear all of what he says because of the screaming in my head. 'Eva, you know that even if you and I had been together properly, it wouldn't have worked. You know that, don't you?'

I don't admit to that.

'What you feel for me is need, not love,' he says. 'All I am is a distraction for you, that's all. What's happened doesn't need to turn into a disaster. You've changed. You don't know that, but I can see it. You think you love me, but really you love something I've done to you. That process of change is going to continue with or without me.'

He tries to touch my hand but I pull away from him.

'Eva, you know that very often, passions of the type you feel don't respect the person who is loved. If you can't let go of something, then you don't really love it.'

I'm not listening. My mind is sorting through the future. All I can see is blackness. 'You've always thought that this is just about my father.'

'No. Your father is incidental, just as I am. There are always layers and layers to these yearnings.'

My eyes blur and my head throbs. I wipe my hand across my eyes. Jack shakes his head and drinks some of his coffee. For a moment I raise my eyes from the table and look over at the church with its jeering ray of sunlight. Yes, I think, I know where I am, I know what's happening. I've done this before, I know how it goes. I must stay bright and calm, not make it too difficult for him, appear to be taking it well. That ray of sunlight dances at the side of my vision, jabbing at my eyes. Words begin to join up in rhymes in my head. Yearnings-learnings-turnings.

Jack watches the knife in my hand. 'Are you going to eat that?'

I shake my head without looking at him.

'Please, eat it.'

I take one mouthful but the meat tastes of soap, so I lay down the knife and push the plate away. 'All your talk about the difference between need and love, that's rubbish. You can push me away all you like, but you need me as much as I need you. Because without me, what's going to happen to you? You're just going to get more and more ill, and lie in some rented room waiting to die.'

'No,' he says. 'It won't be like that.'

The pain is making it difficult to breathe. A pressure is building behind my eyes but this is too bad for tears. The music from outside thumps in my ears and the man with the dogs gets up to go. Still he hasn't noticed, still the waiter hasn't noticed. Yearnings–learnings–turnings. I sit staring at the red checked tablecloth.

Jack looks at his watch. 'I must go. I don't think I'm going to be able to take the Metro. It'll be better to walk.' My lips feel swollen, my throat thick. The bill comes and Jack picks it up, but I take it from him and pay. We stand on the pavement outside. 'Jack, I can't – please, let me come to the station.'

He shakes his head and closes his eyes. His face is white and shrivelled. Beads of sweat have gathered beneath the line of his hair. I stretch out my hand. For a moment he stares at it, then wraps it in his. He walks fast, pulling me with him. The protesters are behind us now, but the streets are swelling with people leaving work. The sun has turned red and is sliding down behind a cliff of stained walls and dirty windows. The streets are littered with bottles and paper. My feet are unsteady, my fists clenched. We cross a wide square, passing under the shadow of one of the Stalin Skyscrapers. Jack lets go of my hand, looks at his watch, then catches hold of me again, and hurries on.

In Komsomolskaia Ploshchad', we push our way past

taxis, food stalls, prostitutes and homeless drunks. A veiled
woman, dressed in black, kneels on the pavement and bangs
her head on the ground again and again. Under heavy coats
and fur hats, men wear brightly coloured trousers which
glitter with gold. Above us, the fairytale tower of the Kazan
Station stands up sharp against the evening sky.

We enter the marble hall of the 1960s Leningrad Station
and Jack's eyes scan the departure boards as they flicker and
roll. Around us, people sit on wooden slatted benches. Whole
families huddle around piles of plastic bags, sacks and cardboard boxes. A woman cooks on a gas camping stove. I hear
the scream of a train braking and am caught in a shuffle of
hurrying feet.

We push through towards the platform. I wonder how I
will get on to the train without a ticket or an internal passport, but I'm sure that if I give Jack some of my dollars to
use as a bribe then he can sort that out. A guard at the
entrance to the platform is checking tickets. I keep tight
hold of Jack's hand. He produces a couple of kopeks from
his pocket. The guard hands me a platform ticket and together
Jack and I are swept through an arch towards the train. It's
fat and green, with ridged sides and high windows. People
hurry past us, scrambling for the doors. It's a long train, and
we walk the length of it, as Jack tries to find his seat. Doors
are slamming and women in khaki uniforms, holding flags,
stand at the end of each carriage. We reach the door of the
last carriage. A khaki woman stands close to us. From further
down the train, a man hollers and a child wails. Jack's breath
is short and he wipes at his forehead. A man in a fur hat
pushes past us, bundling his wife and two small children on
to the train.

'If you go, you know what will happen, don't you?'

He looks at me and his eyes are steady. 'Yes, I know.'

The khaki woman comes up to Jack and he produces his ticket. Two young men, dragging a heavy box between them, jostle against me and push their box up on to the train. Jack lifts the heavier of his two bags up the metal steps. I keep hold of the smaller bag and place my foot on the bottom step. The khaki woman blows her whistle. Around us people shout, arms wave, the hum of a diesel engine shudders through the train. The khaki woman is asking me for my ticket. I cling to Jack's hand. She shouts and pushes. Jack eases the bag from my hand.

I'm shoved aside and the metal steps are pushed up, fitting into the side of the train with a clank. The door slams. I reach up to open it again but the woman hits at me with her flag. I look up and see Jack at the window. His face is transparent in the darkness of the glass. I imagine throwing myself against the side of the train. *Jack, Jack.* But instead I raise my hand to him as the train creaks into motion. His face stays in my eyes as I watch each carriage pass – flashes of light, faces, waving hands, carriage doors. Then the train is gone and I'm left alone, staring into the black tunnel at two red lights, flickering smaller and smaller, dissolving into the dark.

Just concentrate on putting one foot in front of the other. Right, then left, then right again. Keep your body steady. Do not look to either side. Most importantly, do not look down. Around me, everything has been shaken loose. The city is jaunty, its balance perilous.

So he has gone. It's finished. I rub my hands together, twisting my fingers as though washing myself clean of him. As I walk, I whistle silently, convincing myself that I don't care. I'm light as a leaf, the wind could catch me and blow me away. The rustle of feet and the murmur of car engines press against my ears. Bare trees zig-zag above me. The lines of buildings sway and contract as though reflected on water. Dance music plays in my head. Keep them gathered together, the arms and legs, don't let them wander off. I catch at my hair as though it might blow away. How I wish they would turn the music down, switch the lights off.

I walk all the way home and don't feel tired. When I get to the flat I have difficulty organizing my hands to open the door. The keys juggle, my fingers slip on the catch so that I graze my knuckle. That music is still playing inside my head. I feel a desire to dance, to spin around in a circle on one foot. The inside of my head is turning and turning. The flat is just as I left it. My cardigan still hangs on the back of the chair, unwashed pots remain stacked in the sink. Everything is just the same, nothing has really happened.

In the bathroom my feet slip. I grab at the loo seat, head bent down, eyes shut. He has split my mind in two and the past is spilling out. In my mouth I taste soapy meat, and a rush of acid. My stomach rises up and then dives down. Liquid rushes into my nose and presses inside my ears. The back of my throat burns, my stomach gathers itself together and I feel myself turning inside out. Everything empties from me. I spit and then fall back, crumpled up beside the loo, my head against the wall.

The child hides beside the cupboard on the landing. The stick of the lolly is still gripped in her hands. From below she can hear Mrs Reynolds calling. She mustn't go up to her father's room. He's busy and tired. He mustn't be disturbed. But a light shines through his half-open door. Mrs Reynolds calls again and the front door bell rings. Her mother's shoes tap over the hall floor. The child steps across the landing towards that strip of light. The air smells of dust and mulled wine.

She moves forward and looks through the door. The curtains are open and the telescope is assembled at the window. A figure moves close to the telescope but the child can't see his face. He's dressed in a frockcoat, blue satin knickerbockers and a three-cornered hat. On his feet are black shoes with square toes and silver buckles. The figure is her father but she's never seen him wear those clothes before. The blue silk shimmers in the light. Gold buttons glitter on the back of the frockcoat and a line of blue lace edges the deep sleeves of the coat.

Her father is adjusting the telescope, talking to himself. The child knows that the sky isn't clear and that he's frustrated because he can't see what he's looking for. Books are open on the desk, and charts, and maps. The child wants to call out to him but she also just wants to stand there watching. From below she hears the front door open. Laughter and voices swell across the landing, and a cold draught moves the curtains.

The child knows that soon she will go away with her father. She hears the back stairs creak. Mrs Reynolds is coming up to look for her. And now her mother's voice is calling as well. Eva must go to bed, she must go to bed. The child steps forward into the room. She wants to touch the silk of her father's jacket. She wants to look more closely at the gold buttons and square-toed shoes. She calls to him and he starts to turn. The lace on his sleeve flutters, his hand hovers in the air. She puts up her arms to him.

But the man is not her father. Instead, she's standing in front of an ogre with the wrinkled face of an ape. The child raises her hands to her neck and chokes on a scream. The ape has tiny eyes, a jabbering mouth, strands of thin black hair. His face is waxen, his teeth long and yellow. He reaches out towards her. The child stumbles back, turns across the landing. She wants her father. Her *hand reaches for the stair-rail but it closes around air. Pictures on the wall swivel upwards, the landing window drops down, rolling like the wheels on a slot machine. The child's cheek bruises against the stair-rail, her fingernails scratch against the threads of the carpet.*

12/20 rue de Lausanne, Geneva

November 1991

My question is this: how is it that I knew him through to the marrow of his bones and yet now, as I come to assemble the facts, I realize that most of them are missing? I kneel on the parquet floor in the hall with the contents of his boxes spread around me. That grey plastic filing tray, his blue notebooks, newspaper cuttings, letters. So many pieces of paper but no answers. The truth is that I don't even know what these boxes are doing here. And I never even knew his real name.

That day in the No Name Café, when he was there with that man and woman, he made it all into a joke, but he never did tell me who those people were. And how did he always have access to things other people couldn't get? I think of the hotel room, that air ticket to Vilnius, Estelle and her gossip. Then later – those days in August – he felt them coming. And that last morning, he was so determined to go back into Moscow. It's only now that I begin to ask myself – why was that? The truth is that even the kindest face, seen in the wrong light, begins to take on the look of an ape.

I open the cover of a book, hoping for an inscription which might place him somewhere. Instead I find a letter. It's in a brown envelope, addressed to him, and the postmark is 23 August 1991. Surely that can't be right? Then I see that the letter was sent from San Francisco and has never been opened. I know what it must contain. I should open it, of course, because it's intended for me, but the risk is too great. You can pursue someone through the unending labyrinth of your mind and theirs, but finally all you discover is a child's shoes kicking against the back of a chair.

Just write it down and you'll understand. How did I ever believe that? Shiny, shallow words. They go up like fireworks, exploding in a hundred meanings. There are no conversations, only monologues. I start to hate you now, Jack. You said that we'd go away to France together. We had it all planned and then in that café . . . You didn't care, you just didn't care. All of that Gypsy Rose act, that cheap mumbo-jumbo. Those theories you had – you needed to try them out, and I was the beagle with an electrode taped to its head.

My father and I, far out on the beach, in the bronze evening sun, waiting for the tide to turn. You should have left us alone, Jack, for we were happy there. Maya was right. You pass the same point again and again. What was it you said to me? *You think all men leave?* Well they do, they do. Jack, you promised you'd wait. You promised. Just one night. I thought it couldn't make any difference.

The easy writing is finished with now. These words are scratched in blood and tears. The story of that day at Tsaritsyno – oh yes, we all want to hear that. Or the day my father carried my mother through the flooded porch at Marsh End House. But no one wants to know what happens afterwards. No, of course they don't. Secretly we all believe that grief is infectious. Don't stand too close, or you'll catch it as well.

30/16 Ulitsa Pravdy, Moscow

1 April 1991

The first two or three days were not the worst. It takes time to discover the dimensions of a loss. I walked through my life as though it were a house which had been burgled. At first the damage didn't seem too serious, but then I saw the locked drawer prised open, the curtain hanging loose, the crack in the glass door. Slowly I realized that the job was thorough. The diamonds had gone from the safe, the gold bracelet from the jewellery box, the cash from the knife drawer.

Most days, after teaching, I went to Sibirskii Pereulok and sat in the doorway of the flats opposite his building. Of course, he'd only said that he was going to Leningrad for two months in order to get rid of me. He was already back in Moscow, I was sure of that. I tried to learn the exact patterns of those curtains at his window so I'd know when he'd been there. Surely when I came yesterday, the curtain on the left was fully drawn and the other one was a quarter of the way across? Now both curtains were a quarter drawn – but was that right?

Every minute of the day I longed for him. Behind my forehead a nerve was plucked again and again, its rhythmic pain reverberated through the muscles of my face, my neck,

the roots of my teeth. On the palms of my hands, I found
half-moon cuts made by my fingernails. Food tasted of cardboard, the edges of it stuck in my throat and I gagged. Every
day I asked the *babushka* if a letter had come for me. I was
waiting for the solicitors to find the right address for my
father. If he were here he'd understand. He'd know what
it's like to live in fear of your own mind.

One day, as I arrived home, I heard a noise from above. A
shadow loomed and Mrs Balashova appeared. Her shoes
were shiny black stilettos and her puffy flesh stuck out
around the edges of them. Her bra, clearly visible through
her Lycra dress, was too small and created the impression
that she had four breasts instead of two. I don't remember
her beckoning to me, or asking me to come up, but somehow
I finished up stepping through her front door.

The flat was exactly the same as ours, except that their
kitchen and sitting room had been knocked into one large
room. Just in time I remembered to take off my shoes.
Everything smelt of nylon, and in the corner a television
fizzed and crackled. Mr Balashov was behind me,
hovering in a corner. The whole place was crammed full
of empty bottles, cardboard boxes, old newspapers, broken
chairs. A vase of yellow plastic roses stood on a table near
the television, and goldfish swam in a weedless, stoneless
bowl.

Mrs Balashova sat down in an armchair, filling it entirely.
She picked up a cigarette which lay smoking on a marble
ashtray, took a puff and wheezed. Boxes of pills, and bottles
of medicine, were lined up on the table next to her. A second
armchair was pulled up close to her own and she motioned
to me to sit there. I kept my hat on and my coat wrapped
around me, although the room was badly overheated. She

asked me if I wanted tea and, without waiting for any response, shouted at her husband to get it. I stood up, thinking to help him, but she wouldn't let me. As she shifted in her chair, there was a sound of nylon rubbing against nylon, a puff of asthmatic breath, the creak of chair springs. She wore several rings on her sausage fingers which were too tight and cut into her flesh. Behind her was another door, veiled by a curtain made of strips of brightly coloured plastic. The bedroom. I thought of the noises we heard in the night.

Mr Balashov made tea in that strange Russian way – pouring out half a glass of hot water, stewing tea in it, then adding more hot water. He served it on a tray with a tiny lace mat and some jam to put in it. His wife opened her mouth and was about to shout at him but I stood up, making it clear that I would leave, and she stopped. Instead she instructed him to give me some food, and a slab of sawdust cake appeared. After he'd given me the cake, he hovered. I was determined that he should sit down and so stood up myself, motioning to him to sit with us. Mrs Balashova watched suspiciously but didn't comment when he sat down.

She showed me an unidentifiable garment she was knitting in baby pink wool, then handed me a folded piece of card and a half-unravelled jumper. It was clear that I was to unravel the rest of the jumper and wind the wool on to the card. Mrs Balashova's needles clicked as she knitted and I unwound the jumper. I didn't want to eat the cake but from past experience I knew that refusing food could cause grave offence, so I pushed it down. On one side of my forehead a nerve throbbed and thumped. The pain was so bad I had to put the wool down and shield my eye with my hand. Mr Balashov poured out some kind of alcohol and eased my coat off. The wool and the card had got in a knot and Mrs Balashova leant over to untangle them for me.

The next day she invited me in again, and I went. I heard no shouting, either when I was there, or later at night. After that I went there often. The crinkled wool wound on to pieces of cardboard. I put jam in my tea and discovered that it tasted rather good. One day I tried to engage them in a political discussion. It wasn't like this during the good Communist days, Mrs Balashova said. After that she seemed to say that the Army needed to restore order, and that the scum needed to be cleared off the streets. For once I was glad that my understanding of Russian was inexact.

Sometimes I talked to them in English about Jack. I went on and on, explaining the same things again and again, as my head thumped. They nodded sympathetically without understanding a word. Mrs Balashova became almost grandmotherly. They always offered me tea, and cake or sweets – food that must have been difficult for them to obtain. I didn't hear them shouting any more and I wondered how I'd brought about that change, just by sitting there.

Without warning, the heating in our building was switched off. For a week it was cold in the flat but not unbearable. Then the temperature dropped, as winter gave a brief encore, and Rob and I slept in our coats and cracked ice from the loo in the morning. In the evenings, after my visit to the Balashovs, I went home and lay in bed under duvets and coats, trying to keep warm.

One night Rob tried to make love to me but he couldn't do it. Physically, he couldn't do it. I was so frozen up that he couldn't get inside me. We both tried to make a joke out of it. Out of luck, better luck next time.

Maya telephoned several times. Each time I said, 'Oh

sorry, I'm just going out, I'll call back.' I thought of that evening at the Smolenskaia Hotel when she'd been so sure that Jack and I had no future together. I couldn't bear the fact that she'd been right.

One day I was sitting with Mr and Mrs Balashov when we heard the scuffle of boots coming up the stairs, and then shouting. I thought someone might be trying to get into our flat so I went out onto the landing. Down below, a policeman in a grey uniform was knocking on the door of the Lady with a Hundred Relatives. No one answered and the man knocked again. Below him, two soldiers appeared on the stairs.

Mr Balashov came to stand beside me. *'Ne idi tuda. Otoidi, ne meshai.'* Don't go down there, he said. Keep out of the way. Downstairs, the policeman thumped on the door again and it was pulled open. I caught a glimpse of the Lady with a Hundred Relatives as the soldiers forced their way in. Questions were being shouted again and again. A soldier with a gun stood at the door of the flat, guarding it. From inside, a woman's voice rose in a long wail and a man cursed. The merciless glow of the strip-lights above made every detail distinct. Outside, rain battered down, pouring in through the broken landing window.

I started to walk down the stairs, and when Mr Balashov caught hold of my arm, I broke away. Downstairs, I went up to the soldier with a gun and asked in Russian what was going on. He ignored me. Through the door I caught a glimpse of closed curtains, cooking pots and mattresses spread on the floor. I wanted to know where the hopscotch girl was. I pushed my way in front of the soldier, 'What are you doing? Tell me – what are you doing?'

The soldier shouted into my face, his spit splattering on my forehead. From above Mr Balashov pleaded with me –

'Ne idi tuda. Otoidi, ne meshai.' Soldiers were yelling instructions. Inside the flat, a feverish scrabbling started – clothes were pulled from cupboards, plastic and string bags stuffed, arms pushed into coats. I stepped forward, but the soldier forced me back against the wall. People started to tumble out of the flat, carrying bags and suitcases. The soldiers barked and grunted, pushing them down the stairs. One man wore his pyjama top under his jacket, another had shoes but no socks. As they stepped across the cracked floor, I imagined it giving way beneath them – the soldiers, the suitcases, sections of concrete, all dropping down into the void below.

'You can't take them away. You can't do that.' The soldiers wouldn't look at me. People continued to file out of the flat. The hopscotch girl came with her mother. She was wearing the coat I'd given her and she skipped a few steps, carrying a pink frilly pillow under one arm. Her mother was cursing and wailing, shaking her fist. The man with no socks hissed at one of the soldiers and pushed him. The butt of a gun slammed into the side of the man's face so that he reeled against the wall.

I jostled my way down the stairs, trying to lay my hands on the girl. 'You can't take them. You can't take them.' One of the soldiers shoved me to the floor, his boot crushed my leg against the edge of the steps. Pain fired up my shin and into my knee. The strip-lights wavered far above my head. My hands scrabbled on the concrete floor as I tried to get up. I shouted again but it was already too late. I wasn't brave enough to go and question the soldiers again, or pull the girl back.

I don't know what happened then. Shouting, a gleam of green light, that star-shaped crack in the landing window suddenly grown large. I sat on the stairs with my head in my hands and in my mind I was hearing the hopscotch girl, her feet slapping across the landing. She was holding that pink frilly pillow in her arms and laughing. And I was re-membering the pride on her face when I'd given her that coat which was twenty years old and six inches too long.

Then I heard Rob's voice and Mr Balashov explaining to him what had happened. I unlocked my hands from my eyes and rolled up my jeans to examine the damage to my leg. My shin was raw, and an ink-smudge bruise was already spreading, but it was nothing really. I waited for Rob to come and comfort me but he didn't. Instead he came down the stairs and ordered me into the flat.

I got up from the stairs, hopping, and followed him. The door slammed behind me with such force that a cup moved on the kitchen table. 'Eva, what the bloody hell were you doing? For God's sake – you don't have a visa.' Rob spat each word. I sat down in the kitchen and started to explain – the hopscotch girl, the coat – but he wasn't listening.

'I've told you again and again. Don't go anywhere near anyone in authority. Why don't you get it? What's the matter with you?' He was standing by the window. Outside, rain streamed down the glass and bounced off the sill. Rob's arms were waving and his mouth was wet. A blue vein stood out on his forehead. 'This doesn't have anything to do with us. Finally you need to understand that it isn't our problem.'

Rob was waiting for some response, but I didn't have one. A phrase from our childhood appeared in my mind. *She became involved in politics in a way which was inappropriate.* My mother's comment on Amelia. Up until now, I'd never thought it strange that Rob had never said anything at all about his mother. Rob was a practical man, a man of the future; he didn't waste time with things that couldn't be changed. But now I began to wonder. Perhaps because neither of us had any knowledge of the past, then we didn't have any grip on the present? I couldn't work it out and the only person who might have been able to help was Jack.

Outside, water gathered and sloshed in the gutters. I thought of the hopscotch girl and longed for the tap-tap of her shoes on the concrete landing. I rolled up my trouser leg again, and said that perhaps I'd go and find some antiseptic cream. 'You should have just kept out of the way,' Rob said.

I looked up at him, his colourless face outlined against the raining window. 'OK. OK.' But he was right. My gesture was pointless. What could I ever have done against a policeman and three soldiers? Rob stamped towards the kettle and clattered around finding mugs. I stood up and said I'd make the tea but he wouldn't let me. When he'd found mugs and tea bags he went to get the antiseptic cream. In silence he pushed it at me. He made the tea and then sat opposite me, stirring so vigorously that tea slopped and he had to get a cloth. As he wiped the table, I stretched out my hand, took the cloth, and put it in the sink. 'Rob, please. What's the matter?'

He sat down again and his shoulders sagged. 'Sorry. Sorry.' Under the table, I pushed my knees against his. From outside, water crashed down from an overflowing gutter. 'You know, I've just started to think – maybe the Russians are a race of corrupt, stupid people, who are more interested in dish-washers than democracy, and have got the political system they deserve.' Rob was staring past me, watching the rain coming down the window. He said again that he was sorry, then he told me that he'd found out that Sasha's arrest didn't have anything to do with the newspaper. For some time Sasha had been involved in stealing cars. He'd certainly been doing it all the time Rob had known him. Rob told me this quite calmly but I knew he was bitterly disappointed. Sasha was meant to be a close friend, Rob had had faith in him. And yet for some reason I wasn't surprised.

'Yeah, so there's that – and then today my contract finally got renewed.'

'Well, that's good news, isn't it?' I should have been racing to Room 815 to tell Jack the news.

'Well, yes. Except they wait until the week before it runs out, then they give me virtually no pay rise . . . And I had vaguely suggested that I could do with a car – I mean a proper car, because everyone else has one, but apparently that's not possible. And . . . well, I'm just pissed off about it.'

'Did you tell Bill that?'

'Yeah, I did, and he's embarrassed. But I can't go on at him too much because Sarah screams at him every night that she's going to leave. And anyway, it's not his decision, it's people in New York, and they don't have a budget, or that's their excuse anyway. And once I wouldn't have minded but now . . . I don't know.' He sighs and shakes his head. He asks me if I want some toast. That's the only food we've got.

'But you don't really care about the money?'

'No, no. Of course I don't care about the money, but . . . Listen, is your leg OK?'

'Yes, it's fine.' He came to look and made me put some cream on it. He wondered if he should go out and look for a shop which might sell a bandage, but we both knew it wouldn't be possible to find one. We sat together eating toast while the rain continued to come down. My mind moved outside itself and I saw Rob and me from above, with the rest of our building around us. The Balashovs, the old couple from downstairs, Rob and I, all trailing in and out of the building, day after day. And from there I could see that Rob and I had become indistinguishable from everyone else. We had the same blank eyes, the same shrug, the same way of swallowing sadness whole and then turning away.

'You know, with the job, it's just – I met this guy from the UN last week and he asked me for my CV. And I don't know why but yesterday I left a meeting early and went back to the office and typed it up. Because, you know, if I worked for one of those organizations . . .'

'But you wouldn't really work for the UN, would you?'

'No, not really. No, but . . .' Rob started to tell me then about an old schoolfriend who he'd met up with for a drink. The friend was on business for a couple of nights in Moscow. He worked as an accountant in Clapham and was married with two children. 'And you know what?' Rob said. 'I wanted to feel so superior to him. I wanted to say, "Look at the amazing places where I've lived and the things I've seen." But then it just wasn't like that. Because, you know, that guy . . . well, he was somehow thoughtful and grown up and . . . he was happy. And I suddenly thought, maybe that's what happiness is – just being dull?'

After they took the hopscotch girl, hours of my life went missing, sometimes whole days. Mrs Balashova was ill and so she and her husband were often at the doctor's or the hospital. A man who looked like Jack stalked the maze of my mind but he had the face of an ogre. I spent whole afternoons lying in the hall with my face pressed against the skirting board. Every day I decided to go to Leningrad to look for him but I couldn't find the energy. My mother's voice rang in my head. *You must listen to the doctor, dear. You really shouldn't go to Moscow. You know how you are.* I longed for drugs so strong that if you put your hand on a hot-plate you wouldn't feel it. I didn't want to live in the same head as myself any more.

Rob pleaded with me to go to the doctor but I wouldn't. He was working less because, although he still helped with the newspaper, he was barely on speaking terms with Sasha. He didn't know that Sasha still came round to see me sometimes when he was out. The first time he came, I wondered if I should ask him about the stolen cars but decided against it. Rob had judged Sasha too harshly, I thought. A few months ago I'd probably have been the same. But Moscow had made me wary of certainty. It no longer seemed possible to know the difference between good and bad. Committed radicals do steal cars, good Catholic girls do have affairs with men twice their age, friends can turn into ogres overnight.

And I'd missed Sasha — his shambling walk, his stained-tooth smile, the way he stooped to listen to me. He laid a hand on my shoulder and peered down at me intently. 'You are been very sad,' he said. How did he know that? I thought of those late evenings when he talked about his childhood. *So cold, always so cold. Always I'm waiting for them to light a fire.* We sat in silence at the kitchen table. I gripped my thumping head, while he drank our vodka, chainsmoked, and played music on our tape recorder.

Rob started to walk to college with me, carrying my bag. During the day he came home from work to make me lunch. My bones stuck out and my skirt started to fall down. He found a safety pin for me and helped me put it in place. In the evenings he prepared meals, made tea, did the washing up. Neither of us could be bothered with shopping so for days at a time we ate nothing but tinned pilchards. Bill came round to see us quite often and talked politics with Rob in a voice that was determinedly cheerful. One night, after he'd gone, Rob told me that Sarah was being treated for depression. Maya telephoned but I put the phone down as soon as I heard her voice.

The crack in the concrete outside our door opened further, revealing a wire mesh. I could look down through it to the landing below. A man with a shaved head, tattoos on his hands, and thighs like tree trunks, moved into the flat next door. He had a Dobermann-type dog, with a spiked collar, which smelt and lay outside on the landing, slobbering. He left his rubbish on the stairs and shouted at me when I asked him to move it.

Rob came home one day and told me that one of his colleagues from New York, who was black, had come to Moscow for a meeting, and had been spat on twice in the street. Then Rob got involved in a row with our landlord who was trying to double our rent. One day we came back to find that someone had tried to break the lock off our door. As always, when we asked, no one in the building had seen or heard anything. Moscow – an echo chamber, a hall of mirrors, an unending game of Chinese whispers. I was fed up with being broad-minded and culturally aware. I wanted to go home.

I kept praying for spring – sun on my skin, a glitter of green in the trees. But winter only faded into days of mud and slush. Paving slabs rocked on the street, throwing up spurts of dirty water. I jumped over the gutters, avoiding one puddle after another. The debris of winter was scraped into small bonfires which smoked and spluttered along the sides of the roads.

At night I lay awake watching the five-armed lamp above me, the brown carpet stuck to the wall, the red digital numbers on the alarm clock. Or I sat at the window staring out at the monochrome lines of roofs and windows, balconies, television aerials. If Rob was away then I'd get up at four or five o'clock and go to look for Jack. I'd take the first Metro and then walk south along the Liusinovskaia Bol'shaia, seeing the streets turning grey then pink as the dawn came.

In Jack's street the bones of a car lay by the side of the road. Windows were grey and dusty. Everywhere was littered with cigarette ends, plastic bags, empty vodka bottles. I'd go to his building and sit in the doorway opposite with my head propped against the wall, watching. A rusted children's swing in the playground next to his building moved one inch back, one inch forward, in the sullen breeze. Today the curtain on the left is fully drawn, the other one pulled halfway across. But is that how they were yesterday? Once I took a piece of paper with me so I could draw their position but the next day I couldn't find it.

At the college, rumours circulated that someone had been defrauding Mr Baloni and that they would be sacked. The staff were called in to see him one by one. When it came to my turn, I sat there quite casually, staring across the expanse of his desk. His face was mottled grey and pink, and his eye was half-closed up by a sty. It was rumoured that his Russian girlfriend had left him. She'd found an American banker who'd bought her a BMW. Mr Baloni rubbed a weary hand over his sore eye and explained to me about the mysterious numbers on the phone bill, and the paper missing from beside the copier. 'Really?' I said. 'How extraordinary. Of course, I've no idea who would do that.' My act was convincing but, as I was leaving the room, I tripped over a wastepaper bin. I steadied myself, but the throbbing in my head was so bad I couldn't see where the door was.

Mr Baloni called me back and enquired after my health. Moving around the desk, he laid a fleshy hand on my arm. Then, from the fridge behind his desk, he produced a bottle and poured me some sickly pink alcohol. It was quite all right, he said. He understood that many people in Moscow needed photocopying facilities. He was worried about me – why was I so sad? I didn't answer him. He rubbed again at his sore eye. I thought of the Leninskii Prospyekt, the new condominium, the empty apartment. He wandered over to the bay window. From there he could see out towards the Garden Ring, the road dipping down into the underpass, the tower blocks of the Novyi Arbat. He stood there for a long time, staring out, then turned back to me and shrugged. 'People are run over by buses. And they fall off cliffs. And then there is love . . .'

Jack possessed every inch of me. In my head I talked to him all day. Sometimes I spoke in tenderness but more often in anger. I wanted to know, Why did you do it? Why, why, why? I tried so hard to hate him. But even before that word was fully formed in my mind, it dissolved into tenderness. Love, hate – the pendulum swung back and forward. At the extremes, these things are close.

I longed for my mind to break. They'd taken my father into an institution, perhaps they'd do the same for me. The idea seemed attractive. I hoped to collapse in the street, choking on my swallowed tongue, my body twitching, my lips babbling and dribbling. Instead I kept on going to the college each day, there and back, there and back. I thought of myself like a clockwork rabbit banging a drum, on and on.

One day when Rob was away, I was returning from the college, and stopped close to the high arch which led into our courtyard. I needed to try again to button up my coat. This should have been simple – the coat had six buttons and six button-holes. Except that sometimes there were five buttons and six holes, or six buttons and five holes. Under the shelter of the arch I counted up. Six buttons but only five holes? I'd already stopped three or four times on the way home to re-do it, but still I couldn't get it right.

Beside me, a car rolled through puddles and drew to a stop. It had smoked-glass windows and, as the door opened, I thought of Mafia kidnappings. A voice called my name. I looked into the car and saw, in the gloom, Maya's hand with its snake-head ring gripping the curl of her walking stick. 'Eva, get into the car.' I was turning away when the end of her walking stick hooked itself around my neck. I pushed the stick away but then I saw the look in Maya's eyes, and knew that there was no point in resisting any longer. As the car pulled away Maya was leaning back, her neck craning upwards. 'You live there? It's ridiculous. To-o-tally ridiculous.'

The car swept through the streets, the chauffeur using the central lane, despite the rule which says that that part of the road is reserved for members of the Communist Party only. The leather seat was slippery beneath my coat. We passed the American Embassy, then turned right, past my college. From the bridge I saw the White House down on the riverbank, like an ocean liner with a curved prow. Then we moved on towards the Triumphal Arch and the wide sweep of the Kutuzovskii Prospyekt.

The car stopped outside Maya's building and we went up in the lift together. I chatted about the weather, the college, the political situation. The clockwork rabbit banging its drum. The heating was off in the flat and the air felt damp. The rooms were full of Jack – the night of the party when I'd seen his shoes moving close to Maya's sofa, the door to that bedroom where he'd touched my spine. The clockwork rabbit faltered, but then asked politely about Harvey. Maya's hand fumbled, and she swore in French as she tried to force the plug of a blow-heater into a socket. She placed the heater beside the sofa, where it breathed hot air and a smell of burnt dust. Then she stood up and looked me over inch by inch. 'Oh my God, whatever has he done to you?'

'Nothing. Nothing. I'm quite all right.'

The clockwork rabbit banged its last bang. Tears flooded down my face. I cried in noisy sobs, with my head against Maya's bony chest. She made me lie down in that same room where I'd first talked to Jack. The bed was piled with blankets and duvets, and Maya moved the blow-heater next to me, but I couldn't get warm. She said to me that she was going to call a doctor and I let her do it. By the time she came back with tea and vodka, I was calmer. She found me a handkerchief and I blew my nose and wiped my eyes. Sitting by the bed she shook her head, and tapped her finger up and down on her glass of vodka. '"Yet each man kills the thing he loves . . ."'

'But why? Why is it like that?'

'Oh, I don't know. If you love someone then you tend to lay bare parts of that person they'd rather keep hidden. And then they can become brutal.' She leant over to straighten the blankets and then pushed a cup of tea towards me. 'But you know, Eva, don't you, that no-o-thing done in love is ever wrong, or ever wasted?'

We heard Harvey coming in, clearing his throat, and creating that familiar clattering in the hall. When he opened the door, I sat up and started wiping my eyes. 'Well, here you all are then,' he said. Maya looked at him and raised her eyebrows. He waved a hand, said something about work, and shuffled out again.

'I just don't understand why I'm like this,' I said.

'I'd say it runs in the family.'

'What? Madness?' I didn't like that word but I forced myself to use it.

Maya turned wide eyes on me. 'No, not that. Is that what your mother said about your father? You shouldn't think that. Too often, what is labelled as mental illness is just a legitimate reaction to the circumstances someone is living in.'

'But he was in a hospital.'

'Well, no, that was the problem. It wasn't a hospital, just some Catholic institution, and if he didn't have a problem before he went there, they certainly ensured that he so-o-on did. For myself, I always knew there wasn't anything the matter with him, and I don't think there's anything the matter with yo-o-u. Some people are passionate by nature and I don't think they should have to apologize for that.'

So that was it. Some people are passionate by nature.

'But what am I going to do? I can't just forget about all this and marry Rob.'

'I don't know. When I married Harvey I was probably in much the same state as you're in now. Not a great start for a marriage. But, you know, for all that, we've been happy enough. Fulfilment doesn't come through love alone. Family, community, work – these things are ne-e-cessary as well. There's love, and there's life, and sometimes the two don't go together.'

'But I won't ever forget.'

'Of course you won't. For every woman there's always the man she should have married.'

I blew my nose, wiped my hair out of my eyes, and settled back under the blanket. 'You know, the truth is I often didn't even like him. That must be what drugs are like – the more you take, the less effect they have, but you keep on taking more and more because you want to get back to that first feeling.'

'Well, yes,' Maya said. 'Addiction. That's what it is. My son's doctors say that if you can only get pleasure out of one thing, then the pleasure you get is very extreme. What you need is to be able to feel with *all* your senses, and then you can get enjoyment out of a wider range of experiences.'

'So theoretically I should be able to get the same feeling if I go for a nice walk in the country or look at a vase of flowers? Is that it?'

'Yes. One should be able to reach that place in one's mind.'

'And you believe that?'

Maya considers this question, her head on one side. 'Yes, oddly, I do. Although I myself have never discovered that place.'

10/38 Kutuzovskii Prospyekt, Moscow

May 1991

Maya's doctor gave me tranquillizers which dropped me into a dreamless sleep. I woke more tired than before, and slept again. Night, day, sleep, wake. I was in that room where I'd first talked to Jack. Occasionally I thought, I really should get up, but then Maya appeared with those yellow pills and I slid back into warmth and stillness. I suspect that Maya and Rob had a row about where I should stay. I heard voices tangling in the kitchen one afternoon before I slid back into darkness.

Then one morning I opened my eyes and summer had arrived. The window of the bedroom hung open and the sun burned down on to the stained concrete wall of the building next door. Maya came with a glass of water and I sat on the bed, enjoying the light and watching the curtain blowing in the breeze. Soon after that, Rob came and I went home with him. Maya didn't want me to go but Rob insisted. I didn't really care where I went.

Our courtyard had become a different place. Washing hung from balconies, people walked with their heads up and looked each other in the eye. Dust blew up in sudden spirals, and the drains smelt. For a week the whole city was covered in lumps of white fluff, like cottonwool. My colleagues told

me that this was *pukh* – which is spores from poplar trees.
It lay on the ground, inches deep, like a kind of summer
snow. When the wind blew, it rose into my eyes and mouth
and made my nose itch. If I went outside for even five
minutes then I had to pick handfuls of it off my clothes.
Everyone was relieved when a torrent of warm rain cleared
it away.

I removed all of our landlord's junk off our balcony and
sat out there through evenings which were long and light.
Women came out into our courtyard, hung up carpets and
beat them with hooped carpet-beaters, raising clouds of
dust. Men with motorbikes revved their engines outside our
building, their leather jackets decorated with swastikas and
Tsarist eagles. Our new neighbour sometimes went out to
join them, leaving his dog, slobbering and panting, tied to
the stair-rail outside our flat.

I put on summer dresses and felt as thin as a pipe-cleaner.
When I wasn't at the college I slept for long hours in the
June heat. Sometimes for a whole quarter of an hour I didn't
think about Jack. A stray dog took up residence in our courtyard. In the afternoons it lay in the sun, twitching its ear
occasionally to remove a fly. I took down a bowl of water
and some stale bread. A man in the flats opposite shouted
at me and I stuck out my tongue.

One day I sat on a low wall in the courtyard reading a
book of translated Russian poetry which Jack had lent to
me. The *babushka* from downstairs came hurrying out.
'*Devushka, ne sidi na stene,*' she hissed, and flapped at me,
waving her handkerchief, until I got off the wall. What was
she saying? *If you sit on that wall then you'll never be able to
have children?* Surely I'd misunderstood. When Rob came
home he confirmed that all *babushka* firmly believe that if
a young woman sits on a wall or a railing, even in the middle

of summer, then she'll finish up infertile. That made me laugh more than I'd done in months.

Most evenings I went to see Maya. In her flat the windows were sometimes open, but the blinds were still down. Lounging on the sofa, she wore elaborate safari-style suits made of pale linen, and complained about the heat just as bitterly as she'd complained about the cold. She was reading an e-e-xcellent new book about the Russian Revolution. Su-u-ch a tragedy. All that hope and possibility all brought to nothing.

One evening my mother rang and Rob talked to her, then put his hand over the mouthpiece. 'Please, Eva, speak to her. She's so worried about you.' I took the phone and heard my mother's voice. 'Flu can really be so very lowering, can't it?' She told me about the wisteria along the back of the house – better than ever this year, although she hoped it wouldn't damage the brickwork. And she had had some lovely walks on the marsh. So nice to have a little more time to spare, what with her job coming to an end. Wisteria, coastal walks, worries about the brickwork. I suppose that after my father left she had to decide to take an interest in such things. What else could she do? But probably she didn't find it that difficult. She'd always wanted a small life.

Around us, Moscow was changing. We heard more Western voices on the streets. The new joint-venture hotels were full of businessmen. Advertising hoardings sprang up everywhere. Prostitution became more public. Porn magazines and pirated videos started to be sold in the Metro and underground walkways. Cars with smoked-glass windows rolled idly by. Strip clubs were opening and cinemas showing bad Western films. While most people continued to earn the equivalent of one hundred dollars a month, some could afford to spend two hundred dollars

on one bottle of French champagne. Rob said that democracy was becoming nothing more than a theatrical perform-
ance designed to mask the emergence of a gangster society.
I began to ask myself whether the old couple downstairs,
with their Lenin pictures and medals, were not as mad as
I'd thought.

July came and Moscow was fractious in the heat. Lines of
cars filled the roads heading out of town, their roof-racks
stacked with rakes, brushes, and bags of concrete, flapping
under tarpaulin. I'd thought only rich Russians had *dachas*
but it seemed that everyone had somewhere to go. Rob said
that growing vegetables at *dachas*, pickling and preserving,
had once been a hobby for the Russians but now it was a
means of survival. The city was quiet and listless. Mosquitoes
buzzed and the air was sticky.

One day I got back from the college to find Rob already
at home. 'Listen, you know that UN guy who asked for my
CV? Well, he rang to offer me a job.'

'Really? Here?'

'No, not here. Probably Belgrade or Zagreb. The problem
is, that the situation in Yugoslavia is changing so quickly
they just don't know where their offices need to be.'

I looked out across the courtyard. The elderly couple from
the ground floor were sitting out on the bench. He wore
his medals, as always, and she wore her yellow dress and
matching headscarf. I suddenly wanted to take the silver
birch trees, the grey-green concrete blocks, the whole city
in my arms. Rob was still talking, telling me that if he took
the job, then I might not be able to go with him at first. I
might have to go back to England, but that would only be
for a month or two, not longer.

'And when would it be?'

'Beginning of September – but it depends. We need to talk about it.'

It was already the middle of July. Zagreb? Belgrade? *Shake up the world and pick out a city.* Despite the evening sun shining in through the window, I shivered. If we left Moscow then it was certain I'd never see Jack again.

'Do you want to take the job?' I asked.

Rob sat down at the kitchen table. Well, of course, the UN is a hopeless organization, he said. The bureaucracy would drive him mad within a week. But the work did sound interesting, and the job was a real promotion. He probably needed to do something like that for a while, if he wanted to be taken seriously. I looked at Rob and wondered what had happened to him. With him it had always been freedom, democracy, civil society. Now it was experience, and bureaucracy, and being taken seriously. Was it him or his political commitment which I'd always found attractive?

'But nothing's decided,' he said. 'Not at all. We've got to be sure this is the right move for you. You've been brave about Moscow . . .'

'Yes, but if you want the job you should take it.'

What else could I say? I wandered through into the sitting room and found the atlas. Yugoslavia was coloured pink. It didn't seem like a proper country at all, just a ragged piece torn from the fabric of a formless peninsula. But if we weren't staying in Moscow, then what did it matter where we went? And so it was all agreed. Tomorrow Rob would tell Bill he was leaving and we'd give notice on the flat. I hoped that we might be able to go back to England, or somewhere else, for a couple of weeks before Rob started the new job, but Rob said he'd probably have to work through August. Maybe we'd have a week to spare, not more.

Rob opened a plastic bag and produced a bottle of Soviet champagne. He'd also been to Stockman's and bought a ready-made lasagne, chocolate brownies, proper coffee, sliced white bread. 'We're celebrating – a fond farewell to tinned pilchards.'

He put the lasagne in the oven and popped the champagne. We moved our chairs out on to the balcony. The sides of our glasses clinked together and, when Rob leant to kiss me, his mouth tasted of champagne. 'Is it awful of me to take this job?' he asked.

'No, you deserve it. It isn't about money, it's about being valued. You deserve that as much as anyone else.' We gulped a glass and then another. From a window below, a poor quality recording of a Beatles song played. When the lasagne was ready we started to wolf it down, but after so many months of sparse food, we both felt sick after four mouthfuls. So we put it back in the fridge, and, taking the remains of the champagne, we went out on to the balcony again.

'Rob, there's something . . . Before we leave. I'd like you to invite Sasha round sometime. I know you were angry with him, but he just wanted something more, something he's never been allowed. It's not really such a crime, is it?'

'No, I suppose not. You're right – I should patch things up with him.'

The champagne was gone and we started on the vodka. 'To Yugoslavia.' Rob raised his glass in a drunken toast. Then he burrowed with one hand in his trouser pocket. 'Actually, I've got something for you.' He held up a ring made of blue moulded plastic, with a flower on it. 'It came out of a cracker at Christmas and I put it in my pocket, then I forgot about it. I thought you might like it.' I reached out to take it but he caught hold of my left hand and held it up. I watched as he slid the ring on to the fourth finger. 'Not exactly the ring I'd have chosen, but I suppose it'll do for now.'

And that was how it was decided. All so easy. Rob was right really. It was time to leave Moscow. Belgrade or Zagreb, or wherever it was, would be a new beginning. And if we were going there, then we should get married. That would enable me to look for a proper job. I'd start doing some research now and get Rob to help me with my CV. I stared at the ring on my hand. We put on a tape but we didn't have any dance music. Most of Rob's tapes had been stolen in the various burglaries. So instead it was Vivaldi. We shuffled around the room to it, laughed, then collapsed on the bed.

Rob asked whether I'd be sorry to leave Moscow. I mumbled regrets about never seeing much of Russia. Rob said we could still do that. When the college closed in a week's time I could go back to England to see my mother and get my visa renewed. Then we could go off on a trip somewhere.

'And while you're home,' Rob said, 'you'll be able to get a dress and invitations and all that stuff.' Those words sounded strange. Rob and I had always had a contempt for the whole business of weddings. But still we discussed whether we'd get married in the local church, what kind of party we'd have. We agreed, stretched out on the bed, that we'd get married on Twelfth Night because we'd anyway be in England for Christmas. And the honeymoon? Somewhere really exotic. Bognor Regis? Yes, Bognor. We were suddenly talking like guests in our own lives.

Rob poured himself more vodka and decided that he'd ring his father. He booked a call with the international operator, not expecting to get a call back for several hours. But then, surprisingly, the operator rang back after only five minutes and Rob was put through. After he'd put the phone down, he did the usual impersonation. '"Married? Oh hum.

Yes. Jolly good. Might be best to do the exams for the Foreign Office. Must get back to the Hungarian subjunctive. I've put a cheque in the post".'

I realized then that Rob often made me laugh. Jack had never done that.

Rob then rang the operator again and, a second time, the response was rapid. He passed the phone to me and a voice babbled in Russian. Then I spoke to my mother and heard the tears in her voice as I told her the news. 'A dress? Of course. Something straight, I think. I'll start on a pattern and you can look at it.' Then I rang Maya as well. I'd had so much to drink that I hardly heard what she said. But she was pleased, of course, and took care to express no surprise. It was as though there'd never been any question about it – and really, there never had.

'So where do you want to go?' Rob said. 'How about Leningrad?'

'Yes, Leningrad.' My voice was quite steady but I needed to keep talking. And then those words I didn't want to say fell from my mouth. 'What about my father? Would we invite him?' For a moment the evening paused and held its breath. The moment floated on champagne and shock.

'Ask him?' Rob said. 'Well, yes, of course, why ever not?' The evening recovered and rushed on. Rob said he'd write to my father, if I wanted. I knew that he wanted to expunge those awkward conversations we'd had about the past. 'Oh no,' I said, 'don't bother. It doesn't really matter. And anyway, it isn't possible – the solicitors haven't got an address for him.' But Rob said it must be possible. He'd telephone his father and tell him to get the address. It was as easy as a blue plastic ring sliding on to your finger.

We drank more vodka, and I tried to teach Rob to dance the tango, but I stumbled against the bed and the broken leg fell off its box. Together we tried to put it right but we couldn't do it because we were laughing so much. So instead we lay on the tipping bed, and made love in a drunken rush of zips, and shoes hastily pulled off. Then we lay there wrapped up together in one sheet through a night that never quite got dark.

Marsh End House, Malthouse, Norfolk

July, 1991

My mother sat at her sewing table with wedding magazines spread around her. She'd already made a dress in calico so that I could see if I liked it. She was just redoing one of the side seams because it wasn't quite even. 'Yes,' she said as she cut into the calico. 'Manic depression is really the cruellest of illnesses because the people who suffer from it don't want to be cured.'

Snip–snip. My mother's scissors moved through the material. I sat opposite her, close to the open window, lolling on a wooden stool. The room smelt of ironing and oil from the sewing machine. I couldn't believe the change in my mother. Strands of hair fell from her bun and she didn't bother to put them back. She wore a cardigan with a hole in the sleeve. On Sunday morning she'd said she didn't feel like going to Mass. Instead, she'd walked on the marsh and then sat out in the garden reading a book. And now this conversation.

'But you always knew he had a problem?'

'Not when I married him, no. But from early on. You see, he went through a major depression only a year after we married and . . .' She lifted the foot of the sewing machine and placed the fabric under it. 'Well, I suddenly didn't know who I'd married. And, you see, I was alone here, and so I just couldn't afford to see what was happening. All I could do was to cling to the idea that as long as I loved him, then everything would be all right.'

'And then?' I fiddled with a piece of green ribbon tied around a dusty box.

'Well, often things were fine. Good. Far too good. But then the black times got longer, and he got lost in his work, and in Mexico and astronomy and all these wild ideas . . . I mean, we'd both been brought up Catholic, of course, but with him it got out of control. He had all these ideas about pagan religions in Mexico. He wanted to know things you just can't know. Then when Amelia died, he had to go into hospital . . .'

And at that time he'd lost Maya as well. She'd gone away to Rome. But my mother wouldn't say that and I judged it better just to let her talk.

'At the time, the hospital seemed like a disaster but actually it was a great help, at least to me, because I met this priest there and he was the first person I'd talked to who really understood.' My mother put her foot down on the pedal and the sewing machine hammered through the material. She stopped, lifted the machine foot and cut off the threads.

'The priest had red hair?'

My mother stopped still with the material half-lifted out from the machine. 'What? You remember him?'

'No. Just a man with red hair.'

She gave me a searching stare and then went to the ironing board. 'Father Michael, that was his name. He saw that I was pretending there wasn't a problem and encouraging your father to do the same. And he was furious with me. "If you love someone, you see them just as they are," he said.

And it was like a slap in the face – but he was right. The only problem was, other people didn't want to see the truth either.'

'People like Maya?'

'Yes. She was one.'

'But she loved my father?'

'Did she? That kind of love is only about losing yourself . . . Certainly she wouldn't listen to anything I said. She wouldn't be told.'

I didn't like my mother talking about love. I was sure she couldn't know anything about it. In the distance I could hear the shouts from children swimming in the lake by the caravan park. I stared out of the window at the monkey puzzle tree and the pinewoods blurred in the heat, thinking of that photograph I'd seen at Maya's. It must have been taken here – the spider's-web gate, the monkey puzzle tree. But then why was everything in it the wrong way round?

'Of course, what that priest didn't say was how high the costs would be.'

'Yes,' I said, looking her in the eye. 'Very high.'

My mother was busy with the iron. I just wanted her to admit that perhaps her decision had been difficult for me, but she wouldn't do that. I thought over what she'd said. Another turn of the kaleidoscope. This wasn't the truth, it was just a story she needed to tell. Of course, if a Catholic priest had told her all that, then she would have believed it. The Church at that time would have been quite capable of confusing adultery and mental illness. The iron hissed as my mother pressed it down and the room filled with the smell of pressed material. My fingers twisted the green ribbon on the box. 'What's in here?' I asked.

'Oh, that. It's the veil I wore when I got married. I thought . . .'

I opened the box. Inside, pale pink tissue unfolded to reveal a veil as fine as a cobweb, and an ivory satin bodice stitched all over with seed pearls. 'It's beautiful. Did you make it?'

My mother had finished with the iron. She came to stand beside me, and laying the veil aside, she lifted the bodice out of the box. 'I never got it quite right. You see here . . .' her finger indicated some invisible fault. 'It was too ambitious, there wasn't time.' She stared around her, as though trying to work something out, still holding the pearl-crusted bodice in her hands. 'It wasn't just him, you know. It was this place as well. All the stories your father told about his father and his grandfather, and their furniture, pictures, books. The past all still here.' My mother laid the bodice back down in the box, carefully folding the straps and the long ribbons at the back. 'But after a while I came to question even that. Your great-grandfather killed in Mexico in circumstances which were never explained. And your grandfather drowned, out on the marsh here. How could that have happened? I just don't understand. The man grew up here – he knew how dangerous this coast is. I don't know. The doctors can't say whether that kind of illness runs in families. And then Amelia as well . . .'

My mother shook her head, and placed the veil on top of the bodice, her hands briskly stroking the fabric into place. 'Come on,' she said. 'Let's see how this looks.'

As I began to undress, I thought of Jack, his hands touching me. I stepped into the dress and my mother made me stand on the stool. The material felt stiff and scratchy against my skin. She hovered with a box of pins. 'For the general shape, I think – yes.'

I turned and looked at myself in the long mirror on the wall. Although the dress wasn't even cut out from proper material, it made me look tall and slender. My neck was long, coming up from the low V at the front. I didn't look like those silly women in the wedding magazines, I looked better than that. I wished I could wear this dress for Jack. My mother started to search around for various fabric samples that she wanted to show me.

'Just put that box out of the way, will you?' she said. I tied the green ribbon around the box and took it over to the cupboard. Every shelf was full of different materials, all neatly folded. Silk with gold thread running through it, chiffon, shot taffeta. Other shelves were stacked with transparent boxes full of feathers, beads, cottons, and bindings. I went to get the stool and reached up high to put the box right up at the top, on a pile of finished clothes. The wedding dress scratched under my arms. I saw a flash of sky-blue silk, and swayed on the stool. As I pulled at that material, it slid out from the pile. My hand gripped the deep cuffs, sewn with tiny buttons. I'd never been sure that this jacket really existed. I didn't want it to exist. Looking down, I saw my mother staring up, her eyes held by that sky-blue silk. I pushed it back into the pile. *I'm getting married to Rob. I'm going to Yugoslavia.*

'Come here a minute,' my mother said. 'I'm not quite happy with that neckline. It'd look better with more of a heart shape.' She made me get back on the stool and produced a black pen and pins. She drew on the calico, a line appearing under her hand, close to my collar-bone. Two pins were inserted at the shoulders. 'More this shape perhaps?' My mother had ceased to be the woman with a hole in her cardigan wandering on the beach. She was back in her world now, creating dresses for cardboard cut-out women. A black pen and pins. Shoulders a little higher here, waist a little lower there. Just fold the tabs over and she'll walk away.

'Mum, you know what you said about my father? I understand it all much better now except – why did you decide that he should go away?'

My mother stood with one hand on her hip, and sighed. 'It was . . . I couldn't trust him, he was out of control . . . Oh really, this heat. It's too much. Let me just sit down for a while and then I'll have another go at that seam and we'll decide on some material.'

I looked at her, making it clear that I wanted an answer to my question.

'It was just – I wanted to lift you out of this in one piece, complete. For myself, I could have gone on, but I had you to consider.' She wiped her hand across her forehead, then got up to start on the dress again. So she hadn't wanted me to finish up like him, I thought. She'd fought so hard for that. The little red devil who looked so like him. She could prevent me from being an art student, she could make sure I got married to Rob, but if she was fighting genetics, could she ever win?

'You know, Eva, I really think it would be better for you to get married before Christmas.' The dress was pulled tighter at the waist as pins were inserted. I felt them close to my skin. Calico, black lines and pins . . . The room seemed to turn around. My mother's hand, moving my hair, touched my spine exactly where Jack had touched it that first night. I looked up at the cupboard but I couldn't see that blue silk any more. I didn't want to start asking more questions. My father was mentally ill so, of course, everything I remembered about him would seem confused.

'I've looked in the calendar. The fifteenth of December is a Saturday – wouldn't that be better?' she said.

But Rob had been certain about Twelfth Night. 'No, I don't think so.'

'People might find that date difficult. If the weather is

bad the travel could be a problem.' I said – Oh well, if they want to get here, they'd do it somehow. But my mother insisted that it just wasn't practical.

I felt a pin slide close to my skin. When was it that my father had worn that jacket? I couldn't be sure if the question mattered. I thought I'd seen an ogre, but it was only my father wearing a rubber mask. But still I wanted to know. Something had happened on the night he wore that jacket.

'Mum, you know that costume – the blue silk jacket?' I looked at myself in the mirror. The pale girl in the cream dress did look beautiful, but she wasn't me. However had I thought I could do this?

'Stand still now.'

'That belonged to my father, didn't it?'

'Yes, it did. At first it seemed like a joke – Beauty and the Beast.' My mother sighed and reached for another pin.

'Where did he wear it? Here?'

'I don't know, dear. He wore it several times. I really can't remember. Stand still, will you?' A pin stuck into my ribcage. I thought of the 1967 diary in his room and that day early in the year, the names and train times.

'Eva, I need you to keep your arms up, please.'

'Mum, I can't. Sorry. I'll have to . . . I've got a headache.'

'Oh sorry, dear, have you? I didn't realize.' My mother was all concern. She wanted me to go and lie down. 'Yes,' I said. 'Yes, that's what I'll do.' I pulled the dress off and reached for my T-shirt and skirt. The dress lay collapsed in a heap, stiff, like a Victorian lady, swooned on a sofa.

But I didn't go to my bedroom, I went to hers and pulled that cardboard box from under the bed. 1967. I flicked through its pages to 6 January. *Exhibition. Boltons, two crates of wine, a barrel of beer, six bottles of champagne. 15.30 Hislops and Carrs. 17.02 Rachel and Edith.* Then, afterwards, only those three entries which had been scratched out. So there'd been a party on Twelfth Night, 1967 – the night of the red lolly and the ogre face. Beauty and the Beast. But where was the path where I had stood?

I hurried down the stairs, across the drive and out into the lane. A gentle wind rattled the masts of the boats in the yard opposite. A group of ramblers were setting out to walk across the marsh. The air smelt of salt and dried mud. I walked inland to where the lane curves and the gate leads through the pinewoods back to the house. I opened the gate and stood on the overgrown grass of the path. This wasn't the moonlit path I remembered, but it was the only path. I climbed through the collapsing post and rail fence and into the woods themselves, pushing my way through briar and thicket. Prickly twigs caught at my hands as I moved them aside. I trod down brambles but thorns still dug into my shins. After I'd gone a few yards I looked back. What was I doing? But I went on, manoeuvring myself past the trunks of trees, stumbling on roots half-covered by sand.

What did I expect to find? There could only be more woods, and more woods, until eventually I reached the fence to the lake and the caravan park. Under the cover of the trees the air was cold and still, the light dim. My hands were ripped. I stopped, gasping for breath. I wanted Jack, I wanted him to help me. I looked up and saw a flash of sky above. I longed for a hand to stretch down and lift me up into the light. This is just your imagination, I thought. Your memories are all confused. You need to calm down, go to bed, see a doctor. But still I went on.

My foot caught on the stump of a tree – or was it a brick? I looked down. Yes, it was just as I'd known it would be. A line of bricks ran through the undergrowth, their jagged tops standing up from the sandy earth. I could only see three or four bricks but, when I edged some brambles away with my foot, I saw more. And here the woods were less thick. A path. Traces of gravel under my feet. I shuffled my shoes, testing the reality of this place. Branches of yew and laurel scratched at my face as I moved forward. I knew what I would find – a door in a brick and flint wall, with ivy growing thickly across it. And there it was. The door was shut but I ran my hand down over the rotted wood. I wanted to be able to touch the long-ago shadow which once slid down that frame.

I stood there listening and the wind called my name. A wall of earth had built up against the bottom of the door. I kicked at that, wanting the door to open just a crack. *You must never go through that door.* I fell on my hands and scratched the earth away. In my mind I could see the lake – the path down to the jetty, the black water, and, in the far distance, the boathouse. Standing up, I thrust my fingers into the gap beside the frame, but still the door wouldn't open.

'Mum, in the woods – there was a path, wasn't there?' I tried to stop myself from shouting but my voice was shrill. I was sitting in my bedroom staring at the threads of red on my hands where the thorns had cut me. The smell of pine needles clung to me.

'A path where?'

'A path to the lake. To a door – and the lake.'

'Eva, you're going to have an asthma attack.'

'No, I'm not. I don't have asthma. Tell me – I want to know. There was a path, wasn't there? It went through the woods to the lake.'

'Yes, of course. Don't you remember? When you were a child we used to walk that way down to the lake.'

'But then what happened? What happened?'

My mother crashed a tray of tea down on to my desk in frustration. She spoke as though I was a child who couldn't understand properly. 'Well, the land was sold, and Wyvelston Hall was demolished, and the new owners didn't want people from the village using the lake so they put up fences everywhere and boarded up that gateway.'

'And so then how did the path in our garden get covered up?'

'Well, I had it closed up.'

'But why? Why?'

I'm shouting now because I'm frightened that I've got this all wrong. Perhaps there are no symbols carved on trees, no kidnapped princess, no piranha lake.

'Because the path didn't lead anywhere,' my mother said. 'Think about it, Eva. Why would anyone want to walk down a path leading to a boarded-up door?'

'But the gate with the spider-web pattern? It used to be at the entrance to that lake path.'

'Yes, it was moved. There was an old wooden gate leading out to the lane, and it was rotten right through, and so when the lake path was closed up, we decided to move that iron gate there. It was the obvious thing to do.'

I remembered Rob's voice. *This isn't the Montezuma Mystery.* Jack, Jack, please make this stop. I leant my head back against the wall. The rocking horses on the wallpaper spun around. I gripped my hands over my eyes. I thought of that book lying on the shelf. The story of Bluebeard and the new bride discovering the castle with the fountains and peacocks and chandeliers. But there's that one locked room and she can't leave it alone. She has to know what's inside. A room full of dead and rotting brides. And now she knows the secret, she must join them.

From somewhere far away I could hear a heaving sound.

Was it the distant roar of the sea, or that sound my father had heard as we stood on the beach? The monster, far out in the evening distance, but waiting, waiting.

'Eva. You're making yourself ill.'

She was right, of course. I needed to stop imagining things. People who imagine things have court orders made against them. They get sent away. They go down paths that don't lead anywhere. 'Mum, I invited my father to the wedding. Rob got in touch with the solicitors.'

'What?'

In the distance, a whistle blew and a dog started barking. At the window, the sky was a garish blue. My mother's face broke open and tears spilled over her cheeks. She wiped at her face with the back of her hand and immediately she was calm again. 'Don't worry. It's all right. I'll get in touch with your father – I'll explain.' She kept repeating those words. 'It'll be all right. I'll explain.'

Leningrad Station, Moscow

August 1991

It's only two weeks now until we leave Moscow so I won't see Jack again. I mustn't hope any more. That's what I've decided. So when I see the outline of a head which looks like his, I take care not to notice. The head remains poised above us on the Metro steps. Rob and I are ten steps below, rucksacks on our backs, feeling too hot. We're pushing our way up the side of the staircase, close to the rail. A throng of people elbow their way down towards us. The outline of that head touches on the edge of my vision. But Moscow is such a vast city you never bump into anyone you know.

A checked shirt, a brown case with a broken strap. He comes down towards us, but still I'm sure it isn't him. I hold on tight to Rob's hand. A Tannoy announcement echoes up into the roof of the platform above. The straps of my rucksack cut into my shoulders. Two steps more and I hear his voice. I don't look at him. He's the ogre with the blank eyes, the jabbering lips, the long brown teeth. Rob is talking to him. I wrap myself up tight inside. The air around us is wrinkled by the smell of hot bodies and soot. I look down at my foot resting on the concrete step, worn into a dip by years of tramping feet. Rob and I have become small and white, our bodies shapeless, our muscles slack. We are the

rag doll and the plastic soldier. Leave us alone, Jack. Leave
us alone. Let us have our small world of occasional shy sex,
and cooking supper together. Leave us alone in the attic
bedroom, with the model aeroplanes, and the biscuit-tin
drum and the pine-cones in the grate.

He asks me something, and the rag doll opens and shuts
her mouth, but I still don't look at him. Instead I watch his
hand gripping the metal rail beside us. His sleeve is rolled
up and my eyes follow the route of a familiar vein which
stands up on the back of his hand. I see us together in
Room 815. The sheets on the bed are tangled. I'm standing
between his legs and his hand reaches out to touch my hip.
My heart is beating between my legs. A train sweeps in and
the crowd surges towards it.

'We must go.' I grip Rob's hand. 'We need to get home.'
Again an announcement echoes through the station. Rob
and I are swayed by the movement of the crowd. A man in
a dirty military uniform pushes against us, cursing at the
obstruction we cause. Above us, someone shouts and metal
clanks against metal. Jack says that perhaps he'll write down
his address for me. I look up at him then and he isn't an
ogre. Instead he's a man with death staring from his eyes.
His cheekbones are sharp, his eyes far back in his head. A
part of me is disappointed. The ogre image is easier to deal
with than a real person.

'It's all right, I have the address.'

'No, you don't. I'm staying in Malakhovka.'

I don't have any idea where that is. Ahead of us, we can
see people pushing and stumbling onto the Metro. Jack's
hand is fumbling with the strap of his bag. His skin is thin
and the colour of putty. The blade of his collar-bone sticks
out where his shirt is undone at the neck. He pulls out one
of his blue notebooks, his hands fumbling as he tries to rip

a page from it. I support the weight of his bag. His fingers tremble as he takes off the lid of his fountain pen. He writes clumsily, then hands the piece of paper to me. The side of his finger brushes against the pad of my thumb. The touch of it fizzles up through my arm. Again I see the hotel room, the tangled sheets, his hand reaching out to me.

I turn and Rob pulls me towards the waiting train. But we're too late and the doors close. When I look back, Jack has gone. I keep his paper held tight in my hand. The departing train seems to have sucked all the air off the platform. Only a few people sit on benches, or pace along the wide platform. Rob is watching me as though he's never seen me before. His eyes are clouded by a look of quiet horror. I push Jack's address into the pocket of my skirt. Both of us struggle for words and can't find any. Rob knows, somehow he's seen. Perhaps it was there in the way that Jack fumbled with his pen, or in the touch of his finger against mine.

I want to talk but my jaw is locked. I stand staring at Rob, my tongue straining. Then words come and I gabble, trying to push back the silence. Rob responds but his voice is empty. Our eyes come together, move apart. I may be scared of the accusations he may make, but he's more frightened of what I might admit. I want to take that knowledge back from him. I want him to pretend he hasn't seen anything. 'Only two weeks to go now,' I say. 'Doesn't it feel strange?' Another train sweeps into the station, bringing with it a gush of hot air. I keep talking, even in the silence of the carriage.

As we walk back to the flat through the evening sun, we talk about our week in Leningrad. How good it was to get away. How strange it feels to be back. The two cities are so different. This afternoon we must start to pack. Tomorrow he'll fly to Kiev, but he'll only be there one night. We both know all of this but still we repeat the details again and again in voices as serious as prayer.

We've been away for a week. Our landing is piled with fly-infested rubbish bags, doubtless left there by our next-door neighbour. His dog lies stretched across the landing, chained to the stair-rail, slobbering. In the flat, dead flies lie on the sitting-room windowsill and the loo smells bad. Rob and I rattle from room to room, opening windows, chasing the dust and the stillness away. I unpack some bread, pickles and *smetana* we brought in Leningrad. My mouth still babbles comments about how we should do this – or perhaps that? But Jack's sunken eyes flash in my mind again and again. The piece of paper he gave me rests against my thigh. In my mind I'm already on a train going to find him.

It's six o'clock and Rob and I didn't have much lunch so I make sandwiches and we sit down to eat. I cough and my head thumps. I must be getting a cold or flu. Even with the windows open, the air wraps around me, tight as a woollen jumper. While Rob and I were in Leningrad it seemed possible that we might slip through the barriers unnoticed into happiness.

'That guy – Jack,' Rob says. I wince, ready for the blow. 'He looked ill, didn't he?'

'Yes, he did look bad. I think he's been ill for some time, in fact. I was thinking I ought to try and see him before I go.'

'You won't have time.' The way Rob says that is so calm and definite, a statement of fact. But I hear it as an instruction and it makes me angry. I must see Jack. I want to see him now. It's Sunday 18 August today and we leave on the twenty-ninth. Twelve more days.

The phone rings and I go to answer it. It's Maya and she wants to know about Leningrad. Yes, we went to the Hermitage, and the Akhmatova Memorial Museum. Yes, the city was spectacularly beautiful. Yes, we took a boat along the canals. As we talk my mind calculates – if I make an arrangement to go and see Maya this afternoon, then could I use the time to go to Jack instead? But the address he's given me is somewhere miles out of town. Maya asks me if Rob and I want to go round for supper on Wednesday. I say I'll ask him and ring her back. Rob has finished eating and is sitting behind a newspaper. 'I'm busy that night,' he says.

The heat and my cough make me so irritable that I feel ready to scream. Some demon inside me wants to punish Rob for having seen too much. 'Why don't you like Maya? What's the problem with her?'

'I don't have a problem with her.'

'Yes, you do.'

He lowers the newspaper and glares at me. 'OK. You want to know? She doesn't know where her life stops and another person's begins.'

'Why? Why do you say that?'

I wait for him to say, 'Oh, I can't really remember,' but he doesn't. 'When you were ill she wouldn't listen to what I said. And she was just the same with your mother.'

'No, she wasn't.'

Rob sighs and, for a moment, shuts his eyes. 'Eva, she insisted on his having exhibitions, and parties, even when your mother didn't want it and your father had been ill. Even when people were grieving . . .'

'Yeah, but Rob, Maya wasn't even in England then. She went away to Rome the summer before.'

'No, she didn't. She organized that exhibition, didn't she?'

No, no, no. The kaleidoscope is turning again. Maya did go away to Rome the summer before, I'm sure she did. I stand staring at the back of Rob's newspaper. I go into the bedroom and take out that photograph which is in the back of my address book. I'm close to my father now. Soon I will know him. Fear breaks like sweat over my skin.

From upstairs, a sound like splintering wood judders through the air, followed by a crash which makes the ceiling vibrate. A scream hangs in the sullen air. It's followed by another, then another. The sound is like an animal in pain. Oh my God, Mrs Balashova has murdered her husband, I think. But it's a man making that sound.

Rob runs up the stairs ahead of me. Mr Balashov is stumbling against the banister above us. Bent double, he's screaming, his hand flailing against the wall. Other doors open below us. The Communist medal man and his wife appear and stand holding hands, uncertain whether to come up the stairs or not. The man with the shaved head crashes out of his flat, unties his dog from the stair-rail and pulls it inside.

In the Balashovs' flat, the yellow plastic flowers stand up stiff in their vase, the goldfish still swim in their bowl. Orange hair spreads on the floor. Mrs Balashova is lying face down, filling all the space in the kitchen. Her flower-scattered dress has risen up to reveal an expanse of mottled thigh. Her inflatable arm lies stretched to one side. Her leg is twisted, her red stiletto bent against the kitchen cupboard.

Rob goes to her and, kneeling down, starts to take her pulse. Behind me, people hurry up the stairs, crowding forward. The heat clings to my skin, a sour smell fills my nostrils. I cough and steady myself against the wall. Voices are coming to the boil. Mr Balashov is on his knees, his head pressed into a corner. I go to him and lay my hand on his shoulder, but he doesn't know I'm there.

Rob comes to me. 'She's dead.'

His words vibrate inside me. 'She can't be.'

This is all so senseless and random that I suppress a desire to laugh. The bottles of pills, the visits to the hospital . . . but I'd never thought it was serious. I've seen a dead body before in a street in Lima, but that wasn't someone I knew. People I've never seen before are coming up the stairs. Mr Balashov pushes towards his wife. A space is cleared for him. He kneels beside her, kissing her hungrily, pressing his lips against her red-painted mouth.

Hours seem to pass before anyone in authority arrives. Under the strip-lights people hurry back and forth. Silence, then weeping, then silence again. Everyone wants something to do, but there's nothing to do. I start to cough and can't stop. A grimly festive air develops. People make bitter cups of tea and pass around vodka. A woman I've never seen before starts mopping the floor. The Communist medal man and his wife continue to stand outside their flat, stiff and formal, heads bent in respect, as though they're already attending the funeral. The shaved-head man tries to get Mr Balashov away from his wife's body, but he won't be moved. The goldfish swim round and round in their bowl.

Eventually, men dressed in a collection of different uniforms arrive. Two of them stand smoking while the others assemble a stretcher which is nothing more than a patched piece of canvas between two poles. The corridor is narrow and the door of the flat narrower still. They push and pull at Mrs Balashova but without success. *'Nyet, poverni yeyo siuda.'* No, move her this way. They pull her around so that one of her legs sticks out of the doorway. *'Nado budyet dver' sniat'.'* They argue about whether the door should be taken off its hinges. From above I hear shuffling and swearing, then something scraping along the floor. I start to cough again and my throat burns.

Mrs Balashova is no longer a person, she's debris to be cleared away. They sit her up and, with two men shoving from behind, and one pulling in front, they push her lolling body through the door. Spit runs from the corner of her mouth, down her chin, and into the folded flesh of her neck. She's stripped of her watch and jewellery. Her rings are more difficult – the men twist at her fingers, pulling them off. Mr Balashov lies in a heap on the floor, moaning. As they try to take her down the stairs, one of her legs slides off the stretcher and her red stiletto falls to the floor. They heave her leg back into place, but the shoe is left on the stairs.

Mr Balashov gets up from the floor and staggers down the stairs after the stretcher. His hands grasp the jacket of one of the uniformed men. He's shouting and trying to tug the man back. He's reaching out for his wife's body. The shaved-head man takes hold of him, but grief has made Mr Balashov strong. I expect Rob to help them but he doesn't. He's standing watching and his face is green. Finally, some of the neighbours manage to drag Mr Balashov away from the stretcher. Now she's gone and the crowd on the landing stand, hands hanging by their sides, uncertain what to do. No one looks at the shoe. Mr Balashov is lying on the floor of the flat, exactly where she lay, his fist thumping up and down, as he sobs and yells.

Ten, eleven, midnight. He doesn't stop. Rob and I go up the stairs to him. We offer the only painkillers we've got, but he won't take them. We try to get him to eat, or to lie down, but he doesn't even know we're talking to him.

Finally we come back downstairs. Rob sits in the swivel chair in the sitting room pretending to watch television. I lie on the bed in the ochre light, my eyes following one arm of the five-armed lamp and then another. To me there's something strangely comforting in the undiluted and abandoned quality of those sounds from above. I want to add my voice to his and scream until I'm emptied out.

At one o'clock, Rob comes to bed. He needs to be up at six to get his flight to Kiev. The wailing is less but enough to keep us awake. The night is heavy and still. We cover ourselves with the duvet, take it off, pull it back over us. The wailing changes in tone but it doesn't ever stop for more than a minute. Footsteps scuffle on the landing, doors open and close. Conversations scurry along the pipes like mice. Rob and I pull pillows over our heads and try not to hear.

In my head I'm talking to Maya, asking her why she lied to me. Even that first night, at her party, she was so insistent that she didn't know why my father left. She wasn't there at the time, she said, she'd already gone away to Rome. But that wasn't true. It was as Rob said. She *had* organized that last exhibition, against my mother's wishes. I couldn't understand why she hadn't told me that. What did she have to hide?

From below, someone bangs on the wall and curses. 'I'll have to go up there,' Rob says, and goes to get some more vodka from our fridge. When I get upstairs, Mr Balashov is sitting in a chair and his fingers dig into Rob's arm. He's looking into his eyes, repeating the same words again and again. I intend to leave them together, but something about Mr Balashov's words holds me. I look over to his wife's armchair, which still has her shape pressed into it. Mr Balashov's voice is rhythmic and insistent. The sound of it

unnerves me and I head back down the stairs and go to
bed.

Finally the noise from above stops, and Rob comes down.
We lie side by side without touching. My throat feels as
though it's stuffed full of dust. I shiver and pull the duvet
around me. I know that we're never going to sleep. Perversely
I begin to yearn for the sound of falling furniture, the crack
of a breaking glass, even a scream of pain. Anything would
be better than this silence weighing down. 'What was he
saying?' I ask.

Rob turns to look at me but his eyes are obscured by
the shadows of the room. 'He said that he loves her as the
dry earth loves water. That no pleasure can be left for him
now. That he is dead as well.' Rob's voice is flat as he repeats
these words. I want to know what he's thinking, but the
shadows tell me nothing.

'But she was vile to him,' I say.

'I know.'

'So he couldn't have cared that much. He couldn't have
done. People don't love people who make them unhappy.'

'No,' Rob says. 'No, of course they don't.'

'It's like someone being in love with pain, isn't it?' I say.

'I don't know. Relationships are probably never as random
as they might look,' Rob says. 'Perhaps she liked to wound
and he liked to be wounded.'

'And that's OK while no one upsets the balance?'

'Yes, but once the balance is disturbed then it's gone for
ever.'

And that's how we go on, insisting that what Mr Balashov
said was only really theatre and shock. That was all. He may
have thought that he loved her, but he didn't really. But
even as we lie there, arguing, Mr Balashov's words are still
with us and that image of his hand gripping Rob's arm. As

I slide into sleep they whisper in my ears. He loves her as the dry earth loves water.

The beep-beep-beep of the alarm sounds at six and wakes us from shallow sleep. Rob switches it off and doesn't move. Lights are on across the courtyard, but their shape is furred by a low mist which hangs at the window. Rob sits up, yawns and rubs at his eyes. 'You know, I'm not sure I'll go to Kiev. I'd rather stay and get some sleep. I was only going to say goodbye. I can telephone instead.'

'Oh, but you really should go.' If he doesn't go then how will I get to Jack?

'Really?'

'Yes, because you've come to know the people there quite well, haven't you?'

'Perhaps.' Rob's eyes are staring into mine. He knows that I need him to go. We're sitting up, with the duvet wrapped half around us. I take hold of one of his hands and rub it between mine. A breath of air moves at the open window and we both shiver.

'If you don't go, won't it always feel like something unfinished?' I hate myself and I hate Rob as well, because he's allowed this to go on and on, although he knows it's no good. Some bitter thread ties us together and won't let us part. Rob stares into my eyes, then suddenly reaches out and holds me. His head pushes against my neck, butting me, while his hands knot around me. I hold him, feeling the warmth of his skin and breathing in his smell of morning sheets and Moscow soap. My hand strokes his hair.

'Yes,' he says into my neck. 'Yes, you're right – of course I should go. It's only . . . you will be OK, won't you?'

'Yes, of course I will. Why wouldn't I be?'

'Yes, of course. Just as you say. Silly not to go.' He's up off the bed and heading for the bathroom. For a moment I lie quite still with every muscle tensed, my jaw locked tight shut. Then I get up and make tea for Rob. I butter bread and wrap it in tinfoil. His coat is in the hall and I put it ready on the sofa next to his bag. We stand together while he sips his tea. 'Listen,' he says. 'Sorry. Sorry about yesterday. I didn't mean to argue. It was just the heat and the journey.'

'Of course. It's quite all right.'

I can't bear him apologizing for something that was my fault. He was right about Maya – he'd been right all along. Why didn't I see? Why do I never see?

He picks up his bag and I follow him into the hall. I want to thank him but the words would be too specific. We kiss before he goes, clinging to each other in the hall, the stiff material of his jacket pressed against my nightdress. My cold feet come off the floor because he squeezes me so tight. 'Don't worry about me,' I say. 'Of course I'll be all right. You know I will.' It's not surprising that he doesn't believe that because I don't believe it myself.

As soon as the door closes, I go into the bedroom and pull on my clothes. In the fresh silence of early morning, I can hear my own heart thumping in my ears. I find Jack's piece of paper and a guidebook with a map of the area around Moscow. I work out that I need to get to the Kiev Station, which is near where Maya lives.

Maya, Maya, I don't want to think about her. Perhaps nothing she told me about my father was true? I was always so sure that she was the one who understood him, and that my mother knew nothing. Maya told me that she didn't take that photograph of my father wearing his blue frock-coat. Maybe she did, maybe she didn't. But I'm certain that she was there that night and, for some reason, she's never wanted to admit that. But why? Why?

I push my travellers' cheques into my bag. The morning air at the windows is sharp so I reach for a coat. The one Maya gave me is hooked on the back of the door, but my other one seems to have disappeared. I look for it in the wardrobe, on the back of the kitchen chairs, under a pile of Rob's shirts. But it isn't anywhere. I must go, I must go. I reach for Maya's grey velvet coat and slide my hand into its silk-lined sleeve.

The child is lying in bed, a prickly blanket pulled up to her chin. The speckled glow of the toadstool night-light rises in an arc up the wall. The door opens and a black shoe with a gold buckle appears. The child starts to pull the covers up over her head, then she hears her father's voice. He comes to stand beside her but she can't see him clearly. The silk of his jacket rustles as he kneels down and reaches for her hand. Come, he says.

She feels her father's hand wrap around her own. As she climbs out of bed she shivers and looks down at herself. She's wearing a short red tunic and red tights — her costume for the party. Red shoes are lying near her bed and she puts them on. They're too large but she pulls the straps tight. Although the radiator is on, the room still feels damp and icy.

Come on, her father says. Come, quickly. The gold buttons on his jacket catch the light. The child knows that the sky must have cleared and that her father can see the stars he has been looking for through his telescope. This is the moment they've been waiting for. She imagines the picture in the atlas, the fat, pink country with the long tail and the stars which come down to earth. Her father can see that star through his telescope. He will see it tonight. You must find a coat, her father says. She follows him to the

door, then turns back to look again at the familiar shapes of her
room.

As she steps out into the hall, freezing air rises from below. The
house smells of grown-ups and parties — spilt wine, cigarettes, wax.
Music thumps from the sitting room, its beat making the floor-
boards vibrate. But she can't see her father. She heads towards the
back stairs, stumbling in the darkness. Voices from outside on the
drive are muffled — a car engine coughs, splutters, dies. Down below,
the back corridor is lit by night-lights in jam jars. Streaks of yellow
leap up from the bottom of the walls. A lady in a Victorian gown
sweeps past, her skirts catching against the jam jars so that they
appear to be licked by flame. The child takes two steps down the
stairs, then hears her mother's voice. Now she will be sent back to
bed.

She turns and runs across the landing to the front stairs. Below
her, a woman dressed in a tinsel skirt tumbles out through the
sitting-room door. The table in the hall is crowded with empty
glasses, and a candle drips wax on to the floor. The White Rabbit
and March Hare stand by the front door. Then Maya appears,
dressed as a witch. She wears a long black evening dress, black
pointed shoes, and spikes of black paper stuck onto her fingernails.
The child knows that Maya won't make her go back to bed. Maya
will help her to find her father. She helped her to put her costume
on earlier and brought her a packet of crayons from London. As
she moves down the stairs, Maya holds a camera in her spiky-
nailed hands. The child looks into the lens and hears the shutter
click.

As her feet touch the tiled floor, she explains to Maya that she
must go with her father, she must hurry. But first she must find
her coat. In the back corridor, coats are piled on to hooks, they hang
over the stair-rail and are heaped on the wooden chest. The child
trips in her too-big shoes and stretches her hand up to the hooks,
trying to find her duffel coat. Her head is buried in wool and she

can't see anything. She throws her weight against the coats on the wooden chest and they slide on to the floor. But hers is not among them. Her father will go without her. She'll never get to the place where stars come down to earth.

What's the matter? Maya's voice slurs behind her.

My coat — I must find my coat.

Maya shakes her head. You'll never find it here, she says. It'll be under all the others. But take this — it'll be all right. Look. The child stands while Maya drapes the short cloak around her and ties the bow under her chin. The cloak — light and warm — folds down over her shoulders. The child hides her arms under it. She runs back into the hall.

Her mother stands near the front door. She wears a long dress of floral cotton which is laced tight at the waist. Her shoulders are covered by a chiffon scarf which falls almost to the floor. Tiny shoes, embroidered with flowers, poke out from under her gown. Her mother's face is taut and pale. Eva, what are you doing? she says. You should be in bed.

She's all right, Maya says. She's quite all right.

The child dodges into the sitting room and hides behind the door. She watches her mother and Maya through the crack which runs between the hinges. They stand on either side of the hall table. The child thinks of dogs — the way they circle and growl before they pounce. Wax drips down in a spreading pool.

She's all right, stop worrying, Maya says.

No, no. She must go back to bed. You don't understand, you don't understand. He can't be trusted, he doesn't know what he's doing. I don't want her anywhere near him.

Just calm down, Maya says. Stop trying to control everything.

No, no, no. Please just stop interfering. This is my house and my family.

The child turns her head away from the crack in the door and waits. When she looks again, a man in a top hat and tails is

*speaking to her mother. Jump leads? Anti-freeze? Her mother shakes
her head and follows the top-hat man.*

*The child goes back into the hall. Two musketeers and a man
in pyjamas block the front door. She asks Maya. Where is he?
Where is he?*

*Don't worry, dear, we'll find him. The child is sure that he'll
have gone down towards the lake, to the boathouse. That's where
he goes sometimes at night to watch the stars. The child tells Maya
that she needs to go out into the garden and Maya guides her
through the sitting room and out through the French windows. The
cold is raw as a wound. A bonfire smell rises over the frosted lawn.
The garden is alight with torches and candles. The child looks up
and sees a perfect round moon, large and low in the sky. Shadows
dance in the light of the fire. She steps down from the terrace and
on to the lawn. A face painted in gold flashes in front of her and
then is gone.*

*She turns back towards the lights of the house and sees the familiar
shapes of the sitting room – the sofa, the wall-lights, the mirror above
the fireplace. Maya is standing near the front windows, watching her,
and she waves. The child moves through the shifting shadows. The
blue frockcoat appears in the distance, near the path to the lake and
the spider's-web gate. Under her feet, the grass is stiff with frost. Her
nose runs, her lips are numb. Trees are patches of dark against the
darkness. Wait for me, wait for me. Behind her, someone shouts about
fireworks. The child reaches the spider's-web gate. Her father is ahead
of her in the trees. Behind her, the sounds of music and laughter fade.*

*She hurries down the path, through stripes of moonlight. A brick
and flint wall and an open door appear ahead of her. She stops
still, looks down at her red shoes, feels the cloak around her. She
must never go through that door. She must never go through that
door. Her shoes will not move. Her father has gone, his shadow
sliding down the frame of the door.*

Then his voice calls out to her, breaking the night air, spiralling upwards into a sky heavy with stars. Its sound grows and spreads, drawing her to him. They will go to that place and a star will come down to earth. Her foot hovers by the gate. The voice comes again. Then she's running down the path, through the tall marsh grass, towards the edge of the lake and the jetty. A light shines out from the boathouse. That's where he's going. He'll have turned left onto the path which runs around the lake.

But that's not where he's gone. Instead he's ahead of her, far out on the lake, walking on water. He turns in the moonlight, glittering. She hears his call. Eva, come, come. His head is tipped back and he's staring upwards, pointing. He's floating above the water, riding over the top of it. Eva, come, come.

Then from somewhere far behind her, a woman's voice screams. Fear comes down on the child like cold water. Her father is standing on ice, and ice can break. She knows that the lake is shallow at the edges but at the centre it's deep as the ocean. No, no, no. He doesn't understand. He doesn't know. She must tell him, she must stop him. His hand is on the hot-plate, but he cannot feel it burn.

Ulitsa Spasskaia, Malakhovka

August 1991

I take the *elektrichka* from the Kiev Station. The train is wide and brown. It rocks and sighs on its rails as it passes pylons and factories, smudged by the morning mist. At a chipped and peeling wooden station it stops to pick up families laden with boxes of tools, wire, bags of sand and planks of wood. The landscape changes – a stretch of green, a tunnel of silver birch. A dank river is clogged with fallen branches, plastic bags and petrol tins.

I turn over that fragment of memory in my mind – red shoes, a bonfire smell, the light from the sitting room, shadows moving across a dark lawn. I thought that what I saw that night was a magician who could walk on water, who could bring down stars from the sky. But what I really saw was a sick man running out onto a frozen lake. And the two women – Maya and my mother – who should have stopped him, were too busy arguing to see what was happening. Which is why neither of them will talk about that night.

The station at Malakhovka is deserted except for one *babushka* sitting on a bench in front of a bucket of potatoes. I walk over a level crossing, past a shop and a line of houses. In my head I describe to myself everything I'm seeing. I need to keep my mind occupied by external details to stop it being pulled back again to the frozen lake, and the sudden screams. A redbrick church is topped by a dome spiralling up into the sky like whipped ice cream. I turn into a half-made road which dissolves into mud at the edges. Around me, the land is forested and has a gentle roll to it, like the sea on a calm day. In a yard full of rusted cars a man works with a welding torch, which flashes sparks into the still air.

Behind falling-down fences, I see wooden houses painted blue and green. They have steep tin roofs, lace curtains and strips of wood carved in intricate patterns along the windows and eaves. Occasionally I catch a glimpse of a woman working with a hoe or a rake, a man hammering or laying concrete.

Although the directions Jack wrote were brief, I find the *dacha* without any trouble. It's the same as the others but larger, with an acre of garden, a garage and a glassed-in veranda at the front. I walk to it through yellow flowers scattered across an overgrown lawn. The doors to the veranda are open and Jack is there, propped in a chair, asleep. His glasses are pushed half off his nose, and his book has fallen to the floor. His face is all bone, the skin of his neck loose and wrinkled. I know now that I've found him I'll be safe.

The steps up to the veranda creak under my feet. The floor is wooden planks, painted brown. Various objects from his Moscow room are scattered on a table – that shell paper-weight, a vase, piles of papers. I bend to pick up his book and he wakes, blinks several times, then slowly reaches out to me. For a moment I stare at his fleshless hand, and hesitate. The sun coming in through the glass above is so bright it dazzles our eyes. I reach out and pull his fingers up close to my face and kiss his knuckles. He catches me around the waist and pulls me towards him, burying his face against my hip. 'Oh my dear, I'm so glad you've come.'

I lean down and kiss his hair. The last five months cease to exist. He and I are back in the life we were meant to have. I pull up a low stool and sit close to him. Although he looks ten years older than when I last saw him, a glow radiates from inside him, illuminating his skin and eyes. He looks as he did at the Church of the Resurrection. His fingers stroke my neck, just below my ear. 'Such lovely weather. Just look at the flowers.' He points up the garden and smiles, that familiar first-time smile. His cheeks are hollow, and dark blue shadows have gathered under his eyes. I look down at those raw fingers and remember how they touched me, cupping my breast, or sliding down over my hips.

'I'm sorry,' he says. 'I'm so sorry. You know, I wanted to spare you this.' I pull my stool closer to him, listening to the familiar sound of his breath. In the distance, a hammer strikes metal and a train rumbles into the station.

I tell him then about my father and the ice. 'You need to go and see Maya,' he says. 'You need to insist that she tells you exactly what happened. It isn't good enough to have some vague idea.' I tell him that I won't be able to speak to her, I'm not strong enough.

'I don't know why I always believed her,' I say. 'I suppose it was because I was sure she loved my father.'

'But of course,' Jack says. 'We tend to forgive anything if passion is involved.' He shifts in his chair, coughs, draws in a short breath. 'Do you think that this party you can remember was on the sixth of January 1967?'

'Yes, it was.'

'I wonder if that night had some particular significance for your father? Something to do with his work or his astronomy? I don't know. Perhaps I'm wrong. I could find out, but there's information I would need. I could ring someone in America and ask them to send it.'

I should ask him what information he needs but I'm frightened to keep talking about that night. So instead I tell him that I'm leaving Moscow in two weeks, but he doesn't seem to hear. 'I can stay tonight,' I say. 'At least I can do that.' That pleases him, although he warns that the house has no electricity, and only an outside loo.

For a long time I sit in silence, holding his hand. I know that I should be making some kind of plan, but I can't let my mind move out of this moment. I suggest to him, once again, that he should go and see a doctor but I only do it out of a sense of duty. I know that he won't agree. The wind stirs the long grass of the lawn and the nodding heads of the yellow flowers. I look out down the garden at the tin roofs of other *dachas* visible through the trees.

'I don't want this to end,' I say.

'Eva, you don't understand. You think that time is measured in minutes, and hours and days. But it isn't — it's measured in intensity of feeling. Some moments always remain with us, they become the backdrop to all the other days.'

'But why isn't it possible just to make time stop?'

'It is possible. We have. Time is driven by desire, isn't it? So when you have everything you want, then time ceases to exist.'

And that's how it seems as we sit together staring out down the garden.

'Jack, you know about my father. This thing between you and me — it isn't only about that, is it?'

'No.'

'What then?'

He turns to kiss me. 'Most things have an explanation. But not this.'

★   ★   ★

The day slides past in scattered sunlight. We eat bread and cheese at the table under the hot glass roof, and carry buckets of water from the tap near the gate. The drowsy buzz of a mower sounds from next door. I drink glass after glass of water because I can't stop coughing. Jack jokes that I'll die before him. As the sun cools and the shadows lengthen, he says he'll walk to the shop near the railway station. He wants to buy us some supper. I think it's too far for him but he insists, and he wants to go on his own.

I watch him heading up the lawn, his steps still straight and energetic, then I step through the double doors into the house. It's smaller than it appears from the outside. Downstairs, there's a bedroom and a sitting room and upstairs, two bedrooms. It's all simple and austere, unlived-in, decorated a long time ago. The smell is of damp wallpaper, moss, and unaired beds. Flies buzz against the windows. In the sitting room, wallpaper with a fine stripe is peeling in places. It feels like a house where someone has died.

When Jack gets back we eat garlic sausage and bread and tomatoes. As the day fades, he lights candles and stands them on the windowsill. The damp sitting room smells of earth and garden and wax. Now, for the first time, neither of us feels any need to talk. All evening Jack is restless, wandering from the bedroom to the sitting room and back, staring out at the navy sky. An ancient radio, the size of a television, and made of mahogany, stands on the top of a cupboard and Jack fiddles with the knob but it only crackles and fizzes. It usually works, he says. What's wrong with it? It's a warm night and he opens the doors to the veranda then shuts them again.

'What's the matter?' I ask.

'I'm not sure. Perhaps there'll be a storm tomorrow.'

We go to bed in the downstairs bedroom. The walls of

this room are thin, and metal windows are cut into them at the front and the back. Jack brings in the candles from the sitting room and places them on the bedside table. A crooked wardrobe stands cramped in next to a chest of drawers. Above us hangs an oval mirror with a curly metal frame. The carpet is patterned in squares of brown and gold. The trees grow close to the back window, their branches tapping against the glass. On top of the chest of drawers is that wooden box with the ivory clasp, three Metro tokens, a green toothbrush with splayed bristles, Jack's fountain pen. He sees my eyes wandering over the room.

'I'm not sure now what I'm going to do with this stuff,' he says. 'I'd planned to burn everything but I don't know whether I'll be able to do it. I would ask you, but I'm not sure you'll have time.'

I try to remain steady. 'I would do, of course, but you'll need them . . .' My eyes fix on that wooden box. A wisp of conversation floats back to me from the day when that ray of sunlight slanted over the façade of the church. *You're going to get more and more ill, and lie in some rented room waiting to die. No, no, it won't be like that.*

I lie down next to him in the short and lumpy bed, beneath the oval mirror. The bed is damp and hard so he gets up and puts his overcoat over us.

As I lie awake, watching an oblong of light from the window moving up the wall, I think again of that wooden box, of his plan to burn all his possessions, and I'm seized by a sudden fear. It seems to me that something apocalyptic has been woven into the details of the room. My mind travels back to that long-ago newspaper article about Stalin's Terror and the twenty million bodies. I hear the dead close up at the window. I drift into fretful sleep and wake with sweat running down my back and words gabbling in my throat. Jack is staring down at me and I grip my hands around his arm. 'I need your help. I need your help.'

'Of course,' he says. 'Of course.'

And then we start to talk, and we don't stop. Our words go on through sleeping and waking, through the branches tapping at the window, the sounds of birds, the creaking of the wooden house. Jack, I'm frightened. What will I do? After you've gone, what will I do? You'll get married to Rob, he says. Just like that, so certain and calm. I twist in his arms, staring at him in the darkness. I won't. Not now, I won't. I can't do that. Our relationship has only ever been about protecting each other from the past. But then I wanted to know, and that has changed me. But he hasn't changed at all.

I'm not so sure, Jack says. I think if one person changes, then others automatically change as well. It's just we can be slow to see it. Everything that you see in me is there in him as well – it's just that you haven't yet uncovered it. He hasn't left you, has he? Something keeps him there. You have something he wants. You could help him if you decided to. It's up to you to choose.

I wonder why he doesn't leave me? I say. I don't know, Jack says. Sometimes people accept a situation of minor pain in order to avoid some far greater pain.

I doze, wake, hear those branches on the window, see that oblong of light high on the ceiling. My sleep is clouded with half-seen images and I wake again, crying, biting my hand. I tell him then about what happened when he left. And now it's going to be the same again, isn't it? No, no. I didn't cause the pain, you know, I only uncovered it. And it doesn't have to be the same this time. It's your choice. You need to go and see Maya. That's what you need to do. I can't, I won't be able to. You can. You will. You're much stronger than you know. This long journey – most people would never have come this far. You're saner than just about anyone I've ever met. You've been trying to find out the truth and no one has helped you. That is hard beyond anything else.

The hours slide by. I wake, cough, doze, cough. Those words I heard as the child's shoe banged against the kitchen chair. Jack, that's in the genes, isn't it? That kind of illness? No, no, no. Jack's voice is firm and he's gripping me tight. That kind of illness may be genetic and it may not. But there's nothing wrong with you. You didn't inherit that from your father. What happened is quite different. Your mother was always terrified that you would inherit his problem. And you know the strange thing is, when someone is frightened of something, they often create conditions which increase the chances that it'll happen. You've been lied to all your life. Don't you consider what the effects of that must have been?

All along I wanted to make sense of it, I say. I wanted to understand, but once I found out about his illness I realized that maybe there isn't any sense. Jack moves my head back from him, and fixes his eyes on me. No. No. Don't think that. It isn't right. Why? I say. Because the mad are really sane? My voice is weary.

No, not that. But the mind tries to heal itself – and the process of healing can be very strange. Things do happen for a reason. Promise me that you'll believe in that? Do you promise? Yes, I do. I do.

But you and I? I ask. Why has our friendship always been thwarted? I pull the sheets up over me. Thwarted? he says. I don't think so. I think in time we'll find this is all exactly as it was intended to be. He runs his hands over my spine. Eva, I know you can't see it now, but you must have faith – in some overall goodness, some abundance.

Oh, because it's all going to work out right in the end, is it? No, not that. Absolutely not that. But there will prove to be reason in this. As he says this, I understand that he's talking as much to himself as to me. You know that despair is perhaps the one sin for which we can never be forgiven? We all know that nihilism, hopelessness, cynicism exist . . . But we must never lend our spirit to those forces. You understand that, don't you? Now go to sleep, he says.

And strangely I do. And through the night his words stay in my head. I hear them repeated again and again. You must speak to Maya. You can do it. You have far more strength than you know. There's nothing wrong with you, nothing at all. I know that Jack's right. I'm going to be all right. I don't know how it will happen, but I'm sure that it will.

I wake to find that Jack is already up. My neck aches and my throat is raw. At the window, the sun is large as it emerges over the tops of the trees. Dew flashes on blades of lolling grass. I pull on my dress and go out to the veranda, taking a towel with me so I can get some water and wash. A faint wind shivers over the garden. Smoke rises from the chimney of a distant *dacha*. The sound of an axe chopping wood breaks through the air. The morning is so full of blessing that it makes me happy, despite myself. Jack is sitting in the veranda armchair, his feet bare, his shirt hanging out. He's staring down the garden, soaking it all up. 'When I'm gone and you see flowers like that, will you look at them and think, he would have noticed that?'

'Yes, I will.'

'Are you sure?'

'Of course. I'll always think of that.'

For the first time I have the sense that Jack is frightened. It's as though he's given me all the strength he had, and now there's nothing left for him. Yet still he walks down the path, with his sleeves rolled up, and he's carefree and easy, swinging the bucket. As he passes the *dacha* next door, he raises his hand to greet someone there. Then he bends down and puts the bucket under the tap. After he's filled it, he moves back to the neighbour's fence, and stops again. The edge of a Russian voice, suddenly questioning, unsettles the air.

Jack picks up the bucket again and walks a few more steps. He's got more water than we need and his shoulder is pulled over to one side. He stops and looks back towards the fence. I start to walk across the grass towards him. He picks up the bucket and takes two or three steps. The bucket tips, spilling water on to his feet. He stops for a moment, puts the bucket down, stretches out his arm, flexes it. He draws a short breath and I hurry towards him. He's leaning to pick up the bucket again, but I catch hold of the handle. 'Jack, let me—'

He pulls at my arm, his eyes wide and blank. 'Eva, listen. That man . . . It's on the radio. Yesterday, Gorbachev was deposed.'

'What?'

'An announcement – he's unable to continue as President due to ill health.'

I'm not really listening. This is just one more Moscow rumour. It doesn't necessarily mean anything. I shrug and reach for the bucket again. 'Oh yes? And so what happens now?'

His fingers dig into my arm. 'Eva, there's been a coup. Yesterday.'

I make an effort not to laugh. That word has floated around me all the time I've been in Moscow. But a coup can't happen now – not in August, when everyone is away on holiday. Anyway, what exactly *is* a coup? What happens? The bucket standing on the grass suddenly seems dangerously innocent and vulnerable. Around us the morning is still waking, the mist dispersing, the sun climbing up above the line of the trees. Birds are chattering on a telephone wire, and in the next-door house a child is crying. 'We need some water,' I say. 'Let's carry the bucket back.'

'Yes. Let's do that.' We walk back together, holding the bucket between us. Our feet move in time, we keep the bucket steady so it can't bang against our legs. But just as we're getting close to the house, my ankles tangle and water splashes across my bare feet. We put the bucket down and I sit on the table, reaching for my towel. Jack takes it from me and bends down to wipe my feet. His breath is tight and his hand clutches at the table, but he dries my feet all over, moving the towel over my toes, the tops of my feet, my ankles. When he's finished he lays a sombre hand on my knee.

Then he walks into the house and turns on the radio. The sound of classical music swoops and falls through the sparse room. A clarinet plays a swirling melody, violins tremble. Jack fiddles with the knob, the radio fizzles, then the music starts again. 'This is what they always do,' he says. I want to take the radio from him and stop that music. 'We need to go into the city.' Jack stumbles into the bedroom and tries to pick up some books from the floor but he can't bend down. He sits on the bed, his hand pressed against his chest. 'The plotters have closed down all the television stations and the newspapers. They're taking control of the city.'

To me, the idea that anyone could ever control Moscow seems ridiculous. 'Jack, surely the best thing we can do is stay here?'

'No. I need to go back. There's Mrs Pastukhova. And Kashtanka.'

The dog? But there's no point in arguing. Jack's already far away from me. Sweat has gathered on his forehead and his hands tremble. He goes through to the sitting room and crashes his finger down on to the radio button. The silence is full of questions. Images I've seen of the 1917 revolution flash in my mind. Blood in the snow, flesh ripping, metal against bone. And those fuzzy pictures of Vilnius, stick figures dodging, caught between the tanks and a high wall, the sound of gunfire, screaming.

I stand at the window and stare out at the treacherous sun. Only those few hours of happiness yesterday. And even that was unreal, because the coup had already happened. Jack says that people are gathering at the White House to defend it and that we should go there and join the protest. But I can hear defeat in his voice.

'The West won't let this happen. They'll support Gorbachev.' But my cheap optimism can do nothing for Jack. This has shocked him at a level beyond my understanding. Where I come from, tragedy is a train strike or a hospital closure. For people here, it's twenty million dead. I think of those china cups in his room, edged with their line of gold. And the photograph of the pony and trap, the women in long skirts, the small boy in his plus fours. For him this is history repeating itself.

'Jack, please, just sit down. I'm going to get everything ready, then we can go.' He sits on the bed, uncertainly, while I gather together his books. I find his suitcases under the bed and pack everything into them. I want to wrap my hands around each object, register its exact feel, so that I'll remember later. I make tea, find a clean pair of socks and his shoes. He sits like a small child, fumbling with his socks.

I try to help him, touching those alabaster feet. But the socks are stubborn, they catch on his toes, the heel finishes up on top. Suddenly he's crying, tears pouring down his face. I remember when he cried once before, in that hotel room. I was embarrassed by him then. Now I'm envious.

'I never wanted to get old,' he says. 'I didn't want that.' I want to comfort him as he comforted me during the night. But we're both at the end of comfort. My eyes follow the pattern of the carpet — squares of brown and gold. I hold onto his shins, pushing my head against them.

'I can't do anything,' he says. 'I can't do anything.'

'You've done something for me. You know that. You have.' He nods his head and half-smiles. He mumbles apologies. I take hold of the socks again and put them on, fitting the heel carefully in place.

Liusinovskaia Bol'shaia, Moscow

August 1991

Moscow is still happening, just as it always has. At early-morning stations, the sun spreads a generous light. Men board the train, yawning, their eyes still heavy with sleep. On the platform a stray dog rummages in a paper bag, two women swing a small child between them, laughing. Don't these people know what has happened? Is violence usually this quiet?

The Metro is running and people are on their way to work. I tell Jack that I'm going to walk home with him to help him with his bags. He wants to argue, but he hasn't the energy. Sometimes he shuts his eyes and draws in a deep breath. When a seat comes free, I make him sit down. I stand among creaking leather jackets. Somewhere further down the carriage a man strums on a guitar. My lungs feel as though they're full of tar.

As we come up from the Metro at Dobryninskaia, Jack stumbles and nearly falls. He reaches out for my hand and I steady him. The air rumbles as though a plane is circling overhead. In the street Jack tries to insist that I should go back. But I say, 'Just let me carry your bags as far as the flat.' As we walk, I stare up at the sky, trying to locate the source

of that uneasy sound. Jack's face is set hard and he's trying
to walk faster than he should.

We reach the turning to his street. I try to tell him to
slow down, but he can't hear me. I shout the words at him.
'What is that noise?' I stop and feel the muscles of my legs
tremble, and realize that the road is vibrating. A growl fills
the air. I steer Jack off the main road in the direction of his
flat, but he won't go, and turns back. Two women have
moved to the edge of the pavement, and stare down the
Liusinovskaia Bol'shaia as it heads out of town. I look up
at the windows around us and they seem to rattle in their
frames.

A tank appears on the main road. It's gone in a snarl
and a flash of khaki, but it's followed by another. And
another and another. A stream of faceless steel boxes
stretches for as far as we can see. The tanks dwarf the cars
parked at the side of the street. They leave trails of blue-
grey smoke which spread a distorting haze across the
morning air. Their caterpillar tracks score marks in the
tarmac. Up towards Dobryninskaia there's a place where
the road narrows. There the tracks of the tanks catch against
the kerbstones, cracking them open and leaving them
splayed in the road.

Along the pavement, people stand watching. An old
woman is close to the kerb, shouting curses, flapping her
apron, crying. Looking up at an office block, I see blank
faces crowded at every window. Jack puts out a hand to
steady himself against a railing. I reach out to him, hoping
that I might pull him away, take him to his flat. But
he wants to see the full extent of this. Eventually the
noise lessens and we see the end of the line. The last tank
rolls up the street. Then all that's left is a pall of diesel
fumes.

Jack turns to me. 'Eva, do you already have a ticket booked to England?'

'Yes, why?'

'You must go to the airport and get it brought forward – and if you can't, just buy a ticket out of here.'

'No. I'm just going to explain to Rob that you're ill and that I need to be with you.'

'No. No. Don't do that.'

'Why not? It's what I should have done months ago.'

As Jack raises his hand to wipe sweat from his face, his arm shudders violently. For a moment he looks at me, and his eyes are like tunnels which run far back into his head. In his mind he's running through a hundred calculations. I have the feeling that he's coming up against some new idea, but it isn't one he wants to contemplate. 'Listen, Eva. I'm sorry, I can't talk about this now. Let's just leave it until tomorrow. I need some time alone.'

I agree to that. One night can't make any difference. 'Give me your phone number so I can call.' He puts his suitcase down and starts to look for a pen. I find one in my bag and he writes on the back of a receipt from his pocket. He's staring away from me into the street. 'You promise to do what I've said?'

'Yes.'

He nods his head vigorously. 'Go now. Please go.'

I put his suitcase down on the pavement and turn to leave. He steps back, but then he stops and puts his hand out to me. 'Eva?' His voice sounds strange, saying my name. He comes towards me and kisses me, his tongue feeling my lips, his hand cradling the back of my neck. 'I just wanted to say – you know what you said, at that café, with the sun shining on the church?'

'No, what did I say?'

'That all my talk of love without need was rubbish. Well, you were right. How do you think I understand you so well?' He kisses me again and holds me against him. 'I'm sorry,' he says. 'I'm so sorry.' His voice is muffled. 'Remember what I said last night, won't you?'

'Do you really believe all that stuff?'

He shrugs and rubs at his head. 'No. No, I'm not sure that I do. But I think we have to live as though it's true.' Then suddenly he kisses me once more, picks up his bags, and walks away. I watch him go, waiting for him to turn back and wave. But he's determined not to do that. Instead, he just walks on with his crooked, old-man step and his shoulder pulled down by his bags. And although he's sick and frightened by what's happening to his city, he's still the only thing I see in that bland and jumbled street. A black post standing up straight in the sea, and the rest just so much flotsam washing up against him.

I go back to the flat because there's nowhere else to go. My throat is choked by a ball of pain and every breath stabs in my chest. In the kitchen I pour myself a glass of water. I try to call Rob at his office. He should be back from Kiev by now but he doesn't answer the phone. I try Sasha's flat. No answer. It occurs to me that Rob and Sasha are among the first people who the plotters will arrest. The phone rings and I pick it up, hoping to speak to Rob but instead I hear Maya's voice, an octave higher than usual. 'Eva, I've been calling and calling. Are you all right?'

She starts to insist that I should go to her flat. It isn't safe where I am. Where is Rob? Why isn't he looking after me? Her voice rises higher and higher. I should go to the British Embassy. What is the Democracy Foundation doing to protect its staff? I must come round to her flat right now and she'll see what she can do. Harvey will know what's best. I remember what Jack said and I know that I'll be strong enough to speak to her. I need to do that now or it will never happen.

'OK, I'll come. I'll come now.'

In the Metro, photocopies are pasted on the wall and a man hands out fliers denouncing the coup. A woman in a khaki uniform hustles a drunk who is blocking one of the doors. In the train, three Germans carry cameras, lights and a thing like a furry caterpillar on the end of a stick. They get off at Barrikadnaia, which is the stop for the White House. I travel on to Kutuzovskaia and come up from the Metro to find two tanks parked in the street. Teenage soldiers lean against them, yawning and smoking in the sharp sun. Small boys swing from their sides, making tak-tak noises with pretend guns. In Maya's building I speak to the floor lady then climb the cracked marble stairs, coughing and sweating.

The building is filled with a fresh silence. I wonder if some people have already left. I imagine clothes left unfolded on bedroom chairs, a window hanging open, a kitchen chair overturned in haste. When I knock at Maya's door, I hear nothing for a while, then a rustle and the door eases open six inches. A slice of red silk dressing-gown decorated with a golden Chinese dragon appears. The door opens wider and Maya pulls me into the flat. 'I don't know what to do,' she tells me. 'Harvey says that the Embassy people have been moved into secure accommodation, so maybe I can go there.' With fidgeting hands she lights a cigarette from a pack on the hall table and takes a long drag.

'Maya, there are tanks, but that's all. Nothing is happening.'

She rolls her eyes and disappears into the bedroom where cases are flung open on the bed and silk dresses hang from the backs of chairs. Gold jewellery lies in a pile on the bedside table. Maya sits down at her dressing-table and picks up an eyebrow pencil. Foreigners are being detained and thrown into prison, she tells me. As from tonight there'll be no more flights out of the country. More than half a million troops have been mobilized from across Russia and the Republics, and they're surrounding the city.

I'm not listening to her. Instead I'm staring at the canvases propped against the wall. I know which one is my father's. From the corner of her rolling eye Maya sees me looking at the picture and her eyebrow pencil hangs in the air.

'Maya, I want to know what happened to my father.'

It's easy to say that now. Maya's snake-clad hand is unsteady and a black line veers up above her plucked eyebrow. 'Damn, damn.' She scuffles among her make-up and pulls out a cotton bud. Her hand knocks a powder compact and an empty glass to the floor.

'There was a party,' I say. 'After Christmas in 1967. You were there – and my father ran out onto the frozen lake.' My words fade into a cough and blood thumps in my forehead. My mind tips and a chasm opens. For a moment I'm back on that moon-striped path. The ivy-covered door, the sudden screaming. Maya gets up and scrambles clothes into a suitcase. Her dressing-gown, half-undone, falls open to reveal a shrivelled breast. 'Eva, da-a-rling, you don't seem to understand. The government of this country has been deposed.' She sits down at the dressing-table again, picks up a tube of lipstick, then looks at me, shaking her head. 'Just look at you. You need to see a doctor. You're ill. Come on now, co-o-me on. I'm sure I've still got some of those pills somewhere.'

She's moving towards me, stretching out her hand. I long to let her give me pills, make me tea, look after me. I want

us to be back where we were before. Of course, she didn't
lie to me. We should laugh and drink vodka and she should
tell me how pretty I am and lend me clothes. She goes to
get me a glass of water. Now the pills, the pills, where would
those be? I think of all the times in my life when someone
has said, 'Pills, tea, sit down and rest, you're ill.' But I'm not
ill and I never have been.

'Maya, what happened? Did he fall through the ice? I
just want to know.'

An image forms of my father's hand burning on that hot-
plate. Except now it's not his hand, it's mine, and I'm pushing
it down on to the burning metal again and again. *Maya-liar-
fire.* She slams a drawer shut and turns to look at me. 'Eva,
you think you want to know but you don't. You re-e-ally
don't. I've done my best to help, I re-e-ally have. But you've
always been the same. You could never be told anything.
Push, push, push. You've never known when to stop. You'd
been told so many times.'

Yes, of course, I might have known. It all turns out to
be my fault. The little red devil with her forked stick and
too-big shoes. It was all your fault, if it hadn't been for you,
everything would have been fine. My mother had said that
as well. *Eva, I had to think of you.* They've both been so kind
to me, and made such sacrifices. And I've always been such
a problem. Except I don't believe that any more. I may have
been the tiresome child who wouldn't go to bed that night,
but I was also the only person who was there when he went
out onto the ice. Maya and my mother – they both cared
for him so much – but they weren't there when he needed
them.

'Harvey will be here in five minutes and I must be ready.'
Maya grabs at a bottle of vodka which is standing on the
floor near her chair and pours some into a glass. *Maya-liar-*

fire. Her doll's eyes roll as she smears lipstick across her mouth. I start to see the child standing on the ice. I press my hands over my ears and stare down at the pattern on the carpet. An ape face leers in the corner of my mind. The front door opens and Harvey marches across the hall. 'All right, dear? It's only me. Are you ready?' He enters the room with a purpose I've never seen in him before. The time for strong men has arrived. 'My dear, we must go now.'

'Yes,' Maya says. 'We re-e-ally must leave.'

I go to the door and I try to shut him out. His pale eyes don't see me, but he moves his foot forward and blocks it against the door. I wrestle with the door but he doesn't move. Maya shuts up her suitcases and shovels her make-up into a travelling case. I stand in front of her. 'Tell me,' I say. For a moment she looks straight at me. I know her then as I've never known her before. Our minds are touching and I think she might speak. I need to hear her tell me exactly what happened. Tell me. Harvey picks up the cases and ushers Maya out of the room.

I'm shouting now. Words tumble out. 'You lied to me. You and my mother — you didn't watch him, you didn't take care.' I follow them out onto the landing and the words keep on coming. 'You lied to me, you lied, you said you weren't even there that night. You said you'd gone to Rome. But you were there, you were.'

Maya is tucked in close against Harvey as he steers her down the stairs. She looks back at me once, then they've gone and I'm left alone on the landing. I see myself from far above, standing in the stairwell, next to the cage of the lift. Like a woman in a Greek tragedy, I'm wringing my hands, tearing my hair, shouting out all the rage of twenty long years.

★   ★   ★

The entrance to the Kutuzovskaia Metro is sealed by barriers and guarded by soldiers. The sky is solid grey now, and soft rain is starting to fall. I walk on towards the bridge, but the road is blocked by bulldozers, lorries and buses. Some lie on their sides across the road, others have had their wheels removed. I turn right along the embankment. As I approach the next bridge, cars are being stopped but no one seems to care about pedestrians. Patrol boats chug through the gleaming black water. As I cross the bridge a helicopter drones overhead. The White House and the Ukraina Hotel are faint as sketches in the thickening rain.

I know now what happened. Maya didn't say any words, but her silence spoke. My father nearly drowned in the lake that night and, after that, he left my mother, and Maya, and went to Mexico and didn't come back. There is such power in knowing. I am equal to anything now.

As I walk towards my college, the city is being uprooted. Chairs and sheets of corrugated iron sail down the streets. Doors are passed from hand to hand. The branches of a tree are dragged along the ground. The panels of a rusted car, a park bench, a lamp-post, an iron gate, a telephone box – everything is travelling in the same direction. I'm swept up in a crowd of people all heading towards the White House. Young men, straight out of their offices, still carry their briefcases. Elderly ladies grip their string shopping bags.

On the bank of the river the White House – a four-storey building with two wings – sails like an ocean liner, tranquil above the crowds. It's surrounded by barricades ten feet high. Two tanks are at the front of the building, one of them draped in flowers. Television crews push up against the white marble steps and flashbulbs pop. Lines of women, all wearing the same factory uniforms, stand to attention, linking hands. Young men with long hair huddle around

fires, or sit on coats in the mud, strumming on their guitars.
A woman with bouffant hair and a sleek fur coat hands
out boxes from McDonald's and Pizza Hut. Close to the
building, armed men wear black masks with holes cut for
their eyes. A man in a wheelchair is chained to the railings. An orthodox priest in full robes is surrounded by a
group of worshippers.

An overexcited English journalist, who knows Rob, tells
me that although three tanks have decided to defend the
White House, not many more will do the same. Most of
the soldiers are from the Urals, the Volga, Siberia, so they
care nothing about what happens in Moscow. A solid
Scandinavian woman, mistaking me for a journalist, intro-
duces herself and explains that she is a delegate to an international conference of librarians which happens to be taking
place in Moscow this week. Rumours run through the
crowd – the KGB are using secret tunnels to enter the
building. A special Alpha Force will come in from the air.
Thousands of riot troops are massed in Red Square and will
soon move this way. Planes will come over spraying poisonous
gas. The English journalist points to snipers on the roof of
the Ukraina Hotel.

I feel a hand on my shoulder. Vladimir, the newspaper
boss, is staring down at me. He speaks in Spanish. What am
I doing here? Where is Rob? I say that he was due back
on a train arriving at midday. Vladimir tells me that I look
ill. I nod and cough but I don't feel ill. I feel better than
I've ever felt in my life. Vladimir is insistent – I must go
home, at least for a while. There's no point in staying,
nothing will happen for several hours. I will be needed
tonight. I should come back then.

I wake with a jerk. My head drags up from the pillow.

Thump, thump, thump. For a moment I think that the sound is in my head. But no, someone is banging on the door. I stand up and stare down into the darkness of the courtyard. I look at my watch and it's past two o'clock. Thump, thump, thump. I struggle into my clothes, open the door, and find Sasha standing there. He's unshaven and looks as though he hasn't slept for weeks. The birthmark on his face is crimson and his hair hangs loose. Where is Rob? He's definitely in Moscow because Sasha spoke to him at the Democracy offices at two o'clock. But now no one is answering there. Sasha needs to find him now. Where can he be?

We agree that he's probably at the White House but what hope is there of finding him? Sasha sinks down on the steps, cursing. He's close to tears. He talks but I can't make his words into any shape. Above us, the strip-lights buzz, filling the landing with their green glare. Sasha's feet are close to that ever-widening crack. I think of the hopscotch girl and hear the tap of her feet. I stare down at Sasha and remember how he used to talk to me. Those memories of his child-hood. A man who's seen so little kindness that he has diffi-culty even recognizing it. And yet even with his drinking and car stealing, he keeps on trying to speak the truth.

He's telling me about the newspaper. Soldiers came and tried to seize the machinery. But most of it had already been taken away. He climbed out across the roof with one of the typewriters. Now tape has been tied across the door and a soldier is on guard. But they don't know that they have come too late, he says. Most of the text of the newspaper has already gone to the printers. Yeltsin is calling a General Strike, and in Moscow people will support him. But outside Moscow, people don't know anything. All news is cut except for official channels, and everything that is said is lies.

Voronezh is a city of one million people, Nizhnii Novgorod has two million – but none of them knows anything and so they can't support Yeltsin.

He says that if the plotters stay in power then everyone he knows will be arrested and sent out of Moscow. All the journalists will be sacked from their jobs, no one will have a trial, many people will die. All the work of the last three years will be wasted and Russia will be back in silence, in lies. There will be no hope for the future, no one will be able to write, or speak. They will not even be able to think. This can't be allowed to happen. Everyone must stand firm – but how can they do that if they know nothing? These faxes must be sent.

Rob's office is all closed up and so they can't send any faxes from there. What can he do? His voice is suddenly weak with despair. He doesn't know – maybe none of this would make any difference. Most of the people don't even care, they don't even know. He curses the Russians and their lack of interest.

'Give me the faxes,' I say.

Sasha says no, I mustn't do that, but I'm determined. I must do this for him, I must do it for Jack, I must do it to compensate for all the time I've watched and felt nothing. I'm powerful now, I can do anything. 'Give me the faxes,' I repeat. My hand shuffles through my bag, looking for the office key.

'No, no,' Sasha says. 'You don't go.' But I insist. 'Your office is near the White House,' Sasha says. 'And you are sick. A curfew says that no one must go in the streets.'

I make him give me the papers. 'You go back to the printers, and I will do this.' He's still protesting but I take the papers and walk away down the stairs.

Stepping out from under the arch and into the waiting night, I listen to my feet on the pavement, concentrating

on the sound to keep my mind clear. I give myself instructions. Don't walk down the Garden Ring, it's certain to be
full of soldiers and tanks, roadblocks, and overturned ve-
hicles. Walk through the back streets. I head in towards the
centre, avoiding the yellow pools of streetlights, and the glow
from the windows of buildings. The air smells tense. At one
corner soldiers are massed, their cigarettes flickering in the
dark, but then the next street is deserted. The curfew doesn't
seem to have had much effect. People slide through the
darkness, their shadows flaring across pavements, or up against
walls. Light rain still floats down, but the air is warm and
sticks to my skin. I listen to the scraping of my breath. The
streets are braced, waiting.

I round a corner to find three soldiers on the pavement
opposite. It's too late to turn and go back. I keep my head
down and walk. My mind fills with half-remembered stories
of Soviet prisons, meat-grinders, electric wires, tooth drills,
dazzling lights. A bed like a hospital bed but with leather
straps across it, and below it the black stains of dried blood
on a concrete floor. One of the soldiers shouts at me. Fear
rises in my throat but I look across at him, mumble a
greeting. He nods and I walk on. Don't walk too fast, don't
look as though you're frightened. I wait for him to shout
again but he doesn't. A street appears to my left. I turn into
it and start to breathe again.

As I come out on to the Novyi Arbat, the whirr of a helicopter sounds. Spotlights sweep across the street, crossing and
merging, their translucent ovals highlighting one detail after
another. The air explodes in a rattle of gunfire. The sound
comes from several blocks away, but my feet falter and I press
myself back into the entrance of a shop. Now it starts. Now
people will die. Ahead of me, tanks are clearing roadblocks,
pushing against overturned lorries and cars, shovelling aside

uprooted trees. I need to cross the Garden Ring to get to my college. Because of the river there's no other way. Sasha's faxes crumple under my coat. I hurry along the pavement, keeping close into the buildings. Around me I feel the air pull tight. A ball of fire sails through the air and crashes down into the roof of a building. The junction ahead is crowded with protesters. Feet trample, banners wave and the air throbs with the sounds of idling tank engines.

I'm coughing and shaking, dripping with sweat. For a moment I just want to go home. What I'm doing will make no difference anyway. But I think of Jack and I go on. Voices echo from inside the underpass. An armoured personnel carrier runs out of control, its engine roaring, as it jerks back and forth across the road. Protesters crowd on top of the underpass, hanging over the metal rails. They hurl stones down at the tanks, and throw lighted bottles of petrol. A Russian flag is draped over the side of one wall. Dark figures stand in the path of a tank, smashing at it with metal bars. A tarpaulin is heaved over the edge of the underpass. I watch for a moment, then stumble on across the road and reach the pavement on the other side. I go up to the door of the college building. From behind me I hear shouting, the sound of a horn blaring and the crash of metal against metal.

The code works, the key slips into the lock. I fall into the building and stumble on a pile of post. I go up in the lift, open a door and step into the office. The shadows of cupboards, chairs and rubber plants stand waiting in the dark. Everything here is small, neat, normal. I turn the light on, then switch it off. I flick the button on the fax. It buzzes and clicks, its dial pad glowing green in the dark. I put a chair next to the fax and find a bottle of water. My head bends low as I dial in the glow of the streetlight outside. The numbers are engaged again and again. My fingers lose their way on the keypad. The engaged tone beeps in my head. My eyes are sore and my breath rasps. Occasionally I receive a response, and hear a muffled voice, then the paper starts to scrape through the machine. But after two pages the line always cuts and I don't know whether the sheets have been received or not. Every time I breathe, a sharp pain digs in under my ribs. I watch the dark shapes of the room, and the lights from the street shining up on to the ceiling.

When I'm sure that all the pages must have gone through, I turn off the machine and go to the window. The sky is turning grey at the edges. The air is smoky and helicopters still hover. I look out towards the White House and see a halo of light but the building itself is obscured. As I come out of the door the sound of an explosion blasts into the night, echoed by shouts and screams. From deep inside the underpass, an engine roars. The protesters dangle from the rails above. Gunfire stutters. I cross the road, dodging behind a lorry and a tank. Another explosion rips through the underpass. On the railings above, a man falls, his body twisted, one arm flung out. The crowd around him buckles. The scene is frozen there. The purple sky, the orange glow of the streetlights. The roar of engines. The ebb and flow of the crowd. A petrol bomb sailing like a fiery comet through the sky. Banners dropped in the street. With my hands gripped to the side of my head, I start to run. But I know now that the plotters will not succeed. No amount of tanks and soldiers can win this battle. The people of this city have made up their minds.

Sibirskii Pereulok 1/8, Moscow

August 1991

As I put on my clothes, my limbs feel no more substantial than the air around them. It's early still, and the courtyard is damp with dew. I've only slept two hours but I don't feel tired. I slide my arm firmly into Maya's coat. The day hangs uncertainly between sun and rain. The air is full of rainbow light. People push into the Metro, lost behind blank eyes.

I want to know what happened last night, but the newsstands are empty and that snatch of conversation I'm waiting to overhear doesn't come. Jack will be able to tell me. He'll have listened to the news, or telephoned someone. In the Metro, my foot hovers above the wooden slats of the escalator. I've never got used to the fact that from the top of these escalators you can't see the bottom. I step forward and my stomach turns as I drop down into a brown fog lit by circular, moon lights. Crowds press onto the platform. The train comes in, bringing with it a blast of sweating air. I fight my way into a carriage. Beneath me, the train bounces over the rails. I break into a sweat and start to cough. I pass through station after station − marble pillars, chandeliers, mosaics and statues flash into sight then fade. Surely I'm passing through the same stations again and again?

Then suddenly I emerge at Dobryninskaia and stand staring at the street as though I've never been there before. As I walk the road to Jack's flat, I pass all of Moscow on the way – the tower blocks, the stunted silver birch, the kiosks, the building sites, the blank stretches of sky glimpsed between the concrete outlines of buildings. Occasionally a man or a woman looks into my face, raises a hand, or opens their mouth to call out. I don't have time to listen, and hurry on. The touch of their questioning eyes follows me down the street. I feel as though I'll keep walking past these same scenes for ever. It's like in a cartoon where the characters appear to be running but the same backdrop rolls behind them again and again.

I'm spiralling towards Jack now like water drawn towards a drain. Around me, the streets are blurred by slow summer rain, and the air is clotted with the smell of smog and oil. The lines of buildings sway and expand, as though reflected in water. A street vista opens like a gaping mouth – a sudden dazzle of grey sky and buildings stretching away into the distance.

I have no memory of turning off the main road, or walking down Jack's street, but then suddenly I'm opposite his building. Its cold-eyed windows stare down at me, the few trees around it are parched and ragged. No children play on the swings and slides. Before I key in the code, I repeat it several times in my head. I identify the buttons I'll need to press, memorizing the pattern they make. My fingers shake, but I get it right and the door clicks open. Bags of rubbish are stacked in the green-tiled hall. I wonder how I will get up those four flights of stairs.

My feet move, but they hardly touch the concrete floor. The light is dusty and the building is touched by a strange chill, as though frost has settled there unseen. The silence reverberates, as after the sounding of a bell. I stop on the third-floor landing, my chest heaving. From above, mottled light falls through the glass roof. Jack's door is shut. I move forward, lay my hand against the green paintwork. The door opens and the corridor narrows ahead of me. I step into the hall and move forward to his door.

And there he is – sitting in an armchair by the window. And this is all exactly as it's meant to be. Time has folded in on itself, and I'm back at the *dacha*, standing on the veranda, and the whole day stretches ahead of us. Time to walk down to the standpipe and fill the bucket, or watch the yellow flowers, or light candles in that damp sitting room, which smells of earth and wax.

I step forward. The silence holds words on the tip of its tongue. Jack's head is leaning back, exposing his throat. On his chin is a tiny smear of blood where he's cut himself shaving. His glasses are propped on the bridge of his nose, his lips slightly parted. His legs are stretched out in front of him, crossed at the ankles. One hand hangs down beside him. My eyes trace the folds of his blue shirt, the edge of one cuff which has come undone. A spectrum of light shines in on him through the sun and rain at the window. I move towards him and take hold of that dangling hand. I want to fold his fingers up in mine, but his hand is cold.

I step back from him. He's ill, I say to myself. Then I say it again to make sure I've understood. I need to look after him and make him better. It'll be difficult, but I can do it. Soon I'll make everything all right. I issue instructions to myself. *First you must make sure that he's warm.* I pull pillows from the bed and then lay a blanket over him, tucking it in all around.

I straighten his glasses and lift his head, feeling the thickness of his hair. I slide a pillow under his head. My finger runs down over his cheekbone, and I bend to kiss his lips. I tell him that he'll be warm soon, that everything will be all right. *Now you must make him a cup of tea.* I go behind the screen and struggle to pick up the kettle. My skin is flooded with sweat and I tug myself out of Maya's coat, leaving it draped over a chair.

The few things in front of me – my wrist, the kettle, the cups – seem like objects exhibited in a museum case, or projected on to a large screen. They're spectacular in their lack of significance. I light the gas, find a bowl and a cloth. I fill the bowl with warm water and go back to him. Everything will be all right-white-height. Gently I wipe around his wrists, rubbing the warm water into each of his fingers and the palm of his hand. I wipe the bruise on the inside of his middle finger where his pen would normally rest. He will soon be warm. I move around to wash his other hand, running the warm cloth along the ridges of his fingers and the pad of his thumb. Then I wash his face, run the cloth across his lips and over his eyes, then below his ears and his neck. In a minute he will wake.

I go into the bathroom to fetch a towel. White-right-sight-light. How strange that this flat is suddenly cold as midwinter. A syringe lies next to his watch and razor, on the side of the sink. I look up at the one window in the bathroom – a tiny square high up in the wall filled by opaque glass. A pipe runs down the wall near the sink. I notice that it has a strange curve to it. The tiles on the wall are crooked. My hands, as they stretch out to pick up a towel, have become as large as dinner-plates. *You must go back to Jack and make sure that he's warm. You have to look after him, you have to be there when he wakes.* I repeat these instructions again and again. But the syringe is burning on the white ceramic surface. And on a shelf below the shaving mirror stand two tiny bottles, their reflection doubled in the mirror behind them.

I stare at his wristwatch, lying on its side, the second hand climbing around the face. You must pack up his things for him so you can take him away from here. But I can't keep control of my eyes. They escape and fix on that syringe, on the narrow gleam of the needle, the figures marked on the tube. My fingers close around a bottle. I turn it upside down. It's empty and drops with a clatter into the sink. I try the other bottle. Empty.

The crack is so loud that it sounds as though the crust of the earth has broken. The child sees her father go down. She shouts, Dad, Dad, Dad. He will drown, with black water filling his mouth, his fingers slipping against sharp-edged ice. The child knows that she must help him, but fear holds her still. Behind her, she hears screams ripped from her mother's throat. Feet scrabble on the icy path beside the lake. The planks of the jetty clatter. In the freezing air, each sound is distinct. Dad, Dad, Dad.

A sucking noise and then a splash. Far out across the lake a form rises, falls, rises. Shaggy and slow-moving, it is blurred by fronds of weed. Again a splash, and that shape is struggling towards the far bank. One leg detaches from that shape and lifts, rises above the ice. The child knows that soon her father will be safe. He is in shallow water, he can make it to the bank. She watches his figure rise and fall, struggling through weed and broken ice.

And then it happens – the child stares down at her feet and finds them resting on ice. Shock jolts through her. Surely she hasn't come out across the ice? Surely she didn't follow him? She wouldn't do that, she knows that ice is dangerous. But her head turns and all around her is nothing but air. She's far from the jetty, far from the boathouse, far from her father, far from the star-sprinkled sky.

She stands in an infinite space, attached to nothing except the ice. She looks back towards the bank and sees a shadow, hears her mother screaming.

Oh, she thinks, it's me. It's me. I am the person on the ice. I should never have followed him. I knew that I must never go near the lake. But someone will come, they will come soon. She slides one foot forward, just an inch. The ice is covered with a sprinkling of snow. Underneath is transparent blackness, deep without end. All is quiet and the child holds the stillness inside her head. Someone will come soon. Her father, her mother. They will come.

A ripple, the faintest movement. A creak as though a door is blowing in the wind. Another ripple, something shifting, then settling again. She feels it in the soles of her feet. Above her, the moon and stars waver. Her mouth opens ready to shout, but her lungs fill with a rush of cold air. The creaking is quiet, a slow easing. Her foot moves, ready to run. Then a crack and the stars jerk back over her head. The darkness grips her legs and tugs her down. The cold of the water scalds her. The ribbon of the cloak cuts into her neck. Her body collapses as the cold presses into it. Her hands push against the yielding water. The sliding mass of the cloak clings to her face. Air is shocked from her lungs, bubbles rise around her. Her head will burst. She reaches up, her fingers scrabbling against a wall which has no shape, no edges. Help me, help me. She thought that her father would die, but she is the one who is going to die. Her hands scratch, her nails break. She can't grip, she is falling.

Down, down. Warmth floods through her. She is suspended in light. All is still. Her hands float above her through the water. They swell with a gentle heat. The water is dissolving her, soaking through every sinew. All around her, the light increases. It welcomes her. She wants to be absorbed into that light, to be lost in it. Somewhere far above, people scurry back and forwards, like ants, along the side of the lake. They scream, their arms wave, their hands are pressed against their mouths. A ladder is lifted down from the wall of the boathouse. *Torches are carried through the woods to the banks of the lake. Their light dances in the trees and spills across the ice.*

The child wants to leave those people behind and stay in the warmth and the light. This is the place her father told her about, the place he was going to take her to. A turquoise and gold beach, a place where the sun's rays spread like the spokes of a wheel. Dad, Dad. I'm waiting for you. Take me there.

12/20 rue de Lausanne, Geneva

December 1991

Silence. His pen has stopped. My bloodless fingers uncrumple. I sit back, raise my shoulders and stretch my arms. The words are all out. I've set this story free. I look around this pale apartment – unwashed plates on the floor, clothes strewn across chairs. I listen to the noises of the building. The lift sighs up and down its shaft, someone is running a bath, a small dog yaps. I yawn and stare down at my pyjamas and cardigan. When did I last sleep? I'm so tired I can hardly stand. This feels like putting down a heavy bag.

Tears come suddenly and I welcome them. I know now how high the cost of unshed tears can be. If you don't grieve for someone properly, then in future you'll make someone else stand in their place.

I pull open the window and breathe in the winter air. It tastes of pine trees and mountains. Sharp as peppermint, it clears the nose and lungs. Could there actually be more air here than in other cities? Strange that I never noticed it before. I go to the kitchen, sobbing noisily, my eyes and nose running. I slop milk into my tea and it gathers in lumps. I fling the tea down the sink, sob, wipe at my eyes, and go to the bedroom to put on my clothes. I can't find socks but I put on Wellington boots.

Outside, the day is giddy with wind and splatters of rain.
Soggy leaves and stray paper bags drift along the pavement.
I start to enjoy the brisk wind on my face, but I can't allow
myself that. It feels like betrayal. I'm insulted by my own
capacity for rejuvenation. I was never going to enjoy anything
again. I stamp down the pavement in my Wellingtons, still
crying. Clouds scurry across a low sky. I buy milk, bread,
tinned soup, cheese and oranges. Then I walk down to the
lake and stare out at its receding lines of blue and grey. In
the far distance, a line of sun touches the water.

I lay my hand on the metal rail and savour the feel of its
cold, chipped paint. The wind catches at my coat, and creeps
in under my scarf. I take off a Wellington boot and put my
foot on the wet tarmac. Taking off the other boot, I walk
a few steps. My feet are icy, the stones of the tarmac deli-
ciously sharp. I move my foot back and forwards, heel toe,
heel toe. I feel the geometry of my leg muscles shift. The
earth is satisfyingly firm beneath me. Heel toe, heel toe. The
wind buffets at me, tugging at my bare ankles. A man in a
suit walks past, trying not to stare.

I go back to the flat, warm a tin of soup and eat it with
some bread. Then I wander into the hall. Jack's things are
still spread all over the floor, just where I left them – when?
Weeks ago. His sea-shell paperweight, the tin which
contained the shortbread I gave him. I kneel down on the
floor, bury my face in his overcoat. It's only now I begin
to understand that he's gone. I find that brown envelope
postmarked 23 August 1991 – the information he said he'd
get for me. The last piece of the puzzle. Except it doesn't
seem important now.

The envelope contains a blurred photocopy of a page
from a magazine. In one corner the date has been underlined – *December 1966*. Two asterisks have been scratched in

Biro next to an article beneath it. The text is so faded I can hardly read it. *The planet Venus . . . completing its eight-year cycle . . . 6 January . . . a planet associated with reconciliation and renewal . . . sometimes called the bearer of light.* So that was what my father was looking for that night. In his diseased mind, he thought that he could become like a Mayan shaman and harness the power of Venus. To bring a star down to earth, to find peace inside his own head. I stare at the paper again. As so often, Jack was right. But my question is – how could Jack have understood my father when he'd never even met him?

I open one of his cardboard files which is lying on the floor. Inside are faded photographs, documents on yellowed paper, letters written in Cyrillic script. On a list of names I find one underlined in pencil, marked with a star. I manage to decipher the letterhead. These papers relate to an asylum. Not a place where Jack worked recently, a place from long ago. Was he trying to find out where his mother died? My story. His story. The two may be more similar than I ever understood. Both of us searching for the past. All those Katias and Svetlanas. Layers of yearning. Did they take him back, however briefly, to some moment of perfect love? Perhaps Jack needed to save me in order to save himself?

The truth is that I never knew him.

The thought comes at me sideways. It has the lemon-sharp sting of revelation. I turn it over in my mind. I loved him, I'm sure I did. But I didn't know him. His words come back to me – *love such as yours doesn't respect the person who is loved.* I remember that last day at the *dacha*. He was dying, and yet he comforted me, and I never really saw what was happening to him. Some words of my mother's drift back to me. *If you love someone you see them just as they are.* I didn't want to listen when she said that. Maya's version of my father was so much easier to accept. But finally it was my mother who knew my father. Maya merely loved him.

I pick up one of his notebooks. I turn the pages and see my name. Eva, Eva, Eva. I shut the notebook then open it again. Every word is about me. I always thought that I was the lover and he the beloved, that I kissed while he turned his cheek, but maybe it was always the other way around.

An image comes into my head of a globe, and voices are shouting from everywhere, and pleading hands are raised – *love me, love me, love me.* But next to every single one of those pleading people there's someone who loves them but the pleading person never sees. They just go on and on, shouting, stretching out their hands. It's so much easier to give love than to receive it. I think of Sasha, and his *I don't have any shelf to put that on.*

As I move through the flat, I become aware that something extraordinary is happening. I'm alive now as I've never been before. The truth is energy, it is life. The kitchen table, the tiled floor, the wide windows and white walls – everything is exaggerated, enchanted. It's as though I'm seeing it all for the first time. In the bathroom, I look in the mirror and, for a moment, I see the shadow of Jack's face behind my eyes. And both of our faces are like that day at the Church of the Resurrection – luminous, immediate, exalted. I've spent all of my life locked in my own head and yet it's only now that I know myself. I am here, I am here. Welcome home.

I go back into the sitting room, trying to keep a hold of this feeling. I flick through this pile of paper on my desk, each page scrawled with knitted words. Changes are written crooked in the margin, asterisks and arrows dig into the paper. I think of Mr Balashov, weeping over his wife's scraps of coloured wool and her magnifying glass. He had his grief, this is mine. *Once a feeling becomes a word, then we are released from its grip.* And somehow, without my knowing it, the words did turn into a story. My story. Me. And it isn't just the truth I can bear. It's all of the truth. Because Jack would have expected no less.

And something more – some other change – has happened while I've been writing. I can't say that a pattern has emerged, but now that I've stopped trying to explain that time in Moscow, it has started to explain itself. The answer is not a blurred photocopy in an envelope, nor a mathematical equation or an intellectual argument. Instead it's the feeling of spiky tarmac, the wind flickering against my ankles, the rain under the sole of my foot.

30/16 Ulitsa Pravdy, Moscow

August 1991

The body breaks when the mind won't. Jack and I – we were both of us dead. I lay in that carpet-covered Moscow bedroom, still as a corpse. Why didn't he take me with him? A wedge of yellow light widened and then narrowed as the bedroom door moved back and forth, clicked open and shut.

Sasha, Vladimir, Bill. Voices told the story of the coup again and again. How they waited at the White House for the attack. How women and children were sent home. A blackout was imposed. But then the coup leaders lost their nerve, fled. Then Gorbachev came back from the Crimea. This story was repeated until it could be believed, until it was real and the mind could digest it.

Sasha came, brought me a bowl of soup. He told me the faxes had gone through and that the newspaper had been produced in Voronezh and Nizhnii Novgorod. 'What you did,' he said, 'it was very brave.' I woke and slept, woke and slept. Gathered my limbs together under the duvet, stuck my fingernails into my leg to check I was still there. Brave. Everyone said that, while the light at the window changed from day to night and back again. A journalist friend of Rob's wanted to interview me. But bravery, I thought, implies choice. And wherever I was that night, I was in a place far beyond choice. And yet still they said it. I'd become a heroine by accident.

Rob's face appeared sometimes in the numb haze which surrounded me. His eyes hid from mine and he said nothing about bravery. Some fragment of memory from the night of the coup came into my mind. We'd been standing in the kitchen. His hand had gripped the collar of my shirt. His face was close to mine. *Eva, where were you? What were you doing? You shouldn't have gone out. You were crazy to go anywhere near that place. How could you? How could you?* Amnesia-Rhodesia-catfever. Water splashing over the side of a sink. I had nearly become a woman who involved herself in politics in a way that was inappropriate. Above me, the five-armed lamp swayed and contracted like the tentacles of an octopus. Did that scene in the kitchen ever happen?

I slept and woke to find Bill bringing me some bread and cheese. I knew, although I couldn't have said how, that Sarah had left him and gone back to America. His trainers were dirty and his smile brutal. A glass of vodka seemed to have become part of his left hand.

'Wasn't there shooting?' I said to him. 'And someone was killed?'

'Yes,' he said. 'Three people were killed. God only knows how it wasn't more. A man was crushed right under a tank and another brought down by a ricochet bullet. Outside the American Embassy – that's where the worst fighting was. But you know for me,' Bill said, 'the strangest thing was that no one here really knew what was happening. There you are, right in the middle of the damned thing, and you don't have a clue. Truth is, I spent most of my time on the phone to New York trying to find out what was going on. And, you know, that's why the coup failed. The plotters should have cut the power, or the international tele-phone lines. They didn't understand that they needed to control information.'

Rob was dismantling our lives, packing our books, bundling clothes into boxes, taking pictures down from the wall. We talked briefly about whether he should try to change the flights. Would I be well enough to travel? I couldn't think why he was talking about flights. What did that matter? He decided to leave the flights as they were. Above me, the five-armed light dissolved and reformed. I heard Rob on the telephone. Who was he talking to? My mother? He seemed to be repeating the same words again and again, and his voice had a serrated edge. For a moment I felt the whole flat falling away from us. I opened my mouth to shout at Rob, 'Take care, take care.' But no words came and I dropped back against the pillow, helpless.

The radio crackled, cut into silence, then a voice reported that the Communist Party had been banned and the head-quarters of the KGB had been sealed off. The people working there had been told to leave, the building was being searched. The reporter described a statue of Dzerzhinskii, the founder of the KGB, standing in Lubianskaia Ploshchad'. It was being covered in a net of ropes and men were hacking at it with metal cutting equipment. A crowd had gathered, chanting, waiting for the statue to fall.

I woke and blue evening light shone at the window. Rob was sitting on a chair near the bed, reading a book. I watched his down-turned eyes flicking over the words. His hand moved to turn a page. His shoulders, his spine, his head, were twisted up, like pieces of metal after a car accident. A bottle of vodka stood on the floor beside him and he reached down and filled his glass. He looked up and saw me watching him. Are you OK? Yes, I'm fine. And you? How are you? Fine, fine, how are you? But that old refrain could do nothing for us now.

With a sudden clarity I understood that he knew about the party and the lake and the ice. I said, 'You talked to my mother?' And he said, 'Yes, I did.' And we sat in the half-darkness, staring at each other with horror growing in the reflected light of our eyes.

'Your father nearly killed you,' Rob said. 'He took you out onto a frozen lake. But your mother never told you that, and she never told me. I didn't even know he was a manic depressive. There was always some story about him being ill . . . But what I can't believe is that your mother thought she'd get away with it, and that neither of us would ever find out.'

'I know,' I said. 'Yes, I know.' Rob and I both know. The facts sink through our skin, and right down into the marrow of our bones. But we don't want to know, and the only way to hide from that knowledge is to hide from each other. And really that's how it's always been.

'I asked her the question directly,' Rob went on. 'When you were ill over the summer I rang and I asked her several times, because I'd always wondered. And I said then, "Tell me, is there something specific? Is there something I need to know?"'

I should have walked over to the chair then and gathered him into my arms. Pain brings people together – isn't that how it's meant to be? I knew that it was worse for Rob than for me. I'd probably always known, at some level, that my mother would lie to me, but Rob had believed in her entirely. I watched him shift in his chair – that twist in his body, that wince which he suppressed. For him, the world had always been so simple. On one side stood the dramatic and unreliable – my father, his mother, Maya. And then on the other side stood the good woman, my mother. But now the plastic soldiers had all been mown down and lay scattered on the carpet.

'I thought that the truth would somehow be splendid,' I said. 'I thought it would be spectacular.' Those were my words, but I wondered even as I spoke what I had really expected. After all, whoever heard of a happy secret? The human mind is so very ingenious in its unending games of hide and seek. I looked at Rob and knew how it must be for him, and I wanted to save him from it, but it was already too late. Far too late. From that night when I'd first met Jack, when he'd touched my spine, questions had started and now they could never be stopped.

Rob and I talked then about who was to blame for what happened that night. My father took me out onto a frozen lake. Maya encouraged me to follow him. My mother failed to stand up to Maya. For a moment we found comfort in this dry analysis, but our words soon stuttered and came to a halt. Apportioning blame was only a way of denying the pain my parents must have lived through. All we knew for sure was that my mother shouldn't have lied to me afterwards. But how do you tell your daughter that her father nearly killed her?

'But your mother must have known,' Rob said. 'She must have known what the effect of that lie would be.'

'I don't know. She was frightened I'd finish up like my father. But I'm not ill, and I never have been. I don't even have asthma. All I've ever suffered from are the effects of living in a world where the truth couldn't be spoken.'

Rob stood up and moved over to the bed. We wanted to hug then, or kiss, but both of us felt so tainted that we couldn't bear to touch. It seemed that the whole of our relationship had been based on some misunderstanding. We were neither of us the same people we had been before. So Rob turned away and continued to pack shoes into a box. What else was there to do? We needed to move on. Impermanence was the only home we knew. I saw myself walking through the ungrasped days in yet another city, waiting endlessly to turn a certain corner, waiting to think, Oh yes, this is it, the place where I was always meant to be.

Our lives went on, driven by the necessities of each day. And all the time I wanted to help Rob, or at least to talk. Even to say honestly that I had no help to offer. But we were held in an ancient silence, trained from childhood not to know, not to see. We lacked the vocabulary of emotion. Our minds were heavy with shame. We'd been failed, but we'd also failed each other.

Rob, who had always been so vigorous, moved slowly through the flat. He held a tie or a book in his hand and stared at it. Standing at the window, he looked down into the courtyard with unseeing eyes. He lost the ability to take small decisions. Was it worth taking the bookshelves with us or should we buy new ones later? The discussion about that went back and forth. Yes, no, yes, no. What did I think? What should we do? In Rob's voice I heard a rising note of panic.

One endless night as we lay in bed, side by side, not touching, he turned to me and said, 'You know, you've been very brave.'

'What – the faxes?' But I knew he didn't mean the faxes.

Then again, later, he said, 'I understand it now. When I was a child, and I came to stay with you, my father would always say, "Take care of Katarina and Eva now, won't you?

Be sure to take care of them." But I just thought it was
something he said.'

One morning Rob was on the telephone, making calls for
more than an hour. I listened to the radio. The celebration
was over now and the hangover had set in. The radio reports
pointed out that only fifty thousand people had defended
the White House, which was nothing in a city of ten million.
Then it was rumoured that Gorbachev had organized the
coup himself in order to flush out the right wing. Perhaps
more food was now on offer in the shops, but inflation
meant that people couldn't afford to buy it.

Rob came into the bedroom bringing a cup of tea.
'Listen, Eva. We're not going to Zagreb.'

'Why? What happened?'

'I decided against it. But it's a bit complicated. They'll
give me a post in Geneva instead, but I have to go to Zagreb
until Christmas, until they can appoint someone to the post
there.'

'Geneva?' I thought of small dogs, pen-knives, money
laundering.

He shrugged, put some papers down on the top of a case,
and began to push it shut. 'Actually, I think it might be quite
interesting. But the problem is, they won't let you go to
Zagreb.'

'Oh. OK. Yes, I see.'

The moment had arrived when I needed to stop all this.
I had a reason to do it now. Rob hadn't helped me when
he should have done. He'd believed in my mother instead
of me. I had a perfect right to say, Actually, you can go to
Zagreb, or Geneva, or wherever, but I'm not going with
you. But I couldn't summon up the courage to hurt him.
I couldn't bear to see him brought down. I wanted to make

him into the person he'd been before. I'd lost two men I loved and I couldn't lose a third. For better or worse, he was all that was left.

And then the phone rang and it was someone from Geneva. They'd heard that Rob was moving there and they wanted to know if he'd like to take over the lease of their flat. It was a one-bedroom flat in a 1950s' building with a view over the lake, not far from the centre, light and spacious, in good repair. He'd get it painted for us when he moved out. Rob said, 'Sounds quite good, what do you think?'

Buy a flatpack life, read the instructions and fix it together with an Allen key. I should be able to manage that, I thought. I've done it often enough before. Geneva sounded as good a place as any for a posthumous life. So Rob booked me a flight and he organized for our boxes to be sent there. Shake up the world and pick out a city. Hope that when you arrive you won't find yourself there.

I woke to hear a voice with a long American drawl. Harvey. I pulled myself further down under the sheets. Rob's voice in the kitchen was muffled. I heard the clink of china. Then that brash voice again. 'You know, we're moving on as well. Going back to Massachusetts. We'd have gone in two years anyway, but this recent upset . . . No, no, thanks. Sugar but no milk.'

Then I heard – Jack Flame. I sat up in bed.

'Oh, I'm sorry. Didn't you know?' A cough, a shuffle, the clatter of a cup. 'At first they thought he'd just committed suicide, but now they think he was killed. Murdered. Someone else had been in the flat. Seems he had information which somebody wanted and they were even prepared to kill for it.'

I was out of bed, listening at the door, but Harvey had

moved back towards the kitchen. I leant my head against
the frame of the door. It was just as Jack said: *There's nothing
as mysterious as someone with nothing to hide.* People believe
in incredible stories when the real ones are too hard to
accept. Even in death Jack was distrusted and misunderstood. Harvey's voice sounded again, as he emerged into the
hall. I could see his broad back in its well-cut suit. 'Of course,
you know that wasn't his real name? No one ever thought
it was.'

Rob and Harvey were standing with their backs still
turned. 'Now you must give me your address in Geneva.
Maya won't forgive me if I don't get that address.'

Rob went into the sitting room, searching for a pencil.

'Oh, and I nearly forgot,' Harvey said. 'Eva left this coat
last time she was around at our place.' I saw the coat as he
lifted it from the bag. The top of it was stiff as though a
person might still be inside it. I pulled my head back from
the door. I hadn't left that coat at Maya's flat. I'd left it on
a chair near where Jack lay. Why did Harvey have it now?

My mind was running towards a precipice. I watched it,
but there was no way I could stop it. I flung myself back
into bed and lay with my arms wrapped around my head,
my face pushed into a pillow. I was trying not to think
about anything at all, but words pushed through to the front
of my mind. All the time I had thought that Jack was the
one living on borrowed time – but really it was me. I should
have died twenty-five years ago. My life had ended then.

In the kitchen, rubbish bags bulged beside the bin. The nails
were still in the walls where our few pictures had hung.
Rob and I were ready to go, but we still had an hour to
wait. My flight to Geneva was earlier than Rob's plane to
Zagreb and so he'd arranged separate taxis.

The sitting-room curtains, which Rob had taken down when he arrived, had been put back up. The bottoms of them hung six inches above the windowsill. A stain, no different from all the other stains, marked the carpet near the armchair where Rob had spilt a glass of red wine. Fluff lurked on the carpet behind the chairs. On the windowsill, circular stains marked where my pot plants had stood.

Mr Balashov came down and said that he wanted to show me something before I left. I trailed up the stairs after him. He'd been arranging things, tidying up. A little of the junk had gone and he had dusted and cleaned. Mrs Balashova's bottles of pills were ranged neatly on the table. The blanket which had covered her chair had been pulled straight. On a low table near the television, a range of objects were laid out as though exhibited in a museum. Her knitting was there, carefully wrapped up so that the stitches wouldn't slide from the needles, along with rings and her watch. A magnifying glass lay next to a pair of diamanté earrings. Different coloured wools were twined around folded scraps of cardboard.

Mr Balashov gave me two tiny dolls, a man and a woman, stitched together. I realised from the miniature veil which the female doll wore that they must be getting married. I kissed him goodbye, suddenly wanting to cling to him. Then I wrapped the dolls in my handkerchief and put them in my bag – the one souvenir of Moscow I'd always keep.

I went back downstairs and walked through the four rooms of the flat saying goodbye to each of them. The table where Rob and I had eaten so many suppers was wiped clean and pushed against the wall. The corner of a note remained stuck on the door of the fridge under a slanting strip of Sellotape. In the bathroom, steam still hissed from that defective tap and the mirror was still propped on the sink at that same drunken angle. The doors to the balcony were shut and the junk which had always lived there was back in its place. In a panic I searched for us, for Rob and me. Our feelings, our words, must be somewhere, encrypted into the walls or hidden behind the doors. But no, this was just a flat – tables, windows, doors, a bed.

We walked through the flat again and again. Both of us longed to be gone and we longed to stay. We had had all the conversations we could possibly have. Yes, I did have my passport. Yes, I knew the address in Geneva where I needed to pick up the keys. Yes, it would probably take some time to get the phone in Geneva put into my name but, of course, we'd keep in touch. Yes, I had the address of the office in Zagreb.

We stood near the sitting-room window, staring down into the courtyard. 'You know,' Rob said, 'I'm going to have to phone your mother. I left things unclear. Practical things . . .'

'Like what?' I was running my finger around the circular stains on the windowsill.

'Well, you know, she's probably still organizing things.' I looked up and saw him searching for words. For a moment, I imagined my mother in her sewing room, pins held in her pursed lips. She was hurriedly sewing seed pearls on to a cream satin dress. This time the curve of the neck would be absolutely even, this time she would get it right.

'Perhaps I should just say we're going to delay?' Rob said. 'Because, after all, it'll be hard to sort things out while I'm away.'

'Yes, why don't you do that? That's a good idea.'

I thought back to that evening nearly a year ago when he'd asked me to marry him. And I'd sat at the kitchen table turning that coin in my hand. Heads, tails, heads, tails. Surely something must have changed since then? But it hadn't done.

Down below, I saw the taxi man waiting for me under the arch. 'I must go.' We stood staring at each other. Surely all this must come to some conclusion? But no. We kissed each other with an awkward shuffle of cheeks, and arms and knees. And, like people in an unconvincing play, we said, See you soon, I'll miss you, not long to wait. And Rob stood watching me go down the stairs, and inside I was weeping for him, and for us, and for the wretched pointlessness of it all. But all I could do was turn back to him, summon a smile, raise my hand, wave.

12/20 rue de Lausanne, Geneva

December 1991

So this is grief. It rips through me again and again, shaking everything loose. From one day to the next I can make no prediction of what it might do. Sometimes I weep until I'm dry of tears. On other days I'm fired with a fragile energy. His death was not all sadness, there was beauty in it as well.

I telephone a former colleague who now works for the British Council in London. He says, 'Of course, for someone with your qualifications there are always jobs available.' He knows of possible openings in Lima, Sucre, La Paz. I tell him that I'm most interested in La Paz. That's somewhere I haven't been before. He asks me to fax an updated CV and ring back in a week. I go to the travel agent to look at the price of tickets, but it's closed so I sit on the doorstep in the rain, and wail for an hour. I had no idea that grief would be so capricious and impure.

My body feels small and empty. Jack is like some internal organ – heart, kidney, or liver – which has been ripped out of me. I lie in bed cuddling a hot-water bottle just for something to hold. The future pursues me like a persistent man trying to recover a debt. I need to decide something. For three days I spend every hour redoing my CV. The process feels like wading through treacle. I scream at the concierge when she presses me about some service-charge bill which hasn't been paid. To me, it feels as though I'm shot through with bullet-holes, so why doesn't this woman see? Why is she bothering me about a bill? I want to wear mourning so that people will know that they need to treat me differently.

But then, by the next morning, that strange energy has returned and I think, Jack died, so what? Everybody dies some time. What does it really matter? There are things I must sort out, decisions to be made. I can't just keep wandering around this flat waiting for each day to turn itself from the present into the past. I plug the phone back in, and look through a pile of post which lies on the sofa.

I find three letters from Rob and open the one with the most recent postmark. It turns out that he's going to be back in less than a week. The letter doesn't say much more than that, but there's something comforting in his bold, even writing. But I'm going to La Paz. I mustn't allow myself to be drawn back into his world. I open up the other two letters. *You'll never guess what,* one of them says, *but the man in the flat next door has got a smelly, slobbering Dobermann which sits on our doorstep. Home from home?* I shove the letter back into its envelope. I've got a lot of things to organize. I look at flight prices, and find that once I've bought my plane ticket I'll have only fifty dollars left. I consider getting in touch with Uncle Guy because he's the only person I know who'd write me a large cheque with no questions asked. But I can't ask him for money so that I can leave his son.

I feel my nerve failing, but I convince myself that this plan will work out somehow. Jack comes to seem like a powerful force inside me. When I'm frightened, I summon him up and he gives me the strength to go on. I know now that I need to wring every last bit of life out of each day. I need to live because he can't. I'd never have thought it possible to have such an intense relationship with someone who is dead. I'm going to make something out of my life for him and for me. I'm going to turn what happened to us into something more than a series of random events. We suffer losses in order that we may know the full value of what's left behind. So simple, but I never saw it before.

In two days Rob will come back. I telephoned about the La Paz job. The man at the British Council said that, if he recommends me for the job, then there should be no problem, but he won't know anything more for another week. I don't want to be here when Rob arrives, but where else can I go? I have keys for Uncle Guy's flats in both London and Paris but, if I spend money getting to either of those places, then I won't have enough for the flight to La Paz.

And still Jack's boxes are in the flat. I need to get rid of them before Rob gets back. Jack said he wanted them burnt. There's an attractive drama to that idea but the reality is more complicated. This flat has no fireplace and, in this country, if I burn boxes in the gardens, I'll probably be sentenced to five years in prison. I'll have to move the boxes down into the lobby, then hire a car and drive them to somewhere outside Geneva.

I feel Jack inside me and I know that together we're going to do this. I start to move the boxes, sliding them along the floor and edging them into the lift. I move two downstairs and then go back for more. A box is shunted out of the lift, and pushed to the side of the lobby. I cut my hand on a staple and suck at it to stop the blood. As I'm doing that, an old man comes in through the front door. I can't see him properly but, in the pneumatic swish of the opening door, I have the impression that I heard my name. I look towards him but my ears have tricked me. I bend down again to push at a box. When I look up, the man has moved towards me. He speaks to me and I answer in irritation. How does he know my name? His hand moves up and touches the scarf he wears around his neck.

'I'm sorry,' he says. 'I did try to telephone.'

I turn away and I'm about to head up the stairs. Then I turn back. This isn't right, it isn't right at all. I don't know who this man is. His head is slightly turned to one side but he watches me intently. I can't talk to him now. I'm busy with these boxes, I've got too many things to do.

'I should have written perhaps.'

This scene isn't meant to take place in the half-lit lobby of a block of flats. I've always known how it will happen. I meet him at a railway station where he's getting off a train. The steam from the train clears on the platform and I see him there, and I fling myself into his arms. That is what happens.

'I'm sorry,' he says. 'I've shocked you.'

He should be wearing a grey turtleneck sweater with a cable twist down the front. Instead he's wearing a white shirt and a charcoal-grey suit from twenty years ago. He has white hair and skin burnt brown, his beard is knotted and he walks with a stick. He probably smells of mothballs or hair oil. I do not know him, he shouldn't be here. If this is what it means to be cured, then isn't it better to be ill?

But the normal patterns of behaviour surface. 'You had better come upstairs.' That's what I say, but I don't want him in my flat, or anywhere near me. I want the afternoon to go on just as it was. I need to finish moving these boxes, hire a car, drive out of Geneva. It'll probably be difficult for this old man to get up the stairs, but I can't have him standing beside me in the lift. I've always worried that if this person turned up then he might look like Jack. But he doesn't at all. Not one bit. I place my feet carefully on each step and don't look back. The old man walks behind me and I hear his breath, and the rubber-ended sound of his stick. The door to the flat is half-blocked by Jack's boxes. I sigh as I push one out of the way.

'Would you rather I went away?'

Something in the generosity of his question breaks through my outrage. 'No, no. I'm sorry. Of course not.'

He follows me into the flat. 'Perhaps you'd like some tea?' I walk through to the kitchen.

'You sit down,' he says. 'I'll make the tea.' I take off my coat and hang it on the back of a chair. The old man hooks his stick on the door handle and sets about making tea. He seems undaunted by the task, despite the half-unpacked boxes heaped on every surface. He washes up cups, lights the gas with a match, fills the kettle. He rummages through a half-unpacked box and finds the teapot and a mat. In a trance, I stand and watch him. I keep thinking of things I should say, or feel, but all maps, all patterns, have disintegrated. I see the old man bend towards the stove and, like a shadow inside him, I see my father bending down towards the fireplace in the sitting room at Marsh End House.

I clear aside a few of the glasses which are lined up on the table. I move them carefully but that isn't what I want to do. I want to sweep them all on to the floor and see them smash. I pick one up and move it from hand to hand. The old man lifts boxes from the table, wipes the surface with a cloth, warms the pot, pours the milk into the cups, improvises a tea cosy out of tea towels, wrapping the teapot snugly between them.

Then he sits down, with the teapot next to him, as though this is something he always does. He wants me to sit down but I won't. As always, the grand scene is refusing to take place. I stand by the table, moving the glass from hand to hand. I imagine it smashing on to the kitchen floor, then all of the others following it in a shower of crystal. The old man starts to talk and his voice is all wrong. I remember it as fluid, hasty, unpredictable. Now it's precise and careful, his phrases measured, as though English is a language he has learnt with care. His words are too quiet, so that I find myself leaning closer to him in order to hear. He says he has come on behalf of my mother. She wrote him a letter.

I tell him that I also wrote a letter. He got a letter from Rob, he says. No, I wrote. I wrote. But he didn't get that letter. He's very grateful to me for having written and, of course, he would have replied. When did I send the letter? Ah yes, well he moved house around that time. Where he used to live, right on the Pacific coast, there are often violent storms. My letter would have arrived at around the time when his house was flattened for the second time. Perhaps it was lost, or delivered to what remained of that house. The postal service is not always reliable.

The old man's careful voice continues. Before he left England he had been ill, he had been in a violent state of mind, perhaps I hadn't been told that? The tone of his voice angers me. What is this old man talking about? He doesn't know anything about this. How dare he presume to tell me what happened?

'I know,' I say. 'Before you left England – I know what happened.'

He unwraps the teapot. 'Ah yes.'

'She should have told me,' I say. 'She should have told me.'

'Yes, she should.' His gaze is direct. 'She was mistaken in that.'

My voice conceals a shriek of disgust. 'Mistaken? She fails to look after you properly, and then she lies to me.'

'She didn't throw me out. We both knew, even before that night, that I needed to go. And I did go – the following morning.'

Yes, that's how it happened. He went to Mexico without even saying goodbye, and later the pain was so great that every memory of that night was wiped from my mind. I look down and the glass I'm holding has snapped in two at the stem. I want to throw the remains of it onto the floor but the old man lifts the two pieces neatly out of my hands. He pulls out a chair but still I don't sit down.

'Eva, your mother loved us both.'

I bang my hand down on to the table but despite my anger the action lacks conviction. 'Love? Love? I'm sick of that word. I'm sick of it.' My voice shakes and I put my hand on the side of my head. 'What does anybody mean by that? Everyone claims to have loved everyone else, so how did we finish up unhappy?'

The echo of my voice hangs around us. The old man's eyes blink as he weighs my words. He stirs his tea, places his teaspoon on the saucer, then pours a cup for me. I don't actually want, or expect, an answer to that question but he's going to give me one.

'Perhaps love has to do with the opportunity to set another person free.'

His words silence me. I pull a chair further away from him and sit down. That phrase sounds uncomfortably similar to some of the things my mother said when we sat in her sewing room foolishly looking at wedding dresses. I was so sure she couldn't be right, and I didn't want to hear anything she said. I wanted a perfect father, someone absolute, who could explain me to myself. Now I stare down at my hands and long for the comfort of a simple explanation while knowing there isn't one to be had.

'Well, maybe,' I say. 'Maybe. Perhaps that's what my mother did for you. It's just a shame she didn't do the same for me.'

'Yes. You're right. Of course.' He looks out of the window for a moment, his eyes distant, then he turns back at me. 'But you know, your mother had been through a terrible time. She was trying to speak the truth and no one was listening.'

'Yeah, and I've been asking for the truth and she hasn't been listening.'

He stares at me, his head nodding slowly. 'I know, Eva. I know. Nothing can possibly justify the fact that she didn't tell you what happened. But, you see, children are the hope in our lives. We want them to put the past right, we want to make some better world for them. But sometimes in doing that we deny them a fullness of life.' His hand moves to the side, a small gesture, the palm facing upwards. 'And then circumstances made it easy for her. All knowledge of that night seemed to have been wiped from your mind. And then the path to the lake was closed up. Your mother always meant to tell you, but the right moment just never arrived. The tragedy is that you can make a child believe anything.'

The cup of tea he made for me still sits in front of me. I feel I should start to drink it, but I don't want to allow him any victory. I don't want this old man sitting at my table. What I wanted was my father. He wouldn't have said these things. He loved me, not my mother. He is not drab and careful. He is someone who creates other worlds, and has the power to catch a star in a butterfly net. I look at my watch and find that it's already half past three. I haven't got time for this old man with his slow voice. I need to carry Jack's boxes down the stairs and then finish my packing. In a few days' time I'll be on my way to La Paz.

The old man has seen me looking at my watch. He drains his cup and reaches for his stick. 'Tomorrow I leave early. I'm going to England to see your mother.'

Oh yes, of course, that's what he really wants to do. And perhaps they'll laugh together and walk on the marsh, as they did before I was born. Before the little red devil arrived and wouldn't do what she was told. Never mind that little accident, that little white lie. She's always been rather hysterical, Eva. The old man is going now. He has his coat and scarf on, his stick gripped in his hand. The cup of tea he made for me is going cold on the table. At the front door he stretches out his hand and his fingers brush my arm. 'I'm so very sorry, my dear. I didn't want us to meet again in this way. I can only say, for me . . .'

I pull my arm away, but I'm turning to water inside. He steps out of the door. I ought to touch him, to kiss him, but I don't know how. His stick reaches out, and he fixes the rubber point of it on the floor. I can feel the place on my arm where his fingers touched me. 'You know, I always remember . . . I always remember a day on the beach. And you were so happy. And there was that dog. I think it was the Reynolds's dog and it followed us down the beach. It was a red setter. Do you remember?'

He blinks as he considers that question. 'The beach, of course, I remember the beach. But the dog – I'm not sure.

If it was the Reynolds's dog it wouldn't have been a setter. They never had setters, always Labradors.'

I stare down at one of Jack's boxes, my eyes running over the words on the side scribbled in Cyrillic script. It was a red setter. I know it was a red setter. I want to hold on to the old man's arm and make him say that. Yes, I remember that day. Yes, it was a red setter on the beach.

He puts a hand on my shoulder. 'Oh my dear, my dear . . .'

His hand still rests on my shoulder and we're quite still, on the landing of the flats, close to each other and yet endlessly separate. And it seems as if we'll be like that forever now, frozen by the knowledge of what can never be recovered. A patch of sunlight touches on the tiles by the top of the stairs. From somewhere below, a Hoover whirs. He turns and looks at the boxes spread along the corridor. 'You're trying to move? Let me help you. At least let me do that. I've got some time now. I can carry some things.'

'No, no. It's all right. These aren't my things. I was trying to get rid of them. But anyway, I'd need a car and it's too late now.'

'I have a car. I hired one at the airport.'

I don't want him to have a car. He shouldn't make this possible. I look along the landing at Jack's boxes. 'Really, I need to burn them and it's too late to start that today.'

'To burn them? Oh, I see. Yes – difficult, but by no means impossible. We can do that. I'll go and get the car. And some paraffin, we'll need that. Perhaps a rake.'

Yes, paraffin, he's right, and a rake. I hadn't thought of that. One of Jack's shirts lies spread over a box. For a moment I see him sitting on the bed in Room 815, his hand struggling to do up the button on the cuff of that shirt.

'The boxes belong to someone who is dead.'

'Ah, I see,' the old man says. 'Of course. Perhaps not now, then.'

'Yes, now.' I look up at my father and I know he's going to make this possible. A car, paraffin, a rake. 'Yes, please, if you could help me.' I begin to push papers and books back inside a box. I can do this now because I know that these boxes were not Jack's legacy to me. I don't need the information they contain. Was he a drug trader or a spy? Was it purely a matter of chance that he went to Vilnius just before the conflict there? I realize now that I'm never going to know the answers to those questions and I don't care. He was a man who understood the transforming power of the truth. That's all I need to know.

My father starts to move some of the closed boxes towards the lift. He looks so frail but strangely he seems able to manoeuvre them without much difficulty. I pack away Jack's coat, his shoes, a pile of notebooks. Grief, perhaps, consists mainly of things left unsaid. I begin to understand now that between Jack and me, everything was understood. As I rearrange the contents of a box, I find a square tin and open it. Packed away inside newspaper I find that one family photograph and those two white china cups which, amazingly, have made the journey unscathed. I decide I'll keep those things, as a monument to those lost and perfect moments, with their power to soothe and destroy. And as a reminder of the importance of possessing the past, whatever it may be.

My father's already got eight of the boxes into the lift. All this is going too fast. The lift goes down. I close up the last box and push it out of the door. At the car it seems as though they can't all be made to fit. 'Never mind,' I say, 'it doesn't matter. I could keep some of them. Or I could leave it and do it tomorrow.' But my father gets them out of the car, then loads them again, fitting them neatly together as though doing a puzzle. When that's done, he sends me upstairs to get some newspaper and then we get into the car. I feel too close to him but he doesn't smell of mothballs or hair oil. Instead he smells of beaches and sun. He tells me that he spent some time in Geneva as a young man. I never knew that. He suggests that we should drive up into the mountains, to the wine villages.

As we head out of town through the rush-hour traffic, he stalls the car twice and lets it rabbit hop across a junction. Despite myself, I start to laugh and he laughs as well. It's more than ten years since he's driven a car, he says. I tell him that the boxes we're going to burn belonged to a man called Flame, and suddenly that's riotously funny. We stop at an out-of-town hardware store and buy paraffin and a rake. My father is wide-eyed amidst the slug repellent, bird-boxes and coils of wire. He says isn't it convenient for people now, the way they can buy all these things by just giving the cashier a card.

Soon we're in a land of stone farmhouses and fields etched with row upon row of leafless vines. Frost has turned the land white. I consider conversations I should start, but they are all so large that they keep me silent. I open the window so that I can breathe in the spacious mountain air. I find it exhilarating to be somewhere else, in a car, travelling. Oh yes, I'd forgotten, there's a whole world out here. My father is concentrating on finding a place to burn the boxes, but it isn't easy because there are few turnings off the main lanes. He drives down a track, reverses, then explores another unmade road which leads to two barns. He discusses the merits of various options. I'm shivering inside and my hands fidget. I feel the weight of Jack's boxes behind us. This is all a bad idea. It's too late in the day, none of these

places are right; something will come along to save me from
this.

Finally we settle on a place at the end of a track, near
the entrance to a wood. Smoke rises from the chimney of
a cottage nearby, but the land here is overgrown and unused.
We heave the boxes from the car and try to pile them up.
Despite the cold, we're soon sweating and puffing, our
muscles pulled, our hands dry from the cardboard. I can't
lift the boxes high so they finish up in a spreading heap but
my father picks a couple of them up and piles them on top.
Then he screws up pieces of newspaper and pushes them
in between the boxes. Picking up the tin of paraffin, he
looks at me for permission. For a moment I nearly put out
my hand to stop him, but these events have taken on a
purpose of their own and are outside my control.

My father heaves the canister up and soaks each box in
turn. He takes the matches and lights the corner of a box.
The flames begin to eat their way into the cardboard, flaring
higher and higher. Blue and then orange, they splutter and
leap. I feel their light on my face. The boxes turn black,
their shape disintegrating. I imagine tongues of flame wrapping around Jack's notebooks, licking at the collars of his
shirts. The heat touches my cheek and warms my hands.
The flames leap high, blurring the air all around.

But then, quite soon, they begin to die, and my father
and I sit down on a tree trunk and watch as they flicker
lower and lower. The light is changing from white to grey.
Frost is closing its grip. Later tonight – or perhaps tomorrow
– there'll be snow. The cold bites through my boots. My
father sits silently, watching the flames. They die but not
everything is burnt. The corner of one box remains, the
spines of books, pieces of cloth. I stare down into the embers
and see Jack's glasses. The frames are twisted, the glass melted,

but the wire structure still holds them in shape. I feel a sudden desire to reach down into the smouldering heat and take them out. I want to touch them, to hold them to me.

My father has fetched the rake from the car. He uses it to draw pieces of cardboard in from the outside of the fire, and makes a pile of all that remains. Then he sloshes paraffin over that pile and throws a match down into it. He's not going to stop until everything is burnt. He understands the importance of properly settling the dead. Flames flare again but they're uncertain and gentle now. Around us, the light has abandoned the fields. An owl hoots from the woods. I'm stiff with cold and aching with tiredness. This day has gone on much too long.

I sit down on the tree trunk with my hands gripped together. In the darkness my father rakes through the ashes, pours paraffin, lights matches, rakes again. Still the metal skeleton of the glasses remains. He picks it up on the end of the rake and lays it down on the grass beside the canister. I sit and watch him, shivering. Finally only a mound of ash remains at the centre of the grey scar in the grass. My father rakes the ash out so that the earth is flat again.

Everything is finished now. There's nothing more to be done. My father picks up the wire of the glasses and puts it in his coat pocket. I sit on the tree trunk staring at the place where the fire was. Slowly tears gather and roll down my cheeks. But I hear Jack's voice: *Don't live on secondhand emotions.* And so I admit to myself that I'm not grieving now for him. I'm grieving because this is the beginning of the end of my grief.

We drive downhill, heading back to Geneva. The boxless space around us feels infinite. The night is deep and starless. Car headlights flicker on the windscreen. Rain clatters like a round of applause. My father turns on the wipers and they creak across the glass, scattering fragments of light. He says perhaps I won't mind stopping at his hotel, as he has something to give me.

He's staying in one of those small hotels, hidden away in a back street, which exist in every city. A glass door jangles as you open it, the corridors are narrow and hushed, a static fizz rises off new nylon carpets. My father leaves me sitting on a black leather sofa in the bar. I'm alone there, surrounded by electric organ music and palms in brass pots. Exotic fish stare at me from a gently bubbling tank. Christmas cards are looped on a string across the bar. On a windowsill a laughing Father Christmas frolics in a pile of fake snow. Is it Christmas? I hadn't even noticed.

My father comes back with a plastic bag. He takes out a flat package wrapped in brown paper and tied with string. I realize it must be a painting and I'm expecting a miniature version of that canvas in Maya's flat. But it isn't like that at all. Painted in oils on a wooden panel, it might be Mexico but equally it might not. It might depict a beach, but it might not. All the colours are pale, and merge together. I move it into the light but that doesn't help. 'It's wonderful. Really wonderful.'

'It's the scene I see outside my house. I've painted it hundreds of times over the years. In fact, I don't paint anything else. It interests me to see how much I can take out.'

It looks to me as though he's taken out rather too much, but I don't say that.

'You know,' I say, 'whenever I thought about you I always imagined a beach like that. Because that was where I thought you were going to take me.'

'It was unforgivable. I'm sorry. I'm very sorry.' He looks at me and his eyes are old and sad and clear as water. I know that for him sorry is not just a word. But I don't want his apologies and he is aware of that. I want him to tell me that that place does exist, that we will go there. I want him to become the magician who put everything upside down and back to front, and made words jumble together. I look at him, pleading for that. But he's busy putting the picture back into its wrapping.

He offers to walk me home. It's only half a mile, so I say that he shouldn't bother, but he wants to, so I let him. We set off into the damp night. He asks to see the lake so we take a detour in that direction. A string of lights loops along the path, and around us, trees drip. We stand together looking out at the blackness as the water laps close to our feet. Above us, a few stars hang vivid under the low lid of the sky. I see my father gazing up at them. 'Looking for Venus?' I ask.

His head jerks towards me and his eyes open wide in surprise. 'Come on,' he says. 'It's time to be getting back.'

We walk on along the side of the lake. My father moves ahead of me, his head stretched upwards, drawing in the smells of the night. I understand that because he's cured, he's less than he was before – but also more, infinitely more. His head is shaggy and his stride crooked, his arm gripping the picture in its plastic wrapping. I thought he looked nothing like Jack, but I was wrong. Physically there may be no similarity, yet something pulls me back to that day at Tsaritsyno, and the sounds of the snow shifting in the branches of the trees. Despite that crooked walk, my father moves as easily as a bird in the air, or a fish in water. As I follow him, walking two steps behind, our eyes move together over the scene around us.

And I'm back in the strange place where the sole of my foot on tarmac is charged with splendour. Shades of grey merge and contrast – the bruised-grey of my father's coat smudges against the concrete-grey of the path. Railings cast a striped shadow which dances as we move towards it. Pinpricks of light shine out from the distant shore. Brighter lights radiate from cars and streetlights on the main road. Each ray breaks into pieces and shimmers on the wet path, the surface of the lake, the branches of trees. I know now that I'm feeling – really feeling – in a way I never have before.

We arrive at the path which leads back up to my building, and I point it out, but my father and I walk on. We take a fork leading away from the lake and come to a pedestrian crossing. The lines of the shadowed streets ahead are collaged one against another, blurred and suddenly tender. Outside a Chinese restaurant, I smell ginger and fried beef. A man passes with a small dog which wears a tartan jacket and strains and leaps on the end of its lead.

Something has changed, but I don't know what. The façade of ordinariness is cracking away from everything. The world is revealed in all its original strangeness. Fruit and vegetables are displayed under a striped awning outside a night shop. Strands of tinsel weave around the vegetable boxes, and inside, electronic carols play.

On a shelf in the window, robins bob across a chocolate log and miniature reindeers pull a sleigh over an icing field of snow. A bucket on the floor contains one bunch of yellow dahlias. Wrapped in crumpled orange paper, they manage to look both spiky and withered. But still I want to buy them because of Jack. Their smell is bitter but I stand in the street breathing it in. I remember that question, *And can you have the same pleasure from other things? Can you enjoy sunlight on a puddle as much as the kiss of a lover?* Just at this moment it seems that perhaps I can.

What has happened? This is just an ordinary December night in ordinary Geneva, and yet the sound of traffic reverberates deep inside me. And in the rain, the pavements sparkle like spilt jewels, sharp air rushes into my lungs. The smells of the roads and the cars' exhausts go right through my body. Joy blows up inside me like a balloon. I turn to my father, as we stand under the shop awning, and we smile at each other over the vulgar flowers.

When we get back to my building he says goodbye but then both of us hesitate. He turns to go and I want to call him back, but I don't know what name to use. 'Dad.' He turns around and we both listen to that unfamiliar sound. Still we hesitate, watching each other under the harsh electric light.

'Perhaps when you get to England you'll say to Mum . . . Well, I don't know. Perhaps just send her my love.'

'Yes, I'll certainly do that. And I'll see you at the wedding,' he says.

I open my mouth to explain that there won't be any wedding. I'm going to La Paz. But then a switch clicks in my head and I know, with a resounding certainty, that I'm not going anywhere. 'Yes,' I say. 'Yes. It won't be straight after Christmas. But yes – see you at the wedding.' The words have the solemnity of phrases pronounced in front of an altar.

12/20 rue de Lausanne, Geneva

December 1991

The next morning I wake early and get everything ready for Rob. I plug the phone back in and work out how to turn the central heating up. I go out and buy food, candles, champagne and more flowers to add to that bunch of yellow dahlias in their vase on the kitchen table. The flat should be decorated with holly, streamers and strands of tinsel, but I don't have time for that. Instead I assemble the ingredients for a beef casserole with black olives, and a ginger cake. This is the kind of thing that married women do.

I used to make ginger cake with my mother when I was a child but I'm struggling to remember. Soften the butter first and make sure to sift the flour. Jack said that I'd stay with Rob. As usual it seems that he was – oddly, annoyingly, unexpectedly – right. Decisions don't have to be grand and dramatic. You can choose what you already have.

I chop onions for the casserole and then garlic. This is where my life is now. In this flat, doing these things. The cardboard cut-out girl would have gone away, but I will not. No more rented rooms in cities where I don't have to explain. *Isn't a tree in London much the same as a tree in Moscow? The need to be free can be its own prison.* And it's surprising, really, how interesting chopping garlic can be. Unwrapping those tiny layers, hearing that chop, as the knife goes down. The smell is sharp, good, clean. And really you could fall in love with a piece of garlic. And you could spend all day near the window, with the knife coming down, and the air outside so heavy and white that snow must surely fall by the end of the day.

I cream butter and sugar together, beat eggs, sift flour. If I stay with Rob then I can't allow him to finish up like Harvey – a man endlessly clattering in the hall of my life. I have to make it different. One person can save another just by living in reality. That's all it takes. That's what Jack did for me. It would be too easy to move on to some new man. What I need is a different relationship with the man I've got.

I add a splash of milk to the cake mixture and two table-spoons of ground almonds. Is that how you do it? I remember the look on Rob's face as he left for Kiev that morning. Perhaps he knew then that I would go to Jack but still he went. Jack wasn't the only person who wanted to set me free. I chop preserved ginger and fresh ginger, then I add a teaspoon of ground ginger as well. You have to have all three. Perhaps love isn't so much a feeling as a decision you make.

The doorbell rings and I find the concierge outside, obscured by the bulk of a large package. It has come by courier from America. I take it into the flat and put it down on the sofa. With a knife, I cut through the plastic tape. Inside are four cushions made of sea-green silk, decorated with dark blue beads and gold tassels. Maya and her compen-sations and comforts. They could have come straight off that spacious Moscow sofa. I take one of the cushions out of its plastic packaging, put it down on a kitchen chair, then sit down on it and read Maya's letter. Her handwriting contains the cadences of her voice.

She's so ve-e-ry sorry that she hasn't been in touch for so long. The move back to America ne-e-arly killed her. Everything has been in boxes for months. Two armchairs are missing and half of her shoes. The glass dome of the chiming clock which used to stand on the hall table is cracked right down the front. She didn't know what we'd want for a wedding present but she hopes we like the cushions. Massachusetts isn't what it was, the letter says. She knows no one there now. A block of flats has been built at the back of her house and the view is s-o-o ugly she has to keep the blinds down. I picture her sitting there, surrounded by bottles, complaining. *Oh Maya, you will kill yourself with comfort.* But, she continues, she's reading a fascinating book about the early history of America. So ve-e-ry interesting.

Then – almost in mid-sentence – the letter changes. She hopes that I received Jack's boxes. She gave some of his things to the old lady in his flat, and she tried to find out if there was anyone in America she should contact, but it seemed he had no living relatives. She sent the rest to me. After I left, she says, an officious young man from the American Embassy came round asking about that velvet coat. Someone had recognized it as belonging to me. The young man asked what it was doing in Jack's flat. Maya says she told him that the coat certainly did belong to me, but I'd lost it months before – March or April perhaps. Lost, definitely, lost.

Then she says – and the letter blurs in front of my eyes – that she organized for Jack to be buried in the cemetery near the Church of the Resurrection because, as a child, he used to live near there. She's not sure – did I ever visit that church? It was complicated to organize that, and perhaps it wasn't the right thing to do. She went to see him buried. I imagine her standing there in that Moscow churchyard crowded out by the textile factory. The August heat is dusty, and Maya wears one of her neatly pressed linen safari suits, and leans on her stick. The white walls of the church are grubby in the sun. The bell chimes, just as it did when Jack and I were there. A few other people hover – perhaps Anna, or Svetlana or whatever her name was. One day I'll be able to go there and visit his grave.

I think of Maya at her dressing-table doing her make-up while in the street below, the tanks rolled by. As she left the flat that day, there was that moment when she and I under-stood each other entirely. How strange to discover that anger can be more intimate than kindness.

I ask myself now why she ever kept the photographs she took that night? It seems that people as deluded as Maya are arrogant in their lies, and yet at the same time they contin-ually flirt with the truth. Even after all those years she still couldn't accept the truth about my father, and she still couldn't face up to the fact that her delusions nearly led to my death. How can a clever woman be so blind? But I can hardly accuse her because, in other ways, I was just as bad. She is simply the person I'd have become if I hadn't met Jack.

I put on a brightly coloured woollen skirt and a jumper that I never wear because usually I feel it looks too tight. Now I decide that perhaps it rather suits me. I apply some mascara and eye-liner. After that I add lipstick but it looks too much, so I wipe it off. I pace around the flat waiting for Rob to call. I'm hoping I'll be able to meet him at the airport, but he rings to say that his flight is delayed and I shouldn't come. Later I find him at the lifts being harassed by a rucksack, a roll bag and three bulging suitcases. Stupidly, I start trying to deal with the suitcases when I haven't even kissed him. Then I stumble on a bag as I reach out to him. He feels thin and smells pleasantly unwashed. His hair needs cutting and he hasn't shaved.

'Great flat,' he says, as we drag his bags through the door. I suppose it is a good flat. I'd never thought about it much. He walks through every room. 'Fitted wardrobes – and bedside lights.'

'Yes, but don't you miss the carpet on the walls?'

In the sitting room he glances at the telephone.

'Yes, I know,' I say. 'Sorry. I've had so many problems with it.'

'That's OK.' He goes into the kitchen. 'And a dishwasher?' He opens it and looks inside, pulling out the top rack.

'More interested in dishwashers than democracy?' I say.

Rob laughs and I remember how much I like that sound. 'Yes,' he says, with a theatrical shrug. 'Perhaps I am.' With exaggerated attention he runs his finger along the front of the dishwasher rack. 'Actually, dishwashers can be fascinating.'

I want Rob to kiss me and I know he wants to, but it doesn't happen. Of course, it takes time to get back into the habit of someone when you haven't seen them for nearly four months. We open the champagne and stand in the kitchen while he talks about Zagreb. From outside, a car backfires and Rob jumps back from the window. Suddenly I wonder what exactly he's been doing since I last saw him. I'd like to ask, but Rob just shrugs and smiles as though his sudden movement was a joke. I think of all those conversations I planned this morning. I was going to sort everything out, start us off on a new course. It was all so easy in my mind. But now we're back in the same old silence. I need to tell him about my father's visit, but I can't find a way to begin.

Rob starts fiddling with the television. I've switched it on a couple of times before and seen nothing more than a grey-and-black fizzing screen. Rob adjusts various sockets and a clear picture appears. He flicks around the channels and then decides to have a bath. 'Listen,' I say, as he turns to go. 'I just wanted to say I'm sorry I didn't keep in better touch. And sorry I was so strange in Moscow. I'm much better now.'

'Oh good. Good.' He nods and wanders away to open one of his cases. Probably he's tired from the journey. It seems odd to have him in this flat. After he's had a bath we sit down to eat, facing each other across the table, looking out over the lights on the lake. I want to sit close, but we finish up at opposite ends of the table. Low voices mumble from the television. Rob has put it on because he doesn't want to miss the news. I see him looking at Maya's cushions, which lie propped on the sofa.

'Maya sent them,' I say.

He's still staring at the cushions, puzzled.

'You know, as a present . . .'

Rob pulls at the collar of his shirt and clears his throat. 'Eva, listen, I've got something to say.' The spoon in my hand tips and gravy splashes back into the casserole. 'It's great to see you again. But you know we talked about getting married? It's just that now – I don't think it's the right thing.'

My stomach drops down a lift-shaft. But of course. I should have known it couldn't really be so easy. If he doesn't want to marry me, it's hardly surprising. I'll never know now what he knew about Jack and I'll never be able to ask. Probably he knew much more than I ever understood. He'd have felt it, even if he didn't know. When I speak, I'm surprised by how calm my voice is. 'It's all right, I understand. You don't have to explain.'

'No, Eva, it's not that. It's just . . . I know it's not right for you, that's all.'

I put the spoon back into the casserole and stare around me at the candles and flowers. How could I have thought that a few props on a stage-set could make a marriage? Rob comes to my end of the table and serves the casserole for both of us. I watch the neat way in which he does it, with not a drop spilt. Why are we being so well-behaved? He should be shouting accusations at me, calling me a whore. I should be on my knees, pleading with him. Instead I pour a glass of water for him.

'Did you meet someone else in Zagreb?'

'No, of course not. Don't be ridiculous.'

I've made the mistake which indecisive people often make. I thought that because I'd finally made up my mind, then everything else would automatically fall into place. I should have known that this fatherless world would prove a little more varied and vicious than that. I pick up my glass of champagne and see Rob watching me. I put the glass down slowly, wanting to say, Look, I'm not making a tragedy out of this. Our forks scrape on our plates and Rob says how good the casserole is. It occurs to me that he probably went to Zagreb in order to finish this. I wasn't meant to be here when he got back.

'So now you'll go back to Zagreb?' I ask, keeping my voice even.

'No, I'll stay here. I've decided that.'

Rob opens a bottle of wine and pours me a glass. Some ridiculous part of me wants to propose a toast and click my glass against his. A toast to not getting married, to behaving far too well, to a future refusing to happen. I keep my hand steady and drink the wine too fast. The casserole tastes like glue, the table has become as long as a football pitch.

'And you?' Rob says. 'What will you do?'

'I think I'll go back to South America. La Paz, perhaps. I shouldn't have any difficulty getting a job there.' But I'm finished with all that. I was always the one who was going to put an end to this relationship. Rob can't finish with me – that's not the way it's meant to be. I put the lid back on the casserole and tell Rob about the ginger cake. I put it on the table and it stands there, with its lemon icing, mocking me. He says, 'Let's save it for tomorrow.' Tomorrow? There isn't any tomorrow. The music from the ten o'clock news sounds from the television.

I start to clear the table, moving the pots carefully. 'Eva, come and look at this.' Moscow appears on the screen. The ridiculous ice-cream cones of St Basil's, the sinister red walls of the Kremlin, the black Moskva river sidling behind them. This is the Moscow of tourists and journalists. It doesn't look anything like the place we knew. Martin Sixsmith stands in Krasnaia Ploshchad' and explains that, as from midnight on New Year's Eve, the Soviet Union will formally cease to exist. I turn away, unable to watch. I should be thinking, What good news. But it feels as though Moscow itself is coming to an end. I want Rob and me to go back to our flat there, and sit with our knees close under the kitchen table. I look over at Mr Balashov's tiny dolls propped on the windowsill. I want him, Sasha, Maya, Jack. I even want garlic sausage, pickles, pilchards. I loved Moscow. Even in the worst of hardship and scarcity, it remained an unfailingly generous city.

'Rob, sorry. I need a bit of fresh air.' I pull my coat off the hook on the back of the door. Rob turns to look at me. He's glad that I'm hurt and I'm glad as well. This can't be allowed to go too easily. Outside, the sky is low, the air hushed, the first flakes of snow are just starting to fall. Everything feels unsteady, even my feet, my legs. There's always been Rob. He's the default option, a possible end to the story. I suddenly desperately want to stay in Geneva. And the worst of it is that I know I can't allow myself a shred of pity. Don't come crying to me, Eva Curren, you've only yourself to blame. You've finally got what you deserve.

The snow falls in wet flakes, evaporating on the shoulders of my coat. In my head, a roulette-wheel spins. The white ball dances over the slots. La Paz, Sucre, Lima. A world in which the buttons of your coat maliciously refuse to fit into the right holes, where you melt like wax, or bang a drum like a clockwork rabbit, going on and on, when you should be lying on the floor with your mouth babbling and your tongue blocking the back of your throat. I stand under the branches of a cedar tree and wail silently.

'Eva, are you all right?'

Rob's hair is wet from the snow and he's out of breath. He looks at me and shakes his head. 'Oh, for God's sake, Eva. You always wanted out of this – why don't you take your chance?'

'Because—'

'Listen. You know how it is. We can't build a relationship out of the past.'

'But . . .' All the arguments I rehearsed have gone from my head. We stand in silence under the spreading branches of the tree and wait for words to arrive, but they don't come. Rob walks away from me, down towards the lake, through the slanting snow. It seems to me now that he and I have lived in a world of borrowed identities. I loved my father when my mother couldn't love him. And she loved me when he was gone. And I loved Jack because of him. And perhaps Rob loved me because he'd lost his mother. A diabolical game of musical chairs.

Rob stands at the place where a jetty, closed off with a chain, runs out into the lake. Through the darkness and snow I see his head bent, his foot kicking idly at a loose paving stone. I move towards him and, when he looks at me, tears have gathered in his eyes. 'I let you down,' he says. For a moment I want to tell him not to cry, but then I realize that for too long his world has been full of people who rely on him not to cry.

'I'm so sorry,' he says. 'I'm so sorry.'

'It's OK. You can make a mistake. In fact, I'd like you to make a few. I'm fed up with making them all myself.'

'It wasn't a small mistake.'

'Maybe. But things can be different.'

'For you, perhaps.'

'And for you as well. I can help you.'

This idea is quite new to Rob. 'Do you really believe that it can be different?'

I want to insist that I do believe. I want to fill him with confidence, create a dream of a brilliant future. But I must be honest, above all else, I must be that. 'I don't really know. Perhaps. Perhaps not. But I think we had better try and believe it.'

He shrugs his shoulders and wipes snow from his hair. 'Maybe.' He puts out his hand to me. 'Come on, let's not stand around out here.'

As we walk back, Rob takes off his coat, and tries to give it to me, but I don't want it. No, no, I don't want it, I say. All of my life people have been trying to put coats on me. Why don't they just let me get wet, for God's sake? Put it on, Eva, just put it on. No, I don't need it. You keep it. But he's still trying to put it around me. I push it away. Put it on. No, *you* put it on. Will our first real row be about this coat? Just when we're about to start yelling, Rob puts his arm in one sleeve, and I put my arm in the other. We shuffle along, clutched together, like people who can't do ballroom dancing.

And then we're laughing inside the coat as we bump against each other. Rob's cheeks are red and wet and we're both out of breath. We kiss and press close against each other. We take three steps, kiss, laugh, shuffle. Four steps, kiss, laugh, shuffle. But then for a moment we're still, staring around us at the wilderness of white and grey. It seems that even the traffic is silent, the streetlights dim. We're suddenly alone – alone together – in a way we've never been before. And we grip each other tight, suddenly taut with fear, daunted by the future. It's in this city that we'll make our longest journey.

I pick up Jack's pen for one last time. I do so hate a happy ending. But perhaps this is one. Except this is the beginning of a story, not the end. I stare down at my pile of scribbled pages. Jack said once that writing is just a bad habit. By watching life you avoid it. He was right and he was wrong. I don't want to turn into my Uncle Guy – a man obsessed with words and yet devoid of all ability to communicate.

My hands flick through the pages. It may happen that someone will read these sentences long after they have cooled. And if they do, my words might lead them out on to those parts of their mind where the ice is thin – and who knows what lies beneath? And if that happens, then they may recover some part of themselves, lost long ago, which might weep or sing or dance. That is the most I can hope. It is everything.

And as for Jack, I should say that I'll never think of him again. But, of course, I will. And I'll feel him, imprinted in my flesh. Time is not measured in minutes, hours, days. Beyond what we see, there's a place of certainty, of silence, of union. It is a place words can't reach. And there we are together. Just as we were that day at the *dacha* when we sat together looking out at the garden of yellow flowers.

Propped on the windowsill is the picture my father gave me. By now he will be at Marsh End House. Will my mother be overjoyed to see him? Or will she be shocked, as I was, by what time does, as it passes? I try to imagine them together in the kitchen, sitting at the table, but the image won't form. It occurs to me that I could ring them up, but I won't do it now. Tomorrow, perhaps. Maybe they'll go out and walk across the marsh, despite the cold. Yes, I think they will. My father would want to go there. That I can imagine, the two of them walking down the lane in the darkness, as the wind sweeps across the flat land and out towards the sea.

My eyes are still held by his painting. All day I've found myself drawn back to it. There seemed so little on the canvas but, as I look, more appears. My father hasn't just painted a stretch of coastline, instead he's painted what lies behind it. Perhaps that's what he found during all those long years on a beach in Mexico.

I stand up and put the lid on Jack's pen, then go to the bedroom door and watch Rob sleeping. Light from the uncurtained window falls on his face, the pillow cradles his head. I could stand here watching him a long time. To me the scene seems perfect – the whiteness of the pillow, the tender way in which the light fits itself to the shape of his face. In the silence, in the stillness of the night, I'm back again in that world where something quite ordinary seems beautiful. Except that world is only this world. It's the place my father painted, and which Jack knew, and wanted me to know as well. That place which I used to think was lost in the past, or hidden on some distant beach. But is here – now – if only you can find it.

POCKET
BOOKS

Alice Jolly
What the Eye Doesn't See

What happens to a family when its private tragedies become public scandal?
How much do you really know about the lives of those closest to you? Three
generations of a family take turns to tell their story.

Max Priestly – charismatic, ambitious and amoral – has always lived close to
the edge, building a glittering political career while hiding the complexities
of his private life. But when his best friend's wife dies in a fire, the suspicion
that he may know more than he has admitted leads to disgrace.

Maggie, his 28-year-old daughter, suspects her father has lied about the night
of the fire but is determined not to betray him – until she falls in love with the
journalist who is writing his biography and begins to understand the cost of
hiding the truth. Only Nanda, Max's elderly mother, preparing for death,
remembers the hidden family secrets which lie at the root of Max's deceit.

This beautifully-crafted, unsettling – and ultimately uplifting – novel
explores the elusive nature of truth and reveals what happens when family
loyalties are tested to the limits.

ISBN-13: 978-0-7434-5071-3

ISBN-10: 0-7434-5071-X

PRICE £6.99

POCKET
BOOKS

Rachel Hore

The Dream House

Everyone has a dream of their perfect house – in the heart of the countryside, or perhaps a stately residence in the middle of a wonderful city?

For Kate Hutchinson, the move to Suffolk from the tiny, noisy London terrace she shares with her husband Simon and their two young children was almost enough to make her dreams come true.

Space, peace, a measured, rural pace of life have a far greater pull for Kate than the constantly overflowing in-tray on her desk at work. Moving in with her mother-in-law must surely be only a temporary measure before the estate agent's details of the perfect house fall through the letterbox.

But when, out walking one evening, Kate stumbles upon the beautiful house of her dreams, it is tantalizingly out of her reach. Its owner is the frail elderly Agnes, whose story – as it unravels – echoes so much of Kate's own. And Kate comes to realize how uncertain and unsettling even a life built on dreams can be: wherever you are, at whatever time you are living, and who-ever you are with . . .

ISBN-13: 978-1-4165-1099-4

ISBN-10: 1-4165-1099-0

PRICE £6.99

**POCKET
BOOKS**

Ronlyn Domingue
The Mercy of Thin Air

In 1920s New Orleans, Raziela Nolan is in the throes of a magnificent love affair when she dies suddenly in an accident. Immediately after her death, she chooses to stay between – a realm that exists after life and before whatever lies beyond it.

From this remarkable vantage point, Razi narrates the story of her lost love, and life, as well as the relationship of Amy and Scott, a young couple whose house she haunts almost seventy-five years later. Their trials compel Razi to slowly unravel the mystery of what happened to her first and only love, Andrew, and to confront a long-hidden secret.

'Fans of *The Lovely Bones* and *The Time Traveller's Wife* now have another classic . . . a wonderfully powerful depiction of true, heart-wrenching love and the grief experienced when it is lost.' EASY LIVING MAGAZINE

'Superbly constructed, this is a story about the power of first love and the potency of memory. Ronlyn Domingue is a first-class writer' IRISH EXAMINER

'A truly original voice and a truly original story' Jodi Picoult

ISBN-13: 978-1-4165-1125-0

ISBN-10: 1-4165-1125-3

PRICE £6.99

POCKET
BOOKS

This book and other **Pocket** Books titles are available from your bookshop or can be ordered direct from the publisher.

Please send cheque or postal order for the value
of the book, free postage and packing within
the UK, to SIMON & SCHUSTER CASH SALES
PO Box 29, Douglas Isle of Man, IM99 1BQ
Tel: 01624 677237, Fax: 01624 670923
E-mail: bookshop@enterprise.net
www.bookpost.co.uk

Please allow 14 days for delivery. Prices and availability
subject to change without notice.